PENGUIN BOOKS

The Best Possible Taste

Sam O'Reilly is a journalist and writer, living in Brighton with her husband and two children. A former *Cosmopolitan* magazine New Journalist of the Year, she is also a runner-up for both the *Cosmopolitan* short-story prize and the Ian St James Award. She freelances for magazines and newspapers including the *Guardian* and *The Times*.

The Best Possible Taste

SAM O'REILLY

PENGUIN BOOKS

PENGUIN BOOKS

Published by the Penguin Group
Penguin Books Ltd, 80 Strand, London WC2R ORL, England
Penguin Group (USA), Inc., 375 Hudson Street, New York, New York 10014, USA
Penguin Books Australia Ltd, 250 Camberwell Road, Camberwell, Victoria 3124, Australia
Penguin Books Canada Ltd, 10 Alcorn Avenue, Toronto, Ontario, Canada M4V 3B2
Penguin Books India (P) Ltd, 11 Community Centre, Panchsheel Park, New Delhi – 110 017, India
Penguin Group (NZ), cnr Airborne and Rosedale Roads, Albany, Auckland 1310, New Zealand
Penguin Books (South Africa) (Pty) Ltd, 24 Sturdee Avenue, Rosebank 2196, South Africa

Penguin Books Ltd, Registered Offices: 80 Strand, London WC2R ORL, England

www.penguin.com

Published in Penguin Books 2004
1

Copyright © Sally O'Reilly, 2004
All rights reserved

The moral right of the author has been asserted

Set in 12.5/14.75 pt PostScript Monotype Garamond
Typeset by Rowland Phototypesetting Ltd, Bury St Edmunds, Suffolk
Printed in England by Clays Ltd, St Ives plc

For my father, Michael Platt
1931–2003

Acknowledgements

Thank you to Veronique Baxter, Harrie Evans and Louise Moore, whose support, insights and ideas made it possible to publish this book. And to my friend Sue Eckstein, whose perceptive comments made it possible to write it. Also to Philip Taylor and Amanda Powelly at Terre-à-Terre restaurant in Brighton, for allowing me to watch a civilized, vegetarian kitchen at work, and to everyone at Secrets lap-dancing club at Grays Inn Road, London, for the chance to take part in a 'one-to-one'. Finally to Georgia and Declan for letting me eavesdrop on childhood, and to Noel for everything.

Preface
Stoke-on-Trent, 1977

In the seventies, normal people went out once a week and bought Wonderloaf, corned beef and Blue Band margarine. Supermarkets existed, but only to sell food under one roof – no one had yet thought of defining a whole social class by its appetite for ciabatta bread and organic mange tout. Children ate Bird's Instant Whip without complaining. Fanny Craddock and the Galloping Gourmet were the best-known chefs on TV, and a young journalist called Delia Smith wrote a book called *How to Cheat at Cooking*. It was an unassuming paperback, with line drawings of cheat's asparagus soup and similar, aimed at people in bedsits or working mums with no narcissistic investment in what they fed to their children.

So who could blame Mrs Rose Beckett for parking her Austin 1300 at a strange angle outside her terraced house and running inside with a cardboard box full of tinned tomato soup, boil-in-the-bag fish and Heinz Spaghetti Hoops? Her children could, that's who. On the carpet, Carmel, eighteen years old and twelve stone in weight, staring dreamily at a picture of Farah Fawcett-Majors. Lying on the sofa, Stephen, weird, skinny and seventeen, who, as a silent protest against the naffness of his home, specialized in refusing to eat any of the meals his mother cooked. And Rose, as is the way of despised mothers, did her best to make her children happy. For Carmel she had bought Slim-Fast, which her daughter would later quaff during a Sugar Puffs binge. For Stephen, mini-pizzas and strong Cheddar, which he would eat at the dead of night, alone, or with his silent friend, William Warren, who had a fringe that came down to the end of his nose and a love of mystic sci-fi.

'Give me a hand, can't you?' cried Rose, as she hurtled past them towards the kitchen. Neither of them could ever work out why there was so much hurtling. The dog, also recumbent, lifted her head idly and flopped her tail up and down as if she too was underwhelmed by the thought of dinner: yet another plateload of Winalot.

'In a minute,' said Carmel, not moving an inch. Stephen just groaned and furled himself into a foetal position among the ruched velveteen cushions. He knew already that these were the marks of the taste-free home, along with room dividers and textured wallpaper. Teenage boys aren't usually aware of such things. William Warren certainly wasn't. But William Warren's parents were arty people, recently returned from Jamaica, where they had taken monochrome photos of Rastas in hammocks. There was no call for class aspiration in the Warrens' shabby, book-filled house. Whereas it was class aspiration alone that kept Stephen sane.

'Stephen,' said his mother, rushing in the opposite direction to relieve the car boot of more shopping. 'Come and help. Carmel, put the kettle on –' And she disappeared through the door, a beige blur in her fur coat. Stephen moodily followed her to the car, extracted a single, lightweight bag containing toilet paper and an Arctic roll, and staggered back into the house, weighed down by tedium and the fawn-to-brown world of grown-ups and weekday meals. Inside, Carmel, having filled the kettle and ignored the stainless-steel teapot, had returned to Farah Fawcett-Majors.

'Carmel!' Rose Beckett's voice ripped through the house as she slammed the front door shut. She came running back into the living room. 'Can't you do anything except lie there sulking? Didn't I ask you to put the kettle on?' Standing by the sofa, face white with strain, she was seventies mid-thirties. To Stephen, she looked about a hundred and ten. Her hair was always perfect – she was a hairdresser, so it had to be. She was wearing it in the Purdey style favoured by Joanna Lumley in *The New Avengers*. It reached her tired eyes in an unflattering golden helmet.

'I did put the kettle on,' said Carmel, her voice swooning with inertia. 'Like you said.'

'But where's the tea?'

'You never mentioned tea.'

Stephen, now mooching in the hall, idly kicking a row of desert boots out of line, sniggered. This was unwise.

His mother turned from Carmel to him. 'That's it! That's the last straw! I've had enough of your rudeness! You've been ruined by your father running off, and there's not a thing I can do to change you! Spoiled brats, that's what I've brought into the world! Just do what you bloody well like. Get your own dinner. I've got a migraine. I'm off to my bed!' With that, she stormed up the stairs. Their mother's level of Irishness varied, depending on how much stress she was under. Shouting at her children had the same effect as talking to Auntie Bridie in Dublin: it made her very Irish indeed.

Stephen and Carmel looked at each other with slightly guilty glee. 'You've done it now,' said Carmel. 'She'll go into one of her three-day stinks.'

'Oh, right, blame me,' said Stephen. 'All I did was laugh.' There was silence for a moment. They both tried not to look at the lurid picture of the Holy Mother that hung in the hall. She had a sheeny, 3-D complexion and sad eyes that followed you everywhere you went, like Catholic guilt. 'Let's put the shopping away, just to show that saying we're spoiled brats is a pile of crap,' suggested Stephen.

'Okay, creep.'

And so it was that, when the doorbell rang and Carmel answered it, Stephen was in the kitchen relieving the shopping bags of all the horrible food his family would be enduring over the next seven days. Hearing a female voice, he assumed one of Carmel's friends had arrived – Christine, probably, the speccy one who got pissed at parties. He turned, with a can of stewed steak in one hand and a packet of Jammy Dodgers in the other, to see none other than Fay Cattermole staring at him with horror as if she thought that it was only in *Steptoe and Son* that people ate such things. Fay Cattermole was the most beautiful girl in his class, an icy Pre-Raphaelite with a piss-off profile and the deportment of a prima ballerina. She was also the most spikily bourgeois person he knew. Her father was a moody English professor with very short legs.

She stood, framed in the doorway, erect and correct as a Victorian doll. This was the era of flicks and curling tongs, shaggy perms and the layered look. Fay Cattermole was above all that. Her long red hair fell down her back in natural ringlets. Sometimes she wore it down, so it formed a soft halo around her face. Today she had looped it into a bun, and looked like the portrait of Virginia Woolf that, three years later, Stephen's tutor at university would have on his study wall.

'Oh!' he cried, in a high, stricken voice which revealed everything – his love, his virginity, his nightly masturbation sessions inspired by a photo of her in the school play.

'I am not here on my own behalf,' she said. She was looking at their breakfast bar. There was no hope of passion now.

'No?' Perhaps she was here to tell him of the devotion of one of her less attractive friends. This was bearable – but unlikely. 'Who are you here on behalf of, then?' asked Stephen, his voice still shaky.

'Of everyone,' said Fay Cattermole. 'Of the group. We're having an end-of-term party and all of us had to invite a certain number of people. You were on my list. We're inviting the entire class.' (She gave great emphasis to this, as if realizing how overexcited he would be at the sight of her.)

'I see,' said Stephen. 'Well. Thanks. When is it?'

'Next Saturday,' said Fay. 'Is that dog food?'

'Is what dog food?'

'That tin you're holding.'

'Oh – yes – I think so . . .'

'No it's not,' said Carmel, who had come in unseen behind Fay. 'Don't lie, Stephen. That won't get you anywhere with the opposite sex. You know tonight is curry night.' The dog, who had followed her, gazed at the tin with sorrow.

'You make that into a curry? The sort they have in India?' Fay's incredulity had got the better of her snootiness.

'Yes.' Red-faced, Stephen reached up and placed the tin in the well-stocked cupboard, noting for the hundredth time that it contained geological layers of processed food that never got eaten. 'Mum mixes it up with sultanas and stuff,' he said, turning back to face her. 'It's okay, as long as you make sure you have plenty of rice and bananas. But I don't eat any,' he added hurriedly. 'I only eat cheese. In the middle of the night.' He didn't want to mention the mini-pizzas.

This was the longest speech he had ever made in front of Fay Cattermole. It didn't appear to impress her. 'Good God,' she said. 'Can't your mother cook?'

'Not really,' said Carmel. 'She's more of a warmer-upper. People in our family aren't really interested in food. We lead busy lives. We're a single-parent family, you know.' Stephen knew this was only partly true – both Carmel and Rose were rather keen on food, especially anything sweet. It was cooking they couldn't be bothered with.

'God,' said Fay Cattermole again. 'How obscene. No wonder you both look so pale and spotty.'

'There's no need to be rude, Fay,' said Carmel, with the hauteur of a person who is a whole school year ahead. 'There are more important things than what people have for dinner, you know.'

'More important? I don't think so. Not everyone knows how to eat – it's part of knowing how to live. My father learned how to live when he was at Cambridge.'

'Food's definitely less important than politics, and world pollution and Rock Against Racism,' said Carmel. 'It's just fuel – and it makes you fat. The less time you spend cooking it, the better.'

'A good meal with a glass of decent wine is one of the greatest gifts of civilization, my father says. And he should know. Ted Hughes came to dinner last night. He spent the whole evening talking about dead sheep.'

Neither Stephen nor Carmel could think of a reply to this. Stephen stood awkwardly over the piles of shopping, not wanting to put anything else away in case he drew attention to its inadequacy. From the corner of his eye he could see such incriminating items as sandwich spread, which were best left in the bags. Carmel, leaning against the breakfast bar, was pulling at the loose skin on her double chin as if deep in thought about calories and anti-racism. Her wavy brown hair was sticking up like a broccoli spear.

'Anyway.' This was a characteristic expression of Fay's, a preparation for leaving. 'I'll tell the others you can come. It's at my house, and it's a fondue party. Which is a Swiss thing – you have a big dish of cheese sauce, and you dip bread into it. Very rich; you don't need much. And you have to bring a bottle – not cider and not Liebfraumilch, please. Proper wine.'

Stephen nodded, already nervous as hell. He knew that William would refuse to go. And that he would not be able to stay away.

'Thank you for inviting me,' he said.

'I had no choice,' said Fay, with her prim, antiseptic smile.

Perhaps, had she left then, cycling off on her old-fashioned bicycle, Stephen would not have been scarred for ever. But, sadly, his mother chose that moment to rush down the stairs in her migraine outfit. This consisted of a quilted nylon dressing-gown, covered in green and purple daisies, and a pair of fluffy mules. To complete the look, her hair was hidden under a mauve chiffon scarf, and her face was slathered with cold cream. When she saw Fay, she shrieked with horror.

'Aaaagh! Oh, hello!' she cried. 'Ignore me, I'm having one of my off days. Oh dear! Aren't you going to introduce me?'

'This is Fay Cattermole,' said Stephen, in a tone which was meant to be the equivalent of giving his mother a warning kick in the shins. But she pressed unstoppably on.

'Pleased to meet you. I've heard so much . . .' Her voice trailed away. 'Have they offered you anything – tea, Nescafé, custard creams? We've got some Wagon Wheels somewhere in all that shopping – which I see you haven't put away, you naughty things. Or a Cupasoup? Or would you like to stay for dinner? We're having our special curry tonight, with a vanilla slice each for pudding. I got an extra one because I know Carmel sometimes gets hungry at night, especially when she's on one of her diets.' She came to an end at last, breathless with the boundless reach of her hospitality.

'No, thank you, Mrs Beckett,' said Fay. 'My father is expecting me. He's making omelettes *aux fines herbes*.'

'Your father – ooh, yes. He's even more famous than you are! We saw him on *Read All About It*, didn't we,

Stephen, with young Melvyn Bragg? Nice smile, but fancy wearing a cord jacket on television. Melvyn, I mean, not your father – *he* looked beautiful! We switched over to *Poldark* in the middle.'

Stephen made a noise of some sort, a kind of mooing sound. Fay was looking at Rose in frank amazement. 'Marvellous,' she said. 'Now, I really must dash.'

'So nice of you to drop by,' said Rose, following her to the front door as if on some inescapable kamikaze mission. 'We've been hearing nothing but "Fay Cattermole this, Fay Cattermole that" for months!'

As Fay cycled slowly away, the three of them stared after her, and Rose trilled, 'Do pop round again! We have boiled mince on Tuesdays! Stephen would love to see you!'

Stephen had known for some time that he had been born into the wrong class, just as some people know from birth that they are the wrong sex. But, until that day, this urge to turn his back on three-piece suites had been a vague, unacknowledged yearning. From that point onwards, his battle to be bourgeois would begin in earnest. What's more, he saw that there was no point in learning to like Puccini if you were still eating Pot Noodles. And his instinctive knowledge that the food in the Beckett house was uneatable had been confirmed. Somewhere out there, in the bigger, posher world, there was better food, and superior people were eating it. He would find it, cook it, consume it. He would acquire taste.

It wasn't going to be easy. He went alone to the fondue party. He scrutinized the Cattermoles' house, committing everything to memory. The upright piano, stacked with recently thumbed sheet music, in the stone-flagged hall. The Indian rugs worn thin on stripped floorboards. On the walls, the paintings that weren't Athena reproductions. In the kitchen, the scrubbed wooden table and the chairs that didn't match. The cookery books on the kitchen shelf. (He furtively noted the titles.) He listened to Fay and her friends showing off and talking about the films of Antonioni. Fay ignored him, as he had known she would, and flirted with a dwarfish, opinionated boy called Nigel Nunnelly who was studying economics and favoured market forces – an unfashionable view at the time. Watchful and withdrawn, Stephen dipped his bread into the rich sauce, drew out the gluey strings of melted cheese, and found that the taste was exquisite, a nutty, creamy flavour unlike anything he had tried before. He dipped his skewer again – and again. Later he was sick outside, retching like a dog among the Cattermole shrubs. Wiping his mouth, he stared through the uncurtained kitchen window at Fay. Sitting below a hanging row of pots and pans, she was feeding Nigel Nunnelly green olives. It was an image of casual *savoir-faire* that would haunt him for years to come.

1. Brighton, April 2002

The cyclist was clearly an amateur on two wheels: the bike was barely under his control. Head down against the oncoming wind, he wobbled dangerously as he approached the traffic lights by the Palace Pier and came to a shuddering halt to allow some pedestrians to struggle across the road. He wasn't even properly dressed for the job – he wore no helmet, his chinos were flapping around his legs, and his black leather jacket did nothing to keep him dry. He glanced around him briefly, his bespectacled face puckered into an unconscious frown, then looked at his watch. It was Friday evening, and the lights on the seafront glittered against the wet sky. On the road that hemmed the empty shingle beach, where traffic was jammed to a halt, rear lights shone jewel red; their blurred reflections spilled over the wet tarmac. The cyclist muttered something that was whipped away by the hurtling rain. He looked as if he had jumped on the bike only as a last resort.

Which was indeed the case. For this was Stephen Beckett, twenty-four years older than the boy curled up on a settee in Stoke-on-Trent. He was now the co-owner of Earthsea, an organic vegetarian restaurant which was his ruling passion. Most nights he would have been at work at this time, supervising the tearing of lettuce leaves and the whipping-up of obscure dressings. But tonight, reluctantly, he was to entertain at home. It was his wedding anniversary, and his wife had invited their two oldest friends for dinner. In spite of his lack of enthusiasm, he had planned the evening with his customary obsessive attention to detail; he had worked out the menu weeks before, and had even sent an email to himself containing a reminder to buy black rice and tamari. These were stashed away in his backpack now. However, Stephen lived his life in the futile hope that he could do more in each hour than was humanly possible. His quest for good taste and bourgeois living still had him at full stretch. No matter how well planned his meal was, he still needed to be there to cook it. Instead of leaving at the time he had written into his Tate Modern diary in his careful, italic handwriting, he had been drawn into a bad atmosphere in the kitchen, caused by a late booking for a hen party of eight, and had lost track of time. At ten past seven, he had realized his mistake. His car was out of action, so he'd leaped on to one of the restaurant's delivery bikes. Only when he was outside, pedalling through the shining black puddles, had he realized just how heavy the rain was. Stuck at the traffic lights, he looked at his watch again. Unbelievably, it was suggesting that it was already seven thirty. His guests were due in one hour. 'Christ,' he muttered to himself. 'Nightmare.' There was a mobile phone in his pocket, but he didn't use it to phone his wife. He knew what mood Rachel would be in, and he knew that excuses would be useless.

When he got home, dripping and half blind from the downpour, the house was unusually quiet. 'Hello?' he called experimentally, peering up the stairs as he propped his bike in the hall. 'Anyone here?' No doubt the children were hiding somewhere upstairs, trembling with merriment. 'Rachel?' He peeled off his jacket, prised off his shoes, placed them neatly side by side in a fast-growing pool of water, and padded through into the kitchen. Rachel was sitting there, silently, at the kitchen table, trashing out-of-season strawberries. Stern-faced, and with long spirals of black Medusa hair, she was a forbidding prospect.

'I know,' he said. '*Sorry*, and all that. I know I'm late. I know they'll be here in . . .' He hesitated.

'Forty minutes,' she said, beheading a strawberry and adding its leaves to a pile by her right elbow. (What was she doing?) She did not look at him.

'We'll just have to eat a bit late, that's all,' said Stephen. Rachel picked up another strawberry and began to disembowel it. He tied on his butcher's apron without taking off his wet trousers. His physical discomfort was beginning to seem trivial. 'There's no need to panic,' he said.

'No one is panicking,' said Rachel, in curdling tones. 'I don't see myself as responsible for this evening in any way.'

Stephen suddenly remembered that he should kiss her. He bent down to do so, but she moved her head to one side, so he missed her and kissed the air like a fashion PR. At the same second, he remembered that he had forgotten to buy her a present. Not even flowers or chocolates. He sighed heavily, and turned to the fridge. The menu for the evening was attached to the door with a Virgin Mary fridge magnet, a present from Vinnie, the co-owner of his restaurant and a fellow post-Catholic. He began to assemble the ingredients for the starter, sorting them into methodical little piles on the granite worktop: chopped tomatoes, aubergines, red onions and fennel. Even under pressure, rushing was not his style – though he had neglected to wash his hands, something he would have done in the restaurant. Good food could not be hurried. The trouble, however, started straight away.

'Rachel, have you thrown away the basil?'

'No, Stephen, I have not thrown away the basil.'

'Where it's disappeared to is a total mystery, in that case.'

'As domestic responsibilities are *allegedly* shared fifty-fifty in this house, I don't see why the fact I'm female automatically means I should know.'

'It's nothing to do with being female, Rachel. But, if you have a fatal flaw, it's your tendency to throw out perfectly good food.'

'And if you have a fatal flaw, *Stephen*, it's attempting to poison your own family with E. coli. Call me old fashioned, but I just don't feel comfortable feeding my children with mouldy food.'

'Basil isn't going to give anyone the E. coli virus.'

'I haven't touched the fucking basil, I just told you.'

'I hope you realize the children can hear everything we say.'

'Don't worry, they already know you're a pompous twat.'

Sighing again, he busied himself with his heavy-bottomed frying-pan, in which shards of garlic were frying in extra-virgin olive oil at precisely the right temperature.

4

If only the rest of his life could be controlled in the same way! But beyond that perfect circle of sanity, chaos threatened to overwhelm him. Needlessly, he tweaked the gas flame, thinking about Rachel's tiresome method of cooking, which involved having everything on full blast, including the radio. (And Radio 2 at that – she was seriously downwardly mobile in intellectual terms.) No subtlety, no patience. Like him, she came from a family who treated food as a chore; but, as they were middle-class socialists who spent mealtimes banging on about the genius of Arthur Scargill, he hadn't noticed till it was too late. He turned to add the onion, but was stopped in his tracks by the sight of two little figures slithering round the door-frame. Eight-year-old Elsie had her dark hair in masses of tiny plaits, kept in place with coloured bands. Stanley, who was six, was wearing a pair of pyjamas decorated with a Tyrannosaurus rex. His curly hair was hidden by a baseball cap. Each was clutching a coloured plastic beaker.

'Hello, Daddeeee . . .' said Elsie, in a squirmy voice.

'WE'RE THIRSTY . . .' said Stan, who only had one mode of speech: a high-octane demand for attention.

Stephen kissed them both, and their warm little bodies surged towards his wet legs. 'Careful, don't get your jamamas wet,' he cautioned.

'I'm sick of this!' said Rachel. 'This is the third time you've been down! Now you'll spend the whole bloody evening on the toilet. There'll be no cinema tomorrow if this happens again.'

'BUT WE'RE DESPRUT!' said Stan.

'We're *dying* of thirst up there,' said Elsie.

'REALLY WE WANT RIBENA, BUT WE DON'T MIND HAVING WATER!' said Stan.

'Just to make life easier for you,' said Elsie, 'in case you're worrying about our teeth.' Stephen filled their beakers, and they tried to look in the frying-pan.

'What are you making, Daddy?' Elsie was standing on tiptoe.

'Food for grown-ups. Go to bed.'

'Horrible smell. Is that garlic?'

'EEYUK! WE HATE GARLIC, DON'T WE, ELSIE?'

'Go to bed!'

As he shooed the children out of the kitchen, Stephen caught sight of his reflection in the large, gilt-framed mirror on the wall opposite the double-fronted cooker. There he was, a smallish, slightly fussy-looking figure, even in his wet trousers. He had always suffered from being over-neat, though in his youth he had been thought dishy by girls who liked boys with a Brideshead feel who could do humour. (He had worked on his accent from day one at college – no one could believe he came from the mean streets of Stoke.) His mother liked to tell him that he had classically good features, and he was glad of this now that his hair was thinning a little. He adjusted his glasses and squared his shoulders. Beyond his own reflection he could see Rachel, sitting at the kitchen table, surrounded by plastic bags, dirty dishes and various cooking utensils. Big-breasted and dark, she looked as if she ought to be good fun. In fact, Stephen reflected as he returned to the cooker and added the finely chopped onion to the gently hissing garlic, she had been a huge amount of fun when they first met, and still could be, conditions permitting. Sadly, conditions rarely were. Why was their life like this? So rushed, and mad, and bitty, and so lamentably sex-free? Over and above all his usual nagging concerns, he had recently experienced a new undertow of feeling, which almost told him something was extra-specially not right with Rachel. But, as well as having that male gift of tuning out emotional messages which were likely to cause additional angst, Stephen had the parallel unconscious policy of waiting to be confronted by superior female insights. So he hadn't investigated.

He thought instead about the meal. There were several issues which were adding to the tension. As they were typical Brighton people, meat was definitely off the menu. But getting the combination right had been made more challenging by the fact that Tamzin, their female guest, was allergic to gluten, while Clive, her husband, loathed 'fish with a strong taste'. And there were other problems, too, which Stephen preferred not to think about at the moment.

'I'd just like to know what "fish with a strong taste" actually means,' he said, mainly to break the silence. Rachel looked up and caught his eye for the first time. The invasion by the children had brought them together slightly, giving them a common enemy as it did.

'Oh, you know Clive,' she said. 'His greatest fear in life is that he isn't very interesting. He's spent years honing all these fascinating little quirks, so we'll all know he's a true eccentric.'

'So this is a signal that he's totally wacky and off-the-wall ... Bit subtle.' Then, buoyed by the almost-friendly tone

7

of the conversation, Stephen took the plunge. 'What are you making, by the way?'

A silence.

'I'm not trying to interfere; I'm just curious.'

'Well, it was meant to be one thing, and now it's going to be something else.' The tension had returned to Rachel's voice. 'Just let me get on with it, and don't start on that expert-chef crap. Remember who does the cooking all week.'

This was the real killer, and the fundamental reason for Rachel's irritation: Stephen, who cooked for a living, rarely produced any food in his own home. Earthsea was his third child, his obsession. It had been open for two years, had once been listed in the *Observer*'s Top Ten Places to Eat Organic, and was popular with time-starved, GM-aware Brightonians. As well as being a proper restaurant, bang in the middle of the bohemian North Laines and right opposite the fashionable Komedia theatre, it was an upmarket takeaway, sending such vice-free delights as Cajun corn-cakes and roast-nut terrine to any address in the area. On environmentally sound mountain bikes, of course. Success seemed within Stephen's grasp – Earthsea was busy every night, and weekends were usually booked up in advance. It seemed that his reverence for food was paying off, in spite of his lack of business skills. Rachel, on the other hand, had no interest in cuisine, or in the restaurant. When they had first met, at university, he had been astonished to find that she didn't even know what to buy in supermarkets. Once she had invested in coffee, spaghetti and half a pound of Edam, she would wander vaguely up and down the aisles, unable to find anything else she liked or recognized. At the time – in the early eighties – this had seemed a respectably feminist stance. What's more, it had given him the chance to show off his ability to roll his own cannelloni. So he had not held it against her. But, since then, it had driven a wedge between them. Her sloppiness in the kitchen enraged him – surely it couldn't be natural? It must be put on, exaggerated. She didn't even turn off the taps properly. He glanced across at the sink now – sure enough, water was plopping noisily into the overloaded washing-up bowl. He huffed across and turned it off with an angry flourish of his wrist. He didn't look at Rachel, knowing she would see this as a hostile act. Instead, he sneaked a glance at the piles of squashed strawberries that stood among the bowls of half-eaten mashed potato left over from Elsie and Stan's tea. How had he come to be married to someone with whom he was so incompatible? It wasn't as if he hadn't worked at fancying the right people. Rachel stood at the highest point of his sexual and social aspirations. Vulgarity didn't turn him on, even when he was seventeen. Leela, Tom Baker's slightly raddled-looking assistant in *Dr Who*, had inspired his first crush. Later he'd had a yen for Sigourney Weaver in her early Ripley days. Classy, stroppy women, both of them. More recently, though, he had realized that he wanted more. He wanted someone who shared his obsession with food. So the obvious choice was Nigella Lawson. While he knew it was unfair to compare her to Rachel in any way, he couldn't help indulging in the occasional fantasy that, instead of a wife who had once managed to incinerate a saucepan of baked beans, he lived with a raven-haired temptress who could rustle up a casual lunch for twenty without smudging her eyeliner. He felt slightly guilty about this mental infidelity. But what a team he and Nigella would have made, in some parallel culinary universe. And putting up with a wife who couldn't even do something decent with two punnets of fresh strawberries was hard work. He shook his head to clear it of these unwelcome thoughts, which did not do justice to the wonderfulness of Rachel. At that precise moment, he couldn't bring to mind the exact components of that wonderfulness; but he knew that this was just the result of pre-meal tension and the fact that she had been sniping at him more than usual this week, for reasons yet to be revealed.

He probably deserved this. He was working too hard, not at home enough and talking too much about his work when he was. His habit of leaping out of bed and rushing downstairs to experiment with new angles on chilli marinade was probably quite annoying. And, sometimes, he even complained about the food which Rachel gave him. This was very bad. He was too fussy. He knew he was too fussy. What the hell, he *prided* himself on being too fussy.

He looked at the clock. Fifteen minutes to go. When they ate *chez* Tamzin and Clive, all was haloumi and harmony. Tamzin – once a City broker – had re-branded herself as an earth mother the minute the line had turned blue on the Predictor kit, and had never looked back. Perhaps, Stephen thought for the first time, she too had been inspired by the example of Nigella. Certainly, there was an air of charmed competence surrounding Tamzin which was notably absent from the vicinity of all the other women Rachel knew. Her house was run with the suave efficiency of a merchant bank; a suaveness aided by all the money they had. No one quite knew where their money came from. But Clive was one of those people who combine an apparent social stupidity with an uncanny intuition about turning a fast buck. Stephen had known Clive for nearly twenty years, and he'd always radiated prosperity, even when he was definitely broke. Now, he and Tamzin were burnished with a certain celebrity gloss, resulting from domestic help, weekends away and a regular Saturday-night babysitter who enabled them to stroll along the seafront before sitting down to eat in some fashionably understated restaurant, hands twined on the natural-linen tablecloth. (They never came to Earthsea, presumably because it just wasn't expensive enough. This rankled.)

The doorbell rang. It was only a quarter past eight — they were fifteen minutes early.

'Shit — I just cannot believe this!' hissed Rachel. 'I'm going to throw on something decent. When I've got ready, you can finish the food off on your own while I entertain them. *Pissing* shit, how *could* they do this! Why aren't you letting them in?' She ran out of the kitchen, tearing the bandana out of her hair, and rushed up the stairs.

Stephen removed his apron, sighed, and hurried to the front door, wondering, not for the first time, whether everyone suffered from a social life which was far more unpleasant than their day job, or whether this was a problem he had stumbled into all on his own.

'Hello, early birds!' he grinned cheerily, throwing open the door. Tamzin and Clive were standing suspiciously close to each other on the doorstep, giving the impression that they had just emerged from a snog. Clive was tall and tanned, with receding yellow hair and horribly voguish spectacles, which gave him the look of a former pop star you really ought to recognize – a long-lost member of Duran Duran or someone from Heaven 17, perhaps. And Tamzin appeared to hail from an even earlier era – with her dead-straight red hair, heavy fringe and tidy, cat-like face, she looked like a perfectly preserved sixties hippie chick. In fact, she was one of those rare people who look younger as they get older. When she was a tense, commuting City girl, there had been something indefinably middle-aged and frumpy about her. Now she was a thirty-something housewife with four children, she sometimes looked a gamine seventeen.

Ushering them into the living room, which was toy-free apart from the remains of Buzz Lightyear lying prostrate on the coffee-table and a nude Barbie perched on a lump of coal in the fireplace, Stephen struggled to find the right cosy, host-like tone. 'Rachel is just getting ready – she'll be down any second.'

'Sorry we're a bit early. We would have phoned but we've got some news that we just had to tell you in person,' said Clive, handing over a clanking Oddbins bag. 'Couple of really nice South African clarets in there, by the way, mate. And some bubbly for you two love-birds.'

Stephen winced. 'News?' He looked from Clive to Tamzin.

'We're not going to say a *single* word till Rachel comes down,' said Tamzin. Always on the fey side, she was this evening wearing a curious floaty outfit in green and beige mottled with gold. She gave him a mysterious smile.

Stephen opened the bag. 'Okay, let's crack one of these

open,' he said, still affecting a hearty tone. 'Red good for now? I'll stick the champagne in the fridge.' He had taken the precaution of keeping the corkscrew in one of the pockets of his trousers. A few months ago they had had the unfortunate experience of completely losing the only corkscrew they owned, on just such an evening as this. Clive had had to drive, half-cut, all the way home to East Hove to fetch his own, ultra-super one, which was made by Le Creuset or something. So this evening Stephen produced it without fuss – one less trauma to dog the evening. He uncorked a bottle, and handed each of them a glass of claret.

'I'm afraid the food isn't quite ready yet – once Rachel comes down I'll have to dash back to the kitchen and . . . add the final touches . . .' he said.

'Oh, fine, fine, no worries,' said Clive. 'Just hang loose and relax – we're not in any hurry, are we, Tamz?'

'Of course not,' said Tamzin. 'You know we love to see you. We've been looking forward to this evening for weeks.'

'Certainly have,' said Clive, plumping down beside her on the leather Ikea sofa and squeezing her leg. 'And not only because it gave Tamzin the chance to splash out on yet another outfit.'

Tamzin giggled.

'Oh, Clive, don't be so outrageous,' she said.

Clive smiled around the room, looking very pleased with himself. His quest for interestingness, as outlined by Rachel, was extremely irksome. It had led him away from the dull path of IT consultancy – for this was his job – and on to more obscure routes, including ghost hunting,

13

paganism and solo camping trips to Winchelsea. Tamzin's mission to be girlish was almost as wearing. Although she had once run the entire back office of a leading broking firm, during which time she had coolly sacked weeping staff whenever necessary, and earned enough money to buy their current house for cash at the height of the eighties housing boom, she now put all this energy into motherhood and self-maintenance. Even though her steely side remained, her only topics of conversation now were children, clothes and calories. She had lobotomized herself – through sheer strength of personality.

Stephen realized that she was giving him a long look. 'How *are* you and Rachel doing? We've been worrying about you lately.'

'Worrying?' Stephen looked from one smooth, well-sunned face to the other.

'Yes – you always look so tired and washed-out.'

'Thanks!'

'Don't be silly, I don't mean it like that. It's just . . . you never seem to have time to be on your own together . . . Which is probably . . .' She stopped, glanced at Clive, then seemed to change tack. 'Are you sure you're not overdoing it in that restaurant of yours?' Clive coughed and straightened out his legs.

'Well, it's certainly pretty hectic,' said Stephen, feeling his irritation levels rise, and making a mental note to call Vinnie when he had a chance. He had a bad feeling about that hen party.

'Trouble is, you're so like me,' said Clive. 'Dynamic. An entrepreneur. At the end of the day, that makes it hard to switch off.'

'It can be hard to know when work should end and real life should start,' said Tamzin. 'Believe me, Stephen, I've been there.'

'I know, I know all that,' said Stephen. 'But starting your own business is incredibly tough. It's still early days – two years is nothing. It'll calm down soon.'

'When it does, make sure you take time to mellow out and find the real you,' said Clive. He took a slug of wine, raised his glass jokingly and affected a port-soaked, aristocratic tone. 'Time to enjoy the finer things of life.'

'And indulge yourself a bit,' said Tamzin. She certainly was determined to push her point home. Stephen hadn't seen her so animated since they had had a drunken discussion about celebrities with a passion for plastic surgery, and someone had suggested that the fashion for dinky Disney noses wasn't aesthetically pleasing. 'Do whatever men do instead of having a leg wax or a shiatsu massage.'

Stephen laughed. 'You mean watch football or go to the pub? Rachel would be thrilled.'

'Whatever turns you on, Steve,' said Clive. 'Personally, I like to get my walking boots on and get in touch with myself on the South Downs Way. Stride out among the boulders, and listen to all those relaxing sheep. But that's the kind of guy I am – outdoorsy and spiritual.'

Tamzin and Clive exchanged one of their special smiles. They were – alone among almost all the couples Stephen could think of – gratuitously happily married. They were so compatible it made you sick. They had both voted for every single political party, in sequence, at the same time. First Tory, then Lib Dem, then New Labour, and finally, in the last lot of local elections, they had plumped for the

15

Green Party. They both agreed, after a long agony about the failings of state schools, that investing in a Steiner education was far more socially acceptable than paying for your children to go to an ordinary private school. And – most important of all – they thought as one on the matter of children's names. Some couples would have been divided by the selection of Noah, Tallulah, Zuleika and Yorick. But these choices had served only to bring Tamzin and Clive closer together.

However, the biggest difference between the two of them and what Rachel called 'normal couples' was their keenness to stroke each other at every opportunity.

Now, as Stephen was inserting his Buena Vista Social Club CD into the stereo, Clive was tucking an errant strand of dark-red hair behind one of Tamzin's white pointy ears, while she smiled at him in a misty way. Later, they would doubtless sit wrapped around each other at the dinner table. This was a feature of their togetherness that Rachel particularly loathed. 'It's just plain rude, flaunting your conjugal bliss like that,' she would say. 'They're even worse than the Blairs.' She was surprisingly down on blissful monogamy, considering she was a Relate counsellor. She might have been expected to be all for it.

'Stop that, you two,' said Rachel, zooming into the room perfectly on cue, trailing an over-strong odour of Coco by Chanel. Perhaps she hadn't had time to wash properly, and was using it to disguise less beguiling whiffs. Stephen had known her resort to this ruse before, when their social schedule had left her time for only the most cursory splash in the bathroom. All part of the mad chaos Tamzin objected to, he supposed.

Tamzin sprang up and embraced Rachel. 'Don't be cheeky!' she said. Then, standing back, 'But you look great! You diet's going brilliantly!'

Stephen, who knew nothing about any diet, noticed for the first time that Rachel had indeed lost weight. She was wearing a long black dress, an unfamiliar one, in a shiny, clingy material. Her hair – always her best feature – was swept up away from her face. But, somehow, he couldn't say anything flattering. He realized he was standing in the middle of the room, giving her a long, hostile stare.

'Shall I go and finish the food?' he asked.

Rachel aimed a glance at him. 'I've left a note for you in the kitchen, so you should know what to do,' she said.

He left the room as Clive was opening a second bottle of wine, and the two women were sitting close together on the sofa, whispery and affected and full of secrets.

In the kitchen Stephen found the note, scrawled on the back of a school circular about head lice.

Stephen,
    Frankly, I don't give a shit what we eat tonight. As you no doubt noticed, the strawberries are a write-off. And if you were thinking of giving them swordfish, think again. It was two days past the sell-by date, so I've given it to the cat. As long as I live here, you won't be giving anyone food poisoning. What would it take to get you to see things as they really are? There's no place for me in your anal little dream world. Our life together is driving me to the brink of insanity — which you probably haven't noticed, as my mental state is of less interest to you than the contents of just about any recipe

17

I can think of. By the time you read this, I will be on the
way to getting pissed out of my mind.
   Over to you,
   R

Stephen stared at the note, his mind at first failing to
register what it said. After a second, a question swam into
his mind. Just what was eating Rachel? Why was she so
angry with him, *all* the time, instead of just some of the
time, an arrangement he had grown used to over the years?
He knew that the note meant they were shifting into a
new gear in their journey towards total marital breakdown.
He knew it, but he kept the knowledge enclosed in a small,
cool, part of his mind. He looked at the strawberries. They
were beyond repair, scattered across the chopping board,
like human fragments after a terrorist bomb. What should
he do? Admit all to Clive and Tamzin, phone for a curry?
Whip up some pasta carbonara, in an offhand, cheffy sort
of way?

But he looked across at Claudius, their unpleasant
cat, and the desire to even the score took over. The cat
was sitting hunched over his bowl, which stood by the
French windows. The expression on his back was one of
intense loathing born of expert discrimination. Claudius
and Stephen had always hated each other. Stephen peered
over the cat's shoulder. Sure enough, he was tackling
four pieces of pale, thick fish. Over them someone had
thoughtfully poured a large quantity of double cream. It
was unlike Rachel to pay so much attention to detail.
Claudius, ignoring Stephen completely, was caught between purring and tearing at the expensive flesh, and

began a mild choking attack. He sneezed, snatched at another piece, and raised his purring to a higher volume.

Stephen straightened up, aware that war had been declared. But he was not – no, he was not – going to let Rachel make a fool of him. He opened the French windows and stepped out into the dank garden. What he was about to do would annoy the hell out of Rachel, but she had left him with no other choice.

2

As Stephen closed the door quietly behind him, sudden angry memories tangled up in his mind. Memories of Rachel, mainly, of the person he had first seen delicately dismembering a ham roll in the refectory of Goldsmith's College in London, her back half turned towards him.

His first words to her had been 'Don't you want that?' and she had looked at him over her shoulder. She was wearing army trousers and an old white shirt, and was leaning over the balcony that bordered the mezzanine area of the refectory. With her dark skin and sarcastic expression she looked beautiful, but not in a reassuring way.

'Want what?' she had responded, not smiling.

'That roll.'

'Why? Are you hungry?'

'No – I just hate seeing food wasted.'

'Oh really?'

She had detached a long strip of white fat and dropped it into a silver-foil ashtray, where it lay curled into a disturbing, snake-like shape among the fag butts.

That might have been it. Now, looking down at his mobile phone, unable for a moment to focus his mind, Stephen thought maybe it would have been better if he had just casually sauntered away on that day, eighteen years before, leaving their children unconceived, their holidays in foreign cities unbooked and argued through, and gallons of lager and wine undrunk.

Instead, he had said: 'If you really don't want it, I'll finish it.'

She had handed it to him, speechless, as if in contempt. Still, she had her back turned half towards him. But instead of moving off, as she easily could have done, she took a Marlboro out of her woven shoulder bag, and lit it with a throwaway lighter. And, as he stuffed the final fragments of the roll into his mouth, she finally turned to face him, her elbows resting on the ledge. The sheer impact of her full attention made him dizzy.

'D'you know how many calories there are in one of those?' she asked.

'No.'

'Three hundred and fifty.'

'Is that good or bad?'

'Christ. Haven't you ever heard of calories?'

'Of course. All food's fattening. But that's not the most interesting thing about it.'

'About what?'

'About food.'

'Oh, for fuck's sake.'

In his garden he pressed the buttons on his phone, imagining the hectic scene at Earthsea. He should have been there, overseeing everything and interceding if Vinnie threatened to make the waitresses cry. But he couldn't be in two places at once, couldn't be two people.

'Hello?' Vinnie's voice; unmistakable, due to his ability to sound morose and manic at the same time. In the background was the noise of pans being bashed around, some shouting and, more faintly, the soothing ambient music they used to calm the diners.

'Vinnie, hi, it's Stephen.'

'We're fine, so there's no point in calling. And if you're in a paddy about the frigging cinnamon sticks and stuff, that's sorted.' Stephen had met Vinnie ten years before when working – briefly – for a steakhouse with a Wild West theme near Charing Cross. Although they were so different – Vinnie a gay miserabilist prone to disastrous relationships, and Stephen a happyish husband with a garden shed – their friendship had continued since then. They had started working together again only when Stephen set up Earthsea and asked Vinnie to join him. Luckily for Stephen, Vinnie had just fallen in love with Marc, who lived in Brighton; otherwise he would never have made the move from sirloin steak to silken tofu. He was an aggressive, combative person in his day-to-day dealings with the world, but this concealed the passivity of a natural drifter. So, although he was an unreconstructed carnivore who loathed vegetarians with a passion, he had thrown his energy into the restaurant. His vegetarian cooking was brilliant, but he ate a donor kebab every day, chewing with relish at the long twists of overcooked lamb. Stephen was afraid that one day Vinnie would storm out and work somewhere that served genetically enhanced cholesterol to meat-eaters. So he treated him with respect. If Vinnie left, everything would fall apart.

'I knew I could rely on you,' he said. 'How busy is it?'

'Ten tables in, nine bookings and seven takeaway orders. Hen party late, but *c'est la vie*. Nothing we can't handle.' More shouting in the background, a waitress yelling, 'So you can get stuffed, and get me more guacamole!'

'Great.' Stephen hesitated, wondering what to say next.

'So, Steve, hate to be rude, but what exactly is the reason for your call? I know you love me and all that . . .'

Stephen hesitated. 'I don't know how to say this, really, but I've had a bit of a row with Rachel, and she's thrown away the dinner we were meant to be having tonight. For our dinner party, you know. She seems to be having some sort of – I don't know. She's on the warpath.'

'Is she really?' Vinnie seemed cheered by the thought. 'I knew it was only a matter of time before she kicked you up the arse. But . . . what d'you want me to do about it?'

'I was wondering if you could put me at the top of the takeaway list and send over something from the à la carte menu. In fact . . .' He drew a deep breath and plunged in. 'It would be really, really good if you could do a nice mezze to start – hummus, broad-bean dip, tzatziki – then those cauliflower and turmeric fritters we tried out this morning, and some baby onions in tamarind, then a spicy aubergine salad with couscous, and for pudding some chocolate torte, and prunes in brandy . . . Er, that's all.' Stephen got all this out as quickly as possible, trying hard to sound matter-of-fact. He co-owned the damn place, after all. But he knew he was embarrassingly in the wrong.

The mobile was mute in his hand.

'Please, Vinnie. I'll do anything you like – just tell me what you want and I'll do it.'

'What you are asking will screw up our takeaway rota, and means making food that isn't even on the bloody menu tonight, so we'll be arse over tit for the rest of the evening,' said Vinnie.

'I know. I know that. I wouldn't ask if I wasn't desperate.'

'Two nights in Paris, then, for me and Marc. All expenses paid.'

'Vinnie, you know we can't afford it.'

'Then I can't fucking help you.'

'Okay. Okay. I'll fix it.'

'Right – you're on.'

'Thanks. And – well, try to find somewhere cheap to stay. I'll fill you in tomorrow about . . .' Stephen wondered what there would be to say tomorrow.

But Vinnie had heard enough. 'Catch you later,' he said.

'Just one more thing.'

'What?'

'Can you ask whoever delivers it to bring it to the back door? I don't want anyone to see them.'

'You are a strange, sad man,' said Vinnie. The phone went dead.

Stephen was left clutching his mobile to his ear, standing in his dishevelled garden. He felt suddenly lost and foolish, and put the phone back into his pocket sheepishly. The garden, like other domestic areas, was a joint effort. And the result was no more satisfactory than in any of their other marital projects. Their efforts were parallel, rather than complementary. Rachel, with characteristic impatience, liked the idea of instant gardening. So what she had brought to their small, square patch with its truncated lawn and steep, sloping borders was architectural plantage, bought at vast expense, and statues. For several obsessive months, she had rushed around antique fairs, junk shops and even car-boot sales, in search of *outré* and – she had assured Stephen – ironic stone or plaster figures of all kinds. Now their garden, which formerly contained nothing more pretentious than some random clumps of fuscia and a rhododendron bush, featured a host of well-known faces from the Italian Renaissance, including The Three Graces and a dinky version of Michelangelo's David. Meanwhile, Stephen, with his eye for detail, had planted lots of dainty ferns, and herbs for his kitchen, which were separated from Rachel's wild, theatrical sections of the flowerbeds by rows of sensible white shells, collected by Elsie on various trips to the seafront. The effect, he thought now, feeling a sense of impending doom, was overcrowded and absurd. Like displaying your minimalist furniture on a swirly floral carpet. It was an experiment that could never have worked, even if their original good intentions hadn't been overtaken by neglect. In the summer, the tiny David was half suffocated by rampant mint and the giant arum lilies that Rachel had been so keen to plant wrestled with a rosebush. It was painfully obvious that he and Rachel couldn't even nurture a border of flowers, never mind a marriage containing two other, small human beings.

He shook himself. Time to go back inside.

'Stephen – what have you been up to?' said Clive when he reappeared. The second wine bottle was almost empty, and Rachel and Tamzin were still sitting side by side on the sofa, their cheeks flushed and their eyes bright. There was an air of unsavoury excitement in the room – what had they been discussing while he was out of earshot? Clive – as always happened when he had anything to drink – had gone into hyperactive mode, and was pacing up and down the room.

'I've been sorting out the food,' said Stephen, without looking at Rachel. 'It'll be ready in about an hour.' Rachel made a strange noise, halfway between a laugh and a growl.

'Well, now you're back, perhaps we should let you in on our secret.' Clive was now standing behind the sofa. He wrapped his arms around Tamzin's neck, almost as if he was about to throttle her, in a manner that Stephen had previously seen practised only in glossy 1970s TV dramas in which flash males would wear navy blazers while the women – usually unstable heiresses – sported cream trouser suits. Tamzin smiled up winsomely from the crook of Clive's elbow.

'Yes, tell us!' commanded Rachel, who seemed more the worse for wear than anyone. 'I demand to know what you two have been looking so smug about all evening.'

'Shall I?' Tamzin twinkled up at Clive.

'Go on, darling.'

'Well . . . our first little news item is that we're going to renew our vows in a special ceremony for a few close friends – how many people are we inviting, Clive?'

'Fifty-nine.'

'A small, informal crowd, nothing over the top –'

'Just a marquee and a string quartet, and a little champagne –' Clive shrugged, as if apologizing for the modesty of the concept.

'And Clive's already given me this fantastic eternity

ring –' Tamzin held up her left hand. It was white and freckled, each fingernail a perfect oval painted royal blue. Above her wedding and engagement rings flashed a circle of diamonds.

'Great . . .' Stephen said. 'That's really . . .'

'Wait!' Clive nodded emphatically towards Tamzin. 'There's more . . .'

Tamzin hesitated. 'The other thing is – I'm pregnant again.' She smiled at her wine glass, which, Stephen noticed, was still full.

'Just one of those silly mistakes,' said Clive. 'Carried away on the spur of the moment . . .'

'Like a couple of teenagers!' said Tamzin. 'You know how it is.'

The atmosphere tightened. Stephen felt a stab of sharp despair.

'How wonderful,' said Rachel. 'Congratulations.' Stephen noticed that the amount she'd had to drink was affecting her ability to pretend to be enthusiastic. Which was fair enough, he thought. Everything that happened to Clive and Tamzin was big news. They suffered the worst service and most excruciating holidays of anyone Stephen knew, but were perked up by their athletic sex life, brood of gorgeous, gifted young children and their beautiful home, which quintupled in value every fortnight. He knew all that. So why did it all seem so unbearable to contemplate now? There was an odd, jerky pause, which probably should have been filled by Rachel hugging Tamzin, but wasn't.

'When is it due?' asked Stephen, limply.

'Oh, in November . . . Are you all right, Rachel?' Tamzin

was peering at Rachel, who appeared to be close to tears.

'Yes – of course – really happy for you!' Rachel kissed Tamzin and sprang up. 'Let's have some Cava! I'm sure we've got some somewhere.'

She rushed out of the room, wiping her eyes with the backs of her hands.

'Shouldn't you go after her, Steve?' said Clive.

'She's fine – it's just drinking on an empty stomach,' said Stephen, who had no wish to go near Rachel, unprotected by guests, while she was in her current mood.

'It's very emotional for women when they find their girlfriends are pregnant,' Tamzin confided. 'Such a bond.'

Stephen had no idea what she was talking about. He looked at his watch – not even nine o'clock. The food would be ages yet. Clive, frowning, bustled out, muttering about champagne. Tamzin smiled and patted the space on the sofa next to her. Stephen sat down, wishing hard that he was chopping coriander at Earthsea, amid the shouting, feuding staff.

'You know, Steve, one thing has crossed my mind,' she said, dropping her voice.

'What sort of thing?'

'Well, have you and Rachel thought about – you know – a third?'

'A third . . . ?' For some reason, Stephen couldn't for a moment think what she meant, and thought of the Third Way. Had that been something to do with the SDP, or was it connected with Adolf Hitler? He had always been woolly regarding factual stuff and current affairs. He had bodged his way through his English degree by somehow knowing what was inside books without reading them – a special talent he still occasionally unleashed on Clive, who read modern novels all the time but found opinions difficult to form.

'A third *baby*.'

Before Stephen had time to respond, Rachel and Clive returned, bearing a bottle and clean, tinkling glasses. Rachel was shiny and smiley, obviously on the brink of hysterics. Stephen noticed that the glasses were the pricey, long-stemmed ones that were meant to be a present for his mother's sixtieth birthday. Rachel had commandeered these, obviously trying to hold her own in the lifestyle stakes.

'Here we are – let's push the boat out for the love-birds!' She was speaking in a strange falsetto. Things were getting worse and worse. They drank quickly for a while. Stephen began to lose track of time, distracted by Rachel looking increasingly dangerous and Clive and Tamzin leching at each other on the sofa. Then he saw through the window at the back of the room that Flint, one of his more gormless employees, was waving at him from behind the micro statue of David, surrounded by ramparts of white plastic carrier bags.

'I'm . . . just off to check how the food is doing,' he said, giving Flint a subtle grimace, intended to encourage him to keep out of sight.

'Oh, nice timing, just as we're about to drink a toast to friends who still have sex,' said Rachel.

But he kept going. They were on a downhill slope now – he could no more control the pace than he could imagine the destination.

In the garden, Flint was full of apologies. 'Sorry – I got

late because Vinnie threw a wobbler. It's a bloody nightmare there, Steve. You're better off out of it.' He paused for breath. 'There are prunes in brandy in the coolbox.'

'Wonderful.' Stephen began picking up the bags. It could have been a year's supply of tripe and chips for all he cared now.

But concern flashed across Flint's angular, undernourished face. 'Is it true you're, like, pretending you cooked this at home?' He craned his neck, trying to catch a glimpse of the terrifying guests.

'Just let me worry about all that. I've got my reasons. Say a big thank you to Vinnie – this has saved me from total disaster. Tell him to have a fag break or something and calm down. Now go, quick, before they see you.'

'Okay – cool.' Flint shambled off around the side of the house, snapping his earphones back into place around his shaven head.

Stephen rushed into the kitchen, bags in each hand, then saw Rachel coming down the corridor, head down. Hurriedly, he backed into the downstairs loo, flushed the chain, piled the bags by the toilet, and came out pretending to flick water off his hands.

'What the *fuck* are you playing at?' she hissed. Her face was no longer shiny. It was lumpy with misery. 'Can't you even go through the motions of behaving properly? What is your *problem*?'

'Where shall I start?' Stephen hissed back. 'How about the fact that you've tried to sabotage the whole evening and make me look stupid in front of Posh and Becks in there. Mr Incompetent, the super-chef who has no food in his own kitchen?'

'Christ, you are pathetic! You pompous, puffed-up little egomaniac! You're the one who tried to give everyone food poisoning! Food's not just about showing off, you know. If you stopped trying to be Marco Pierre White once in a while, you'd realize the rest of the human race is microwaving TV dinners – and is none the bloody worse for that! Just get back in the living room,' said Rachel. 'Drink your drink, and try to look as if you're bloody enjoying yourself.'

'Okay,' said Stephen. 'But just one thing . . .' He thought fast. 'I've done a massive fart in the downstairs loo, so I'd be grateful if you used the upstairs one. At least we can avoid another tirade about the disgustingness of my bodily functions.'

'Why thank you,' said Rachel. 'How thoughtful of you to spare me the stench of your bloody arse.'

'Mmm, that was fantastic.' Clive pushed his plate, which he had scraped clean of wholesome salads, away from him. 'You really know your stuff, Steve. I hardly noticed that was veggie food at all.'

'I try to give satisfaction,' said Stephen. Rachel said nothing, but busied herself with refilling three of the wine glasses on the table. Tamzin was sipping water and gazing at them with a beatific, newly pregnant expression.

'You know, I really am enjoying this evening,' said Clive. He took an extravagant mouthful of wine. 'So nice when we can all get together and totally be ourselves. Although there was a moment earlier on when I thought you two were having a bit of a tiff.'

'Really?' said Rachel.

'Perish the thought,' said Stephen. Each avoided the other's eye.

'It's healthy to express your emotions,' said Tamzin. 'Clive and I are always expressing ours, aren't we, darling?'

'I'll go and get the pudding,' said Rachel. It took Stephen, now blurry with wine, a few seconds to realize what a bad idea this was. By the time he had fully formulated the thought, a sound like a pistol going off was coming from the kitchen. Obviously, Rachel had found the prunes still in their foil container, with the telltale word 'EARTHSEA' and sea-witch logo inscribed on the side. Her loathing of his restaurant was about to go into overdrive.

'Stephen, can you come out here a minute?' Her voice, calling from the kitchen, had a sweetly murderous edge.

'What for?' Stephen called back, sprawled in his chair, casual as a skiving schoolboy.

'Just come here *right now*!'

He gave Tamzin and Clive a cosy smile, and sauntered into the kitchen.

Rachel was standing by the fridge, the container of prunes and brandy in her hand. With her black tousled hair and twisted face, she reminded him of Mr Rochester's mad wife. 'You bastard,' she said, her voice low but growing steadily in volume. 'You utter, total and contemptible little shit. For the last two years, your pretentious little foodery has been driving me insane. You are never here. If you are, briefly, on the premises, you spend the whole time tearing up recipe books and inventing vegan appetizers. You stay awake all night worrying about cash flow and where to source your bananas. The only way to get you to notice me would be to turn myself into a fucking kiwi-fruit Pavlova. And now this: you go behind my back, sneak off and get your little drones to cover up the fact that you can't get a meal together in your own home. All that trouble, just to save yourself the hassle of looking stupid on one of the rare occasions that you can be *bothered* to be here ... You are a complete and utter wanker, Stephen, and this is the final straw ...'

'Now hang on a minute,' said Stephen, who had been trying to speak throughout this outburst. 'There would have been a meal if you hadn't given the fish to Claudius. And if you hadn't destroyed all the strawberries. How you managed that I can't –'

'Don't patronize me, Stephen, or I will kill you,' said Rachel.

'Oh, for Christ's sake!' yelled Stephen, suddenly not caring in the least what love's middle-aged dream could hear from the living room. His futile attempts to show Clive that he wasn't a complete loser were over. 'It's just a meal! It's just one stupid evening, one pathetic, unenjoyable get-together, which you attempted to convert into the night from hell because you are mentally ill, or premenstrual, or ...'

'Premenstrual? Do you even know when my last period *was*, Steve? Because – I'll let you into a little secret – it ended three days ago. If you ever touched me, if you ever came *near* me in bed, perhaps you'd know that. Perhaps I wouldn't have to live my life like a fucking born-again virgin, living with a mincing little prick with the sex drive of a dead slug!' On the word 'slug' she burst into loud, climactic sobs. 'Oh my God!' she yelled. 'Oh my dear

33

God! Is this my life? Is this the way it really has to be?' To his horror, she threw herself to the ground and lay there sobbing hysterically.

Stephen found, with a cold *frisson* of surprise, that he could not stoop down to comfort her. The will, the action, the words, just would not come. He cared, but somehow that feeling was marooned. He could not do what he knew he had to do. Instead, he stared down at her, noticing that, in spite of her extreme behaviour, the prunes still nestled in the silver rectangle, undisturbed.

'Er – what is happening here?' Clive and Tamzin were standing, hand in hand, in the kitchen doorway. Clive was shaking his head, very slowly, as if unable to believe his eyes. Tamzin was oozing womanly concern. 'Maybe we should go,' said Clive. 'Maybe you people need to sort this thing out on your own.'

'No!' Rachel shrieked, from inside her wet, chaotic hair. 'Stay! Don't leave me with him! Stay!' More high-volume sobbing. Tamzin detached herself from Clive and gathered Rachel in her arms, rocking her to and fro, a designer Madonna. Stephen felt sick. It was as if he had committed adultery with his own food.

'This is madness,' he said. 'Rachel, speak to me, this is crazy. It's all about nothing, it's . . .'

'If that's what you really, honestly and truly think, then our relationship is definitely over.' Rachel suddenly knelt up, tossed her hair out of her red, rheumy eyes. 'Because you don't know me, you don't know yourself, and you don't give a shit.'

'What are you talking about? What the hell are you talking about?'

'I'm talking about us, Stephen. I'm talking about our fucking lousy relationship. I'm telling you that I can't go on. It can't go on. You have to leave.'

'*Leave?* Are you out of your mind? I'm not going anywhere! This is my home! This is where I live . . .' But his words were cut short, because Rachel had thrown herself out of Tamzin's embrace and on top of him, and was beating him around the head with the foil container. Prunes ricocheted round the kitchen. Stephen struggled to cover his eyes with his hands. 'Rachel – Christ – Rachel!'

Clive tried to interpose his body between them, being too gentlemanly to restrain a woman, crying: 'Look mate, why not take a turn round the block – breath of fresh air – till she calms down –'

Then someone's hands were wrapped firmly around his upper arms, pushing him gently but irresistibly towards the hall. He felt himself projected by Tamzin's steely embrace towards his own front door, the door he had opened to her just a short time before. He saw it open once more, to the navy night sky. The rain had stopped, but a wind was gathering. From behind him, a sweater stole over his shoulders. Tamzin, demon hatchet woman, mother of all excellence, thought of everything.

'Come back in an hour or so,' she said in her soft-hard voice. 'We'll soon calm her down.' The door closed behind him.

3

For several minutes Stephen walked, flat-out, breathing fast and churning all those terrible words round in his head. Words that he knew, whatever lay ahead, could never be forgotten. He felt physically winded by the ferocity of Rachel's attack, and the thought that Tamzin and Clive had seen it all was an added, angry pain. Phrases like 'mincing little prick' and 'sex drive of a dead slug' weren't ones he could easily forgive.

After a while, however, he started to wonder how his life had managed to turn out like this. In the eighties, one of his favourite songs had been David Byrne's 'Day in the Life', in which a suburban American fails to recognize his beautiful house, and his beautiful wife. One of Stephen's unacknowledged ambitions had been to avoid such stifling conformity himself. But he hadn't known what his beautiful future should consist of, just what he wanted to avoid. Flock wallpaper. Doilies. Boil-in-the-bag TV dinners. Girls who tittered and said 'Room for a little one?' when confronted with a crowded lift. The restaurant idea had come slowly. In every kitchen he had worked in, he would fret over what was done badly, the short cuts, the crap management and the tedious repetition of tired dishes. While working in one restaurant he had vowed that, should he ever become a head chef, he would never shout at his staff. So far, he'd kept that promise. In another job, he decided that he would – when the day came – have six new dishes each day, a pledge he had stuck to ever since, even though Vinnie often cursed him for it. In a third, that he really would make sure that all his ingredients were organic, not just the ones which came easily to hand. This was the hardest of all to stick to, and sadly he had had to compromise along the way. But it was that vision, more than any other, that had suddenly woken him one morning, with the desperate certainty that he must run his own place, a restaurant with beautiful ingredients, tasteful surroundings, gastronomic ideals. He was working as head chef at a hotel on the seafront at the time, and that very day he noticed that a clothes shop for fattish hippie women had closed down in Ship Street, just off the seafront, in the perfect spot for an organic veggie eaterie. He had pushed his face flat against the glass, peered in past the naked, headless dummies that had once sported swathes of kaftan, and – in a flash of inspiration – saw Earthsea for the first time: the tables with their orange linen cloths, the bright, clashing walls, the staff in their matching combats whisking through the half-doors to the kitchen. And the smell of the food was already in his nostrils, combining Middle Eastern exoticism with the subtlety of freshly picked local produce. The day Earthsea opened was the happiest of his life, a fact he couldn't actually admit to anybody. How could launching a restaurant beat getting married, or seeing your children for the first time? But there it was. He remembered Vinnie, on that very first day. Unruly black hair newly trimmed for the occasion, apron lashed around his wiry little torso, standing behind the preparation table with a glass of champagne in his hand. 'Let the ceremony commence!' Vinnie had declaimed, in his usual tone of doleful irony. But the cheers of the staff were anything but ironic, as they stood there, scrubbed up and waiting for the fray.

Their very first customers were a pale twosome who hardly spoke or smiled. They began with mushroom and almond soup, then, looking almost animated, they had moved on to a mezze of pickled turnips, charred aubergine, tabbouleh and wilted herb salad. For pudding, nearly chuckling, they'd ordered rosewater and cardamom ice-cream with prunes in brandy. Prunes in brandy! He wasn't sure whether or not he liked these little patterns life threw up. Not, probably.

Thinking of prunes and pain, he started to notice his surroundings again. He realized he had walked under the viaduct in Beaconsfield Road, which he always saw as the entrance to Brighton proper. He hesitated by the Duke of York's cinema, and looked up at the black-and-white-striped plaster-of-Paris legs that waved from its roof, doing a perpetual cancan. They represented everything he liked about Brighton: the tackiness, the wackiness, the artsy disregard for mainstream people who chose – *of their own free will* – to live in a close. Once, they had lived near this cinema, when the children were tiny and Rachel still seemed to like him. With a bitter sigh, he looked up at the cloudy night sky, and the half-hidden moon. He rarely had time to notice such things.

Which brought him back to the scene he'd just left. Here he was, hardworking, faithful, committed to his family, with no empty spaces for looking at the sky, accused of – what? A low sex drive? A lack of interest in his wife? What was she thinking of? Now he was lost, tossed out on Rachel's melodramatic whim. Where exactly *was* he going? For a moment his legs felt too heavy, too hopeless to carry on. Rachel was stark, staring mad. She always had been, and she was getting worse. Tamzin and Clive were the friends from hell, self-obsessed and stinking rich. What worse combination could there be? He would not go humbly back, knocking on his own front door, to see if he had been forgiven yet. No. He would not play their game. Instead, he would get completely tanked up. Yes. Arseholed. On something like . . . tequila. Or that stuff that had a dead snake in the bottle.

Thoughts of unreconstructed alcohol abuse cheered him up, but he still felt the need for something more, something which reminded him of the world beyond the insane shouting and the wet twists of hair. So – almost without realizing he was doing it – he checked his mobile for messages. And there were two. The bigger, calmer world had not forgotten him.

The first was from his sister. 'Hi, Stevie,' said Carmel. 'Know you're really busy, but I'd like to get together for drink. Got a little plan, darlin', I'll tell you all about it when I see you.' 'Stevie' was new – making him sound like an adorable soft toy. And as for 'darlin'' – what was that all about? But Carmel, who had changed herself almost beyond recognition from the fat, frustrated teenager who pulled at her chin-flab in 1977, had never quite worked out how to treat him. Maybe he hadn't changed enough. Older, louder and at six feet even taller than he was, she had been through so many fresh identities on her way to the current one – larger-than-life lesbian entrepreneur –

that he sometimes wondered if there was anything left at all of the grumpy elder sister he had endured throughout his childhood. She had gone to Queen Mary College in London, making the East End her spiritual home and stamping ground. There, she had put her energies into being a fervent feminist-socialist, the living personification of one of *Private Eye*'s 'wimmin'. At that time, however, she hadn't been gay. In fact, she was much more successful with men than he was with women. She didn't come out as a lesbian until her thirtieth birthday, and Stephen sometimes wondered whether her extreme emotional correctness surrounding all things sexual was the result of that decade spent sleeping with the Wrong Sex. Success seemed to embarrass her less, however. She had recently forked out £3,000 for a private operation to get her bunions fixed without even having the grace to look embarrassed. 'It's just not worth my while to wait around,' she had told him blithely. 'If you run your own business, you have to look at the maths.' It could only be a matter of time before she started running her own think-tank. So far, she had stuck to making squillions of pounds out of a gay dating agency, fairsex.com, trading profitably on the restlessness and fraught relationships of her lesbian and gay compatriots. Carmel did not believe in lifelong romance; this at least was consistent with her performance at college. 'Monogamy is fine for swans,' she liked to say, before dumping yet another hapless lover. Though, mysteriously, her affair with Lise, a shaven-headed salsa teacher with whom she lived in Montpelier Terrace, had now lasted for more than a year.

The second message was from Vinnie: 'Don't know

why I'm bothering, but I thought I might as well keep you up to speed with just how bollocks this evening has turned out since you relieved us of half the menu. Expect you'll be too busy stuffing your face to listen to any of this, but you might like to know that we've lost another member of staff. Briony has just walked out. Don't know why; probably man trouble. Someone has got to try to stop the staff from shagging each other and then splitting up in the middle of a shift. Total fucking arse here. Just so you know. Byeeee!'

Stephen slowed down for a minute. The usually elusive Carmel was threatening to confide in him, and Earthsea was losing all its staff. It seemed that the bigger, calmer world was collapsing too. Should he go into work? He couldn't face it. The two unwelcome messages added to the surreal atmosphere of the evening. He needed a drink. He really needed a drink. By now he had reached the parade of shops opposite St Peter's church at the far end of London Road.

'Give us twenty quid, mate,' said a young man lying on the pavement, wearing torn army trousers and with a faceful of chains.

'Sorry, mate,' said Stephen, feeling prissy and more like Niles from *Frasier* than usual. (Several people had commented on the resemblance.)

Perhaps he would just go. Just disappear from Rachel's life, unwanted, unmissed by her. Live in the restaurant, sleep under the kitchen table, spend the small hours inventing brilliant new recipes, take udon noodles to undreamed-of places. See the children at weekends. Which would be fine. Trips to the park. Or to the Regency Fish

Bar on the seafront, where the Cypriot waiters would entertain the children with peppermints and Mediterranean patter. Being a Weekend Dad was so common these days that it wasn't even corny.

As he reached the bottom of Trafalgar Street, the rain began again, starting almost casually, with individual drops of rain plopping on the pavement around him and only a few, specially selected ones landing on his body. Almost before Stephen had taken in the fact that this was indeed a proper rainstorm, he was soaked through, the sweater around his shoulders heavy with water. He began to run, as fast as he could. With his head down, he dashed into a side street, slithered over the shiny cobbles, and pushed open the door of the Princess Louise, a small, dingy pub where he and Rachel used to drink when they were child-free. Only when he had wiped his face and looked around him did he realize that since then things had changed. The old-fashioned patterned carpets, sepia shots of the Brighton seafront and the landlady's extensive collection of international keyrings had been swept away and replaced with a new, post-Ikea minimalist chic. Now the floorboards were stripped bare, beechwood benches and tables were lined up against the walls and the bar curved dramatically around one corner of the room, covered with a brilliant, multicoloured mosaic. Above the sparkling rows of wine glasses ran a continuous chain of lettering: 'openplan, openplan, openplan, openplan'. The pub's new name. The place had been Stalinized into modishness. He almost turned and walked out. But beyond the door – now painted turquoise and orange – the rain was pouring down relentlessly. So he ordered a drink. A dreadlocked barmaid brought out a bottle of Grolsch from a fridge in which cold beers were displayed in a beguiling, Arctic light. Stephen hadn't drunk designer beer for years, had almost forgotten about the silly white tops. He sat at one of the wooden tables, sipping the eighties. He remembered his first date with Rachel, a trip to see *Accidental Death of an Anarchist*, both trying hard to look amused in a discriminating way, hands not quite touching on the narrow armrests between the seats. (Each had mistakenly thought that the other was a posh, cultural sort of person. They never went to the theatre again.) He remembered the day, years later, when they watched *Live Aid* on TV in Rachel's flat in Brixton, the sun blazing down outside. She had developed such a loathing for Bob Geldof that she ended up screaming 'You sanctimonious Irish git!' at the screen, while the rest of the nation made credit-card donations and felt good about themselves.

Then his mind flashed to Brockwell Park, soon after Elsie was born, the two of them sitting in the walled rose garden while the baby yelled, creasy and scarlet in her pram. He remembered the physical shock of being dragged into parenthood, bereaved of sleep and freedom. Rachel, bent double next to him, sobbing in a dirty T-shirt, old grey jogging pants riding halfway up her wintry white calves. They had gone there to discuss the need to break up, driven to the brink of mutual hatred by exhaustion and the unspoken fear of parenthood. Yes – even then splitting up had been on the cards. They had forgotten it was Gay Pride day, and the park was heaving with gorgeous, sexually charged gaylords and lesbian hard-bodies in little Turkish hats. In fact, they were in serious danger of bumping into Carmel in one of her tribal moods.

Just as he had tried to put his pallid, frail, heterosexual arm around Rachel's shoulders, he had noticed that they were not alone. On the bench in the next alcove two deeply tanned men, both wearing matching outfits of frothy white ballet skirts and black biker jackets, were doing oral sex, silently but emphatically. One was standing up, legs apart, leather arms pressed to his lover's head. The other was . . . well, jerking his head methodically up and down, as you would. Too depressed to move, Stephen had tried to kiss Rachel, but her mouth was full of tears and recriminations. Elsie howled on, oblivious to adult misery and sexual orientation. Above them, shafts of pink and gold drifted across the sky. Perhaps it was only in times of crisis that he looked above head level and noticed what the heavens were up to.

The pub around him came back into focus and he stared covertly at some of the young people who were drinking at the other tables, trying to work out what stage they had reached in the sex war. Mostly, judging from the twined, narrow limbs and the protesting giggles of the girls, they hadn't got far. Not much beyond the sense of wonder and disbelief that comes when you crawl into someone else's bed and find that their perfect, naked body belongs to you for a whole night. Only one couple stood out – they sat at the bar on high metal stools, heads close together but their backs hunched so tensely that Stephen could tell they were arguing. At first, he didn't recognize either of them. Then, when the boy stood up, Stephen saw his tight, regular features and straight yellow hair. It was Andy, one of the waiters from the restaurant – probably their most unpleasant member of staff. He was an aggressive Australian womanizer, with a bad attitude and a low boredom threshold. The girl he was arguing with held her head low, and a dark-red plait hung down her back. Only when Andy had sauntered into the gent's did she turn her head. Stephen saw that it was Briony, the waitress whose abrupt exit had annoyed Vinnie so much. Automatically, he sank lower in his seat, not wanting to be seen. But he was too late. She caught his eye, and visibly winced. Perhaps she thought he was there to demand her immediate return to Earthsea. Stephen waved awkwardly, disentangled himself from behind the table and crossed over to where she was sitting.

'Hello, Briony,' he began, making a hearty gesture with his half-drunk bottle of beer.

Her face was flushed. 'Hi, Stephen,' she said. 'I didn't expect to see you in here.'

'No,' said Stephen. 'No, I didn't expect to see myself in here, either!' He followed this up with a series of nods. 'In fact, I'm on my way somewhere else.'

Where, he wondered?

'Right,' said Briony. Although she, like Andy, was Australian, she was painfully shy in a completely non-Antipodean way. Now, she seemed paralysed with embarrassment. She nodded back at Stephen, smiling without quite looking him in the eye.

'I hear you've left us,' said Stephen. 'Not permanently, I hope. We need good waitresses like you.'

'It is permanent, Steve, I'm sorry,' she said. 'I just can't . . . can't go on with things the way they are.'

45

'You mean . . . Vinnie being rude all the time? I can talk to him about that.'

'It's . . . not anything like that. Vinnie is fine. He makes me laugh. It's not anything you could help with. Truly it isn't.'

'I would be really sorry to lose you.'

'Well, I'm sorry to let you down.'

'So you should be. Tell her to stay, Steve. If she leaves, I'll be stuck with a bunch of wankers and perverts with no one to talk to all day.' It was the delightful Andy, back from the gent's.

'Watch your language, will you,' said Stephen. 'There's no such thing as a pervert in this town.'

'Oh, right, so we'll be getting a nice paedophile in to replace Briony, will we?'

'You know what I mean,' said Stephen. 'Half the staff at Earthsea are gay.'

'Yeah, right, that's what I mean too,' said Andy. He lit a cigarette, which showed up his hard, regular features in a sudden, intense light. Bizarrely, all the other waiting staff thought he was fantastic. Perhaps they all fancied him – he had the dumb, gold face of a professional beach-god.

'Stop being a prat,' said Stephen. 'Have a drink, or something.' He bought beers for them both. He took a long pull of his own drink and realized he was beginning to feel better. The sense of shock was subsiding. 'I agree with Andy that you shouldn't leave,' he said to Briony. 'We need you. I know it's been a bit rough lately, a bit more stressful than usual. But you lot – me and Vinnie depend on you. A team of people we know and trust.

We'll go down the pan if we don't hang on to people like you, Briony. Stay. Please. Stay.'

'I can't.'

'But why not?'

'She won't even tell me,' said Andy. 'And if she won't tell me, she won't tell anyone.'

'Right – the less said about that, the better,' said Briony. 'You don't have to tell Stephen how many girls you've slept with since we broke up.'

'Eight,' said Andy. 'It's eight, right?'

'It's thirteen. You always were better at screwing around than you were at figures.'

Stephen drank more beer. His mind was on the problems at Earthsea now. Running through a mental list of the waiting staff, he realized that Briony really would leave a gaping hole behind her. No one else was as quick, or as unflappable. And she exuded a subdued sweetness that diners warmed to.

'Isn't there anything I can do to make you stay?'

'I don't think so.'

'Why? What happened?'

'Nothing happened. Things – well – they got out of hand.'

'Things?'

'Feelings,' she said.

'Feelings like what?'

Briony's gaze didn't leave the floor. 'Feelings like emotions for someone you shouldn't have.'

Stephen nodded sympathetically. He remembered Vinnie's comment about the shagging staff. It must be hard for her to deal with Andy's endless stream of conquests. 'I quite understand if it's . . . you know. Relationship stuff,' he said.

Briony sniffed. 'I can't say anything else. Sorry.'

Feelings. Yes. He glanced across at Andy. Too much of a doom-brain to see that she was still in love with him. He remembered them arriving a year before, arms around each other, nuzzling in the street. No wonder she wanted to move on – now Andy was nuzzling someone different every time you looked at him.

'You know, you really do have a knack for the job,' he said at last, desperately searching for ideas. 'Tell you what – suppose I trained you? Would you like to be a chef?'

'A chef? Me? I never thought about it.'

'Yeah, but you're a bloody good cook. She's a bloody good cook,' said Andy, putting one arm matily around her shoulders. 'I know you think all us Aussies do is chuck stuff on the barbie, but she can do the real thing.'

Briony was looking thoughtful. 'I still don't know what I want to do in the end – after all the travelling and stuff,' she said. 'I suppose I could be a chef. Maybe. But there's nothing to stop me learning . . . Somewhere else.'

'Not everything I could teach you,' said Stephen. 'Or Vinnie. He is the best. Although he does complain that it's like being asked to cook with one arm behind his back, not using fish or meat.'

She looked miserable again at the mention of Vinnie's name. 'I don't want him to teach me anything,' she said. 'But . . . if *you* would. Yes. I would like to learn. I would.' She thought for a minute. 'So, I could wait tables on Vinnie's shifts, and help you in the kitchen a bit when you're on?'

'More than that — I'll teach you everything I know. And, of course, if you're cooking you'll get a bit more money, too.'

'I'll give it three months,' she said. 'Just three months.'

'Thank you,' said Stephen.

'Good girl,' said Andy, planting a kiss on her cheek. 'You can go back to Sydney and open your own place and I'll be head waiter.'

'Yeah, cool,' said Briony. She flashed an ironic smile at Stephen.

'Well, that's settled, then,' he said. 'Thank God for that.' He looked at his watch. It was ten o'clock. Still time to go and rescue Vinnie. 'Look,' he said. 'I'm going to Earthsea now. Will you come? Just to show there's no hard feelings. And shake hands with Vinnie. He thinks you're brilliant, too, you know.'

'Okay,' said Briony. She chucked her long red plait behind her shoulder. 'Guess I was being a big coward in the first place, running away from him like that.'

4

A scene of controlled hysteria greeted them when they walked into the kitchen at Earthsea. Three people were working with Vinnie in the low-ceilinged, steamy room: Dan, the seedy sous-chef, Robin, the assistant chef, and Philippe, the French intellectual they employed as a kitchen porter. Dan was frantically frying cauliflower florets, aubergines and okra in separate black skillets on the six-ring stove, wearing the Earthsea chef-grunge uniform of baggy check trousers, torn white T-shirt and black skullcap. Robin was squirting dressing at a bean-sprout salad. Philippe was squeezing past him, loaded down with clean metals. He was smiling benignly to himself, as if carrying out some internal philosophical debate. Dividing the kitchen was the pass on which the meals received their final garnish before being whisked into the restaurant or loaded on to the dumb waiter that delivered food to the upper floor. The pass was crowded with meals; Robin was a keen but slow worker. Some plates were even resting precariously on the salad-preparation area, balanced on plastic containers of pickled plums, sundried tomatoes or gooseberry paste. Apparently oblivious to this log jam, Vinnie was deftly placing a sprig of parsley on top of a sorrel tart with his long, bony fingers, his face folded into an expression of determined concentration. When he saw Briony and Stephen in the doorway, he raised his eyebrows at them but made no other sign.

'Vinnie, hi –' Stephen began, but then realized that he didn't know what to say next. Instead, and with a complicit glance at Briony, he dived into the cloakroom, wriggled out of his wet clothes and into his own kitchen uniform. (Though he didn't wear the skullcap; Stephen felt a fool in hats.) When he came out, Briony had tied on her white apron and was scrutinizing the orders pinned to the wall.

'One eggplant terrine, one goat's cheese with mint, table nine,' said Vinnie, thrusting the plates into her hand. 'And good decision to come back. Might have had to hire a fucking hit squad if you hadn't.' Briony took the dishes and fled.

'I suppose that's your idea of an apology,' said Stephen, adding baby mozzarella and basil to two dishes of iced plum soup and, after checking the orders, placing the bowls on the dumb waiter. 'Frightening the poor girl with stupid comments like that. We're lucky to get her back. I've promised to teach her how to cook, by the way.'

'Oh, sorry, didn't realize we had fucking Oprah Winphrey in our midst,' said Vinnie. He glooped some French dressing on to a dish of hummus and chickpea relish with a plastic drizzler that looked like a transport-café tomato-sauce bottle. 'Fresh from the field of battle in war-torn Chester Terrace. Dinner party finished early?'

'Just don't ask,' said Stephen. 'It's totally off limits. Right. Where are we?'

Vinnie was wiping lentil salsa off the rim of a soup dish with one of the cloths that dangled from his apron like a collection of scalps. 'Five more tables have come in since you called. Worst thing – apart from young Briony having an attack of the sensitives – is that fucking hen party. Won't eat anything till the bride arrives. Even turned up their noses at olives – not the regular Earthsea sort at all, darling. All they want is Pringles and fucking cocktails. In the end, I sent Flint round to the pub to get some crisps just to shut them up.' He studied the orders again. 'Right. Can you speed that risotto up, Dan? And I want two soufflés – and can you do me some beans for one of them?' Stephen had been expecting more aggro than this. But he supposed that, having bawled out Briony earlier, Vinnie had got a lot of the tension out of his system – and he wasn't given to prolonged histrionics. Highly strung, perfectionist and utterly focused on his job, he would sometimes scream and shout at a hapless commis chef or waiter. But at the end of the shift he would be cackling with them about some outrage committed by a diner, his elbow resting on their shoulder in that curiously sexless way of his. Somehow, he managed to be tactile and distant at the same time, as if his body belonged to someone else. The staff accepted his moods without question, and usually without complaint. He was Italian, after all, though his accent was pure Basildon.

'So the best thing I can do is work with Dan – right?' said Stephen. They couldn't both be head chef, and if he suggested that Robin should move to another station he would be running the risk of another walk-out.

'Yeah. If you could do that for the next hour, then go out and keep an eye on things at the front,' said Vinnie. 'Got a feeling it's not going to be an easy ride tonight.'

'Looks quiet enough for now.'

Through the half-door opposite the pass they could see the bar and a couple of tables. A woman with big hair was drinking something pink out of a glass at the far end of table seven – Stephen knew without asking which party *she* belonged to. He consulted the orders again, found himself a clean skillet and began to fry baby leeks in the thick, golden olive oil. His hands were steady; here, he knew what he was about. The earlier part of the evening had begun to blur in his mind: this was a method of dealing with being married to Rachel that until now had served him well. He knew the game had changed, but the familiarity of the restaurant reassured him. He was needed here. People respected him, and when he asked them to do something they did it. For a while, he let the noise and bustle of the kitchen soak up all his attention – the persistent roar of the fans, usually noticeable only when they were switched off at the end of the shift, the clatter of metals in Philippe's sink, the ceaseless chopping of Vinnie's knife, like a woodpecker on amphetamines. Zam, zam, zam, the wide, pointed blade falling ruthlessly. But leaves and vegetables were the only things to suffer blows in this kitchen, not bits of murdered animal. Perhaps that was the reason that no one was really bullied in the kitchen at Earthsea, even during stressful times like tonight. There were no dead things here. Stephen couldn't help but see the moral connection between chopping meat and behaving like macho bully-boys. He had turned vegetarian while still at college, after working in a meat-packing factory in his summer break. It had been the stuff of Hieronymus Bosch nightmare; the stiff, frozen carcasses winched around the factory walls had reminded him of the human beings processed and slaughtered in Nazi concentration camps. It had been his job to make burgers from a vat of mince – mince which, his coworkers cheerily informed him, contained brains, hooves and shit as well as offal. The burgers, neatly packaged, looked misleadingly inoffensive when they left the factory for the suppliers. So burgers had been the first meat dish to go, together with that Tuesday regular, boiled mince. Soon after that, he had found himself gagging on Rose's stewing-steak curries. Becoming a vegetarian was the inevitable outcome – and, once he left home, he was too broke to be much of a carnivore, anyway, and had applied himself to the task of making a pan of rice or pasta taste of something. So for nearly twenty years he had cooked nothing that had been terminated in an abattoir, body twitching, blood pulsing out of its slit throat. At home, under pressure from Rachel, he still cooked fish, but in the restaurant none of the food 'had a face', to use the phrase coined by dear departed Linda McCartney.

For a while he let the conversation ebb and flow around him, joining in himself only when necessary to do the job.

'Can you speed up that haloumi, please, Dan?'

'More leaves, please, on the pass.'

'You read my mind, my friend.'

'Watch yourself, Steve!'

'Got any Anadin? Pain in my gut, mate.'

'Three normal tapas and one vegan. Yeah?'

'Yeah. One vegan tapas, no nuts, no seeds, no dill, no caraway oil.'

'Coming round and away when ready, Steve, one sumac noodles.'

'Okay. Dan – ten seconds on the pasta, mate.'

'Look, Robin, fucking Nora. You put too much on the pass and nothing goes right.'

'I was just –'

'No. It happens every time. There is no "just".'

'*Ça va bien*, Philippe?'

'*Alors, tres bien, merci!*'

To Stephen, this was poetry. This was what words were for – not all that emotional sharing and self-indulgence that Rachel and her book-group friends went in for. It wasn't just that women talked too much (though undoubtedly they did – mostly about kids and interiors, as far as he could tell), but also that they were such profligate wasters of words. Such long sentences! So many names and problems and complicated organizational dilemmas to be splurged out – which you were then, for Christ's sake, supposed to remember! This, on the other hand, was the real stuff – the spare beauty of men saying what needed to be said, and nothing else.

Rachel said he was obsessed with Earthsea and didn't think about her. Well, so be it. If anything, he didn't think about the restaurant enough. He had once dreamed of being the best chef in the world. But he knew he lacked the purity of imagination, the courage, the flair. He knew who the best chef in the world was: a Spaniard called Ferran Adria, who ran a three-star Michelin restaurant near Barcelona. This was a man whose life was devoted exclusively to food. He did not waste time in crowded, muzakked supermarkets, or servicing the demands of children demanding Dip-Dabs or cheesy Wotsits. Reading about his restaurant was like hearing the Arabian nights: gelatine with molluscs trapped inside; chicken consommé solidified into thin, coppery, pasta-like strips; cuttlefish ravioli, injected with coconut milk. In another life, Stephen would have brought the same imaginative genius to vegetarian cusine.

'Order in from table seven.' This was Briony's voice. She sounded apprehensive. 'The hen party? I told them we didn't do this, but they were like, "Hey, we don't even understand what the stuff on your menu is about . . ."'

'Why did they come here in the first place, is what I would like to know,' said Vinnie. 'Vegetable lasagne, for eight,' he read out. 'With garlic bread, fries and green salad. Well, they can have six green salads, fine. And that's it. Tell them to fuck off, Briony. Come on. You know we can't do any of this. Don't let's fall out again so soon.'

'They won't take no for an answer,' said Briony, her eyes beginning to fill with tears again. 'They're not like the people who usually come here. They're like – fierce? And they've already had three bottles of pink champagne.'

'We don't serve pink champagne,' said Vinnie and Stephen in unison.

'They brought it with them,' said Briony.

'Oh, brilliant,' said Stephen. 'Did they bring their own table as well?'

He pushed through the swing doors and went out into the restaurant. Table seven was certainly a sight to behold. There was more permed, shaggy hair congregated in one place than he had seen since the sad demise of Bananarama. Seven women, young, skinny, shrieky, with shiny lips and spidery mascara, were giggling uncontrollably. 'Come on, Suzanne,' said one, who appeared to be the ringleader, sitting at the end of the table talking into a mobile phone. 'Get your arse down here! We can't have a bleeding hen night without the hen!'

'Wer-her-her,' shrilled the other girls. 'Hen night without the hen! Good one, Gabrielle!'

There was a pause while Suzanne appeared to say a good deal.

'Don't know why you want him to phone you, anyway,' said Gabrielle. 'He'll be out with his stuck-up mates by now. Just get out of the house. We've ordered for you, so don't mess about.' Another pause. 'You need some food inside you before you hit the Malibu, sweetheart. Yeah. Veg lasagne. Course they do it. Everyone does it. Mind you, it's a weird place. If it was down to me, we would've gone to Pizza Express. But we told the waitress she'd better sort it out for us.'

'We don't do vegetarian lasagne,' interrupted Stephen, as pleasantly as he could. 'We only offer the meals that are actually included on the menu.'

The woman looked at him as if he was mad. 'I'll catch you later, Suzanne,' she said. 'If you're not here in fifteen minutes, I'll be on the blower again.' She put the phone into her bag. The other girls looked at him, giggling, but saying nothing. 'All vegetarians eat veg lasagne,' she said. 'It's what they have instead of steak and chips.'

'No they don't,' said Stephen. 'I'm a vegetarian and I haven't eaten vegetarian lasagne for years. I don't want to be unhelpful, but you really will have to order something from the menu.'

'Oh, pardon *me*!' she said, putting on a posh voice. 'Let us see what your men-ew has to offer, shall we, girls?' She picked it up and began to read aloud: 'Ash crotin and parsley shooter,' she began. 'Tasha, that sounds right up your street. Congee shiso yuzu puff cluster – how about that, Kelly-Marie?' (She addressed a wraithlike child in a pink boob-tube.) 'Or would madam prefer a kalamata coka or smoked sakuri soba salad? I mean, are you for real? Are you telling me people really come in here and order this stuff?'

'They order it, they eat it, and they love it,' said Stephen, smiling winningly at the four diners at the nearest table, who were beginning to titter quietly to themselves over their fresh mixed leaves. 'I mean, I hate to turn customers away, but you really *might* be better off at Pizza Express. Or even Al Fresco, on the seafront. Lovely view of the breakers.' Just then, he felt a tap on his shoulder. It was Briony. 'Vinnie says we should do it,' she whispered. 'Says we can't afford to turn away a table for eight? It's nearly all twos tonight. Says he's got the ingredients – he was going to try out a Jerusalem-artichoke lasagne this week . . . He can definitely do it . . .'

Stephen turned back to table seven with an artificial smile. 'Well, it looks as if we will be able to help you after all,' he said. 'Eight vegetable lasagnes it is. But I have to insist that you drink our wine – we usually charge corkage for people who bring in their own.'

'Oh, go on then,' said Gabrielle. 'Anything white with a bit of fizz – right, girls? And not too pricey.' They tittered again, their big earrings tinkling in their busy hair.

The decision to make vegetable lasagne from scratch put everyone under a degree more pressure. Dan grabbed a plastic vat of pre-prepared tomato sauce from the cold room. Robin began chopping extra courgettes and mush-rooms. Vinnie hunted in the dry-store room for the sheets of wholewheat lasagne. But Stephen noticed that he was whistling. What had cheered him up? The additional work and adrenalin rush? The preparation of downmarket food? (Perhaps, he thought, it was only a matter of time before they started producing veggie burgers and used revolving relish trays. But he would fight that to the bitter end.)

'Wholewheat! That'll go down well!' sniffed Stephen, who had taken over the garnishing duties and was putting the final touches to a starter portion of gnocchi with tamarillo and basil. 'I'm sure they're strangers to all forms of wholefoods. They're a right bunch of slappers.'

'Some of my best friends are slappers, if you don't mind,' said Vinnie, racing back. 'Béchamel sauce, Dan – don't forget the béchamel sauce.' Stephen was too busy to pursue the thought that hovered momentarily in his head and concerned the idea of Vinnie as a human being. What made him the way he was? So engrossed in the moment, such a brilliantly perfectionist chef, and yet so uninterested in what happened to food once he had cooked it. Nowadays, all Vinnie's mental energy seemed to go into finding ways of entertaining his boyfriend, Marc. Stephen really couldn't see the attraction here: Marc was a narcissistic fat boy with sociopathic tendencies. But there was no time to think about that now. The kitchen was swirling around him, the staff dancing past each other in their backless clogs; first Flint with two plates of risotto, then Philippe with a clutch of pots, dreamy expression intact, rattling and steaming round the kitchen under the neon lights.

Finally, after this bout of frenzied activity, the eight portions of lasagne were ready. Stephen helped Flint and Briony carry the steaming plates of food into the restaurant. But all was not well with table seven. Gabrielle was on the phone again.

'You what? He said what?' The other girls were craning round her, cigarettes held between French-manicured, heavily ringed fingers.

'What is it, Gabs? What's going on?'

'Well, why did you tell him, then? You know he is a fucking snob, Suzanne. What is it with you – did you take the truth drug or something? None of us would get anywhere without a little white lie now and then . . .' There was another pause, as Stephen lowered the wholewheat lasagne in front of her. 'Of course he doesn't mean the wedding's off! Get yourself down here, have a good cry and he'll have got over it in the morning . . .' The girls all shrieked their support for this. Gabrielle leaned forward in her seat, as if frustrated by what she was hearing. 'I know there is nothing wrong with being a lap-dancer, Suzanne, I *am* a bleeding lap-dancer. But boyfriends can be a bit funny about it. You must have noticed . . .' She flapped her hands at the other girls as if to tell them to give her room to breathe. 'Suzanne, it just was not your smartest-move-ever to pick the day before your wedding to tell him you show men your tits for money . . . Now stop crying. Calm down . . . You're going hysterical. He loves you. Of course he loves you . . . You're hyperventil-ating, Suzanne . . . Pour yourself a nice big glass and put

60

the telly on . . .' She snapped the phone off. 'The problem with that girl is that she's got a bleeding business-studies degree. She thinks too much.'

'She's sensitive,' said another of the women, an anorexic blonde in gold eyeshadow. 'Remember how she always cries when they chuck people out in *Big Brother*? She's not tough like you, Gabs.'

'Yeah, right, that's a laugh.'

'Is it really off?' said the wraith called Kelly-Marie. 'Because of the job?'

'It's really off,' said Gabrielle. 'Because he's up his own arse. And he thinks, if he's going to be a doctor, he is too good for the likes of us. It was all a joke to him, getting married. I mean, they've only been together three months. And he never even invited his mum and dad.'

'Erm – excuse me. Can I get you anything to go with your lasagne? French dressing for the salad? More wine, perhaps?' Stephen was trying not to sound like Basil Fawlty.

'Yeah, great, just one bottle, quick as you can,' said Gabrielle. 'Let's get this down us fast, girls, and get round to Suzanne's before she tops herself.' They began to eat, and cries of, 'Yeeugh! It's not much like the one they do in Marks!' followed him into the kitchen.

'I'm sick of that bloody table,' he said to Vinnie. 'All very well for you, lurking in here. You never see the crap punters; it's all just theory to you.'

For some reason this appeared to irritate Vinnie. 'Oh right! Yeah! Vinnie has it really easy down here, running the whole bloody show! What a skiver! He hasn't got a fucking family to worry about, so no problem for him to slave away, night and day, like a bloody prisoner. Right.' He took off his apron. 'Is there anything table seven would like? Let me go out there and share in the traumatic experience of interacting with the lower classes. See if *I* need therapy afterwards, shall we?'

'Oh, fuck off,' said Stephen. 'They want some wine, but there's no need to . . .' But Vinnie had already disappeared, heading for the cellar.

'Don't know what all the fuss was about,' he said when he came back. 'Quiet as mice.'

'Quiet as . . . ? You're pulling my leg! What about the chief strumpet at the end?'

'There was no one at the end of the table. But there was someone underneath it. Thought she must be pissed, after your description, but she'd lost her contact lens, or something. The rest were munching away quite happily. You need to get out more. Mix with people who don't use extra-virgin olive oil.'

'Right. Well. Perhaps they just warmed to your salt-of-the-earth persona.'

'Maybe they did. Or,' Vinnie said, retying his apron rather vehemently. 'Maybe you are just a pain-in-the-arse professional whinger, Stefano.'

'Table seven have just gone,' announced Briony, rushing by with a pile of empty pudding plates.

'Gone? But they haven't even had the bill – God – they've done a bloody runner . . .' said Stephen, charging back into the restaurant.

When he saw the table, he realized that this was far from being the truth. A pile of £20 notes had been left among the crisp crumbs. Counting the notes out in his office, he found they had overpaid by about £30.

'Weird,' he said to Vinnie, stuffing the extra notes into the tips box and swigging from the whisky bottle he had just opened. The whisky tasted good – more than that, it tasted like salvation. Of course, it was anything but that. When Stephen tried to piece together the subsequent events of that evening, it always seemed as if they had actually occurred inside that bottle. They took on a bilious, orangey hue. Years later, he would still have sweaty flashbacks to a series of film stills of himself, carousing and cavorting with all the evolved panache of Gazza in his heyday. Where he slept that night, he never could recall. He was sure of one thing, though. He slept alone. It wasn't a night on which any woman would have willingly allowed him into her bed. And in any case, he was married. To a lovely wife. With two children and an inconsistent garden.

5

'What's going on?'

Stephen ran his furred tongue over his teeth, blinked at the angry phone. How should he know? Voice was familiar – but he couldn't place it. Spirit of the phone, maybe. (His stomach was writhing, his hot brain fermenting. He was a dying animal, diseased, rejected. In his mind, he saw himself dancing alone in the middle of a vast space, glass of wine in one hand, bottle of whisky in the other.)

'Stephen, are you there? What's happening?'

He realized who it was. Carmel. Like the time she caught him masturbating with a copy of *Jackie* in the wardrobe. When? Nineteen seventy-six possibly. Those girls with their centre partings, innocent blue eyeshadow, tacky platforms in pink or pale blue. He shifted his bottom around on the lumpy shingle.

'Hello? Say something! Where are you?'

Stephen's eyes were on the sea as he replied. 'Good question.' The sea was grey, flat, heaving gently as it filled the space between the cloudy, drizzle-heavy sky and the jumble of stones that served Brighton for a beach. What *had* happened last night? He saw faces, bottles, cigarettes, heard his own voice spilling out, confessions, betrayals. Saw young bodies dancing in the smoky club. Remembered offering himself as a 'father figure' to Briony and one of her glossy Australian chums. Christ. The oldest swinger in town.

'Oh, grow up! You're a big boy now, Stephen, with big responsibilities, in case you'd forgotten.'

'Nope. I haven't forgotten.'

'But you still stayed out all night.'

'Yup.'

'And where, exactly, were you?'

'Not sure.'

'Not sure?'

'Dunno. Memory loss. Bearings loss. Just – dunno.'

'God, you've got some serious explaining to do.'

'Yes.'

For a moment the phone went silent. Perhaps it would leave him alone, and take its moral judgements elsewhere. He watched a dog dragging seaweed into the waves, shaking itself, prancing with high, merry paws. No living creature happier than a dog at the edge of the sea – what do human beings have to do to get into that state? Take a hell of a lot of drugs, that's what. Or be loved. Loved and loved and loved.

Slightly more gently, Carmel spoke again. 'Rachel's in a terrible state. She didn't go to bed last night. She knew you'd go to the restaurant, but thought that you'd be back at some point. When she realized you were staying out all night . . . She nearly phoned the police . . .'

'I'm sorry – none of this was . . . planned.'

'No.'

'I hope she's told you it was *her* who threw *me* out. Said I was a dead slug.'

'I've heard all about it. She didn't think you'd just disappear. You still haven't told me where you are.'

'On the beach.' All washed up.

'Where on the beach?'

'Near the West Pier. Admiring a fellow ruin.' He stared bleakly at the pier's dark, truncated outline as he spoke. He did admire it, the supporting pillars holding out gallantly against the crashing sea, the crumbling theatres and other faded pleasure buildings looking as if they would collapse into the water at any moment, taking with them the ghost of Graham Greene. Clouds of starlings were wheeling ceaseless patterns in the sky above it. They had a melancholy *joie de vivre*, like the atmosphere of a disappearing dream.

'Coincidence! We're about twenty yards away, in the café by the peace statue,' said Carmel.

'We?'

'Me and Rachel and Your Children.' Some mumbling from the other end. 'But they're just going, apparently.'

'Does Rachel want to talk to me?'

More mumbling. 'Er, no. But come anyway – I'll be here.'

As he shambled along the seafront, his memory threw some images of Carmel to the front of his mind. Her schooldays had been marked out mainly by bolshy swottiness, and a determination to get better A-levels than her thin, rather catty friends. At college, where she had been extremely unhappy, she wore flowery dirndl skirts and men's lace-up shoes. When the lust for other girls began, he never knew. In their university days, Stephen and Carmel developed a sporadic sibling intimacy, never phoning or writing to each other, but spilling out confessions when they met in the holidays. So Stephen tracked her sexual development with some astonishment over the years.

Her first lover was a failed rugger bugger, who because of a gastric condition couldn't drink beer. Later, he turned into a high flyer with the BBC, in charge of repositioning nature programmes. The second was a very small Scottish man on a break-up from his hometown honey. After three months with Carmel, he rushed back to Glasgow and was married within a year. The third – bizarrely – was the hottest boy in college, a drop-dead-gorgeous misogynist from Hebden Bridge with Byronic brown curls. In fact, he and Carmel were still in touch – by email – and he was now semi-happily married to a gym-addicted blonde and running his own management consultancy.

In 1988, Carmel read *Fat is a Feminist Issue* by Susie Orbach. At that point, she was sewing two size-eighteen skirts together and wearing them with a man's extra huge Guernsey sweater. Susie showed her the way. She stopped dieting for two weeks, and within six months she'd shrunk to a modest size eighteen. When she was twenty-nine, Carmel went on a world trip and had a painful, virtually wordless affair with a waitress in Sydney. When Carmel broke off the relationship before a jaunt to Fiji, she broke the girl's heart. Carmel had made an important discovery: women are not looks-ist about who they shag. Overnight, she had become a heartbreaker. Her passion unleashed, she dyed the front of her hair blonde and bought a lot of Victoria Wood-style silk jackets in Hong Kong. Finally, she returned to Hackney, her old home, ready to lay waste to lesbians in the E9 area.

In the following years, Carmel slept with twenty-seven women (she was precise about the number), most of whom adored her passionately. Many of them had small, exercise-enhanced buttocks, Stephen had noticed. And then, last year, she had met Lise, the salsa baldie, at a gay club near the seafront. It seemed that Carmel, whose mantra was that 'love can't last', had met her match. They were ideally suited – both of them were addicted to *The Archers*, hated *EastEnders*, and were lapsed vegetarians who disliked clutter. Above all, they both loathed the idea of having children. This devotion to the child-free life was the bedrock of their relationship: they laughed at lesbian friends who had gone down the IVF route or adopted children. But Carmel stressed that she and Lise would only last as long as the pure flame of passion. When that went, the relationship would be scrapped, and each would find a new lust object. She had even made a career out of this idea, for it was the basis of the online dating agency she'd set up to find true love – strictly on a short-term basis – for the gay community. According to Carmel, sticking with one person was a sign of fear. Passion was worth living for; mundane domestic piss, as she called it, wasn't. So, in 1998, fairsex.com was launched at a small but commanding party at the Sussex Arts Club. One year later, Carmel was a paper millionairess.

'Hi.' He stood in front of her, clutching his arms around his body. A chilly April wind was whipping in from the sea, and his jumper – which reeked of stale booze and nicotine – wasn't thick enough. It felt more like autumn than it did spring. In fact, he wished it was. He couldn't face the thought of summer: long days, young people, sun, sea and sex. No thanks.

Carmel was wearing a maroon cardigan with bat's wings,

decorated with a pattern of what looked like Liquorice Allsorts. (She had a weakness for celebrity knitwear). As usual, she seemed to be on a different scale to all the people around her. Not fatter, but grander. She was drinking out of a white cup, looking out to sea. She put her cup down deliberately before speaking. Stephen could see it was half full of something scarlet – herbal tea, designed not necessarily to be enjoyed but to give the drinker a better digestive system or a stronger sense of purpose.

'Well,' she said, turning to look at him at last. 'Don't say I didn't warn you.'

'Warn me about what?'

Carmel pointed to the plastic chair next to her. 'Sit down. Stop looking hunted. It never was going to work. I've done your profiles.'

Stephen sat down heavily. 'You never warned me about anything. All you said was that I was lucky to get Rachel, even though you couldn't stand her. Mostly, you just told me off for not behaving in a worthwhile way.' Something twisted in his head. Too many words. But it was hard to deal with Carmel monosyllabically.

Carmel sighed and nodded to a teenage waiter at the same time. 'Tea?' she asked.

In normal times, Stephen actually had a penchant for herbal tea, particularly fennel and red bush. But right now he felt the need for comforting, builder's tea, the sort that Rose had inflicted on him during his childhood. 'Yes – ordinary, overbrewed tea; not anything life-enhancing.' He studied Carmel cautiously. He didn't understand his sister very well. Most of the energy he put into the relationship went on trying to avoid being bossed about. Now, for the first time, he wondered what she really thought about Rachel and him, their marriage, their children, their Victorian house with the pink exterior walls and the aspirational garden. All his life, he had struggled to get beyond Carmel's opinions. It was easy to reject Rose's ideas – a cosy version of Catholicism based on no actual religious faith. But Carmel was a harder case to answer; she knew everything there was to know about sexual politics. He'd managed it, though. He'd grown out of her cardboard world of gender extremes. He was as opposed to Carmel and her chums sitting smugly round the perimeter fence at Greenham Common, laying claim to all human virtue, as he was to men who saw the average woman as a tiresome, chat-addicted shopaholic. And so it was that, while Carmel refused to learn to fry an onion or boil an egg, on the grounds that this was a short-cut to female oppression, Stephen would happily work his way through all the recipe books that his mother owned, but had never opened, starting with family basics like beef Wellington and lemon meringue pie. During the holidays in Stoke, Stephen had served up curries and couscous and savoury stuffed pancakes and syllabub, while Carmel had picked at the edges of everything he produced, lecturing him about the politics of penetrative sex. Even in the days when she slept with men, she seemed to think that the penis was overrated.

'Anyway,' Carmel was saying as his tea arrived. 'Let's cut to the chase. As my mentor said at the last self-leadership seminar I attended: I'm going to hit you in the face with a wet fish.'

'You what?' This was the best that Stephen could do. He hadn't been near a seminar since the Thatcher years.

'Why did you marry Rachel?'

'Why . . . ?' Stephen saw a flat in the early-morning light; in it was Rachel, naked, sitting up in bed with her breasts barely covered by a sheet, eating toast and marmalade and slagging off everyone she knew. That was the moment he had thought, *I love you so much.* A solid joy, the idea of a life together, rather than a selection of argumentative nights. 'I don't know,' he said. 'I liked the things she said.'

'Right. The things she said. You thought she was on your wavelength.'

'I suppose so.'

'And was she?'

'I don't know. But it wasn't just a wavelength thing, it was to do with the fact that all the other women were just . . .' He hesitated. Now was not the moment to be needlessly negative about collective female characteristics. He was feeling much too psychologically and physically damaged to deal with one of Carmel's onslaughts.

Carmel nodded at him, as if reaching a silent decision. Then she produced two neat sheets of A4 from an Italian-leather rucksack that was one of her trademark business accessories. 'Profiles – His and Hers,' she said, smoothing out the paper on the table. 'Usually we fill these in after doing a brief interview with any would-be client. Bear in mind that these are done to see if people would get on for a few months, not their entire future life. I felt I knew you and Rachel well enough to fill one in without doing the interview.'

'You did, did you? Bit of a liberty.' But Stephen was already staring at his own name on the computer printout.

His address, the bald ordinary facts of who he was. Profession. Interests. Personality. It was a strange sensation, almost like reading your own obituary. Carmel placed Rachel's profile alongside it, in a perfectly parallel position. One of the things that she and Lise had in common was love of order and straight edges. When they wanted to relax, they piled all their books into neat columns in the middle of their living room in Montpelier Terrace, and invented new and ever more cunning ways of cataloguing them.

He focused his mind on the two pieces of paper lying side by side, not quite touching, like he and Rachel in their frigid double bed. At the top of each sheet were the words 'fairsex.com – the lesbian and gay agency for likeminded lovers'. Underneath, the following:

Profession: restaurateur/businessman/food expert/organic entrepreneur.
Interests: food; wine (high quality); interiors (in bid to conform with bourgeois friends – no real visual sense); film (aspires to arthouse, but secretly likes *The Blues Brothers*); art (limited knowledge); books (mainly by men); music (Talking Heads and non-user-friendly jazz); sleep; foreign travel (not much recently).

Where was all this leading? Then he noticed what she had written under 'Personality'.

Stephen is a dreamer who has spent his life trying to convince himself that the battle of the sexes is irrelevant to him, due to the fact that he has always believed that men and women are completely equal. This has not endeared him to the women in his life. His attempts to foster smooth relations between the sexes are, at best, patronizing. This is a man who loses no opportunity to say that women are – surprise! – actually better drivers than men. At worst, he is offensive. He has even referred to himself as a post-feminist – which places him somewhere between Ben Elton and Peter Stringfellow on any thinking-woman's hate list. His worst failing is wilful blindness to what is going on around him: he spends most of his life ignoring the people he has injured or irritated. He is an emotional illiterate, well-meaning but fatally naive.

'Well!' said Stephen. He looked up at Carmel, unable to speak for a moment. 'You missed out anally retentive compulsive, but then I guess that's because you're even worse than I am. Do you get many takers for your services? Or do you give most of your clients an easier ride than this?'

Carmel laughed. 'I must admit, I did rather enjoy filling that in,' she said. 'Usually I'm trying to put a good gloss on people – so that I've got a fighting chance of finding them someone similar. In your case I indulged myself in accuracy.'

'Yeah, right,' said Stephen, imitating one of Elsie's catchphrases. He turned to Rachel's form. For her profession Carmel had listed 'Mad housewife'. (Surely that wasn't very politically correct? Wasn't there some more inclusive, *empowering* form of words that people like Carmel used these days?) And under 'Interests' she had written:

children; interiors (homes better than hers); wine (quality immaterial); film (George Clooney/Russell Crowe); books (anything by Isabel Allende or Michelle Roberts); relationship therapy; female friendship; conversation; cranial osteopathy; Ikea; aqua-aerobics; flea markets; flat stomachs (His and Hers).

Shaking his head, Stephen braced himself for the final section. (How did Carmel know all this? Why didn't he?)

Rachel is someone who took a wrong turning in life, many years ago, and is paying the price for being too cowardly to admit it. It's so long since she has been happy that she isn't even sure what it feels like. Apparently assertive and noisy, she is in reality a passive-aggressive who finds it very difficult to tell anyone what she wants. She makes up for this by getting pointlessly angry, usually with Stephen. Work does not fulfil her, though she has been pretending to be an interior designer for some time. Recently, after starting to work as a volunteer relationship counsellor, she has improved on her previous track record and made it clear to Stephen that he has to be at home more often. But she still hasn't begun to address all the other things that are wrong between them. Loud, emotional and quick to complain about the small problems of her life, she is still stuck in the role of traditional housewife, hemmed in with children and chores, desperate, but clinging on angrily to the wreckage.

Stephen pushed the two pieces of paper away and looked at his sister with a growing sense of doom. 'What does this all go to prove, exactly, other than the fact that Rachel has obviously spent a lot of time whinging on to you about her terrible life?'

Carmel was finishing her tea. 'It doesn't "prove" anything,' she said. 'I just wanted to see how you measured up on our compatibility table. Needless to say, I wouldn't put the two of you together for a single date, never mind a marriage.'

'But who the hell would you put us with? Social Services? You've written the whole thing in such a negative way that the chances of us getting on any better with anyone else than we get on with each other seem a bit remote.'

'Don't overreact, Stephen. People are looking at you.'

'Let them look. I've just read a character assassination of me and my wife, which adds up to a demolition of my whole life. I'm sitting here on the seafront with my bonkers workaholic sister, who thinks she's Jesus Fucking Christ, come to save us all with her bullet-points and computer printouts and pissing psychobabble. So I think I can just about put up with a few people looking at me.'

'I am going to have some shortcake now. Would you like some?' asked Carmel, in a low, professional voice.

'No. Fuck off.' But Stephen felt a bit calmer. 'Go on, then. See if they've got any with cherries in.'

When she returned, Stephen was touched to see she had bought him two pieces. He bit into the first slice, feeling tears welling up from inside his wrecked insides. The glace cherries burst on his tongue, reminding him of a long-lost afternoon when Rose had inexplicably allowed him to eat all the cherries in her baking cupboard while they watched *Now Voyager* on the television. For a moment, he superimposed Bette Davis's brave black-and-white face on to Carmel's round, pink one, as she chomped on two equivalent slices. He licked the sugar from his lips in silence.

At last, he said, 'So, the verdict is that: a) I am a boor-ish twat with hypermale characteristics; and b) Rachel is addicted to being unhappy, but should still move out a.s.a.p. for mental-health reasons. Is that it?'

Carmel was still chewing. Ever since she had read a

book about the benefits of thorough mastication she had been impossible to communicate with while she was eating. Eventually, she said, 'I get the impression that you don't want to split up after all.'

'Of course I don't! Where did the idea come from in the first place? We're grown-ups. We've got children. Anyway, we love each other. Or I love her, at least . . .' He remembered the list of interests Carmel had made. 'Although, I am surprised about the aqua-aerobics. And apparently she's been on a diet . . .' Was knowing everything about your partner a good thing? Was not knowing a bad one? Carmel seemed to be the only person in possession of the rules.

'I'm afraid the idea came from Rachel,' said Carmel.

Stephen looked at his hands. Narrow-fingered and white, with freckled backs and little girly nails. The first time he properly held Rachel's hand had been at a firework party in a hall of residence in Blackheath. In the damp, gunpowdery dark, he had slipped his hand out of his pocket and found hers, cool and covered with colder silver rings. They had twisted their fingers together, looking up at the falling green stars of a rocket.

He put the palms of his hands over his face. 'I don't want this,' he said. 'I don't want to lose her.' Then a thought struck him. 'And, for Christ's sake, don't tell Mum.'

'I won't. No need to involve her, or the wit and wisdom of Auntie Bridie. Not yet, anyway.'

For several moments he sat, paralysed, looking into the darkness of his own hands. Then he heard the scraping sound of Carmel pushing back her chair. He felt her arms around him, a clumsy, unfamiliar sensation. He realized, numbly, somewhere, that she loved him.

'Come on,' she said at last, pushing herself gently away. 'Your tea is cold, Stevie.' She sat down in her chair once more. 'Now listen to me. You don't want to split up. Fine. But the problem is that Rachel does. She wants you to move out.'

'Not just like that, surely? We've hardly had a chance to talk about it . . .'

'According to her, everything's been terrible for years – since before Stan was born, even.'

'Does that mean it's all hopeless? I just have to do what she wants me to do? What about the kids? Does she want to be a single parent?'

Carmel gave him a look that would have informed him – had he been a woman – that Rachel believed she was virtually a single parent already. But her expression softened when she saw the look of hopelessness on his face. 'If you really and truly want to stay together, then maybe I can help.'

'I wish you would. I wish somebody would.' If Carmel could fix his marriage, he would even forgive her for all the terrible things she had written on the profiles.

'Well,' said Carmel, 'let's go and have a proper talk to Rachel now.'

6

At first, Stephen had trouble pushing open the front door. In his disorientated condition he had a momentary image of Rachel, lying prostrate against it, dead of an overdose. But shrieks of high-pitched, assertive protest revealed that the obstacle was a complex and disruptive game his children were playing in the hall.

'DADDEE, NO – GO AWAY!' was the greeting he got from fearful-but-macho Stan. While Elsie backed this up with a more convoluted set of instructions. Life was more complicated when you were eight.

'You can come in if you really have to but please tread extremely carefully, and you're just about to stand on Barbie's tent, actually, so take a really big step, but not on to this area, which is the dinosaur park, and not over there, which is where we have let the slug out for some exercise.' As he stepped over her game zone, followed by Carmel, Stephen smiled vacantly at his children, feeling a bit like a visiting Royal – pointless, nonplussed, armed only with platitudes.

'That does look an interesting game,' he said, smiling in what he knew was a patronizing and phoney way.

'IT'S NOT A GAME!' yelled Stan. 'IT'S A PARTY! YOU'RE STARTING TO MAKE ON MY NERVES!'

'Lovely party, then,' said Stephen.

'I HATE YOU, DADDEE!'

'I don't think you really hate Daddy,' said Elsie in her ultra-reasonable tone.

'Thank you, darling, of course he doesn't,' said Stephen.

'That's all right.' She turned back to Stan. 'It's only Mummy and Jesus who really hate Daddy,' she said. 'We have to forgive everyone, otherwise we'll never get to heaven. Now, where's that cheeky little slug got to?'

'How long has this being going on?' hissed Carmel as they made their way towards the kitchen.

'How long has what been?'

'This religious stuff. Has Mum been talking to her?'

'No idea.'

'Don't you think that's terrible?'

'Well, I'd rather she'd become a humanist-pacifist, if that's what you mean.'

'I don't mean it's terrible that she's a Christian. Why don't you know what's going on with Your Kids?'

'You get into the habit of tuning them out. If you and Lise ever have children, you'll find out exactly what I mean.'

'Very funny. You know I'd die first. Which seems to be a more responsible attitude than drifting into parenthood and then forgetting to pay any attention to your offspring when they arrive.'

'Don't start on that one. Remember you're supposed to be on my side. Where *is* Rachel?' The house looked curiously unfamiliar, as if something indefinable but fundamental had changed in the few hours since he had left it.

'SHE'S IN THE GARDEN!' shouted Stan, who had

uncannily sensitive hearing. 'SO GO OUT THERE
AND DON'T LOOK AT US!'

The sun had come out; even so, the garden was only
just warm enough to sit in. Rachel was wearing a fleece,
and lying back on a wooden recliner. This was one of
her recent happening garden accessories, purchased from
Edenomics, the annoying florist's and gardening shop run
by Vinnie's boyfriend, Marc. She was wearing sunglasses
and her face bore an expression that was impassive, in an
over-the-top sort of way. In short, she looked pissed off
but contrived at the same time, as if she had spent a long
time deciding how to get her negative mood across to him
most effectively in visual terms.

'Rachel,' said Stephen. Rachel what? Was he meant to
apologize? 'It's me,' he said.

Rachel said nothing.

'Stephen is very sorry,' said Carmel, frowning silent
encouragement to be contrite at him.

'Yes, I'm ... I'm ... I don't want total war,' said
Stephen.

Rachel's face was still a blind mask, facing the sky.

'Stephen knows that he has behaved appallingly. Like
a typical male. With no idea about feelings or his true
responsibilities. In a thoroughly crass, stereotypical way.
For years,' said Carmel, giving him another frown.

'Well, maybe I have been a bit insensitive from time to
time . . .' said Stephen. He was beginning to wonder what
he had let himself in for.

Rachel's mouth jerked. Was she suppressing a laugh?
Or agonized by his lack of self-knowledge?

'On the seafront, Stephen told me he didn't want to

lose you,' said Carmel. 'I know what you've been through, Rachel, but could you ... Perhaps there is room for discussion here. For finding some common ground and thrashing out a few issues. For communication.' The final word came out with more confidence. Carmel was always happiest in flipchart territory, and she was now running through some of her top buzzwords.

Rachel spoke at last, her head bouncing up momentarily from its recumbent position. 'There is no common ground,' she snapped. 'And it's too late to thrash anything out, apart from who lives where and how often Stephen gets to see the kids. Anyway, if he was really so keen to stay here, he would have come back last night.' She fell back into her belligerent torpor once more.

Her coma position was beginning, in Stan's phrase, to make on his nerves. Stephen began to feel anger in its pure form. Why should he put up with being reviled by these two women for his negligible crimes?

'Stop being so melodramatic,' he said. He paused, reined himself in. 'Look, I really am sorry. Sorry about being at work too much. Sorry you've been stuck with the children all the time. Sorry I'm obsessed with work. Sorry about pretending I cooked the meal at home when really it was a takeaway – although I still don't know why that turned out to be the worst thing I've ever done. And sorry I stayed out all night. It was completely innocent. I just bumped into some people I knew and ended up ...' (He had a sudden mental image of himself lying on his back in the middle of a road, looking up into the dark.) 'Ended up getting really ...' None of the words he could have accurately applied to his drunken state seemed

81

appropriate. Try as he might, he couldn't piece together the random pictures that had stayed with him. Wads of money going across the bar. An intense conversation with Briony, which had started with her nodding but had ended with her crying. And was it a dream, the bit where he had been telling a tall blonde girl that he'd like to see her sucking asparagus spears, dressed up as Babs Lord from Pan's People? (Although it was the dark, doe-eyed one he had officially fancied all those years ago.)

Just as he was about to clarify what he was and what he wasn't, the window of opportunity for communication and finding common ground closed. Elsie and Stan came rushing into the garden, Elsie wrapped in an old duvet cover, an expression on her face that indicated that these were priceless royal robes, and Stan making a series of exploding noises, followed by 'CHEEEARGE!' and 'YIKES!' They both let rip with a wall of sound that put a stop to adult conversation.

'Mummeee! The slug is *my* slug, not his, and now it's dead because he was too rough, and he doesn't even understand what slugs . . .'

'IT'S NOT DEAD! IT'S NOT DEAD! IT'S ONLY KILLED!'

'Mummeee, if we have three biscuits now and promise to eat all our lunch, can we have four . . . ?'

'IT'S NOT LUNCHTIME! WE HAD OUR LUNCH!'

'Daddeee, can I have a slug mummy and a slug daddy to come and live in my bed?'

'SLUG DADDIES ARE BOY SLUGS! YOU CAN'T HAVE BOY SLUGS IF YOU'RE A GIRL!'

To attempt to carry on was pointless. But what was the alternative? Rachel was ignoring the children as completely as she was the adults, so he kept going – at a slightly higher volume this time. 'What I'm not is a wife-beater, or an adulterer, or a bankrupt, or a child-abuser –' ('NO, HE'S NOT!' 'Daddy wouldn't beat a slug, would you, Daddy? He might tread on one, but only by accident.') 'I haven't got anything really big to apologize for; only the fact that I've been a bit of a prat. Or even a lot of one.' ('Daddy, that is actually a very rude word which you had better not say. "Prat" is not nice. You're making Jesus sad.')

Carmel and Rachel remained silent. Rachel was still hiding behind her shades. What did these women want – a nervous breakdown or nothing? 'Don't make out that I'm worse than I am. Please. We can sort all this out. Rachel. Look at me.' ('LOOK AT HIM, MUMMEEE! LOOK AT HIM!')

As if in answer to his silence rather than his words, Rachel finally took off her glasses and looked at him. 'Yuk,' she said. 'You look disgusting. To think there've been times in living memory when I talked myself into . . .' She glanced at the children, acknowledging their presence for the first time. 'Into doing S.E.X. Thank God those days are behind me.' As she spoke, she looked beautiful, with her mad black eyes and her coiling hair. Never more so. Stephen felt himself reeling.

'I'm not sure how productive that line of argument is going to be . . .' began Carmel. ('DADDY LOOKS DISGUSTING! DISGUSTING!')

'This has nothing whatsoever to do with you,' said Rachel. She sat up and swung her legs to the ground. 'I mean, thanks for listening, and all that, and thanks for agreeing with me earlier that your baby brother is a prize loser –' (Carmel squawked a protest at this point, but Stephen knew that Rachel wasn't exaggerating.) 'But I don't need your support, or your endorsement, or anything else. I don't need you to approve of this, Carmel. I don't need your permission to chuck him out, either. So shut up.'

This outburst filled the children with joy. Any damage that the forthcoming break-up of their parents' marriage was going to do to them was still to come. Currently, this grown-up spat was one of the most exciting things that had ever happened. Whole paragraphs poured out of them, filling the garden with sound. ('SHUT UP! SHUT UP!' 'Mummy's really cross with you now, Carmel. Totally cross.' 'CHUCK HIM OUT! YEAH! IN THE RIVER – WHERE HE'LL DROWN!' 'Daddy, you really better stop being so bad that no one wants you. You really had better do something good very soon.')

Carmel was staring at Rachel in disbelief. 'Look, I know you and Stephen are a total mismatch, but there's no need to be offensive about it –'

'Isn't there? Haven't I got the right to be as offensive as I like? I'm throwing away security, money, everything I rely on – and I'm supposed to be *polite* about it? Not only are you not as smart as you think you are, Ms Beckett, you're also actually pretty damn obtuse, if you really want my opinion. So go ahead – bullet-point your way out of that one.'

Carmel opened her mouth to speak, but what she would have come out with in response to this outburst will never be known. Because at that moment the doorbell rang. Rachel looked at her watch. 'That'll be Kris,' she said. 'On time, as usual.'

'Chris?' said Stephen.

Carmel and Rachel both rolled their eyes at him in unison. 'See?' said Rachel. 'He doesn't even know who Kris is. He's got no interest in my life whatsoever.'

'Who's Chris?' asked Stephen, his voice rising. 'Why am I meant to know who he is?'

'He's my rock,' 'He's Rachel's Colleague,' said Rachel and Carmel at the same time. At which point a tall, gangly person came strolling into the garden. What did Stephen notice about him first? Male. Black. Rainbow sweater. Mini-Afro. Sideburns. *Black male.* Shocked as Stephen was, he had time to notice that this was a man with a definite seventies look. He had an expression of caring moral superiority, and a high forehead which gleamed with integrity. And he was accompanied by their two leaping children, who were shouting, 'Kris is here! Kris is here! Look, Mummy, we opened the door and it was Kris!' It was as if this bizarre figure was Santa Claus and Gareth Gates rolled into one.

Kris had the grace to look abashed. 'Hi,' he said, waving at them all. 'You must be Steve,' he said to Stephen. 'Great to meet you. Funny thing – you're kind of just exactly what I would have expected. Almost like *déjà* view.' His voice was deep and chocolatey. It aimed to soothe.

'*Vu*,' said Stephen, his face feeling like cold granite.

'Sorry?' Kris was all smiles – fantastic teeth, of course. Presumably he had a huge penis strapped to his leg under those brown cords as well.

'It's *déjà vu*, not *déjà* view.'

'Cool. I'm very relaxed about owning up to mistakes – not letting myself think I know it all already.'

Stephen looked speechlessly at Carmel.

'I think we're going to have to workshop this one,' she said. 'Can I get you a drink, Kris?'

'Kris has his own peppermint tea in the kitchen,' said Rachel.

Carmel bustled back into the house, frowning this time in a private way, blocking out even Stephen. Claudius the cat appeared from nowhere and bounded after her. For himself, Stephen was wondering why his break-up was turning out to be such a busy social event. Wasn't it normal practice to do this sort of thing privately, behind closed doors? Even Hugh Grant and Liz Hurley had split up in front of the cameras only when they were pretending to separate after his Divine Brown lapse; when they had parted for real, no one was invited along to see the empty gin bottles and the balls of tissue. And yet here he was, known only to a select band of organically inclined foodies in the East Sussex area, beginning to feel as if he should have booked a seat at his own marital breakdown. Stephen sat down on the director's chair recently vacated by Carmel. He was now feeling not just physically sick – that had been going on for hours – but also sick in his heart. As if a gentle poison had been creeping into his system, unnoticed, and had finally begun to do its work. The assembly of pretend that was his life – the mugs and plate racks, the suitcases and stair rails, the cameras and bath towels – was going to be dismantled and taken away, item by item. He saw himself, sitting alone on a single bed, sipping Heinz tomato soup out of someone else's chipped bowl. He saw Rachel, striding along a sunny street, laughing at a hilarious remark made by somebody who wasn't him.

'Come on, Stephen – people have come back from much worse places than this,' said Kris. He squeezed Stephen's shoulder. Perhaps Kris was really an alien, who had learned about human interaction by watching daytime broadcasts of European coproductions in which people with phoney accents got off with each other in the manner of wooden aliens. Or perhaps he was just the biggest wanker who had ever lived. But were you allowed to think black people were wankers, without giving them a fair chance?

With an effort of will, Stephen tried to assimilate the situation. 'Remind me again what you are doing here,' he said. 'Only, stupidly, I kind of imagined that this conversation – this whole phase of my life – was something that was no one's business except mine – and my wife's.'

'Try not to be a pompous pain in the arse unless it's absolutely necessary,' said Rachel. She was now stalking round the garden with her arms folded, kicking plants from time to time as if they were the irritating by-products of a dead marriage. Kris squatted on his haunches, scrutinizing their faces and looking like the god Pan or some other force of nature. After a while, he squinted up at the watery blue sky and smiled at it, as if gaining inner wisdom from the eternal verities.

'I know you are both feeling a lot of anger,' he said, returning his gaze to Stephen. 'Rachel's been filling me in about the difficulties you've had, and –'

'Why has she? Why . . . ?' Stephen turned to Rachel. 'Why are you telling complete strangers about our life?'

Rachel looked at him coolly. '*He*'s not the stranger,' she said. '*You* are. Kris knows more about the way I feel than you have ever bothered to find out in all the years you've known me. Kris is – and try to use your imagination now, Stephen – *interested in women*.'

'In people as a whole, really, Rache,' said Kris. 'No gender bias, just an interest in finding out why people are hurting.' (*Rache.* Was that grounds for homicide?)

But Stephen remained sitting, enfeebled, in an over-priced chair. 'Rachel and I have had a tricky time recently, and I've been making more effort to be at home to help us through –' (Here Rachel made one of her loud-explosion noises. But Stephen continued bravely.) 'Last night, there was an unfortunate incident because Rachel gave the cat the dinner I was preparing for two of our closest friends. She's probably told you I ordered something in from my restaurant –' (Kris nodded.) 'Well, okay, maybe you've got a better idea than I have why this was such a terrible crime. I mean, I could see it was a bit underhand, but she went apeshit, it was like having a mad woman in the house. I went off, got drunk, okay, bad idea, naughty boy et cetera, stayed out – and now it's World War Three and my marriage is over. Sheer bloody insanity is what it looks like from my perspective. So perhaps if you are such an expert on Rachel's state of mind you can put me in the picture about how we got from vaguely unhappy to total meltdown in less than twenty-four hours. I mean, please, please do. I would love to have your informed opinion.'

In the uncertain pause that followed, Carmel returned, carrying a tray laden with Tate Modern mugs and a plate of Garibaldi biscuits, with the children skipping along with plastic cups clenched to their faces like coloured beaks.

'Let's all take time to think things through and look at our options in a mature, grounded way,' she said, plonking the tray down on the garden table and spilling much of the contents of the four cups.

'Okay,' said Rachel. Her arms were still folded across her chest. 'I am going to assert myself now,' she said. 'I am going to tell you what my options are, in a mature and grounded way. Elsie and Stan, why don't you go inside and do a lovely drawing for Kris?'

'But we're just –'

'DRAWING MAKES ON MY –'

'*Go inside*!' said Rachel, in a voice that made the grass tremble, the sky shiver. They went, scurrying out of her range without another word.

'Those options,' said Rachel, swinging round to look at the grown-ups. 'There are three of them, as far as I can see. Number one: put up with things as they are. Keep taking the Prozac, keep chucking down the vino, keep moaning to the few friends I can trust with the true story of my miserable life.' She paused for a second, as if expecting an interjection. But none came. Stephen was sitting with his head propped on his fists, wondering if he would ever move again. Carmel and Kris looked expectant.

'Option two: try to change the relationship from the inside. A bit like being in the Socialist Workers' Party rather than the SDP when we were at college. The people who really wanted things to be different – not just no Thatcher, but no poverty, no police thugs, no arms race – joined the SWP. The people who thought that, on the whole, it would be a nice idea if things were sorted out a bit more equally, but who couldn't be arsed to do anything about it, plumped for the SDP. If Stephen and I decide to try Really Hard to make things work, to wear the black negligées and nurture the quality time, et cetera, et cetera, we'll be going down the David Owen route. Things won't change at all. We might have a couple of shags, but that's it.'

'I think I know where this is leading,' said Stephen.

'Well, maybe,' said Rachel. 'And maybe there's a lot you don't know, and couldn't possibly guess.' Kris glanced at her nervously, Stephen thought. 'The third option is the SWP one: splitting up. The only drawbacks there are practical ones – like it would cost a lot of money, and we'd have to run two houses instead of one and all that. But emotionally I can't see that there would be any drawbacks at all.'

'As far as I can see you haven't really brainstormed the alternatives as a team,' began Carmel. 'Clearly, there are big differences between you, but there are lots of things you could –'

'What do *you* think, Kris?' Rachel cut in. 'Speaking as the only person here who knows anything about relationships in crisis.'

'Sometimes clients go for a trial separation. No hard-and-fast rules – just going with the flow,' said Kris. He smiled peacefully at Stephen, as if he was suggesting a stroll down to the seafront.

Carmel shrugged. 'It's one solution. Although, I'm not sure it's what Stephen wants.'

'Of course it's not,' said Stephen. But he looked suspiciously at Rachel. 'What is it that I don't know?' he asked. 'What the fuck is going on? Will somebody please be straight with me?'

Rachel sighed and rolled her eyes. 'Nothing is "going on". At least, not the sort of thing you mean.'

'We just met at a residential weekend on looking for closure in a relationship,' said Kris, smiling across at Rachel.

'And established a rapport – no sex, nothing physical,' said Rachel, radiating love and affection in the general direction of Kris.

'And learned to reeeally admire each other as part of humanity,' said Kris. The space that separated the two counsellors was tingling with Spielbergian intensity – Stephen could almost see the green lightning crackling between them. Carmel caught his eye and shook her head at him, slowly.

7

For Stephen, piecing together what happened to him over the next three months was a bit like trying to make sense of his amnesiac drunken behaviour following the dinner party. Years later, he would try to remember the exact order of things, using both the restaurant diary and the notes in his own, private diary. But he never really succeeded. There were always gaps, inconsistencies. It was as if the story of his life fell apart for a while, and there was no sense to be made of it.

Some facts, however, were clear. He did not go home again. Rachel stuck to her demand that he should go; and, after several more meetings, even more painful than the one in the garden, it was agreed that he would stay in the attic at Vinnie and Marc's house in Kemp Town, rather than crashing on their sofa as he had been doing at first. The assumption that this was a short-term crisis in a long-term relationship faded, and he began to see it as the beginning of a long ending.

His drinking didn't get much better, either. He became so addicted to his bottles of beer during working time and his slugs of spirits once work was over that life took on a hazy, dehydrated quality. He puzzled over films or soaps on TV. Why weren't people drinking more? Watching reruns of *The Good Life* – as he often did before the restaurant opened – he willed them to make loads of homemade wine, as they had in one memorable episode. He wanted them all – Margot, Jerry, Barbara and Tom – to get hysterically pissed with Bacchanalian abandon, and for Barbara and Jerry to shag each other senseless under Margot's gazebo.

But the drinking didn't stop the pain. Instead, it made the pain more abstract, more peculiar, like a strange animal that shared his attic room, his demonic pet. The more he drank, the stranger his life seemed, the more his hands shook and his body sweated. He would wake at three in the morning, his mind rushing around him, swirling out beyond the roof, circling above the houses that separated him from his old home near Preston Park. What was Rachel doing? What were the children up to? He could see their sleeping faces with more vividness now than he had done when he looked down at them in reality, reeling in exhausted from Earthsea at the dead of night. In the mornings, his hands shook, nausea overwhelmed him and he sometimes felt he couldn't swallow. He felt as though his tension had grown into a great tumour, blocking his gullet.

But it was the panic attacks that finally drove him to his doctor's surgery – the sensation that the world was somehow going at a different speed from him, and that he was about to fall off it and tumble into outer space. And, with the panic, the alarming anger that made him feel like an impostor in his own body. Standing behind someone in the newsagent's who had the temerity to keep their money neatly folded in a handy wallet was enough to make him feel like Hannibal Lector, particularly if they were buying an improving publication like the *New Statesman*.

So it was no surprise that he had ended up in the

doctor's waiting room. Stephen had been waiting for his small slice of Dr Astley's meticulously allocated time for (he looked at his watch) forty minutes. He was staring bitterly at some pictures of Jonathan Ross and his lurid-looking family in *OK* magazine. His hands were shaking again. He looked away from them, and wondered what Dr Astley's husband did for a living and what they spent in an average week to stock their larder and replenish their wine cellar. Two high-powered wage earners, eating chicken satay and drinking a nice white Burgundy of an evening, while he was estranged from one bonkers non-wage earner, and had a work/work balance which involved paying for two households (if Vinnie's attic room in Canning Street could be called a household), forcing down a few chips on the seafront in his breaks snatched from Earthsea (currently he couldn't bear to eat his own food – one of the reasons he was here) and running round the restaurant till midnight, shouting at staff, smarming at customers, a regular Jekyll and Hyde. After which he would do the tills, yell some more because they invariably failed to tally (why was this?) and then drink vodka martinis from the restaurant bar till Vinnie reminded him what this was doing to the profits and drove him home.

Last night had been typical: he had sat slumped in the passenger seat, scenes from the evening juddering through his mind, while the lights of the seafront and the Palace Pier glided across Vinnie's moody profile. 'You're cracking up, Steve, you are truly cracking up,' was all he said, before dropping Stephen off abruptly and driving away to meet Marc somewhere flash where they would dance and snog and live in the moment. Stephen had shambled to the front door and let himself in with the spare set of keys Vinnie had retrieved from the cleaning lady. It hadn't taken much to transform Stephen from semi-yuppie-alternative-entrepreneur, profiled in both *Caterer and Hotelkeeper* magazine and the *Evening Standard*'s 'Brighton Special' supplement, to semi-dosser-lodger-from-hell. He had crawled upstairs, knowing that in a few short, feverish hours, seagulls would be skid-landing on the tiles above his head, screaming like abandoned babies.

'Stephen Beckett?' The doctors in the surgery had dispensed with the buzzer system some time ago, presumably for reasons of customer care, and now tiptoed gingerly into the waiting area to collect their patients. Dr Astley – a small, blonde person in her mid-thirties – had her habitual tentative smile.

'Now then,' she said, when they were both sitting down in her room, which was cramped and full of glass-fronted bookcases, 'how are you, Stephen?' In the circumstances, this seemed an odd question. He was crap, obviously.

'I'm, er, I'm having a nervous breakdown,' said Stephen, in a prim, sane voice.

'I see.' Dr Astley looked at him dubiously. Stephen glanced at the framed picture of her children – she seemed to have about seven – that was hanging on the wall behind her, and experienced a serial-killer moment. 'Do you have any particular symptoms you can tell me about?'

Stephen stared at her blankly for a second, then held his hands out towards her. They were rock steady. He could see himself though her eyes: a male malingerer. A whinging, degenerate example of the unfair sex. 'Usually, my hands tremble. In fact, they were trembling outside, just a moment ago,' he said, trying not to sound defensive. 'They started a few weeks ago. I can't eat, either. Not proper food. Nothing with nutrients – or a taste – only chips and KitKats. And . . . and I can't sleep, which is partly to do with the seagulls, and partly the vodka – which is another thing. I'm drinking too much. Which isn't like me. I mean, I'm usually above those safe government limits that I expect you think I should stick to, but not by that much. Now I have my units for three months in one afternoon.'

Dr Astley was nodding and looking at his notes. Feeling that she was sceptical, he felt compelled to go on. 'I feel as if my head's going to explode most of the time. Or my heart. Palpitations – like a pneumatic drill inside my body. And at night . . .'

'Yes?'

'At night, it's as if my whole life is running on a loop – on the opposite wall of my bedroom, endlessly playing, like a cinema screening that just goes on and on and on . . .' He paused. His eyes filled with tears, and to his horror these were spilling down his face. 'Look at me, Dr Astley. I'm cracking up. Vinnie says I'm cracking up, and believe me, he should know.'

'It's your . . . separation that is the problem, isn't it?' said Dr Astley, in a kinder voice. Stephen realized she was handing him a tissue. Presumably not a mansized one. 'I can give you some Prozac, which will make it easier to cope in the short term, but, sadly, I think this is a period of your life which is going to be hard no matter what I prescribe. I wish I could help, but as your GP there is very little I can do. You could see a counsellor –'

'Oh shit, no! Please!' groaned Stephen. 'I'll lose what

little sanity I've got left. I don't want to turn into some airhead like Princess bloody Diana, full of secondhand psychospeak. I know I live in the capital city of counselling and alternative therapy and every kind of rubbish that you can buy for twenty-five quid per hour in the twenty-first century, and maybe I should be pleased about that. But I'm not really very fashionable. I do like food that hasn't been covered in chemicals, but that doesn't make me the sodding Dalai Llama. I thought doctors knew that counselling was crap . . .'

Dr Astley frowned. 'You know, it does sound as if you are letting your anger get the better of you,' she said. 'I really would recommend that you find someone you can talk to – if counselling's not your bag, then a friend. Someone who understands you; a good listener.'

'The only friend I've got is a gay man who's in love with a lump of lard,' said Stephen. 'And even he's starting to hate my guts.'

'Someone in your family, then?' Her expression accused him of melodrama and fattism.

'My sister is trying to help, but she's a lesbian control-freak with her own empire to build. And my mother's a mad Irish hairdresser – we don't even speak the same language . . .'

Dr Astley sighed and handed him the prescription. 'Good luck,' she said. 'Remember: what you are going through is dreadful, but almost the norm. There is life after the death of a marriage. There truly is.' She looked as if she wanted to say more, then broke off. But as he was about to leave the room she called out, 'By the way, Stephen?'

He turned. 'Yes?'

'Some of us found Princess Diana rather brave and inspiring.'

Outside in the waiting room an altercation seemed to be in progress. A man was standing with his back to Stephen, arguing with the steely young receptionist. Wrapped around his legs was a large, wailing child, a girl of eight or nine who looked like a scaled-down version of Britney Spears. 'So you're saying that you don't consider a severe, raging, migraine-type headache an emergency?' the man was saying, in low, venomous tones. 'Can I just ask you whether you have any children?'

'I don't see that my personal circumstances are any concern of yours,' said the receptionist. She was wearing a headset and tapping away on a keyboard while he ranted and his child raged. ('I'm *bored*! You don't love me! Horrible Daddy! Rude Daddy! When can I go *home*?')

'Shh, darling. Very soon. When Daddy gets some medication. If it was my daughter, instead of me, who was in dire need of medical help would you take a different line?'

'It would depend what was wrong. A child with a severe headache would be a greater cause for concern than an adult. However, there's nothing wrong with her. So I suggest you take some painkillers and let the doctors treat the patients who have bothered to make appointments to see them . . . If you do want to make an appointment now, we could fit you in next Thursday.'

'I could be dead next fucking Thursday!'

'If you are going to be foul-mouthed and abusive, I will

98

have to ask you to leave the premises –' Her composure was unshakeable – clearly every eventuality had been covered in her training manual.

'How dare you speak to me like –' The man, struggling to disentangle his right leg from the clutches of his daughter, had caught sight of Stephen. 'My God . . . Stephen Beckett.' Shaking the child away, he came towards Stephen, smiling, apparently forgetting all about his life-threatening headache. 'I didn't even know you were in Brighton! You haven't changed a bit. How long is it? Must be . . .'

'Two decades,' said Stephen. 'You look exactly the same as well.' But then, Nick Fielding was the sort of person who looked like a clever impersonation of himself. It wasn't just that his narrow, seamy face and black, floppy hair would be instantly recognizable anywhere; it was his character. He was one of life's indelible personalities, a rogue of the old school. The sight of him lifted Stephen's spirits more than he would have thought possible. It was like meeting a long-lost member of your platoon behind enemy lines.

'Jesus,' said Nick. 'You have no idea how great it is to see you – of all people! Let's get out of this shit-hole. Come on, Poppy. That's enough. We're going.' And off they went, out into the fitful July sunshine. A pair of shades appeared on Nick's face as if by magic and he squeezed Stephen conspiratorially on the arm.

'Thank God we're out of there. Hell bitches are running the bloody planet these days.'

'What about your . . . headache, and stuff?' asked Stephen.

'Migraine, mate, not headache. Serious business. I was too ill to face the school run this morning, which is why madam here is still in tow. Well, I'll just have to fall back on my usual narcotic props – there's not a lot that Jack Daniel's and heroin can't fix.'

Stephen gave a half-grimace, not sure what to say.

'Only joking, only joking. Are you busy?'

Stephen shrugged. Everything was so terrible at Earthsea these days that he wasn't sure whether being there made it worse or better. Today was a Tuesday, and he dreaded to think how many bookings they had this early in the week – not a single one, probably. At the moment, being somewhere else seemed like a good idea. 'Not really,' he said.

'Well, I've got to give Poppy a dose of fresh air at the park. Otherwise she'll go apeshit all afternoon.' The girl, who had been quiet during this exchange, twiddling her thin fair hair around her fingers and giving Stephen a Lolita-like stare, smiled in a threatening way. He didn't believe he had ever seen a more unsavoury-looking child. Although she didn't look much older than Elsie, there was a quality of the faded starlet about her. She had a wizened, knowing face, skinny little arms and legs and was sporting a sex-toy outfit of sparkly mini-skirt, purple satin T-shirt and sleeveless fun-fur fleece – a strange choice on a summer's day. On her feet was a pair of platform sandals, a mode of footwear strictly banned in the Beckett home.

'I *need* to go to the park,' she said. 'Even if Daddy is feeling like total shit.'

'What have I told you about using words like that?' said Nick. 'You're not allowed to use filthy language and

Anglo-Saxon expletives till you're twelve. Do you want to come with us, Steve?'

'Yes,' said Stephen. 'That's the nearest thing to a fun suggestion I've heard for a long time.'

When Stephen first moved to Brighton from London, he had thought Preston Park very unimpressive compared to the great tracts of metropolitan parkland he had left behind. It didn't have the glamour of Regent's Park, or the scabby, secret charm of Victoria Park in Hackney. Originally, he had thought it featureless and flat, and spoiled by the noisy traffic that rumbled past. But time – and many early mornings spent pushing a buggy among the rosebeds and tennis courts – had changed his mind. There was the Rotunda Café, with its low, circular roof, looking out over a shallow pond full of stagnant weed, handy for children to fall into when the weather was cold. And the Beryl Cook ladies on the bowling green, chuckling in their whites. It was a bustling, small-town park, not a refuge from the big city. Today, it was the sole preserve of parents and children. Even the drunks who usually lay stretched out on benches, comatose and uncomplaining, were nowhere to be seen. Looking around him, Stephen realized that he hadn't been there for a long, long time. He felt the panic he had been unable to summon up in Dr Astley's surgery return, and tried to relax his clenched fists, which were thrust into the pockets of his black leather jacket. Work had eaten away his time – and it seemed ironic that he was here now it was too late, with someone else's child instead of his own.

'So, how are you, after all these years?' During the walk

to the park, Nick had been forced into silence by the whinging emanating from the child-woman Poppy. But once they reached the play area she busied herself by harassing two small boys and trying to bury their Action Men in the sandpit. Nick, with admirable panache, ignored this completely, settled himself alongside Stephen at a rustic picnic table, and seemed ready for a serious chat.

'Oh, you know . . .' said Stephen. 'Older and stupider.' Where to start? If he should start at all. He was almost prepared to draw a veil over the recent breakdown of his entire life, and enjoy a joky reminisce about old times, their misspent youth and all the women who had left him in order to go off with Nick. (At college, Nick had been one of those people whom everybody fancied. Even though he dressed in the manner of Adam Ant, including ruffled shirts and dodgy hairbands. It turned out that, in spite of being skinny, he had been what girls thought of as good-looking.) Carmel would have said this impulse proved that he was 'in denial', but she was in London, co-chairing a forum for pro-pornography lesbians, so she need never know.

But, sitting elbow to elbow with Nick on the narrow picnic bench, Stephen realized he really wanted to tell his former friend the whole story. He knew, before he even started, that this was someone who would be completely on his side.

'Older and stupider?' Nick was shaking a Marlboro 100 out of a packet. What a wonderful sight. 'Stupider in what way?'

'In the way that you are when your wife doesn't want you any more, your children would rather be with her new boyfriend than with you, and you're homeless but still paying the entire bloody mortgage.'

'Aha. In *that* way. A way of being stupider which I happen to know something about,' said Nick, blowing cigarette smoke out of both nostrils with an expression of conscious expertise. 'Have a fag. Join the club.'

Stephen had forgotten how fantastic smoking looked. In his college days that had been the whole point, of course. It was difficult for a speccy to look hard, and smoking was one way of trying to bring that about. But could he still bear the taste, after all those years of eating wholefoods and living in a smoke-free home? He took one, Nick lit it and suddenly he was twenty-one again, united with his fellow man in a battle to sleep with drunken women and then run away as fast as possible. Why hadn't he thought of this before? Being able to smoke again put the whole splitting-up thing in perspective. In all honesty, had he ever, really and truly, preferred being with Rachel to sitting in his room smoking and listening to David Bowie? Fag after fag after fag, till his throat rasped and his mind was a whirl of nicotine and Aladdin Sane? Giving up had been Rachel's idea, and he had fallen in line because it seemed like the grown-up thing to do.

'I don't know when it all started to go wrong,' said Stephen, feeling the nicotine buzzing into his system for the first time for ten years. 'But that's missing a lot out – did you know that I married Rachel?'

'Yeah, think so – from someone or other . . .'

'I know you two never got on; she must have been one of the few women we knew at college you couldn't chat into bed.'

'Well, you win some, you lose some . . . So when did you split up?'

'Three months ago. Seems like a lifetime. On the other hand, I think I'm still in shock. Partly because – although she says she isn't – I think she's seeing this total creep called Kris, who she's been working with.'

'Tell me about it,' said Nick. 'I was dumped myself about a year ago. First time anyone has ever finished with me. It was . . . I can't describe how it was. Total and complete torture. I never knew I could feel that bad.'

'Poppy's mother?'

'Yes. American girl called Clancy. Totally mad. In love with me one minute, hated my guts the next. One day, man's woman in pink stilettos, spray-on dresses, little job in the fashion business – *nice*. Next day, meets some hatchet-faced crone she knew at journalist school and decides she's a celibate Buddhist. Throws me out of the house, refuses to speak to me . . . Like something out of one of those psychological-horror films – unbelievable.'

'Are Buddhists usually celibate?' Stephen was thinking about the Dalai Llama again. Even at times like this, his mind was prone to wander.

'No fucking idea, mate. Do I look like the sort of person who takes an interest in world religion? In any case, Clancy was definitely screwing some of these counterculture types she hooked up with at the yoga centre. Upshot of the whole thing is that she spends three months of every year trekking in the Himalayas – which is where she is at this moment – and I'm left holding the bleeding baby. That's post-feminism for you – and yet still the hellcats go on about how nothing has really changed.'

They sat side by side, watching Poppy kicking a toddler off the cute little rocking horse in the middle of the sandpit. The child's mother whisked him away, giving a blankly hostile stare to the parents sitting nearby but not noticing the two smoke-wreathed men.

'So why did you end up in Brighton?' asked Stephen after a while. 'Always saw you as strictly a North London sort of bloke.'

'Job, mate. Got made redundant, and someone offered me a partnership in an estate agency down here about six months ago. Weird bloke, is Keith. Born-again Christian. We run the business *ethically*, if you can believe that.'

'Doesn't sound like your sort of thing.'

'It's bloody not. But it occurred to me that it wasn't a bad financial move, really. This town is full of hippies, eco-warriers and woolly-minded arses who can't afford to live in Islington – and they fucking love the idea that buying a house is a socially aware thing to do.'

'So you're ethical for cynical reasons?'

'Yeah! Good one! That's me all over.'

Stephen sighed. He didn't have much of an attention span when it came to other people's jobs. 'I don't know,' he said. 'What do women want? That's what I'd like to find out.'

'Are you serious? Why the hell should you worry about that? It's what men want that counts – work that one out, and bloody well go for it. Most of us are made to feel so crap about the sad fact that we're penis-owners that we can't think straight any more.'

'Apparently this Kris knows what he wants. Rachel

says he's in touch with his emotions, and knows how to empower women to feel cherished.'

'I hope you hit her when she came out with that.'

'Very funny.'

'Don't go all PC on me. It's a matter of survival. You look like you've had the stuffing knocked out of you. Fight it. Fight her. Why should she have it all her own way?'

'I don't want to fall out completely. There's the children to think about . . .'

'Children? You didn't mention you had kids.'

A wave of grief swept though Stephen. Why hadn't he talked about Elsie and Stan? It was too painful, too unreal to think that he no longer lived with them. But, in a way, he was still trying to tune them out. Trying to regain his equilibrium, he said: 'Now, she's been to see some mediator, recommended by Kris of course, who says that the best thing for everybody is for me to sign the house over entirely to her. Even though she's never paid a penny towards it. I sign it over to her, walk away, and start again.'

'Christ! Are you going to just sit there and let them do whatever they want? That's not how I remember you – you were never a pushover. What's wrong with you?' Nick leaped up from the bench, as if he couldn't bear to sit in such close proximity to such a feeble-minded wimp. He ground out his cigarette under his shoe as if it was a scheming post-feminist he was crushing into the tarmac.

'What can I do? What could anyone do, that I'm not doing? My hands are tied. All I can do is live from day to day.'

'That's bollocks. Sorry, Stephen, and maybe it's none of my business, but it really is. Number one: get yourself a serious lawyer, and make sure you don't get ripped off.'

Stephen nodded. The very thought of 'serious lawyers' made him feel tired. 'And number two?'

'Number two is obvious. Get fucking laid. Give me your bloody phone number and we'll soon sort you out.'

'Right, yes,' said Stephen, writing in the notebook Nick had thrust into his hands. 'Only problem there is finding someone who'll have me . . .'

Nick raised his eyebrows and made a silent gesture around the play area, as though any one of the young mums wiping snot off her child's chin was ripe for the plucking.

Stephen laughed bitterly. 'Be realistic. I need *spare women*. Women who aren't friends of Rachel or doing the school run.'

'Piece of piss.' Nick had noticed that Poppy was engaged in conversation with two rough-looking boys who appeared to be much too old to be in the sandpit, and began striding towards her. Over his shoulder he said, 'When was the last time you had a serious night out with the lads?'

'Never, probably,' shouted Stephen, as Nick leaped over the low fence to sort out his daughter.

'About time you did something about it, then,' Nick called back. 'Bugger off, you two. This area's for kids, not juvenile delinquents.' The two boys sauntered away. Poppy let out a wail of protest. Stephen sat alone on the bench, and realized that he was smiling.

8

Stephen had plenty of time to reflect on his meeting with Nick over the next few weeks. At first, he had been filled with a sort of righteous excitement. Yes, women really were vile – and it was all right to think so. While Rachel was clearly nowhere like as bad as Clancy, she had still thrown him out, deprived him of his home and taken up with someone else. If not sexually, then in every other respect. What could be worse than the fact that Kris was her new best friend, her mentor, the person who advised her on everything? The exchange of a few bodily fluids was nothing compared to that. But then again. He didn't really like to think about the bodily-fluids thing either. Perhaps the reason he was so quick to assure himself that there was nothing of that kind happening was that thinking otherwise was, well, unthinkable.

Reflecting on Rachel-as-a-lover made his conversation with Nick seem childish and pointless. Her name, her image in his mind, were surrounded with physical pain. Which led – in a wrenching loop – to the children. The children he had mentioned to Nick as if they were merely an afterthought. Every Sunday he took them out for the day. Just like the cliché dads he had imagined when he and Rachel had first fallen out. And, just like the cliché dads and the cliché children who didn't live with their dads, they went to the park, and the Sea Life Centre and the seafront. All in one day. After that, they sat in cafés – anywhere but McDonald's – and the children talked and talked and talked, and fell off their chairs, and blew bubbles in their banana milkshakes. They made him laugh. Better still, he made *them* laugh. There could be no more magical sound in the whole universe than the sound of a six-year-old gurgling with uncontrollable mirth. He hadn't realized how much he loved them. Or how little he could think of to talk about when they were there. When the laughing stopped, he often felt lonely and confused. How did grown-ups manage to talk to children for an entire day? Perhaps it was only the separated dads who tried. He knew that, despite all her protestations, Rachel's idea of quality time with the kids involved getting together with at least two other mothers and cackling in the kitchen over a pot of Earl Grey tea while the children beat each other up in the garden. Maybe he was part of a whole new trend in parenting. He cast his mind back to his own childhood. He had hardly any memories of his father, Giles, who ran away on Christmas Eve when Stephen was nine. Was it normal to remember so little of his childhood? His most vivid recollection was of Giles's square-topped fingers clutching the edge of the *Daily Telegraph*, which was hiding the rest of his body. He certainly didn't remember Giles ever buying him a milkshake. Outings with his mother had been more frequent. They'd often gone to a dark, back-room café called the Globe, where Stephen drank Horlicks from a tall white mug with a solid white handle, like a sticky-out ear, while Carmel read Narnia books, hardly registering the presence of her depleted family, and Rose scanned the restaurant, already on the lookout for those in emotional need.

So what next? Instead of trying to sleep, he had taken to sitting in his bedroom, thinking, far into the night. He saw his children growing up; he saw himself pushed to the edge of their lives. Sometimes, brilliant new recipe ideas came floating to him in the small hours, but he no longer bothered to write them down.

One Thursday evening, at Earthsea, he was scrutinizing his diary, checking up on when he was meant to have the children and wondering for the hundredth time if playing the passive waiting game was the mark of a man or a mug, when Vinnie pushed past him, carrying a steaming tray of baked balsamic red onions.

'If you can't get out of my *pissing* way, Steve, get out of the kitchen,' he snarled.

Stephen stepped backwards, bumping into Briony, who shrieked and dropped an armload of dirty plates. They crashed to the floor. Fragments of china skidded across the red tiles, leaving trails of raspberry and lemongrass trifle in the path of the incoming waiters. It had to be Briony, of course. They hadn't spoken since the evening Stephen had disgraced himself. He knew he was meant to be training her as a chef, but couldn't summon up the energy to get the whole thing started. Now she avoided Stephen's eye, and she would melt away when he entered the room. He wished he could remember why she had ended up crying that night.

'Christ, Stephen!' Vinnie banged the tray down, his face creased with fury. 'If I'm not speaking out of turn, would you care to visit this planet for long enough to clear up that mess? Before one of our valued members of staff kills themselves?'

'It was really my –' Briony began.

'Just shut up, get out there and serve some bloody customers,' said Vinnie, without looking at her. Briony dashed away, her eyes swimming.

'She was only trying to help,' said Stephen. Angrily, he grabbed a sweeping brush from the kitchen porter's corner and began to clear up as fast as he could. But Vinnie was quite right. His mind hadn't been on Earthsea for a long time. He chopped, marinated, fried, tossed and baked in a dream. When he tried the dishes, he had no idea what they tasted like. Only the other day, Vinnie had binned fifty corn-cakes Stephen had produced. This would have been unheard of in the days before he had left Rachel.

As he banged the dustpan against the side of the bin, sending the shards of crockery crashing into the bottom of the black liner, Flint came in, rather more slowly than might have been expected on a busy night. Seeing Stephen, he hesitated, then appeared to be scrutinizing a mole on one of his long, thin arms. Stephen glanced at him over his shoulder. What a gormless boy he was! He had gone off Flint because of his role as meal-bringer on the worst night of his life. It wasn't his fault, of course. But it was hard to untangle the sight of Flint from the memory of that dreadful evening, and of Rachel skimming brandy-soaked prunes past his head.

'Haven't you got tables to deal with?' Stephen asked. 'This is no time to stand around.'

'Yeah, right,' said Flint. He almost looked at Stephen,

then gave a sort of writhe of embarrassment. 'Er, like, there's something I think you ought to know.'

'What?' Stephen was bent double, retrieving some rogue bits of plate from under the preparation table.

'Some . . . new arrivals –' said Flint, looking pained.

'New – what are you on about?'

'I think he's trying to tell you that Rachel has just walked in with lover boy,' said Vinnie, who was peering over the half-door at the side of the kitchen into the restaurant beyond. 'You never mentioned he was black. Looks like Shaft's long-lost brother, the caring social worker.'

'*What?*' Stephen rushed to Vinnie's side. Sure enough, there was Rachel, swathed in some deep-red shawl affair he hadn't seen before, and dreadful Kris, wearing a loud check jacket that looked as if it came from Oxfam. They were sitting down at table seventeen. Both were laughing vivaciously. 'What the hell is she playing at? Is this some kind of game?'

'Isn't that your mate Clive and his missis as well?' asked Vinnie, who looked as if he was enjoying himself.

Stephen looked, crinkling up his eyes. The fact that he needed new glasses was so minor compared to all the other problems that made up his life that it hardly registered in normal circumstances – but at this moment he felt like tearing out his eyes, throwing them to the ground and jumping up and down on them. However, rubbish eyesight or no rubbish eyesight, it was obvious that the other people at the table were indeed his ex-friends Clive and Tamzin. Neither had been in touch since That Evening, and he could only assume that they had decided to take Rachel's side against him. He felt once more as if he and the rest of the earth were going at different speeds, and he was going to hurtle into outer space. Did no one care? Were they all united in a shared loathing for him?

'I can't . . . What's going on? Are they mad?' He realized he was blushing for the first time since Fay Cattermole had refused to dance with him at the school disco. He could still see her now – her lithe body encased in some ruched shepherdess-style frock, her eyebrows arched wryly as if she really had to hand it to him, having the nerve to ask her when he was such a feeble specimen, let alone one who had clearly bought his cut-price loons from C&A. And with the scarlet cheeks went the same nausea rush and sweat trickles sliding down his back. 'Or am I the one who's insane?'

Vinnie patted him on the arm. 'I'll go and have a quick word,' he said, quite kindly.

'No.' Stephen cleared his throat. 'I've been made to look enough of a fool, without you playing go-between. I'll go out and speak to them myself.' Before he could think better of his own determination, he swung through the mini saloon doors, wishing that his legs would move normally – he appeared to be approaching their table in a series of loping bounds, his hands swinging around him, apelike and out of control. But none of them noticed. When he arrived at the table, all four heads were bowed behind Earthsea's large, orange, laminated menus. His feeling of invisibility intensified. He cleared his throat again.

'So . . . erm . . . Clive – you finally made it to my little restaurant,' he said. His voice sounded surprisingly normal. 'Didn't think it was exactly your scene.'

Their heads bounced up at the same time, and all four started smiling at him joylessly.

'Steve –' Clive's face twisted through a series of expressions before he pushed back his chair and rushed over to give Stephen a manly hug. 'Great to see you . . . Been meaning to call you since the . . . But really busy with . . . and then Kris had the idea that this would be . . . Kind of a peace thing . . .'

'A peace thing?' Stephen looked at Kris.

Kris smiled his perfect smile, and the lyrics of 'Sexual Healing' glided into Stephen's mind. 'Sensational place,' said Kris, nodding as if to acknowledge the Norah Jones music, the orange and turquoise linen tablecloths and the waiters and waitresses in their black shirts and matching cargo pants.

'I hope you haven't come out to make a scene,' said Rachel, her voice controlled and chilly. 'Because it just struck us all as a nice idea to come here and show that we can be adult about everything. There's no need to blame Kris or go into one of your strops.'

'And it really is superb . . .' said Tamzin. She appeared to have doubled in size in the months since he'd seen her, and looked less like a delicate Oriental kitten and more like an overfed tabby. Her slightly slanted eyes sparkled out at him over plumped-up cheeks, and a little wodge of white skin marred the usually taught line of her chin. 'A wonderful place. Isn't it, darling? I can't think why Clive and I haven't been before now. Can you, sweetie?' Clive shook his head, apparently unable to speak again. Stephen couldn't help warming to him slightly – his embarrassment did him credit. But then the cold thought struck him that this might be because Clive had lent him £30,000 the year before, ostensibly because he thought Earthsea had good prospects but actually because he could see that Stephen needed help. This was a fact that Stephen had successfully kept out of his mind at the dinner party. Now, looking at Clive shifting uneasily in his seat, it was impossible to prevent the memory from returning.

'Total mystery,' said Stephen. He looked from face to face, a sense of surreal detachment beginning to over-whelm him. What could he do, after all? Shoot them? Lie on the floor and cry? Frogmarch them to the door? He certainly couldn't give Clive his money back. If they wanted to be here – and he still couldn't work out the motivation for this – then he had to leave them to get on with it. 'I hope . . . you enjoy your meal,' he said. 'All of you.' And with that he gave a sort of bow, and walked back into the kitchen. This time his legs felt heavy, like swollen stumps he could only move with a supreme effort of will.

'Well?' Vinnie turned from stirring a sauce on a burning gas ring. 'What are they doing here?'

'No idea,' said Stephen. 'They're trying to make out it's some modern business about being civilized and mature.'

'Bit soon for that old bollocks.'

'Let's just serve them double quick, so they'll leave as soon as possible,' said Stephen, retying his apron and reading the next order on the row of metal pegs above the pass. 'Flint – you seem to be at a loose end. Go and give them the benefit of your skills.'

Stephen was just putting some mung-bean noodles into a saucepan when Flint returned. 'Cool,' he said.

'Considering. Three of them went for the Thai curry. Except Rachel – she wants roasted veg and mozzarella. Only – sorry, Stephen, but they seem to want you to advise them about the wine. At least, the black guy does.'

'For God's sake!' Stephen marched back into the restaurant with his apron on. 'It's all organic,' he said tersely to Kris, who was nibbling at a cheese and sesame breadstick. 'Just take your pick.'

Kris smiled at the wine list in a saintly manner. His forehead was shining with gratuitous integrity. Stephen stood, hands on hips. Was this really the most annoying man who had ever lived? Or would any man who was apparently stepping into his newly vacated life seem equally unbearable?

'The thing is, Steve, I'm not really a wine person,' said Kris. 'In fact, I haven't drunk alcohol for years. But this evening . . . I sort of feel like celebrating the fact that we're all together. *Communicating.*'

'Do you really?' said Stephen. 'In that case, I can heartily recommend the Earthsaver champagne. Speciality of the house. Ten per cent of the price goes to a shelter for alcoholics in a shanty town on the edge of Buenos Aires.'

'Good idea,' said Clive, who was looking more uncomfortable than ever. 'Let's get two bottles. Thanks, Steve – and sorry to bother you again.'

Stephen shrugged and turned on his heel. At least, he thought to himself, there wasn't much more they could do to annoy him now. He threw himself into preparing meals, admonishing staff and adding exquisite visual details to dishes before they left the kitchen to go on public view.

It was amazing, the magic you could work with some spiced dust plantain horns or a handful of Sichuan mizuna leaves. And the busier he got, the calmer he felt. Sod Rachel. Sod them all. He was living his life – the only part of his life that they'd left him, apart from those intense days out with the kids. What's more, the life he had left was all right. The restaurant was full. Waiting staff whizzed in and out of the kitchen with bright, concentrated faces, yelling out the contents of their orders as they spiked them on to the hooks on the wall. When he allowed himself to think about it, Stephen was pleased that the place was bustling and noisy, the music blurred by the buzzing conversation of the diners. Thank God it wasn't one of their dead Tuesdays – he really must do something about the bad turnout they were getting early in the week. Peering over the half-door from time to time, he assured himself that tonight there was a particularly trendy-looking intake – as long as you admitted women who made their own necklaces and men with grey ponytails into this category, along with overtly hip foodsters sporting hooded tops and flares. Rachel would think twice about treating him with contempt when he was publicly fêted as a post-carnivorous Marco Pierre White and as Delia's rightful son and heir – a culinary Everyman for the say-no-to-GM generation. No one need know that, since his meeting with wicked Nick in the park, he had begun to nibble on bacon sandwiches as well as buy his own cigarettes.

But his near happiness was short lived. Towards ten thirty – when he would usually have expected the action to die down, as they stopped serving main courses at eleven – Flint came shambling over again, looking miserable.

'Steve . . . Maybe you want to know this, and maybe you don't . . .'

'I want to know it, Flint, so don't mess about.'

'That guy – with Rachel – seems like maybe he's had a bit too much of the champagne.'

'Oh God.'

Rather than approaching their table directly this time, Stephen affected a breezy, disinterested air and went to the bar in the centre of the restaurant. It was dark outside now, the red wall-lights gave off only a subdued glow, and each table was illuminated by a single candle in a plain-glass sphere. Pretending to scrutinize some papers on the bar – which were in fact a pile of invoices from his lettuce man in Lewes – Stephen squinted sideways at table seventeen.

It was not a pleasant sight. And, if he had any lingering doubts about the exact nature of his wife's relationship with Kris, surely he now had all the information he needed. Tamzin and Clive were doing their usual kissy-kissy routine. His right arm lay along the back of her chair, and they were staring into each other's eyes. Rachel sat opposite, with an expression of benign sozzlement on her face. And behind her stood Kris, kneading her shoulders with his usual aura of beatific oneness with everything.

'Mmm,' said Rachel. 'Lovely.'

'It's a totally relaxing experience, isn't it,' boomed Kris. The champagne had noticeably increased his volume. 'Maggie used to love this.'

'His ex,' said Rachel, nodding comfortably at Tamzin and Clive.

'Great before sex,' said Kris, in an even louder voice.

'Keep your voice down,' said Rachel, glancing nervously

118

around, but still not seeing Stephen. 'Remember where we are.'

'I thought it was all strictly platonic between you two,' beamed Tamzin fatly.

'Of course it is,'/'Are you for real?' said Rachel and Kris at the same time. Then, before Rachel could stop him, his hands still grinding sensuously into her shoulders, Kris yelled. 'Believe me, when it comes to full-on sensuality, this woman is the world's number one.'

'Sorry?' said Clive, who was beginning to look panicky again.

'What I mean is, I truly did not appreciate the power of the vaginal orgasm until I met the person you see before you now.'

At which point, several things happened at once. Rachel shouted, 'Shut the fuck up, Kris!' Tamzin squealed, Clive said, 'Now I really think . . .' and the drunken students at the next table all doubled up with mirth at the thought of Old People Shagging. But Stephen could not move. He held on tight to the lettuce invoices, patches of sweat spreading outwards from his clenched fingers, paralysed with nausea, loathing, penis envy and despair. Then, suddenly, the panic attacks, the night fears, the insomnia, the self-hatred, the voice of Nick Fielding all rushed around him, like some terrible tornado, a distillation of horror and anger and pain. He had no sense of his own movement – rather, the room seemed to sweep backwards, projecting him forwards. By some diabolic force, he was trolleyed towards the four people he least wanted to speak to in the world, and by the same force he was yelling, lips pared back, mouth cavernously roaring, mad, mad, as if dreaming he was the devil in a nightmare. 'Get out! Get out of my fucking restaurant! Get out of my life! I'll kill you all! I swear to God I'll kill you all!' And for the rest of his life he remembered that quartet of shocked, arrested faces, as if he really had killed them, as if everything had stopped at that precise moment.

9

'Careful now! If you looked where you were going, you'd save yourself all these knocks on the head ...'

Stephen backed away from his mother's cooker, hand clutched to his left eye. Her kitchen was lined with orange pine and boasted a slippery tiled floor with tiny rugs which skated the unwary across the floor. All this he could cope with. But she had also installed a brand-new obstacle since his last visit.

'Mum, why is there a plastic unicorn hanging over the cooker?'

'Grand, isn't it?' said Rose. 'It reminds me of home. I got it from the Alzheimer's jumble. Amazing, the treasures you can find if you run the bric-à-brac stall.' It certainly was. Rose's house in Stoke was bric-à-brac heaven. She had lived in the poky terraced house since they were tiny. While their father, Giles, was still in residence, he had indulged in a brief mania for home improvements, and had knocked the old scullery and the back living room into one, then built the breakfast bar which had so humiliated Stephen during Fay Cattermole's visit in 1977. The construction of this rhapsody in hardboard was a project that had made a big impression on Stephen – he could still see his father, hammering away rather amateurishly in his perennially swanky outfit, sporting zipper-sided boots and a rollneck sweater. Soon afterwards, Giles had buggered off, first to teach people to sail in Spain, later to America, where he had disappeared without trace, zipper-sided boots and all. Whether it was a result of the trauma of losing her husband Stephen didn't know, but, since Giles had departed, his mother had progressively filled their marital home with more and more junk. She obsessively hoarded all her own memorabilia, but had a soft spot for the oddments of other people's lives, too. So the photographs on her walls showed not only the sepia-soft faces of long-dead members of the Beckett family and of the O'Dowds, her own people back in Dublin, but also those of complete strangers who had flogged job lots of rubbish at boot sales. And her junk addiction didn't end there. She filled the house with china dolls, overdue library books, embroidered cushions, statues of the Holy Family and shoeboxes stuffed with faded theatre programmes and ancient school magazines. Worse, she favoured things that dangled – mobiles, wind-chimes, dried flowers, bead curtains and now, apparently, a plastic unicorn.

'God, Mother,' he said now, cautiously advancing to the cooker again, where he had six pancakes on the griddle. 'Haven't you ever heard of feng shui?' Even when times were good, Stephen metamorphosed into a snappish, pre-tentious teenager when Rose was around. Now he was being even worse than usual. His awareness of this did nothing to improve his temper.

'Of course I have,' said Rose crossly. 'It's that thing where they make people throw their life away. No! That's more Rachel's line than mine. I like a bit of clutter – brings humanity into a home. Shame she couldn't make it, though. Where was it you said she was again?'

'At a residential weekend for rediscovering desire in monogamous relationships,' said Stephen, poking at the pancakes with a neutral expression on his face. He was determined to preserve his semi-detached relationship with his mother. Her comments or intrusions were the last thing he needed. Anyway, this was only partly a lie – Rachel was indeed spending a weekend considering this important subject. But of course there would have been no chance of her coming to see Rose with him even if her weekend had been empty of such engagements. When he had first realized that they were all meant to be in Stoke for this weekend, he had toyed briefly with the idea of asking Rachel to come with him and join him in pretending that they were still some kind of item. He hadn't been able to summon up the nerve at first – and then two days ago he'd found out that she was mistress of the vaginal orgasm, courtesy of the Love God, so it was out of the question. Even though Rachel couldn't be here there was no need to involve Rose, who would immediately enter full advice alert and start telling him what had always been his trouble. So he had offered the children the chance to earn themselves two Beanie Babies each if they managed – for the whole weekend – not to mention that Daddy wasn't living at home any more. It was now four o'clock on Saturday afternoon – less than twenty-four hours before they could make their escape. He started flipping the pancakes on to a plate. 'Children! Food!' he yelled. From upstairs, there was the sound of something heavy landing on the ground, raised voices, a wail.

'There's something not right with those two,' said Rose.

'Nonsense!' said Stephen. 'They're just squabbling. All children squabble.'

'They're out of sorts, love them.'

'They'll be fine. They should be down here anyway. *Children!*'

At which Elsie and Stan appeared, both dressed in lace curtains. 'He kicked me for No Reason!' declared Elsie. She sniffed tragically, but reached for one of the pancakes on the kitchen table.

'THE REASON WAS I HATE YOU!' said Stan. 'BOSSY!'

'I only said let's get married,' said Elsie. 'Weddings are good fun, aren't they, Nanna?'

'Oh, they're my favourite thing of all!' said Rose. 'I only have to see confetti on the steps of a church and I've tears streaming down my face.'

'Tears of happiness, I expect,' said Elsie, nodding. 'Were you happy when you and Mum got married, Daddy?'

Stephen managed to swallow the tea in his mouth without choking. 'Of course I was, darling,' he said. 'How's your pancake?'

'Oh, lovely, mmm. Was it the best day of your whole life?'

'I should think so.' He remembered it, in fact, as a day of intense fear and stress, with pregnant Rachel throwing up at the reception, Carmel producing a new girlfriend who was dressed like a German expressionist poet, and his mother in a cream-puff hat and bright-orange suit, weeping tears that were not of happiness at all because Giles wasn't there to share in all the joy and sparkly wine. Even years after he had gone, she always spoke of him with a certain awe and gratitude, as if she had never quite got over landing such a catch in the first place. Giles was handsome, the middle son of a wealthy farming family from Yorkshire. He was amusing, clever, stylish, good at listening to women he hadn't yet slept with. All this came out via various, often-repeated anecdotes charting their meeting, engagement, wedding, and ill-fated marriage. It had always been a relationship out of her league, Rose believed. Getting him had been more of a surprise than losing him, an attitude which Stephen found defeatist and annoying.

'I HATE WEDDINGS! THEY STINK!' This was closer to Stephen's view.

'Your mother was a picture on her big day. Beautiful as a princess. Wasn't she, Stephen?' Any minute now she was going to make a dive for the wedding album. He had to head her off somehow. He plunged in desperately.

'So – plans for this evening? I thought – if you don't mind doing a spot of babysitting – I might phone up a couple of people and go out for a drink.'

'Oh, Stephen, I told you on the phone! When will you ever start listening to people? We've got a date with Mrs Cattermole. Sylvia, you know, whose husband just died. He suffered terribly at the end, God rest his soul.'

'Well if she's coming round, won't that be some company for you . . . ? No reason for me to tag . . .' Then he registered the name. 'Cattermole?'

'Yes. You were at school with her daughter, weren't you? In fact, Fay's coming along too. Not here. We're having a little outing to the Tom Thumb – just the four of us.'

Stephen felt his palms begin to sweat. He had envisaged a quiet evening during which he would drink enough to anaesthetize himself; an escape from his mother's perpetual empathy and the chance to dull his own feelings. Dr Astley's pills weren't helping at all, and he was still worried that he was losing his mind. He had had two blackouts now: one the night he had left, and the other the evening he had thrown Rachel and company out of the restaurant. And, each day, he felt heavier and more exhausted, getting up took all his energy, and he had no interest in anything. Earthsea, Vinnie, Rachel – everything just flowed around him. The children were the only thing that could hold his attention, and he felt anxious and jumpy when they were with him. All he could see was that the world was a bad place, that human beings were successful and pitiless predators, preying on the planet. It was as if all his life he had been deceiving himself into thinking that he lived in a safe and normal place. Now he could see it was full of dangerous egomaniacs. The expression on Tony Blair's face, lips pressed close together in a macho, warlike pout; the way that Jeremy Paxman's eyebrows magnificently disdained the news; Ross on *Friends* with his hideously smug hairstyle . . . The world was full of men who had their place and revelled in their alpha superiority. Everything made him feel more isolated, stuck in a void which only he could occupy. Tonight, he had intended to hide his broken marriage, talk about football (he had even bought a paper so he could memorize the sports pages) and soak himself gently in beer. Instead, he would have to experience an entire evening with Fay Cattermole, and undergo not only the embarrassment of hearing his mother talk non-stop for around four hours but also the torture of eating the food in the Tom Thumb, a Harvesteresque carvery that his mother had discovered in Penkhull. It was her idea of serious class.

'The Cattermoles will hate the Tom Thumb,' he said, nibbing a pancake pettishly. He was hungry all the time, but everything tasted, as did this pancake, like cardboard. 'They're proper middle-class people, Mum. Proper middle-class people come equipped with taste-buds. Anyway, what are you doing about a babysitter?'

'Shona from the salon is coming over,' said Rose. 'You know the children worship her.' She was spreading Nutella on her pancake. She had a seriously sweet tooth and would sometimes pick indifferently at her main course, 'saving herself' as she would put it, for pudding.

The Tom Thumb was as horrible as Stephen had remembered. Horrible not in the traditional way that had blighted his childhood, but in the modern, ersatz, interchangeable fashion that solidified his depression. When he grew up in Stoke, in the sixties and seventies, it had been a place of palpable ugliness and poverty, with cramped terraced houses lined up in narrow brown streets. Opposite his school, there had been a Mother's Pride bakery emitting the smell of new-baked, mass-produced bread. At the end of each day, it belched forth hordes of women who looked just like Myra Hindley, their curlers covered with bulging chiffon scarves. Nowadays, the special brand of depressingness conjured up by Stoke was the depressingness of everywhere in the country that had had its identity removed. Instead of squalid corner shops and hard-faced factory girls, the place was full of Coffee Republics and branches of Next, and eateries that sold risotto and tortilla with a Tex Mex theme, heaving with semi-evolved youths with gelled hair and screechy girl-friends who all dressed a bit like Posh Spice. Once, Stoke-on-Trent had been famous as the birthplace of Arnold Bennett. Now its most famous export was Robbie Williams. Only when he took the children swimming did Stephen experience a taste of the forgotten Stoke. While Brighton's public pools were full of glassy-eyed fitness fanatics churning up and down the 'sprint' lane, here there were lots of puffy dads with dodgy tashes teaching their children to do the doggy paddle in the shallow end. Looking around the Tom Thumb now, he saw that this was probably where these flabby non-swimmers spent their evening leisure time. The men wore flattened-down receding hair and casual lemon shirts, and their wives sported flowery frocks and lots of gold chains. This was allegedly a 'family' restaurant, so why did so many people come here in the evenings, without children? The whole place was decked out in a kind of Dickensian Christmas theme, with busy red carpets, dark-brown plastic-wood tables and bentwood chairs pretending to be oak, and pictures of Old Stoke on the walls. Rose was waving cheerily as they made their way across the res-taurant. She appeared to know everyone there. He knew she was a universal agony auntie, but surely they couldn't *all* have had their houses repossessed, or lost a close family member to leukaemia?

'Ah, they're here already,' she said, nodding towards two women at a corner table. Stephen followed his mother unhappily. The music that was being piped into his ears was by Chris DeBurgh. While the kissing and exclaiming went on he had a chance to study Fay Cattermole. If anything, he realized, she was more beautiful now, at the age of something near forty, than she had been when she inspired his first schoolboy crush. She still had the coils of red hair – darker now, perhaps – and the skinny, schoolgirl frame. But while as a teenager she had had a frozen, forbidding air, she now looked softer, calmer. Not, in her plum-coloured lipstick and softly draped grey dress, welcoming exactly, but as if she might be welcoming if you were intelligent enough, or amusing enough, or knew some of the people with whom she mixed. She looked over his mother's shoulder at him.

'I don't suppose you remember me,' she said.

'As a matter of fact, I remember you very well,' said Stephen.

'Of course he remembers you! He had the most –'

'You must be Sylvia,' interjected Stephen, shaking the hand of the older woman. 'I'm really sorry to hear . . . To hear about . . .'

'Thank you,' said Sylvia Cattermole faintly. 'You're very kind.' She was a ghostly creature, wearing some cream creation that looked almost like a sari, and clutching a glass of dry white wine in a veined claw. 'Do you remember my husband?' she asked Stephen as he sat down in the chair opposite her.

He had few memories of Albert Cattermole, though he had once come to their house. But he did recall seeing him poncing round the university bookshop, a scarf tossed over one shoulder in the manner of a Toulouse Lautrec poster-boy. 'Oh, yes, I remember him very well,' he said. 'I always – you know – admired him and everything.'

'He was a complete man,' said Sylvia Cattermole. 'Right up till the end – completely himself. Never – as so many people are – *diluted* by the world.'

'No. No. I can imagine that . . . he wouldn't be . . .' said Stephen.

Fay, who was sitting next to her mother, reached over and took her hand. 'Shall we order some food?' she asked. 'You don't want a late night, do you, Sylvia?' Stephen remembered that Fay had always called her parents by their Christian names, as if they were all civilized contemporaries. The menus were already sitting in front of them on the table. Stephen, heart sinking, picked his up.

The cover was disturbing enough in itself. Against a backdrop of tempting slices of medium-rare beef steak, chips and peas, little Tom Thumb danced in profile. Below, in festive Victorian gold lettering, were the words "PUB MENU – open all day and every day'. And underneath that was a photograph of some recumbent vegetables: mushrooms, carrots, sweetcorn and even fennel. Somehow, the veg looked unconvincing, as if it knew that no one looking at this menu would be expecting anything more nutritious or challenging than a corner of frozen peas. Opening it, he found the contents were even worse than he had feared. At the bottom, for the plebs, was a blue square (hinting at a marine theme?) which tempted the diner with 'Fishes'n Chips' and even 'A Pot Full O'Sea-fish!' (Why the exclamation mark? Didn't it sound quite crap enough with normal punctuation?) Vulgar carnivores could enjoy such delights as a 'Steak Your Claim', or a 'Ranch-House Combo', with rump steak *and* prawns. But it was for foodies like himself that the Tom Thumb saved its most appalling punishments – under 'Pasta, Pasta' some wit had written: 'It's a nice-A dish of ravioli in tomato sauce-A, penne in a light-A citrus sauce-A and capaletti with spinach & ricotta in a cheese-A sauce-A'.

'I *do* like a nice steak,' said Rose. 'Sylvia, you need to get some red meat inside you, dear. You're disappearing.'

'I just don't know if I . . .' began Sylvia.

But then Fay chipped in with 'Oh – look – priceless! Have a "Square to Share" with me.' She proceeded to read out from the menu: '"A whole garlic bread, boozy wings" (what?) "onion rings, wholetail prawns, breaded mush-rooms" (and how delicious *they* will be!) "with sour cream and chives and sweet chilli dips." Fantastic! Sylvia, I know you've hardly eaten for three months, but you can't let an opportunity like this pass you by!'

Rose, pink with pleasure, said sincerely, 'Do you know, I've not brought anyone here yet who didn't have a wonderful time. They make too much fuss about food in all these cookery programmes, don't you think, Sylvia? So-and-so types of olive oil, your woman Nanette Lawson with the eyeliner. Too much palaver about nothing, when you could always come to a place like this and get the best meal money can buy.'

Stephen caught Fay's eye, and she gave him a pursed-lipped, pretend-serious grimace. He was caught between the automatic desire to protect his mother and the gleeful realization that Fay was an ally in loathing this terrible hell-pub. The po-faced teenager had been replaced by someone *ironic*. His resolve was weak. He was nothing more than a near-bankrupt dumpee. He thought about Rachel's orgasms, and about Nick's advice. 'Get laid.' Was it – could it be possible – that this was the hand of Fate? That he was being given a second chance to attract his first, unrequited love? He grimaced back at Fay and said archly: 'For myself, the vegetarian option, of course. I'll have Pasta, Pasta – sounds delish.'

'It's a nice-A dish,' said Fay, twinkling at him like a celeb on *Parkinson*.

'I'll just have some lightly grilled salmon,' said Sylvia, pushing the menu away.

'Sylvia, they don't do lightly grilled salmon,' said Fay. 'You have to have what's on the menu.'

'But I don't *want* anything on the menu!'

'Come on. It's the custom. It's the way things are done. Really, you must have been in places like this at some point in your life. Order scampi or something.'

'But I don't want scampi!' Sylvia's voice had risen to a wail. 'I hate scampi! And I never eat anything deep-fried!'

'Well, you *are* hard to please,' said Rose. 'Have a medium steak instead.'

'I'll have chicken salad,' said Sylvia, in a flat voice. A waitress, dressed in a Dickensian pinny, materialized at their table and wrote this down. When she had taken all their orders and disappeared, silence fell for a while. Fay was smiling waspishly at something in the middle distance, as if she could see a host of similarly naff menus whirling around the room.

'Well,' said Rose. 'This is nice! How have you been, Sylvia? You're looking gorgeous. Those highlights do wonders for you – I told you, didn't I, that they'd take ten years off you?'

'I've been terrible,' said Sylvia. 'Waking at three. Pacing the house.'

'They want to bring a book out with his collected essays, don't they?' Fay interjected, taking her mother's hand again. 'All that stuff about the Beatles and Pop Art in the sixties. Sylvia and I are going to edit it, aren't we, Mummy?'

'Well, *you* are, darling,' said Sylvia. 'I wouldn't know where to start.'

'You should do it; if I had your education I'd leap at the chance,' said Rose. 'I always did want to better myself, you know, in the education department. Imagine if you edited a book about your husband! Him being so famous, you might get on the TV yourself. I could do you something with a bit of height for that – not bouffant exactly; something more subtle. More Judith Chalmers than Judy Finnigan.'

Sylvia seemed to brighten slightly at this. The arrival of a second bottle of white wine appeared to lift her mood as well.

'As long as I didn't look like one of the Gabors,' she said. 'That's always been my fear, Rose.' She lifted her head higher on its long, ruched neck. 'Although, one dares to think, natural class can survive even highlights overkill.'

'Oh! As if you could ever look anything but a quality person! I'd do you something intellectual, but flattering. Like a blonde Joan Bakewell. You'd come over brilliantly. I'd be so proud! The salon's first celebrity.'

Fay dived in enthusiastically. 'We're actually doing a

profile of Sylvia in our next 'Life After Death' slot. Beautiful photograph of her sitting on Albert's favourite seat in the orchard, reading Proust.'

'I shall need new cushions for that bench,' warned Sylvia. 'Something Provençal, or slightly Versailles. It's far too rustic as it stands. And, of course, I don't have the right sort of suit. Black is too clichéd – I think a heavy beige silk would be the thing.'

'My father always read Proust for relaxation,' sighed Fay. 'I don't really think there *is* anything more relaxing, do you, Stephen?'

'Certainly not,' said Stephen, whose current mode of relaxation was quaffing cans of Stella in front of Alan Titchmarsh. 'So, you're a journalist now, are you?'

'Yes – I'm the features editor of the *Carbuncle*.' She filled both their glasses, flashed him an intoxicating smile. 'And I do their food column – great fun!'

'Mmm, I've . . . seen it. Very, er, postmodern,' said Stephen. This was an understatement. In his desk at Earthsea he had a file of practically everything she had ever written.

'Yes! Well done you for having heard of it. A tad obscure, but we've got fantastic writers.'

'I do actually read it,' said Stephen. 'My . . . my wife buys it.'

'I didn't realize you were married.'

'Two beautiful children, too,' said his mother.

'Oh, Rose,' said Sylvia. 'Your genes will echo down the generations. I always thought I should like to pass on my nose. A retroussé nose is such a gift, especially to a granddaugher. But . . . ah well. Not to be.'

'Marvellous,' said Fay. Her smile had faded. Was it her lack of children or Stephen's embarrassment of them that had changed her mood? His mind ferreted about manically for a way of letting Fay know that he was newly youngish, free and separated without letting his mother in on the secret.

'I live in Brighton now,' said Stephen, picking up his glass with a hand he had to work to keep steady. 'Very different from . . . all this.'

'Do you really?' said Fay. She seemed genuinely interested. 'Lots of my friends live there. Brilliant arts scene – and great for children, too. So they tell me.'

'But you don't want any of your own?'

This seemed to amuse her. 'God! No. No wish to go down the motherhood path – wonderful for the right person, but . . .' She caught her mother's eye and laughed. 'Complicated area.'

Sylvia coughed and began investigating her mascarad lashes in a small compact mirror. 'I still think Rufus from the *Guardian* would have made you a very happy girl,' she said, shaking her head.

'Darling, we've been through this already. *Nostril hair.*'

Sylvia coughed again and rolled her eyes. Stephen wondered just how hairy-nosed Rufus from the *Guardian* could possibly be.

'Stephen loves it down in Brighton, don't you?' said Rose.

'Best place in the country. It's got the sea, the Downs, and style, great places to eat. Everything.'

'Thriving gay community, too, so I'm reliably informed,' said Fay.

'Oh, quite – absolutely – it's very metropolitan. You never feel you are stuck in the provinces. Metrocadia, I sometimes call it.'

'He's an organic vegetarian chef,' said Rose. 'Always was a fussy eater.'

'*Really?*' Fay's face lit up at this news. 'Oh, how wonderful! A sort of Gordon Ramsay without the blood!'

'I hear organic food is very anti-ageing,' said Sylvia. 'Chemicals do take it out of one. There's only so much one can do with advanced-formula restructuring cream.'

'Terrible lifestyle, though,' said Rose. Then, to Stephen's horror: 'His wife has thrown him out, you know. I blame the restaurant for that. Oh, look – now the fun really starts. The food is here.'

10

It was the Monday after Stephen's return from Stoke. He lay in his attic room, looking blearily at the blue morning light which edged his curtains and listening to the scaly claws of the seagulls scraping on the concrete tiles. Below, the sound of Vinnie and Marc's morning preparations was muffled and indistinct. He could hear the bath running, and John Humphrys roughing up a Cabinet minister on Radio 4. But no word from his two landlords. Neither Marc nor Vinnie went in for much verbal communication before work – in fact, they were surly in the extreme if called upon to speak. It took Marc a long time to prepare himself for a day among the blooms in his designer-flower-and-shrub emporium, due to his obsession with personal grooming. This seemed to Stephen somewhat incongruous, given that he was doughy and overweight, and that his permatanned flesh puffed over the tops of his tight jeans like a middle-aged Essex tart's. Stephen had always had – along with his love of food – a powerful loathing for gratuitous flesh. Carmel had once told him that this was a sure sign that he was a repressed queer (her word of choice during the Queer Nation campaign in the 1980s). And he had indeed always gone for whippetty little women who looked like tidy gay boys. That is, until he met Rachel. But, unreconstructed body fascism aside, he felt that there was something dubious about Marc. He was what Rose would call 'sly'. He never quite looked anyone in the eye, and had a disturbing air of complacency, as if possessing some secret knowledge which gave him the edge over the rest of the human race. But perhaps feeling like this was just a symptom of Stephen's homophobia, another sin to add to all the others. Perhaps what he had really observed was sex appeal.

Should he get up and join them? He hadn't seen Vinnie since the awful incident in Earthsea – he'd stayed away from the restaurant on Friday, and had gone up to Stoke with the children early on Saturday. (Rachel had uttered not one word when she dropped them off.) He dreaded hearing whatever sardonic account Vinnie would come up with about the hilarious embarrassment of having the proprietor of the restaurant brawling with his wife in full view of the entire world, and about the views of the staff, and the chances of the story getting into the national press. In fact, he had almost decided to leave the restaurant and Brighton for good. He could sell out to Vinnie – except that they were in so much debt that Vinnie might not see this as much of a bargain – and go back to London, and start again as a chef working for someone else. He still knew people who would take him on. He wouldn't earn much, but he wouldn't spend much either. This was always the benefit of working such unsocial hours. So he could send what he did earn to Rachel and the children, and forget all about the life he had nearly had in Brighton – and about the humiliation, the failure and the pain. He wondered what his children were doing now. When he thought of them, his throat ached with longing. He thought of his own unhappy, post-Giles childhood, the lopsided mealtimes with one parent, two children, four chairs, the Christmases when his mother would put out a glass of sherry – not for Santa Claus but for Giles, because he had disappeared on Christmas Eve. Bizarrely, Rose had convinced herself that he might reappear on the same date, like the errant hero of a fairytale. Now the same damage would be done to Elsie and Stan. They would live in a world with the wrong number of people in it, knowing that grown-ups were careless and weak.

No. No, he would not go downstairs, and he would not go to work, and he would not speak to Vinnie, or to anyone at all, about what happened. He rolled himself tighter into the duvet, and snuffled into a different, cooler section of pillow. He would do nothing, just nothing, and see where that took him. Because doing something – which had been his strategy for far too long – had led him to this. Utter and complete failure, in every area of his life. Look at the food he was eating: he had even gone back to snacking on mini-pizzas, in a throwback to the nocturnal eating habits of his adolescence.

However, it wasn't easy to be alone when you were occupying someone else's attic. Moments later, he heard the thud-thud of Vinnie's chunky boots crashing up the top staircase, the door banged open and Vinnie walked in, carrying a steaming mug.

'Here you are, Stevie boy. Glad to see you decided against topping yourself after all.'

Topping himself? God, what had he said during that blackout? But Stephen said nothing.

'Cheer up. She's a silly cow – and God knows what

she's up to. They should have gone to Terre-à-Terre and done us all a favour.'

Stephen still said nothing. He lay still, his eyes shut. Again, he thought of his teenage past, his mother trying to persuade him to go to school before she dashed off to the salon, her powdery scent-smell lingering round his pillow as she removed a cup of cold tea and told him that attitudes like his led straight to hell.

'All right, if you don't want to say anything, that's fine with me. Only, if I were you, I would go in to work today. Don't stay languishing at home with *Trisha* on the frigging box. It's like getting on a horse when it's thrown you. Stay away today and seeing everyone will be that much harder tomorrow.'

There was a pause, then Stephen heard Vinnie's boots clunk to the door over the stripped-wood flooring. The footsteps stopped, and Stephen sensed that he was hesitating again. 'See you, then,' said Vinnie. 'You can drink anything you want out of Marc's drinks cabinet except the Armagnac. Polish that off and I'll crucify you.' It was the nearest he had ever come to showing his sensitive side. Stephen kept his eyes closed. In his mind's eye he could see Vinnie, beating an egg with accomplished frenzy or sticking an unlit cigarette into his mouth with a celebratory flourish as the last dish of the evening was paraded through the swing doors. Vinnie survived the knocks and vicissitudes of life with an elegant toughness that Stephen could never emulate.

After the front door had closed, and the quietness of the empty house seeped around him, Stephen finally rolled on to his back with a groan, flipping half the duvet over in the process. He looked down at his naked white torso and narrow, spindly legs. He had always hated his legs, and was the only man in Brighton who never wore shorts. Even at the height of summer, strolling along the seafront, he kept his knees hidden from view under a nice sensible pair of chinos. He now inspected the whole length of his nude self, his chin doubled to his chest as he did so. Christ. What an unappealing sight. Not only white and not only managing to be both scrawny and flabby at the same time, but also somehow peeled-looking, as if really he should have been covered in fur or some other kind of protective layer. Would it ever do sex again? It was hard to imagine a girlie young thing falling on top of that sorry-looking body in a spirit of sexual abandonment. Or even an ungirlie middle-aged thing who was reasonably broadminded and a bit desperate.

He slouched into his dressing-gown and tracked down the stairs, observing his bare white feet as they plodded from step to step. For some reason his toe hair was the darkest on his body. As he was weeing sluggishly into the upstairs toilet, the telephone rang and clicked swiftly on to the answer machine. The volume was on full blast, and at first Stephen made no attempt to answer it.

First came Marc's message, in his fruity, show-off tone: 'Sorry Vinnie and Marc can't come to the phone right now. We're probably having rampant sex on the hearth rug. We'll call you back – if we've got any energy left. Catch you later!' Then came a familiar voice, cigaretty, with a dark-brown timbre, designed to impress the ladies. Martin Amis on Mogadon. 'Hello, Vinnie and Marc. *Nice message*. You don't know me, but I'm a friend of the strange man who's living in your attic – I've got some news for him about . . .'

Stephen ran down the stairs two at a time, urine dribbling down the inside of his legs, and snatched up the receiver. 'Nick! Nick! Great to hear from you –'

'Hi, Stephen – screening messages?'

'No. Just late getting up.'

'Heavy night?'

'Just the usual kind. Drinking a bit too much all the time. I'll tell you about it when I see you. Basically, everything is worse than it was when I saw you. Rachel flaunting her new man . . . shitty weekend with my mother. So, what's the news?'

'Remember we were talking about a lads' night out?'

'Sort of, yes.'

'Well, we're on. And it's happening on Saturday.'

'Oh God!'

'What?'

'I said, oh great.'

'So you're up for it?'

'Yes. Absolutely. Up for what, exactly?'

'Getting bevvied, bit of a chat. Taking in a lap-dancing club. You know. Boys' stuff.'

'Sounds . . . fantastic.' His mind shimmied around the words 'lap-dancing club'. Vulgar? Sexy? Embarrassing? Terrifying?

'Fine. See you in the King & Queen at seven. You know, the pub near the Pavilion.'

'Right.'

'And Stephen?'

'Yes?'

'Don't go on about Rachel and all that break-up stuff, will you? It's a boys' night out, not a men's group. If you know what I mean.'

'Yes. I know what you mean. Don't worry – I'm just about ready for some serious action myself.'

'Great.'

Stephen put the phone down and emitted a robust and smelly fart. Which seemed like a bit of a lad thing to do. And none the worse for that. But just as he was about to go into the kitchen in search of Vinnie's Coco Krispies, the phone rang again. He picked it up, half expecting to hear Nick's voice once more. Instead, it was Carmel.

'Stephen, how are you?' She sounded tense.

'I'm fine. Considering all the usual stuff that you know about already. Except there's an extra bit of crap from Rachel. And Mum knows. *You* didn't tell her, did you?'

'Of course not. I promised I wouldn't. What kind of crap from Rachel?'

'She came into the restaurant with her new man.'

'With Kris? *Is* he her new man? Perhaps she just wants to bring some maturity to the table. He is an expert on relationships, after all.'

'If you take that line, Carmel, I'm putting the phone down. Rachel is mad and Kris is a wanker, and that's all there is to it.'

'You really do need to speak to someone about this. I can understand where the anger is coming from, but you need to have a good talk. If you were a woman, I'd suggest going out with some *friends*.'

Stephen sighed, then remembered that he did indeed have a social engagement. 'I'm seeing some people on

Saturday, as it happens,' he said. 'Some Lads. Do you remember Nick from college?'

A whiff of a chilly pause came down the line. 'That male-chauvinist twit who thought he was Adam Ant? Who could forget? I suppose it's *possible* to talk to him about your feelings,' said Carmel. 'In between the jokes about tits and bums.'

'Bit sexist. You'd never let me get away with a comment like that.'

She sighed. 'It's not the same thing. If it's the Nick I'm thinking of, he's one of the semi-housetrained polecat persuasion. And women don't spend hours banging on about software solutions and cars. Your life is falling apart – you need human beings to hang on to. Not a seminar about Skoda rebranding. *Talk* to them – and listen, too. It's not difficult. Trust me.'

When he put the phone down, Stephen realized he hadn't asked why she sounded so miserable. But, as he was a man, she probably hadn't expected him to.

Nick and a podgy, dejected-looking man were already in the pub when he arrived, sitting on high stools at the bar, two blurred figures in a pall of cigarette smoke.

'About fucking time,' said Nick, looking at his watch. 'We were just about to give up on you. This is Ian, by the way.'

The other man nodded at Stephen without smiling. 'Been out with Nick on one of these jaunts before?'

'No. I've just left my – I mean, I only met him again recently. We hadn't seen each other since we were at college.'

'Right.' Ian nodded gloomily. 'College. Things were different in those days. We were the hip young studs to their available nymphets.'

'Yes.'

'All that shagging.'

'Yes. Can I get you a drink?'

'Too right. I'm feeling like a rogue elephant who's lost his way in the jungle and wandered miles from his watering hole, searching for the cow of his dreams.' Bearing Carmel's advice in mind, Stephen listened hard to this, but felt that he must be missing something. 'A pint of lager,' the rogue elephant added helpfully, 'and a whisky chaser. I'm going to get ritually slaughtered tonight.' As he paid for the ludicrously long line of drinks at the bar, Stephen felt very strange, as if they were all appearing in an unconvincing TV drama about male midlife crisis. For instance, why were he and Nick having chasers, just because Ian was?

'Thanks, squire – bottoms akimbo. You're my wife now, Dave,' Ian appeared to say when he handed the drinks over. The trouble with really listening, Stephen found, was that it was hard to really hear. The pub throbbed to the sound of the Levellers, a local Brighton band. Most people seemed to have no problem with the intense volume; everyone was chatting animatedly all around him. But Stephen found that he could only pick up fragments of the conversation between Nick and Ian. Even if he could have decided whether it was best to keep his traumas to himself, as Nick had advised, or to let it all hang out, as Carmel had suggested, he wouldn't have been able to do anything about it. Only after a lot of careful lip-reading and frowning concentration did he manage to establish that Ian was a loser in love. Whether all the humiliation, sado-masochistic point-scoring and in-yer-face, anti-male, six-minute hates had been delivered by one woman or by a succession of quickly disillusioned one-night stands, Stephen couldn't be sure. But it certainly seemed to put his experience with Rachel into perspective. And, surely, after attempting to listen to a ten-minute monologue on the subject of being harassed, fleeced, cuckolded and dumped, he would himself be allowed to slip out a few nuggets of information about the specific unfairness and awfulness of Rachel? For the time being, he was happy enough to let it all wash over him, huddled over the drinks he had bought himself to show that he too was a rogue elephant unleashed in the jungle.

After a while, he realized that Nick had taken centre stage, and was apparently giving them the lowdown on The Lads. What Stephen could make out sounded entirely dispiriting. 'Fat Peter – slept with literally every woman he fancied. Keeled over like ninepins. Not one ever put up a snorkel on spinless argot; most of them spoonfed fit as well,' was all he could decipher at first. He nodded sagely, unable to be bothered to find out more about Fat Peter's technique. And so it went on, with the derring-do of Kevin-from-Stow-on-the-Wold, Rory the Sheep-shagger and the hapless Gumboil, it sounded like, all spread out before him in an endless half-heard panorama of unreconstructed arrested development. 'Aha,' said Nick, his voice looming clearly out of this narrative for a moment. 'Looks like we all need a top-up. Looking forward to your first night out with The Lads, Steve?'

'Oh yes,' said Stephen. 'Can't wait to . . .' But couldn't think of any suitable end to the sentence, so took a swig of lager with a manly flourish.

'Got to get these down us pretty damn quick,' said Nick on his return. 'Need to catch up with The Lads. They'll all be loaded. All coming down on the train from Clapham Junction. Going to be completely bloody fantastic when we all get together. Can't enjoy ourselves properly if there's just the three of us, can we?'

Ian and Stephen, slurping from their glasses, agreed that they could not.

But The Lads proved to be an elusive bunch. After a few more drinks, they had still failed to appear and the conversation reverted to Ian's terrible past. Stephen positioned himself as close as he could to him, in an effort to fill in some of the blanks in his knowledge. It soon became apparent that it wasn't just the Levellers who were responsible for his incomprehensibility: this was a man who could be incomprehensible all on his own. 'Thank God I'm completely over her now,' he said, taking a sip of lager. Then, without pausing for breath, 'The Ice Maiden never told me the reason. So I never found out why it was. Coldest winter they had had in Stockholm for twenty years. And she just threw me out into the snow. Horst was nowhere to be seen.'

'What a bitch!' said Nick. 'Did you ever get the money back?'

It was no use trying to catch up with any of this. And Stephen was struggling to care much about the love trials of Miserable Ian. After shaking and nodding his head for some time, he said: 'So . . . where *is* this lap-dancing club, then? And . . . is it some kind of strip club?'

'In a way,' said Ian. The thought of the club they had yet to visit seemed to lift his mood. 'The girls certainly do get their kit off. But they'll dance for you – sort of one-to-one – if you pay them. Haven't you seen them on TV?'

'Not as such . . .' said Stephen.

'He only watches *Newsnight* and Nigella Lawson,' said Nick.

'God, you do lead a sheltered life,' said Ian. 'Believe me, it's fantastic. Pure therapy. Every time I get a girl to do it for me, I imagine it's the Ice Maiden. Whole scenario in my head about how she loses the business, it's the only work she can get, and I walk in and she has to do it for me because I pay her. Shows that I'm totally over her, the way I can just toy with her like that in my mind.'

'Certainly does,' said Nick. Ian's thumbnail sketch of lap-dancing life seemed to have whetted his appetite. 'Can't wait for The Lads to get here so we can get down there pronto,' he said. 'Some of those girls are more than fit.' He glanced at his watch. 'Only twenty minutes to closing time – they're bound to be here by then.'

But at closing time there were no Lads from London to be seen, and no Lads in the adjacent streets, or in the even louder pub round the corner. After a while, Nick leaned against the blank closed front of a travel agent's and scrutinized the passing traffic with an expression of contained rage. 'Fuckers,' he said. 'Can't believe they've let me down like this.'

Ian shrugged. 'We can't wait here all night,' he said. He shivered in his tatty denim jacket. It was a clear, sharp summer night. 'Let's go to the club and stop fucking around. I feel like I'm the king of delayed gratification.'

'We could go to a restaurant first,' said Stephen, preferring to ignore the fact that only a curry house would welcome diners at this hour. 'Where we can – you know – eat.'

But Nick straightened up and visibly pulled himself together. 'Don't be a fucking arse, Steve,' he said. 'We're not here to stuff our faces – we're here to feast our eyes. Let's go.' His tone did not invite alternative suggestions.

11

The club was down a flight of steep concrete steps, in a side turning off Western Road. Traffic was growling and creeping through the darkness, but this street was quiet, a row of redbrick Victorian houses and shabby shops. The doorway opened on to a narrow passage, lit by a row of spotlights. Nick and Ian were ahead of him. Then they came to a hatchway, and a blonde girl with a nose-ring took their money. She had white, chalky skin and Goth eyeliner. No exposed bosoms as yet. Questions kept spooling through Stephen's mind, though he was trying to keep his thoughts blasé, hoping this would have an effect on his expression. Were the girls who worked here all prostitutes? If you gave them extra money, would they have sex with you? What was the dancing like? He remembered something that Rachel had spat out at him during one of their tell-all rows. That men were less interested in sex than they were in not being sexual losers. He kept his hands deep in his pockets, trying to exude non-aligned sexual sufficiency.

They finally reached a long, low room, with red-shaded tables grouped around a small dancefloor on which were three podiums.

'Drink, anyone?' said Nick. Stephen nodded. He was looking at a skeletal waitress, whose skirt was short enough to show her red lace knickers. Suddenly, her appearance seemed to him to be a reinvention of the female form. It struck him like a series of hammer blows. Legs. Long naked arms. White neck. Decades of schooling himself that Women Are People Too fell away in seconds. Until now, he'd been seriously bothered about the food issue. It was against his nature not to make food a central part of the evening, even though in recent months he'd had trouble actually swallowing anything. But now his mood changed. He didn't have to prove anything. All he had to do was sit still, drink his lager, and watch.

'What do you reckon?' said Nick, after setting the brimming pint glasses on the table between them. 'Sleazy enough for you?'

'It's like . . . I'm being dragged by two wild horses, but one is galloping slightly faster than the other one, and I'm not sure which is the speed I'm most comfortable with,' said Ian.

'Mmm,' said Stephen, keeping his tone uncommitted. 'On the other hand, nothing at all seems to be happening now.' He looked around the room, wondering if women as well as men went to lap-dancing clubs. But there were none to be seen. Not only that, but there was also a noticeable lack of variety in the appearance of the male clientele. All of them seemed to be overweight, wearing tight white shirts and with greasy hair scraped back from their flushed faces. Just as he was telling himself it was probably all a con and nothing erotic would happen at all, ever, the lights dimmed, dry ice drifted across the dancefloor and the music – previously something by All Saints played at a lowish volume – switched to Abba's 'Dancing Queen' and became much louder.

A young woman wearing a black leather thong and nothing else came twirling into the room. The first bare breasts of the evening. Hers were disappointing, though, the undroopy sort, pert backdrops for serviceable nipples, but nothing more. Stephen realized with a shock how much he wanted to see pendulous, rounded, heavy bosoms. Like Rachel's? He wasn't sure. But this girl, now simulating intense lust for a metal pole, was like a schoolgirl being naughty for a bet. Which could have been – should have been – very alluring. Instead, he felt like a clean old man, unable to drum up appropriate lust due to dotage and lack of practice.

Nick leaned across. 'Nine and a half?'

Stephen nodded. Clearly Nick's response was that of a well-adjusted, red-blooded male, and his own lack of excitement revealed homosexual tendencies.

The girl processed towards them, in a series of worrying writhes and wriggles. Her naked limbs glistened. She began wobbling her buttocks a few inches away from the face of one of the fat, clammy-looking punters. Stephen hadn't noticed whether he had given her money before this happened, and didn't like to ask the others. She twirled on her heel, turned to face the fat man, bent over and pointed her nipples at his head. The fat man looked up at her, glassy-eyed. He looked terrified, submissive. Shades of girl power? But Stephen had to admit that he wasn't thinking that clearly about the political implications of all this. He was thinking seriously about sex – rather than allowing himself flashes of fantasy and five-second bouts of self-abuse – for the first time for months. Imagine getting hold of that girl when her act was over. Imagine taking a girl like that home. Ideally, of course, one with breasts of the kind that drooped and trailed across your face. The kind that . . . But this was just degrading, really. He was letting himself down, letting Rachel down, just by thinking about it.

'Another beer?' he asked, with studied casualness. Ian and Nick nodded without taking their eyes off the dancer. When he returned, Nick and Ian seemed to be talking about property prices, although it took him a while to work this out.

'If I was an animal, I'd be a snail without a shell on its back, trapped in the Gobi desert in the middle of a drought,' said Ian.

'Yeah, a sand-covered slug,' said Nick.

'Trying to crawl towards an oasis, and wondering if it's all a mirage.'

'Yeah – except I think slugs are blind, mate.'

'That's earthworms,' said Stephen. They both looked round at him as if he was mad. 'Earthworms are blind,' he said, feeling slightly foolish.

'What have earthworms got to do with it?' said Ian. 'You're just confusing the issue.'

'Don't take this the wrong way, but you do come out with some weird remarks, Steve,' said Nick, shaking his head.

'Seems a bit ridiculous to be talking about house prices when we're surrounded by luscious femininity,' countered Stephen. 'I thought the point of the evening was to stop thinking about that kind of thing.'

Ian looked thoughtful. 'Like, as we aren't Prince Charles, where would we rest our tampon, other than inside Camilla Parker-Bowles, if we were one?' he suggested.

'Exactly,' said Stephen.

'All right then, let's start with you, as you're so keen to get girls into focus,' said Nick, sounding faintly hostile. 'Describe your ideal woman.'

Stephen was taken aback for a moment. He was so used to thinking about the non-ideal one he had fallen in love with all those years ago, it was difficult to reposition his mind . . . His ideal woman. Nigella, of course. Too obvious, though. Joan Ruddock used to be nice, but never seemed to be on *Question Time* any more. Lorraine Bracco playing the sexy shrink in *The Sopranos*? A tiny bit too old, perhaps. Then he remembered an episode of *Frasier*, in which the celebrated psychiatrist had failed to pull a singularly eligible woman – beautiful, clever, witty and understated. He launched into a description based on this delightful creature.

'Tall, slim, pale-skinned – the Pre-Raphaelite type,' he began. (Nick groaned, for some reason, at this point) 'Long, red hair – wavy but not curly. She'd have elegant, European style and wear classic clothes – not flash, or trendy. Nothing like those Middle Youth types who start wearing flares in their forties.' (Rachel had a number of fearsome friends who dressed in this way.) 'And clever – intellectual. She'd speak several languages – including fluent Spanish – and play the cello. Humorous, too, in a slightly aloof way. She'd have her own flat in Notting Hill, full of abstract paintings. And a high-powered job in – I don't know – something to do with the arts. A producer for Radio 3, maybe. Or head of publicity at Ballet Rambert.'

He realized that Nick was groaning again. 'None of that boring stuff about what she's like in bed, then?' he said.

'Oh – and of course she'd be a fantastic cook,' said Stephen. 'So I wouldn't have to worry about that side of life in my off-duty hours.'

'Bloody hell,' said Nick. 'What planet are you on?'

'A nice quiet blonde with breasts the size of Manchester would do for me,' said Ian, in a rare moment of lucidity.

'Or a tousled brunette with a temper and plenty of flesh,' began Nick. But he stopped abruptly and studied his cigarette packet.

Stephen was just about to say something in his defence when he realized that a new girl was dancing, replacing the one with the tidy tits. In fact, she was one of five girls who had now taken the floor, but once he had caught sight of her his gaze seemed lodged permanently on her face. Like the others, she was young, impassive, with lots of hair. But unlike the others she was . . . What was different about her? Why did his breath suddenly seem trapped in his throat? She was just a lap-dancer. A tart. A woman so stupid, sorry, so *oppressed*, that, in a time of practically full employment, showing her boobs to a bunch of moronic off-duty builders was the best that she could do.

So what was it that was holding his attention? She had big, round eyes, with heavy mascarad lashes. A neat, snub nose, giving her the look of some sort of American cartoon character or cute toy. And a huge mouth. Perhaps it was the mouth that did it for him – a purple-red gash across her face. He stared longer and harder, and suddenly, she caught his eye, their gaze locked together and he realized who she was. It was the loud-mouthed girl from the restaurant. Gabrielle, was it? It wasn't that he fancied her, or anything, he just *recognized* her. But why was his breath still caught in his chest? She danced nearer to their table, still staring at him, then turned her back to them and waggled her buttocks suggestively, in a manner that simulated anal sex, he supposed. The thing was, she was laughing. Unlike the other girls, with their dead, dead-serious faces, she could see that the whole performance was ludicrous – and that the joke was on the red-faced *Sun* readers at the next table, on the bourgeois, screwed-up *Guardian* readers at his, on him. She had the measure of them all. He thought of the £20 notes that the girls had left on the table at Earthsea, and wondered whether they had once been shoved down their G-strings.

'That one's pretty fit,' said Nick. 'Got a look of Clancy – after she had the nose job, of course.' And, to Stephen's dismay, he fished some money out of his jacket and made some invisible signal to the girl, encouraging her to come over. She danced closer, spinning and thrusting her pelvis towards them. Stephen tried to look away, willed himself to take his eyes off her face, but could not. She bent towards Nick, but Stephen's chair was in her way, so she was leaning over him. He could smell the powdery tang of hairspray, cheap scent – Impulse? Did anyone wear that now? – and beneath that a hint of new sweat. Nick tucked the money into the thong that was all she wore, and she darted her tongue out at him, danced in slow, sensuous movements around the back of the table, and came up behind him, shaking her breasts.

Stephen hadn't looked at them before. Had been too frightened to look at them, in fact. She was leaning over Nick now, so his face was partly hidden by her lusty, pendulous bosoms. Stephen wondered if he was going to vomit, due to the sheer agony of it all, and how, if he did, he would manage to get on with the rest of his life. Finally, he wrenched his eyes from her chest and on to what he could see of Nick's blank, unmoving face. The girl, never once allowing her body to touch Nick, took a step backwards, back into the darkness. But before she disappeared, she caught Stephen's eye again and did something far more shocking than anything that had gone on before. She winked at him. Quite unmistakably, she winked. Then she was gone, sucked back into the ersatz mystery of the dry ice.

'Well,' said Nick. 'Tits on that.'

Neither Ian nor Stephen replied.

'Wouldn't kick *that* out of bed.'

Still the other two were silent.

'Top marks for total shaggability.'

Stephen rolled his eyes. He was utterly depressed, utterly alone. 'Can't you just shut up?' he said.

'What's wrong with you now?' asked Nick. His voice was fugged with drink. Nick was one of those people who slipped from being sarcastically sober to madly stage-drunk without bothering with any transitional signs.

'She's just a girl,' snapped Stephen. 'Just someone earning their bloody living. And here we are, sitting with our tongues hanging out. It's not even as if she's even all that attractive. I mean – she's not exactly Helen Mirren, is she?'

'Helen Mirren could be that girl's granny,' said Nick. 'We're at a lap-dancing club, for Christ's sake. To look at tits. Okay? We're *supposed* to behave like brainless wankers.'

'It's just so . . . so degrading,' said Stephen.

'Oh my God. Step down Germaine Greer,' said Nick. 'Why don't you just loosen up, and get on with fancying some real-life totty instead of some disgusting harpy dreamed up by your warped imagination, and stop whinging? I don't know what's happened to you. You're turning into a complete loser. At college you were a laugh . . . although Rachel mentioned you could be a pain in the arse, even then.'

'When did she say that? I never had you down as one of her confidants.'

Nick's eyes shifted back to the nearest dancer, a proto-anorexic in cream lace cami-knickers. 'I don't know – it's just something she said. In passing. Once. When I was passing her in the corridor.' With that, he stood up, gave a slight, angry shrug, and left the table.

Stephen knew he was getting on Nick's nerves, but there was a limit to how much dumbing down he was prepared to do in the spirit of male solidarity. And then again – perhaps there was a reason for Nick's odd behaviour, the underlying tension and his creeping crypticness. If Rachel had been here, she would have been able to tell him what it was. Silly idea, though. Rachel wouldn't set foot in the place. What's more, he was fed up with having women tell him what things really meant. It was as if all his life he had been provided with dodgy subtitles by his mother, or Carmel, or Rachel. And he'd taken them on trust, in a spirit of spineless, inverted sexism. When he'd gone out on an early, arty date with Rachel, they had seen a film called *La Balance*. It was a cops-and-robbers job, with Gerard Depardieu in it, and lots of blood spurting up peeling Parisian walls. Behind him, a cineaste-from-hell, the sort of poser who could have stepped out of a *longueur* in a Woody Allen movie, was giggling with his girlfriend about the peculiarities of the translation from French to English. After ten minutes of huffing and puffing into her polystyrene coffee cup, Rachel had turned round and told the man, in perfect French, to shut the fuck up or else leave the cinema at once. From that moment on, Stephen had been her slave. The combination of poshness, pissed-offness and Continental *savoir faire* would have been enough to fell any man. Surely. But now, for the first time, he thought about that fraught scene in a different way. Perhaps the translation was funny after all. Not knowing any French, he hadn't been in the position to see the joke. And perhaps women abused emotionally monolingual men in the same way when it came to Life and Undercurrents. You only had their word for it that the hidden minefield of human pain, emotion and nuance was the way things really were. Perhaps the whole human-interaction thing was a figment of their collective, febrile imagination. After all, when you got to know them, most women turned out to be a hideous combination of Virginia Woolf and Geri Halliwell: deep when they wanted to make you look shallow, and shallow if there was a copy of *Hello* magazine in the room. Perhaps blokes were right, and there was nothing much going on at all.

He wondered if Nick had left. But this seemed unlikely,

given that his jacket was still hanging on the back of his chair and he had left his wallet on the table. Still musing on the impenetrable nature of the sex war, and leaving Ian staring happily around him, Stephen went out into the passage leading to the bar. There, he noticed a doorway with a glazed mirrored top, with a sign over it: STAFF ONLY. STRICTLY NO ADMITTANCE. He walked towards the exit, where the Goth girl was still sitting, boredly analysing the peeling black varnish on her fingernails.

'Did a thin bloke with black hair go out a few minutes ago?' he asked.

'No,' said the girl. 'No one's left at all.' She huddled herself down into her spiderweb sweater. 'Perhaps he's gone into a one-to-one.'

'A one-to-what?'

'If you pay twenty quid, you get to go into a room with one of the girls for five minutes. On your own. No touching or funny stuff, but most of the punters go for that at some stage in the evening.'

'Where are those rooms?'

'Knock on the office door and Robbie will tell you,' said the girl. 'He's the boss.'

Stephen returned to the NO ADMITTANCE door and knocked. He wasn't sure why he wanted to stop Nick doing whatever it was he was doing, or whether it would be possible. But he knew he wanted to stop him very much. The whole experience was taking on a nightmare quality. He felt faintly sick, tainted. A red-faced man with a cigarette crammed into his mouth opened the door almost instantly.

'They're all taken,' he said, in a thick Scottish accent.

'I'm looking for my friend . . .' began Stephen, in what he knew was his stage homosexual voice. But before the man could beat him to the ground a female scream tore into the air from somewhere behind the pokey office.

'Fuck off, you filthy bastard! You disgusting pervy little shit! Get off of me – get *off*!' Stephen pushed past Robbie and rushed through the door on the far side of the office. There Stephen saw Gabrielle, lying sprawled on the ground, wearing only her tiny thong. The figure who was collapsed across her, face plunged down between her naked breasts, was Nick. It was such a horrible yet comical scene that for a second Stephen thought he might succumb to nervous hysterics. 'Get this fucker off of me!' yelled the girl. Stephen noticed that the front portions of her hair were dyed blonde, reminding him of a Yorkshire terrier called Mitzi his grandmother had once owned. He pulled Nick away. His body was heavy and undemanding; only his voice protested.

'Look out, it's the Mary Whitehouse Experience!' he trilled, as he was dragged clear. 'Ladies and gentlemen, let's hear it for Stephen Beckett, Britain's most boring man! He wants lap-dancing stopped – and it's all for the common good.' Just as he was about to manhandle Nick from the room, Robbie appeared, with two matching heavies, burly in the manner of the Mitchell brothers in *EastEnders*. 'I'll leave you to sort them out,' said Robbie, before lighting another cigarette. 'Chuck them into the street.'

But Gabrielle stood with her back towards Nick and Stephen, stopping the bouncers from reaching them. 'Do me a favour, Robbie,' she said. Her tone was sarcastic.

'All you do is smoke yourself to death in your disgusting den. You expect us to ponce about in front of shits like him every night. As if one of them isn't going to try his luck from time to time!'

'Gabrielle, darling, just do what you're told,' said Robbie.

'No way,' said Gabrielle. 'You lot stand there and keep the peace, and I'll deal with this the best way I know how.' She flicked a light on the wall, and suddenly the room flashed into a hard, pale light. Her skin was very white, and Stephen could see that she was covered in tiny freckles. Her voice was raspy, fag-deepened, Estuary. She crossed over and stared angrily into Nick's face. For his part, he seemed frozen, unable to react.

'You. Are. Totally. Pathetic,' she said. 'You are the sort that thinks you're too good for people like me – different, special, entitled to something a little bit extra. Aren't you? Aren't you?' She jabbed him in the shoulder. 'Go on, answer me. What are you – social worker? Teacher?'

'What d'you mean, teacher?' he said, incredulity breaking through his drunken catatonia. 'I'm . . . an estate agent, if you don't mind.'

'Estate agent? Should have known. Bunch of crooks and weirdos. It was an estate agent who pissed on me on New Year's Eve. Gave me fifty quid, opened his flies and – surprise! His idea of sexy.' At this, the bouncers began to laugh. While she talked, her breasts trembled, shiny with sweat. Stephen tried to look elsewhere. Her mascara was running. He looked down instead, just in time to see her give Nick a hefty kick in the crotch. On her feet she

162

wore silver platform sandals, not unlike those sported by Nick's sex-toy child. Coincidence – or judgement?

'Aaaah!' yelled Nick. He doubled over and staggered to his knees.

'Get *off* him,' yelled Stephen. He stooped down and put his arms protectively around Nick, who smelled strongly of cigarettes and, he realized too late, vomit. 'Can someone here please stop behaving like this? We'll just go – there's no need for anyone to be hurt, or attacked, or anything.' At this, Gabrielle whirled round and said. 'You are the saddest of the lot! What are you doing here, anyway? Looking down your nose at us. Pretending you're not scared. Staring at the punters like you've landed from another planet. Planet Veggie Burger.'

'If I'd known the place was stuffed with murdering witches from hell, I would have thought better of it, obviously.'

'Obviously,' said Gabrielle, in a mockingly mincing tone. 'Why don't you, you jumped-up suppressed homo, take your friend the sicko estate agent and just piss right off out of here? Go back to your funny little restaurant and serve up some more muck to weirdos. We're not here so that snobs like you can have little day trips to Sin City. We're here to make a living. And we don't need people like you – or him – to do that. So get lost.'

Stephen looked into her pale, freckled face, at her running mascara, her full, pouting mouth and thought he had never seen anyone look so uncivilized. Even the trophy tarts who had hung out with the rugby club when he was at college were classier than this. Whereas she was . . . She was . . . A total tramp. He would not look at her breasts again. There was no need. They were just drooping areas of completely average flesh.

'I'm going,' he said. 'I'm just sorry that anyone has to work in a place like this, exploited, and demeaned, and deprived of dignity –' The bouncers laughed, and Nick looked up at him with disbelief.

'Don't talk to me as if I'm some moron,' said Gabrielle. 'We're not whores, whatever you think. We don't have sex with the punters. We don't need to. This is an honest living. It's entertainment. No different to being one of Atomic Kitten, or Jennifer Lopez, showing off her tush to the whole world.'

'I never said you were a whore,' said Stephen. 'I just said you were demeaned.'

'Demeaned?' Her face came closer, closer. He could smell her lipstick, and . . . something else, hovering on her breath. He realized it was curry. The thought of her eating chicken tikka massala in the breaks between her act was gross in the extreme. 'I'll tell you who's demeaned. The people who come here and don't accept it for what it is. Who think they live in a different world. Who think the women they know wouldn't give a million pounds to look like some of the girls who work here. Who think living in a nice house, in a nice street, with nice kids, makes you into a nice person. They're the people who're demeaned, and they're the people who are a total waste of space. People like you. Smug. Scared. With pretend little problems that no one gives a toss about.'

How did she know? Could she see inside him, just as he could imagine the half-digested curry? Stephen realized that the emotion he was feeling now was fear, a strange, almost superstitious fear. She was worse than vulgar. She was evil. She really was a witch.

At this point, Ian's head squirmed round the door. 'I've been feeling like a seal pup, left behind by the herd, with only some Japanese clubbers for company –' he began. Suddenly, Stephen felt very tired. Ahead of him lay the journey home to his empty room, and the rest of his miserable life.

'Let me know when this bunch of losers have left the building,' said Gabrielle, pushing past him. 'I'm off to show my tits to some real men.'

12

After that evening, Stephen wanted to make his life normal again. But what did 'normal' mean? His assumptions and carefully assembled view of the world had been knocked to one side. Firstly, there was the women thing. He had always prided himself on being if not a new man exactly then certainly someone who liked women and was able to see the world from their point of view. The triumvirate of Rachel, Carmel and Rose had shaped his opinions: there wasn't a single man whom he knew as well as he knew these three, no matter how much they might annoy him. In his teens, he had sprawled on the sofa watching *Miss World* with Carmel, screeching with righteous disbelief at Miss USA's charity addiction and the ghastly judge line-up, which usually included George Best. Of course it was wrong! Would men walk up and down in high heels and swimsuits? Would they be asked for a trinket of an opinion to put their breasts in context? No, sir. And what was pointless, wrong and stupid for a man was pointless, wrong and stupid for a woman. He and Carmel had howled down Rose's protests that these were just 'lovely girls' who wanted to travel and meet a nicer class of man.

Later, though, the issues had become more cloudy. Many women, he found at college, rather liked parading up and down in high heels and skimpy clothes, and were offended if you didn't find this sexy. Carmel, he realized,

166

had been unusual in her choice of swathes of fabric and desert boots, even at the height of seventies hippiedom. Nowadays, you had Trinny and Susannah braying 'Make the most of your fantastic *arse*!' at innocent female security guards, or pulling down women's tops to give their cleavage more airplay. Nick might not be interested to know What Women Want, but Stephen would have liked some idea. Even if he decided, in the end, not to give it to them.

How, for example, did you explain dieting? If women were people too, why did all of them want to lose a stone more than they craved any other achievement in the field of human endeavour? What *was* this thing about shrinking? Why – for heaven's sake – would anyone want to look like Posh Spice, who resembled nothing more than a store-front mannequin mysteriously raised to life by Dr Frankenstein? He wasn't seventeen any more. Twenty-three years had passed since he had thrown up on the Cattermole shrubs, yet what did he know? What lessons had life taught him? The grim fact was that his only area of expertise was in the kitchen. Unless he had a pestle and mortar in his hands, he was as ignorant and baffled now as he had ever been. So how could he analyse the good/bad/indifferent status of being the sort of man who went to lap-dancing clubs? He knew what Rachel, Carmel and Rose would think. But he had no idea how to form his own opinion of this new hobby.

It was August now: four months since his ejection. The lap-dancer's words seemed to be seared permanently into his mind, and he wondered if his problems were 'pretend', as she had said. But every time he tried to work out why Rachel hated him, and why Vinnie was getting more tense by the day, his head began to spin. It didn't seem possible to piece together any of the fragments. He was fed up with Nick, in any case, who hadn't contacted him since the trip to the club. Carmel, too, was lying low. Worst of all, his mother was clearly on the warpath now and was deluging him with unwanted messages. Briony and the other staff at Earthsea had been briefed to say he was 'visiting suppliers' if she called him on the restaurant phone. And when she called him on his mobile he rushed into the kitchen so that there was no chance of hearing her over the pots and pans and yells, and just shouted 'What?' 'Sorry?' and 'Terrible *line*, Mum!' till she went away. It was only a matter of time before she arrived in person to find out what was going on.

Another Bad Thing was that at some point that evening he had lost his diary, in which he had noted all the times when he was meant to have the children. It did not seem like a good tactic to mention this to Rachel, who was currently treating him as if he was a very dim serial rapist. He dreaded to think what she would say if she found out about the lap-dancing trip. So he proceeded by guesswork and his vague memory of the plan they had worked out – every other weekend, except for the weekends when certain things were going on that she wanted to take them to, and certain non-specific weekday afternoons on which he had additional duties for reasons which he could not recall. Or something along those lines. He bought a new diary, and in his neat and tidy handwriting sketched in when he thought his access days might be; but he did this in pencil, knowing that some of it would be wrong. From time to time each day, he would fish the diary from his pocket and scrutinize it, frowning, and when he saw Elsie and Stan he would try to glean more information about their future arrangements. Stan's response to all questions was to say 'I DON'T KNOW! I'M SPIDER-MAN!' Elsie was more verbose, confusing him with lengthy and complicated instructions. 'Well, there's Natasha's disco party at four o'clock on Tuesday, which Mummy can't do because she's having her legs waxed, and Stan's supposed to be learning to swim in the same swimming complex – you know, the one with the large pipes outside near the seafront in Hove – so we'll definitely need you then. And don't be at all late, because then it's just completely embarrassing. And I'll need a two-piece costume, like a bikini with bigger knickers, so you'll need to discuss that with Mummy without anyone being rude and losing their concentration . . .' There were two occasions in the weeks following his lap-dancing trip when he turned up at his old home ready to drive the children to a social event which was not, it turned out, taking place. Both times, Rachel had looked at him with a raised eyebrow and suggested that, as he was so keen, he may as well take the kids off her hands for an hour or two while she enjoyed some quality time with herself. So far, he had not done the opposite and failed to appear when he was meant to. He knew he ought to ask her to give him the dates again. But he couldn't bring himself to do this.

All in all, it wasn't a total surprise when everything fell apart. The day this happened, he was also trying to get to grips with the fundamental but essentially tedious problem that Earthsea was losing more and more money. He and Vinnie were both food men – anything to do with finance made their minds fluffy and muzzy and jangled their nerves. But, while Stephen had been using his collapsing life as a diversionary tactic, Vinnie had been assiduously tracking all the various strands of impending disaster. And this was the day – a hot, turgid Thursday in August – that he had managed to pin Stephen down. They were sitting side by side in the airless office in the basement of the restaurant, perched in front of the computer. Vinnie was clicking the mouse, forehead creased with concentration, a cigarette burning away in his mouth.

'You've got to look at this, Steve, no matter what else you do,' he was saying. 'Basically, we need to take three times what we are taking now to get anywhere near breaking even. And that's without paying ourselves anything . . . Look – that figure at the bottom . . .'

'Which one? There are about four million,' said Stephen irritably. 'Can you get rid of that cigarette – I can't see a bloody . . .' Then the phone rang. He handed the receiver wordlessly to Vinnie, in case it was Rose.

'Earthsea – how can I help?' asked Vinnie with silky professionalism. The fag was still in place. He listened for a second. 'Oh *shit*,' he said. And then, 'Where are they now? Where? That'll go down well. Yeah, right. Tell me about it. I'd like to divorce him myself. Completely useless tosser. Yeah. He's right here.' He handed the phone to Stephen. 'It's your ex,' he said. 'Brace yourself.'

'Rachel,' said Stephen. 'What's wrong?'

'What's wrong is that My Children are waiting for you to take them to a party, which they have been looking forward to for months, and which they have discussed with you on several occasions, and which is to celebrate the birthday of a child they have known since they were foetuses, and which began half an hour ago, and I am in London, having a very important meeting, and you are in your stupid little veggie shit-hole, arsing about doing nothing in particular, and they are hysterical.' Rachel managed to sound chilly and tearful at the same time.

Stephen went cold. 'Oh my God,' he said. 'Where are they now?' Visions of them wandering the streets or dangling from pylons flashed across his mind.

'They are with Kris,' said Rachel, a note of haughty self-defence creeping into her tone.

'With . . . What the hell are they doing with him?'

'The childminder dropped them off there half an hour ago. At this moment, they are sitting in the reception area outside his consulting room. Howling the place down. And it's all Your Fault, so don't even think about giving me a hard time about having Kris look after them once in a while.'

'Why couldn't she have dropped them here?'

'Oh come on, Stephen! Get real! Surely you're too busy doing the extremely important job of running your precious restaurant to bother to look after two small children.'

'Why didn't you phone?'

'It was engaged. No, actually, I'm lying. It was all a devious ploy to dump them on Kris in the middle of a counselling session. I thought it would show him in a really professional light. Have you finished cross-examining me now?'

'What the hell has got into you, Rachel?' asked Stephen. 'What's the point of carrying on as if it's total war? That won't help either of us.'

'How can it not be total war if you can't remember when you are meant to be looking after your own kids? The best thing you can do is get over there and try to calm them down. It's already finished between us – I presume you don't want a complete break with your children as well.'

'Of course I don't. I don't want a complete break with anyone. Stop being so melodramatic. Where is this bloody party?'

'At Clive and Tamzin's,' said Rachel. 'Ring any bells?'

'Just give me Kris's address and I'll be there as soon as I can,' said Stephen. She gave him the details before he clicked her voice away.

Vinnie looked at him without saying a word. Then, still not speaking, he relit his burned-out cigarette. Shaking out the match, he finally said, 'What a total mess we've both made of our pissing lives. Complete load of arse. When you've rescued your kids from the Love Doctor, I'll give you the lowdown on our chances of going to the wall. Which are extremely high. So until then, don't spend anything I wouldn't spend.' From somewhere or other, he produced a small bottle of vodka, which he drained as Stephen hurried out of the room. Only when he was starting the car did Stephen wonder why Vinnie had said both their lives were a mess, but by the time he had reversed out of his parking space he'd forgotten what he was wondering about.

There was no sign of Elsie and Stan, howling or otherwise, when Stephen ran panting into the place where Kris plied his trade, the Holistic Sanctuary. He looked around the reception area. The walls were cream, the floor was stripped and bleached. Instead of chairs, anaemic-looking floor cushions were ranged around the walls, irregular blobs of palest grey. They looked pretty much how Stephen felt, and could have been designed to represent the posture and pallor of the newly single. Sick with anxiety, he rushed over to the reception desk. Behind it sat a frigid-looking blonde, dressed in something white and ethnic. 'Children –' he gasped. 'Lost some . . . dropped off by . . . Elsie and Stan . . .' The words rattled incoherently out of his throat.

'They're in Kris's consulting room,' she said, looking at him as if he was the least holistic person she had ever seen. 'Through there.' She nodded towards a white door.

Stephen didn't know what he had been expecting to find on the other side, but it certainly wasn't this sunny, uncluttered room with a sofa on each side and a pine coffee table in the middle. On one sofa, a middle-aged woman reading a book called *Seven Steps to Impossible Dreams* while eating cookies out of a bag. On the other, Kris, sandwiched between Elsie and Stan, apparently recounting the story of the three billy-goats Gruff. Both children were smiling up at him, transfixed, as he said, in a comedy-German accent, 'Who goes trip-trap, trip-trap over my bridge?'

For a second, Stephen stood there, frozen. Then the children caught sight of him. 'GO AWAY!' yelled Stan. 'KRIS HASN'T FINISHED THE STORY! GO AWAY AND COME BACK LATER!'

Catching sight of his face, Elsie, who was a sensitive child, added: 'We do love you, Daddy! It's just that Kris is really good at doing stories. You can wait outside on the cushions if you like. We did. It's fun.'

Kris smiled and shrugged at the same time. 'It's the last goat,' he said, apologetically. 'I'll be through in one minute.'

It certainly was the last goat. The middle-aged woman flicked her eyes towards Stephen momentarily, mid-chew, then flicked them back to her book. Presumably she had enough miseries of her own, without concerning herself about him.

He went back outside, and tried to crease himself into the sort of shape which coincided with one of the cushions. Reading stories with flamboyant humour and maximum fun injection had always been one of his special Dad talents. Or so he had thought. He did all the voices in *Winnie-the-Pooh*, and was nearly as good as Alan Bennett, if he thought so himself. Once, he had read *The Selfish Giant* with so much feeling that he made himself cry, which had baffled the children. Instead of hugging him passionately as they did from time to time, filled with sheer wonder at his level of fantasticness, they had patted him respectfully on the shoulder, having concluded that his tears were caused by not believing in life after death. Now, it seemed, any fool could enthral his children. There was nothing special or remarkable about his Eeyore after all. He sighed heavily and rested his face in the hot palms of his hands.

The receptionist turned from her computer screen to look at him. He raised his head and tried to smile, but couldn't, and stared at one of his thumbnails instead. Then the door crashed open and his children dived on top of him, yelling 'Daddeee! Daddeee!' and he thrust his tired face between their warm, sweet heads, which smelled of ice-cream and nit-repelling teatree oil. 'You forgot all about us, didn't you, Daddy?' said Elsie. To which Stephen could offer no reply. 'Don't worry; we don't mind,' said Elsie. 'We're used to lots of sorts of grown-ups now.' As they left, Kris handed him something in a John Lewis bag. 'Present, dude,' he said, now speaking in a strange sub-*Wayne's World* accent. 'From Rachel.'

'For me?'

'For the birthday girl.'

'Birthday . . . ?'

'At the party?' said Kris.

'Ah.'

'God, Daddy, it's like you're half asleep all the time,' said Elsie.

As he drove towards the Cathcarts', Stephen ran through the various reasons why Clive and Tamzin were currently his least-favourite couple. First of all, the usual, low-grade irritation stuff: their enormous income, their vibrant and much-vaunted sex life, and their brood of gorgeous, high-achieving children. Then there was the fact that each year they produced a pert little Christmas circular, updating their friends and family on all the above, usually enlivened with a couple of vignettes or nuggets of exceptionally annoying information: the meal they shared with Pavarotti during their Roman holiday, for example, or the fact that Zuleika had last year – at the age of seven – read *David Copperfield*. This harrowing missive was emailed to everyone on Tamzin's database, and inserted into all their

Christmas cards, so there really was no escape. Then there was the specific stuff: such as the £30,000 Clive had loaned him. The thought of this unmentionable act of generosity made Stephen's head ache. He had never let Vinnie in on the secret, and hoped to keep things that way. Finally — and worst of all — there was the business with the break-up. If friends were to be divided up like property, Clive and Tamzin belonged to him. He had known Clive since he was a trainee chef at the Savoy and Clive had come in to do some project for his course in business studies at North London Poly. Even then, Clive had been a diligent entrepreneur, supplementing his grant by driving to Milan in his MG Midget and selling cut-price shirts. (The Cathcart love affair with all things Italian and their fluency in the language provided another undercurrent of under-miningness.)

So how was it that Clive and Tamzin had both decided to back Rachel in this dispute? He could have understood it more easily if he had committed some terrible crime — or *any* crime, in fact, other than working too hard, which surely was a universal male foible. Since that scene in the restaurant, he had been expecting or at least hoping for some sort of explanation from Clive. The fact that he had heard nothing made him worry even more about what he might have said during his blacked-out phase. Or was he guilty of some other unforgivable transgression, of the sort that only women could define, before Rachel had thrown him out? He could still remember Tamzin's fingers as she had half ushered, half pushed him out of his own house. Now they were pushing him out of their friendship as well. However much they had annoyed him, he had thought the Cathcarts would be part of his life for ever. But it seemed that they would be part of Rachel's instead. Clive, if Stephen was honest, had been one of the only two people in the world he could call a friend. (The other, of course, was Vinnie.) Any day now, Clive could ask for his money back. And there was none to give him.

At last, they drew up near the house. Clive and Tamzin lived in a huge Victorian villa that loomed over a section of narrow streets near the seafront. It was surrounded by a high, white wall, topped with spiked railings, painted a tasteful shade of Heritage green. To reach the house, you had to go through double iron gates in a doorway in the wall. Today, the gate was decorated with helium balloons, tied to the iron filigree with coloured strings, and adorned with the faces of the various characters in *The Simpsons*. From the other side of the wall could be heard the sounds of the pop group SClub 7 and the hysterical shrieks of a large crowd of young children. Stephen wondered if Clive had actually paid for the band – a big favourite with Zuleika, the birthday girl – to be present in person. But, as they got near enough to look through the gates, he could see that the Cathcarts' vast lawn was free of recently manufactured pop stars, and was covered with a mass of ebullient under-tens. In a shared ecstasy of anticipation, Elsie and Stan ripped their hands from his and ran whooping through the gates.

'Sorry we're late, everybody!' called Elsie.

'CHEEARGE! YIKES!' yelled Stan.

They disappeared into the crowd. At least they didn't seem to be damaged by his inadequacy as an absentee father. Stephen, still carrying Zuleika's present, was left to shamble up the steps between the twin mosaic water features. (These were two multicoloured pillars twinkling with tiny coloured tiles, with water trickling down their sides, like something Caligula might have had in his garden.) He looked around him. On the far side of the lawn was Rossetti Lodge, the Cathcarts' redbrick house. It had been built by a railway entrepreneur who admired the Pre-Raphaelites, and it was busy with neomedieval detail – mullioned windows, towers, turrets and Gothic archways. Nearer to him stood a clown, on stilts, attempting to amuse a posse of toddlers, most of whom were crying and being handed ice-pops by a girl Stephen recognized as May-Beth, the Cathcarts' American au pair. May-Beth was a moody Californian with serious acne. She kept tossing her long, heavy brown hair over her shoulders and rolling her eyes. It wouldn't be long before the Cathcarts were in search of yet another nanny, Stephen thought. Nearer still was a clump of grown-ups who were having their glasses of pink champagne topped up by Clive, who was wearing a pink suit. When he caught sight of Stephen, he raised the bottle in greeting and came towards him.

'Steve! Better late than never!' he called, slightly overdoing the *bonhomie*. 'Have some of this –' and he poured some champagne into a glass which had been rushed over by a minion. Tamzin and Clive always had minions at their parties, taking coats and serving food. This was a feature of their conspicuous consumption that had once united Stephen and Rachel in contempt. Now each of them felt contemptuous on their own. Still, he badly needed a drink. He took a gulp of champagne. Too late, he realized he had almost emptied the glass.

Clive certainly seemed determined to be friendly. 'Looks like you needed that, mate,' he said, refilling Stephen's glass before he could stop him. 'Don't think we've seen you since, you know. That night you flipped. Screamed like a banshee and ran out into the night. Not exactly the way to make people come flocking to your restaurant, is it?'

Stephen, realizing that Clive was already half-drunk, shook his head. 'Yes, well. Things are on a slightly more even keel now.'

Clive nodded earnestly. There was an intense, heated-up quality to his stare that Stephen hadn't seen before. Was this the drink, or his reaction to speaking to someone on the verge of a nervous breakdown?

'It's so good to see you,' said Clive. 'I've been worried about you.' Then he came closer and somehow squeezed the back of Stephen's left shoulder. 'How are you *really*?' he asked.

'I've been better,' said Stephen. 'But I'm not going to bore you with the details. You've got other things on your mind.'

He nodded across the lawn at the children. There were about thirty of them, fermenting in a great mass like a football crowd. May-Beth and the clown were attempting another game; apparently musical statues, but to little effect. Surprisingly, there was no sign of Tamzin, who usually excelled at children's parties to a degree that Rachel found offensive. Every theme and party nuance had been done to death *chez* Cathcart – everything from animal parties, with live falcons flying over the heads of four-year-olds, and pythons slithering around their necks, to disco-lesson parties, at which lively girls in Lycra taught simple dance routines, which were videoed and copied for all the parents. Last year, Zuleika had had a riding party to go with her brand-new pony, and Elsie's mind had been poisoned by dreams of gymkhanas. Three months later, little Noah (then five) had his birthday bash at Ovingdene beach, where a local artist had braved a gale and led the kiddies in a pebble-painting workshop. On top of this were certain characteristic Tamzin touches: not only did she make and ice a themed cake each year (perfectly ordinary mothers did as much), but she also designed and made party bags for each child. Usually in a basic gingham fabric, they would have a small appliqué picture of the party *motif* – a child in a leotard for the disco event, for example. Rachel took the party bags very hard. In fact, Stephen thought this could be the real reason for her absence.

'Where's Tamzin? he asked. But as he spoke she appeared on the steps of the house, with another woman, and crossed the lawn towards them. As they came closer, Stephen realized with a jolt that this woman was stunningly beautiful. She had waist-length, straight black hair and large, thick-lashed eyes. Everything about her was perfect – her skin glowed gold, set off by a floor-length shift dress of palest pink. When she smiled – which she was doing now – she showed her snowy Hollywood dentition. Tamzin, on the other hand, looked rather strange. Her long floaty frock was formed of a series of panels in various shades of russet and fuscia, and on her hair she wore a wreath of pink roses. Uncharacteristically, she appeared not to be in full command of her headgear, and it was slightly askew. She looked like a cross between Titania and Violet Elizabeth Bott. Her face was distorted into a rictus of manic, fixed determination.

'Hello, darling,' said Clive nervously.

'Stephen,' said Tamzin, as if registering his presence rather than welcoming it. 'This is Sorrel. Our party organizer. You're not wearing pink.'

13

'Pink?' Stephen looked from Clive to Tamzin to Sorrel. 'Why should I be wearing pink?'

'It's a Think Pink party,' said Tamzin, pityingly. 'Didn't you see the pink invitation, with the pink wording and the pink frill?'

'His children aren't in pink either,' said Sorrel, who was clearly nicer on the outside than she was on the inside. With an expert eye she was scrutinizing the crowd of children who were now clustering around the ineffectual clown, demanding ice-pops. She glanced down at a small clipboard that Stephen noticed for the first time. 'There's no use doing a Think Pink party if people turn up in khaki.' But it was hard to hate her. Stephen had half hoped she would have an ugly voice that didn't match her gorgeous face, a horrible Estuary twang, perhaps, like David Beckham's or the lap-dancer Gabrielle's. Nasal Brummie would have been even better. However, she had a faint, hard-to-place European accent, just to add to her sexual allure.

'I'm afraid I just dashed here straight from work,' said Stephen. 'I didn't . . .'

'Yes, we know about all that. You're late because you forgot. And Rachel's livid. But I thought at the very least you would have popped home to get into theme,' snapped Tamzin. 'It really is so annoying, when Sorrel has gone to all this effort, when –'

'Look,' said Stephen. 'I'm sorry. I didn't know anything about the pink thing. *Mea culpa.* My mind's been on other issues – I've been busy getting separated. That takes a lot of energy, you know.'

'You are just so wrapped up in yourself,' said Tamzin, drooping slightly as if with the effort of talking to him. 'You always were. All that time you spent trying to get a Michelin star . . . What was the point? Paying a bit of attention to how people feel might have been a better idea.'

'Darling, have a drink,' said Clive. 'You're taking everything too much to heart. Stephen just didn't know.'

'I *can't* have a drink. I *won't* have a drink! You know that perfectly well!' said Tamzin furiously. She rounded on Stephen again. 'Do you want to know how much trouble she's gone to? Do you want to know?' But before Stephen could say anything she was off, apparently unphased by Sorrel's simultaneous commentary, her wreath trembling as she spoke. 'There's a fancy-hat competition.' ('Self-expression and visual creativity using pink,' said Sorrel.) 'And pony rides.' ('Pink saddle and bridle,' came the interjection. 'Breaking down traditional stereotyping around riding tack.') 'And then Calypso Collective are doing drumming lessons.' ('Interactive, multicultural fun looking at colour in a world setting,' said Sorrel.) Perhaps it was possible to dislike a physically perfect woman after all.

'It sounds great,' said Stephen, wondering why Tamzin wasn't doing anything herself, given that children's parties were one of her top obsessions. Being pregnant hadn't stopped her doing anything in the past – usually she'd think nothing of flying to Australia and stopping off for some light maternity shopping in Hong Kong. 'All that and tea as well.'

'Yes – Sorrel's sorting that out too. My only contribution is a pink Cadillac cake.'

'Oh!' Sorrel let out a sort of yelp. There was an uncomfortable pause. She looked – for a woman of such poise – slightly sick. 'I'm sorry. There was absolutely no mention of food,' she said, looking at her clipboard as if for confirmation. 'I organize events. People. Things. Music. And connect them to educational issues in a global context. Food is not in my remit.'

Stephen looked from one face to another, wondering how the mighty Cathcarts, who probably gave more thought to entertaining than any other family in Brighton, had managed to hold a children's party with no birthday tea. He didn't know who looked the most horrified – Tamzin, Clive or Sorrel. He looked at his watch; it was nearly five o'clock.

'I . . . I thought all those boxes you brought into the kitchen were boxes of party food . . .' said Tamzin.

'It's all stuff I need: prizes and costumes and fancy-hat materials, spare drums and castanets. You name it . . .' said Sorrel. 'Not food. Why didn't you ask me?'

'Because . . . Because . . .' Tamzin was lost for words. Stephen had never known that to happen before.

'Never mind, darling,' said Clive. He put his arm protectively around Tamzin and she leaned her head against his shoulder. 'We have to think of something. What about sending May-Beth round to McDonald's in the jeep? To get thirty children's McMeals or whatever. I'd go myself, but I'm too plastered.'

'No!' cried Tamzin, lifting her head. Her voice rose to a shriek, and her wreath finally became completely dislodged and fell to the ground. 'Think of the parents we've got here,' she said, her voice dropping to a stage whisper. 'Helen Twiss runs her own environmentally friendly babywear firm; Susan Delaney practically *is* the PR department at Barnardo's; and Enrique Lopez is a Channel Four producer. He did that thing about dead babies in China. They probably have *principles*, apart from anything else. I'll never live down offering a McDonald's tea to their children! Oh God – what are we going to do? There's not even enough time to go to Waitrose!'

Stephen sighed, feeling much the way a holidaying GP might if presented with a broken leg or suspected cardiac arrest on his first day at the beach. 'What food have you got in the house?' he asked heavily. 'I mean, I assume you've got something? Bread? Cheese? Biscuits?'

'I've no idea,' said Tamzin. 'Let's go and look.' Clive and Sorrel made as if to follow, but Tamzin was having none of this. 'Go and Organize the Event – I'm sure you've overlooked a Third World theme somewhere,' she said to Sorrel. 'And, Clive, keep the parents primed with drink. If all else fails, there's always the karaoke machine.'

The stone-flagged kitchen was, like the rest of the house, on an absurdly large scale. The walls were a muted turquoise, which, Tamzin had once informed Stephen, was the colour of the universe, according to Gaia philosophy. At one end of the room was a huge olive-green Aga and an open fireplace big enough to have wooden seats at either end. Against one wall was a dresser, painted creamy yellow, on which dozens of handpainted plates and dishes were displayed. In the middle of the room was a vast wooden table, fashionably rough-hewn and broad-legged, surrounded by chairs in the same style. Stephen always half expected a fairytale giant to walk in, pull up a chair and start eating hunks of bread or tiny humans. At the far end of the room, opposite to the fire-place, was a walk-in larder. Which Tamzin duly walked into.

'Come and see,' she said. Her tone was despairing. 'If you can make a tea out of what's in here, I think you'll be vaguely on the same level as Jesus Christ.' Stephen wryly noted the fact that she had already taken it for granted that he was indeed going to attempt to save the day, seconds after she had slagged him off. Which he was, for reasons he wasn't too clear about. He suspected that the fact that he wanted to stay on the right side of Clive was part of it. So no points for altruism there. But, also, he was fed up with being the bad guy. He wanted to do something which put him in the right.

Looking around the larder, he could see why Tamzin had sounded so despondent. The well-stocked shelves appeared to be loaded only with adult-friendly food: Hungarian paprika, canned pimentos, Thai green-curry paste, porcini pieces and even a packet of snails in their shells. He certainly couldn't fault Tamzin for pseudy food shopping. For kids, there were Ricicles, digestive biscuits (three packets, he noted with satisfaction), small pasta shells and several jars of ready-made tomato sauce. He rooted around at the back, and with a cry of pleasure pulled out several sachets of Angel Delight.

'God! My mother buys that filth every time she comes to stay!' said Tamzin.

'Well, you will be eternally in her debt,' said Stephen. 'I need thirty small dishes, thirty little plates and thirty cups.' Without missing a beat, Tamzin produced stacks of drinking cups, plates and dishes from a plastic shopping bag hanging from a hook on the door. 'Got these as back-up,' she said.

Next, Stephen found a carton of hundreds and thousands, another of chocolate buttons. In the bread bin, two slightly stale loaves of wholemeal bread. In the fridge he discovered two large hunks of Cheddar cheese, Greek yoghurt, three red peppers and some tomatoes. From the Cathcart canned-food collection he joyfully produced chickpeas, sweetcorn, pitted olives and morrello cherries. By the time he had finished, the giant's table was covered in piles of tins and packets. He looked at his watch again. Five twenty. 'Right,' he said. 'Can I borrow one of your minions?'

'I think we're out of those . . . Oh – you mean one of our staff?'

'Yes. Quick. Unless you want to open tins and do mixing in that dress.'

'Oh, no. Not at all. I'll go and get a . . . minion.'

Five minutes later Stephen was astonished to see not one of Tamzin's serfs but Sorrel. 'I . . . Are you sure you want to do this?' he asked. 'I thought food wasn't in your remit.'

Sorrel winced. 'Let's call this a damage-limitation exercise,' she said in her crisp, unplaceable accent. 'Or last-minute PR. They don't need me up there – Clive's got the karaoke machine out. It's better for me to help make the food than to stand around like a spare part.'

Stephen nodded. There was no time for conversation. To his relief, he soon saw that Sorrel knew how to cook. For the next half hour, Stephen barked orders at her as if he was back in the kitchens of the Savoy, where the staff would parrot 'Yes, chef' to everything the head chef said, like privates on parade. Sorrel stuck to 'Right' and 'Got you', but was quick and deft. She chopped like a whirlwind once he had shown her how to hold the knife, standing behind her and placing his hand over hers. The touch of her skin underneath his was silky and cool, and looking down her arms he could see the subtle but firm muscles moving as she followed his instructions. Between them – and later Stephen did in fact wonder if divine intervention of some kind might have been involved – they produced dips made from yoghurt, cream cheese, peanut butter and maple syrup, with dainty strips of carrot, red peppers and celery alongside them, and tiny toast squares with different toppings; Marmite, homemade hummus, egg mayonnaise, grapes and sliced cherry tomatoes, arranged like patchwork quilts. There was pasta salad with grapes and mayonnaise, iced digestive biscuits decorated with hundreds and thousands – Sorrel was a dab hand with the palette knife. And of course the Angel Delights: butterscotch, chocolate and strawberry, each in an individual glass bowl, decorated with sliced cherries. May-Beth had been dispatched to the corner shop and reappeared just as they were putting the finishing touches to the food. She was carrying bagsful of plastic bottles of ginger beer, crisps and jam tarts, which they added to the spread.

When they had finished, they stood back and looked at the table. 'Will that feed thirty children?' asked Stephen.

'You better hope so,' said May-Beth. Then, more optimistically: 'It should be cool – kids don't really eat at parties. They mainly holler.'

Stephen, who knew that Elsie ate a vast amount no matter what the social occasion, shook his head dubiously. 'I suppose we'll soon find out,' he said.

To everyone's relief, the food did go round. Stephen looked on with foreboding as the children stormed into the kitchen, leaped into their seats and began eating with gusto, but they all seemed to have enough food on their plates to keep them happy. Screams of 'Juice, juice!' and 'I hate cherries!' filled the air. Paper napkins were folded into aeroplane shapes and hurled around the room. Little figures picked up jam tarts and ran round and round the table, making serial-explosion noises as they did so. Elsie and her friend Maya stationed themselves beside one of the dips and methodically ate their way through it, sucking hummus from crisps with exaggerated slurping noises. Stan and crime-chum Josh struck camp under the table and their filthy little hands appeared from time to time in search of cheesy Wotsits. The minions served the children weak Ribena in Pimms jugs, everyone scoffed the Angel Delight as if it was the best thing they had ever tasted and the iced biscuits were hoovered up in seconds. But there was no yelling for more – once the plates were empty, the small guests surged back into the garden in search of party bags. The table was covered with empty plates, discarded paper cups, piles of coloured straws and little blobs of dribbled-out Angel Delight. On the floor, the oversized chairs lay on their sides, as if beaten in combat.

'God, what a relief,' said Sorrel when it was all over.

'You did a fantastic job – both of you,' said Clive, who had been lurking anxiously in the kitchen door, as if ready to beat a hasty retreat if the children turned nasty. His face was as sweaty and pink as his suit, from the sun. 'Have another drink, Stephen. Sorrel, are you sure I can't tempt you?'

'No, thank you,' she said. 'I'm keeping a clear head till I go out later.' She was drinking Evian water from a long glass in series of carefully modulated gulps, as if drinking water was a special skill. Perhaps it was. Her skin was so clear that she probably drank ten glasses a day.

Stephen gratefully took a flute of cold champagne. He sipped, watching as the minions cleared the kitchen table and stacked the dishwasher. 'Nice to have staff, in a way,' he said to Clive. 'Maybe if we'd had people to do that, Rachel and I would still be together. Sucks up so much of your life, all the sorting out of the crap.'

For a moment, Clive was silent. Stephen experienced the social wobble that still afflicted him from time to time, when dealing with people who were posher or better-off than he was. Perhaps it was totally Not Done to mention the staff? Perhaps he really had broken some bourgeois taboo, thus showing himself up as greedy, chippy and – at the age of forty – gauche? But Clive's mind seemed to be on something else. 'If you've got a minute, Stephen, perhaps we could go and take a stroll in the garden? I just wanted to talk to you in private. It won't take long.' Stephen's stomach lurched, and he took a large gulp of champagne.

As they left the house and crossed the terrace, Stephen

saw that his children were still playing happily with May-Beth and the Cathcarts' brood. They were chasing each other across the grass, the long shadows cast by the evening sun giving the scene an ethereal, dreamlike quality. He could imagine them wearing Victorian pinafores and knickerbockers, like the characters in an E. Nesbit story, instead of the cargo pants and slogan-decked T-shirts they had on in reality. Clive led him to a wooden bench on a rose-covered walkway overlooking the rest of the garden. They sat side by side for a while, looking at the children. Was he plucking up courage to ask for his money back? Glancing at Clive, Stephen realized that his face was drawn and sagging; he had never seen him look so old, or so tired.

'What did you want to tell me?' asked Stephen, with unusual directness. He felt suddenly ashamed of his fears, and protective towards Clive. Something was wrong, he could tell. And he felt without knowing why that it wasn't anything to do with hard cash.

'Well, it's about Tamzin,' said Clive. But for a while, he added nothing to this, but continued to sit and watch the children run in and out of the shadows, squealing and giggling as they went. Stephen watched them too, and felt waves of love for his own children sweeping over him.

'I hope she isn't ill?' Stephen asked, after a while.

'No! Oh, no. Tamzin is fine.' He paused again. He seemed to find it very difficult to say what was on his mind.

'So . . . ?'

'Sorry, mate, sorry. Just find it quite hard to . . . choose the words, you know?' Clive seemed to shake himself and force himself to speak. 'As you might have guessed, we've had a bit of bad news,' he said.

'Bad news?' Stephen realized that he should have expected to hear this, but hadn't. He was so used to regarding Clive and his cosseted life with uncomplicated envy.

'Yes.' Clive stopped again, but this time pushed on quickly, as if he'd finally found the will to say what he had to say. 'Against her better judgement, Tamzin had a test that can tell you whether everything is . . . all right with the baby.' Stephen, beginning to understand what was coming, listened in silence. 'And it wasn't . . . wasn't okay. We had another – an amniocentisis – to check it further, and the outcome was conclusive. The baby has Down's.'

If Stephen had been a woman, he would have been able to digest this information immediately. But, in spite of all his best efforts, he was still semidetached from the expertise and jargon attached to parenthood. Down's – he knew this was something bad. But how bad? And what kind? The fact that his own children went to a state primary called Downs, while the Cathcart brood attended a Steiner school, complicated the situation further: could this possibly have anything to do with the state system? So all he said, very flatly, was: 'Down's.'

'Down's syndrome,' said Clive quietly. 'What people used to call Mongolism.'

'Oh God,' said Stephen. The old-fashioned term carried with it an instant image. Damage. Disability. A misfit. A snubbed, idiot's face with flat hair and slanted eyes. 'Clive, I am so sorry. Really . . . very sorry. If there's anything I can do . . .' He thought again of his 'pretend' problems. Then he thought of the modern ways of dealing with things that go wrong in pregnancies. 'Is Tamzin going to . . . have . . . the baby?' he asked in a hesitant voice. This was the most intimate conversation he and Clive had ever had.

'She won't have a termination,' said Clive, staring ahead again. This time his voice was hard-edged, clinical. Their faces were still turned towards the children, who had disappeared into a shrubbery on the other side of the garden. Both men were staring at long shadows on an empty lawn. 'Mad, really, when you think she had two abortions before she even met me.'

'I didn't know that.'

'No one does, mate. Tamzin has written it out of the script. Once she'd had Zuleika, it was as if she'd crossed a line into a different identity. I think she felt more guilty, once she'd had a baby, than before, when the whole thing was just like some weird theory. Babies don't seem real until you've owned and run one, do they?'

'So that's why she's so against having an abortion now? Because she knows what babies are like?'

Clive sighed, and dropped his head down despairingly. 'Sort of. She thinks it's different because she's had children. She's a mother and she knows how to do it. When she had the abortions, she was a single girl living in Fulham, living it up, sleeping around a bit. But, more than that, she thinks it's different because of the bloody money.'

'The money?'

'Whatever's wrong with the baby, we've got the resources to deal with it. Full-time nurse, special nanny, private hospital treatment, proper equipment . . . Whatever – we can pay for it.'

'Hasn't she got a point?'

'Of course she's got a point, but what about the effect on the other children? A sick brother or sister, taking up all our energy and time. Someone . . . damaged . . .' The term echoed Stephen's own thoughts, and made him wince. 'We've never had to deal with anything like this. But do we discuss it? Do we hell. It's as if I don't matter, the other kids don't matter, the only person she's interested in is this . . . handicapped *thing* that she wants to bring out into the world when she has every chance not to . . . It's the norm not to, for God's sake.'

'I suppose it's her choice. A woman's right to choose.' Stephen felt he had grown up with this phrase dancing round his head. Carmel's belief in abortion rights was about as close as she came to having a religion.

'Bollocks. I could understand if it was her first child and she was worrying about not having another chance or something, but when she has four perfect children already! Why? What's it all about? Seems like she wants to win prizes for being the ultimate sacrificial mother.'

'Poor Tamzin,' said Stephen, to his surprise.

'Up to a point, yes. I mean, on one level, the girl's having the worst nightmare of her life. That's a no-brainer. But, on another level, what about the rest of us? What about poor Zuleika, Tallulah, Yorick and Noah?' asked Clive. His voice was hoarse. It was the first time Stephen had heard a run-through of these names without wanting to laugh. 'We're trapped,' said Clive. His voice dropped to a whisper. 'Trapped with Tamzin's stupid fucking notions about doing the right thing.'

'I don't know what to say,' said Stephen. 'I wish I could help you, when you've done so much to help me.'

'Don't be stupid, mate. I've done nothing. I've been a complete prat half the time. Why we all thought it would be such a great idea to come into your restaurant I'll never know. Kris had some idea about it "normalizing" everything, but . . .'

'You tried to help. You were the only one. And you gave me the loan last year. I haven't forgotten that.' Much as he'd wanted not to mention this, Stephen felt it was now immoral not to.

'The loan is the least I can do,' said Clive. 'In fact, I've been meaning to ask you if you need some more. I get the impression that things are still pretty shaky at Earthsea.'

'I couldn't take any more from you. I just couldn't.'

'Well, the offer's there. One thing I do have is money in the bank. No point leaving it there when people I care about need help.'

'I need help all right. But . . . not the financial sort. Thanks, though. You've been incredibly generous already. You've done more than enough.'

Clive patted Stephen on the shoulder, stretched and stood up. 'Oh well, mate,' he said. 'Life goes on. Kids to bring up. Jobs to take up every waking bloody second. Women to confuse us.' He seemed to shake himself out of his gloomy reflections. Stephen had forgotten about this habit of his, the way he almost consciously shifted gears when he felt the need. It was Clive's own brand of ruthlessness, the way he forced his life into compartments and closed the lid on experiences he found painful. 'Funny that you and snooty old Sorrel got on so well, isn't it?' he said.

'Funny?' asked Stephen, surprised that Clive had noticed.

'I saw the look you gave her when she was helping pour out the drinks. And she seems to quite like you, too. Almost smiled at you once. I wonder what would have happened if things had been different?'

'Different in what way?'

'Different if she hadn't been Kris's fiancée. Funny combination – mixed-race hippie counsellor and gorgeous Euro-babe party organizer. She used to go out with David Ginola, you know, that French footballer with girl's hair? Funny thing is, Tamzin thought at one time that there was something between Kris and Rachel.'

'Amazing,' said Stephen, whose mind was spinning helplessly, trying to reorientate itself around the known facts, his known feelings.

Clive shook his head ruefully. 'Women – always reading between the lines and seeing the *Encyclopaedia Britannica*. Emotional intelligence, allegedly. Surprised girls are so keen on that, because it sounds like some kind of patronizing consolation prize for not having the other sort. The type you need when you're reading what's actually on the bloody lines.'

He looked at Stephen as if hoping for a reply, but Stephen was still running old impressions through his mind in the light of new information.

'Not that I've got any idea what's going down myself,' said Clive, after a while. 'No way. It's all blue-sky thinking to me now.'

14

It was almost ten o'clock when Stephen drew up outside his old house in Chester Terrace, and the evening was growing dark. The Victorian villas glimmered in the street lights, some half obscured by tangled shrubs, others facing the road more openly, their gardens having been modernized and filled with pebbles, architectural plants or some studiedly stylish combination of the two. His former home had recently become one of these. The front garden had once tumbled with a profusion of roses, ferns and lavender, with clematis climbing up the house and, by the gate, an apple tree with a bird feeder that attracted the few songbirds in their street. But, about a month before, Rachel had torn down the clematis, uprooted the apple tree, removed the roses and the lavender, and replaced the whole lot with a square of gravel and a dwarf palm tree. It was now more in keeping with the back garden, with its cornucopia of statuary and dramatic architectural plants. Now, this self-conscious gardenette reminded him of the forecourt of a fashionable hotel. The clinical isolation of the single tree in its weed-free square of stones seemed to represent Rachel's determination to root Stephen out of her life, along with the familiar muddle of foliage. He had loved that damp, messy front garden, he realized now, though he had always cursed it as a paradise for slugs and a possible hiding place for lurking burglars.

As he ushered the children towards the house, he looked around with miserable foreboding. Perhaps she just hated him. Simple as that. With no adulterous arms waiting to enfold her. She would rather be alone than be with him. Over time – months, then years – her anger had built up its momentum so that finally she had managed to throw him out on a tidal wave of spleen. Since then, not living with him had fuelled her loathing, rather than lessening its force. Now, forgetting to pick up the children had raised it to its highest level still. He could feel her rage from where he stood. The lights of the house were blazing, upstairs and down, as if the building itself was angrily waiting for him, staring glassily into the night.

What point had they arrived at now? She wasn't sleeping with Kris. This was good. This was very good indeed. But – ironically – he had found this out only when relations between them had reached a new low. As he walked up the garden path, the front door flew open and Rachel's silhouette loomed out of the lighted frame. He was about to speak, make some self-justifying joke. But Rachel got in first. And her tactic, it seemed, was to pretend he wasn't there.

'Hello, kids!' she called, squatting down. They ran towards her, and she caught them both and kissed them passionately. She loved them. Of course she loved them. Even so, Stephen thought unwillingly of Princess Diana during the period when she was facilitating spontaneous photo opportunities in which she rapturously embraced her children. He was trying to work out whether Rachel had deliberately misled him about Kris, or had been inno-cently describing her relationship with a close male colleague who understood her every mood and need. That hardly described the vaginal-orgasm thing, surely. She looked over the children's heads at him. 'So you got over Daddy forgetting to pick you up, then?' she said, in a neutral-to-spiky voice.

'Daddy was great,' said Elsie, disentangling herself from the group hug. 'He let us play for ages in their garden while he chatted to Clive in the bushes about stuff.'

'YEAH. AND HE MADE THE TEA, HE DID!' said Stan.

'Did he, darling? Isn't that wonderful?' cooed Rachel insincerely.

'Actually, he really did,' said Elsie. 'He did these really cool biscuits with hundreds and thousands on them. And Angel Delight with stripes.'

Rachel straightened up and addressed him at last. 'Back in favour with the Cathcarts, then? Even though you screamed the place down the last time you saw them?'

'Well. Kind of,' said Stephen. 'I don't think Tamzin's speaking to me as such, even now. But I don't think I'm her number-one concern at the moment.'

'No. You've heard, then.'

'Heard what, Mummy?' asked Elsie.

'Heard nothing – just go and play, darling. Daddy will be gone in a second and we can all have a really good talk.'

In a second. Not much chance of a cosy chat, then. Stephen wondered if this was what he wanted. Since he had moved out he hadn't been offered so much as a cup of tea when dropping off or collecting the children. This at-the-door business had an oddly familiar feel. Like visiting America, getting separated was an experience which he had lived out in advance, through films and TV. Standing at the edge of his ex-garden, he felt like a corny archetype, the absentee dad at the end of his shift, lonely and pathetic, but with his immaturity intact. He felt that any lines he might come up with that were designed to placate Rachel were similarly doomed to cliché. But he was desperate to talk to her about Kris, and the relationship that – perhaps – never was.

'Rachel, I . . .'

'What? Rachel what?' She watched Elsie and Stan scurry into the house. Her voice was cold, and there was something in her face he didn't remember. Something hard and artificially composed. 'I hope you are not going to say how sorry you are. As if that would make any difference.'

'Well. I sort of was, I suppose.'

'Save your breath, Daddy. Today you did the worst thing, the very worst thing that you could possibly do to those kids. You let them down.'

'It was a mistake, I –'

'You fucking let them down. Haven't they been through enough? Do you really want them to be completely crushed by what's happened to us? All anyone is asking of you is to turn up on time. Once a week, sometimes twice, turn up when you say you will. And you just couldn't be arsed to do that.'

'Rachel, it wasn't like –'

But Rachel was on a roll. 'I didn't think, I truly did not think, that I could have underestimated how much of a wanker you are, Stephen,' she said, taking an angry step towards him. 'But – surprise! – I did. You have managed to be even worse than I thought you were. So that's it.

Fuck you, Mr Perfect Father. Or should I say, Mr Perfect Ex-Father. You are a worthless piece of shit.'

'Stop it! Stop it!' Suddenly Stephen couldn't stand it any longer. He felt his hands starting to tremble, and then he did the one thing he had promised himself that he would never do when their marriage began to implode. He started to cry in front of Rachel. Great sobs came heaving out of his throat. Even to his own ears this was a terrible sound, like a sick cow baying in a field. 'Stop shouting at me! Stop telling me I'm useless! I lost my diary, okay? I didn't want to admit it, right? Because you were already treating me like the bloody Yorkshire Ripper. I was just ... I was just ...' But another surge of emotion silenced him. Rachel said nothing. His shaking fingers were covering his face; he couldn't see her expression. He waited for the sound of her retreating footsteps, for the front door to close, as it always did, with him on the outside, a fragment of himself. Instead, he felt her hands pulling him gently along the path.

'You'd better come in and calm down,' she said. He followed her obediently into the hall, and sat in a heap on the stairs. She closed the front door and stood with her back to it, looking at him sadly.

'Look – maybe I shouldn't have said you were useless, Stephen,' she said. 'For God's sake. But you have to think of the children.'

'I *do* think of them! I *do*!' he said, feeling like Stan again. 'What else *is* there to think about? I've lost you, but I'm still their father! I'll always be their father! Don't try to take that away from me! I'll go out of my mind! There'll be ... nothing. Just nothing left for me at all ...' The sobs were still coming. They weren't the soothing, cathartic kind. With each one his head ached more.

'Just try to pull yourself together,' said Rachel, more gently. 'It was a mistake. Okay. I accept it was a mistake.'

'Maybe it's all a mistake? Maybe me going is a mistake? Until today, I thought you were seeing Kris . . . But then it turns out he's marrying some party-organizer woman.'

'God! You idiot. I *knew* that was why you blew a gasket in the restaurant. He was just ranting on about something I said in the Sex and Monogamy workshop. Typical! Thinking of yourself so much that you leap to all these paranoid conclusions, rather than paying attention to things that really matter – like the kids.'

'He does pay attention to us,' said Elsie in a quiet, old voice. Stephen twisted round to see both children standing at the top of the stairs, eyes round with wonder at the spectacle below. Without moving, Elsie continued: 'And Kris didn't mind us being in the office, either. And he is very good indeed at story reading and doing voices. So you can stop being cross, Mummy. We all had fun.'

'YEAH,' said Stan. 'STOP IT RIGHT NOW!'

This time it was Rachel who crumpled under the strain. Stephen watched her slide slowly downwards, her back still against the door, till she was folded into a melancholy heap on the mat. He noticed that she was wearing new clothes – a dark-grey dress and high-heeled mauve suede shoes he didn't recognize. On some level he knew she wouldn't want to sit in a creasy pile in that particular outfit. On another, he wondered which credit card she had put them on. But, fundamentally, he knew that it wasn't his enemy who was slumped on the doormat; it was his wife.

'Oh God,' she said plaintively. 'Oh Jesus. How did we get into his mess? What's happened to us all?' And the tears began to slide down her face. She stared up at the children. 'I'm sorry,' she sobbed. 'I'm so sorry.' Stephen shuffled down the hall towards her on his knees, groping towards her. The children were close behind him, unusually silent, like sinless little ghosts. Just as he was about to take her hand, his mobile rang.

Shit. Without thinking, he whipped it out of his pocket. 'Can't talk now, I'll catch you later –' he began.

'Hello, Stephen,' said a voice, cool as lemons on a marble chopping board. 'Sorry if I've called at an inopportune moment.'

'Fay!' he nearly shouted. Then, his face contorting with the effort of being two people at the same time, he modified his volume. 'Fay. Great to – really good to – erm. Can I call you back?'

'Sure. You sound terrible. Is everything okay?'

'Erm, fine. Just some . . . domestic stuff . . .'

'Poor you. Call me when you've got time.'

'Yes – of course I will – bye, er, Fay . . .'

'Cool. Speak soon.'

He hardly dared look at Rachel. Her tears were glittering on her newly frozen face. 'Fay,' she said, deliberately. 'And who might Fay be?'

Stephen responded with a sort of squeak, one hand still reaching towards her.

'You certainly didn't waste much time. Why were you so worried about what *I* was up to, when *you* were fixed up already?' Her words scarred the air between them. He felt sick. The present had won. There was no way to return. His extended hand fell to his side.

'It's Fay Cattermole,' he said, forlornly. 'You know. Just an old school . . . chum.'

'Oh, fantastic. Instead of pining away on your own, you've been chasing after your pathetic little teenage crush . . . Just how low can you go, Stephen? Just how pathetic are you?'

'I've seen her once,' Stephen cried, plunging the phone guiltily back into his pocket. 'In Stoke.'

'Nanna's been talking to her mummy,' said Elsie, helpfully. 'About death and cancer and stuff. Her daddy died, in mortal agony.' She and Stan were now snuggled under Stephen's leather jacket, looking from one parental face to the other, for signs of reassurance and normality.

'I might have known Nanna's oar would be shoved in somewhere,' said Rachel. She hauled both of the children on to her knees. 'If she left the counselling to professionals, we'd all be a lot better off.'

'Rachel, please – let's not leap from me thinking you're seeing Kris to you thinking I'm seeing Fay. I'm not. *Please*. I want to –'

'I'm not interested in what you want. Just piss off.' Rachel's voice was weary. 'I've had about as much deviousness and double-talk as I can take for one night.'

'I thought maybe we could talk – try to . . . I don't know. Understand each other's point of view.'

'That's very big of you. But I think I understand your point of view very well, frankly. And I can't help it if you are too crass to understand mine. Now, say goodbye to the children and go.'

The children kissed him, clung to him as if this was their first real parting, or their last. More strongly than ever, he felt that he could damage them, destroy their innocence. He felt they understood the enormity of what was happening. Elsie stroked his hair with caring, formal little hands. Stan solemnly gave him the rubber ball which was the most prized component of his party bag. As Stephen was leaving, Rachel came up behind him. 'There *is* something I need to tell you,' she said. 'But it can wait.'

He spent most of the following day mooching around Brighton, reluctant to return to Vinnie's house, thinking hard. Surprisingly, he found himself in the Lanes, looking at expensive shirts with gratuitous fashion detailing. Clearly his sojourn with his gay chums was taking its toll. These shirts certainly weren't the kind of thing he would ever buy. Even years of trying to familiarize himself with the highways and byways of taste had left him with areas of utter non-expertise, and clothes came into this category. Surely this collection of wacky garments was suitable only for Engelbert Humperdinck or some dodgy Northern comedian? Put Stephen in a canary-yellow frou-frou number with Regency ruffles and he would resemble not the artful dandy Laurence Llewellyn-Bowen but an aesthetically bypassed Bloke from Stoke, with as much idea about the niceties of personal styling as John Prescott. Midlands blood ran in his veins; there was no escape from inner naffness, not ever. In front of a mirror he held a multi-coloured number that looked as if Kandinsky had been sick on it, and remembered the first disco he had ever been to. His outfit had consisted of cardboard denims from Mr Byright and a cheesecloth shirt that pinged open when he got down to Status Quo. Now he was wearing a sweatshirt from Primark and a pair of Levi's that had frayed badly round the bottom – the sartorial equivalent of sausages and mash, probably. Stephen might have revamped his diet and knowledge of cuisine, but as far as fashion and outfits went he was as naffly unsophisticated as ever. He sighed heavily, watched beadily by the assistant, returned the shirt to its perch and wandered miserably back to Kemp Town.

The following evening, lying on the bed in Vinnie's attic, he tried to assess the situation. He stared at the ceiling, smoking and thinking as hard as he could. So . . . He didn't know what Rachel had to say to him. But he could guess. She wanted him out permanently, lover or no lover. He would never live with his children again. Instead of being with them, with their cold cheeky little feet burrowing into his back in the early morning, their Cheerios and Lego-leavings littering his world, he was here. A barely tolerated lodger in the love-nest of two gay men. The thought that the mess between Rachel and himself was doing his merry little children harm was so terrible that he shrank away from it. He would make it up to them. He would be Fantastic Fun Dad, he would reinvent their world, fire their imaginations, open their eyes to wonder and magic.

He twisted himself into a less comfortable position on the bed and thought about the sex thing, which was nearly as worrying but nothing like as painful. It clearly wasn't going to happen with Rachel. Whether he would ever experience it again with anyone else was unclear. He couldn't imagine how it might happen. With his shaky hands and his sweaty nightmares, he wasn't sure he was up to the job of pursuit, persuasion and penetration, even if he found some woman accommodating enough to let him try. It wasn't just Rachel's contempt which was undermining his confidence; living with the pink pound was an emasculating business. His landlords indulged in more fornication in one weekend than he and Rachel had managed to stump up over the last twelve months. He could hear them now, splashing about in the bath below his attic room. They were giggling and singing snatches of Kylie's latest hit in an ironic way. Vinnie in particular was managing an impressively animated falsetto, which Stephen hadn't heard him do before.

He sighed and exhaled smoke, watched the clouds wafting towards the white ceiling. Smoking was bloody good. Still, it wasn't quite enough to make up for the loss of wife, home and children. More splashing and gasping from below. He wanted to go to the toilet, but was too embarrassed to leave his room. What was the protocol in such situations? He wasn't entirely sure whether they knew that he was in – they'd been in the bathroom when he came back from the shops. Skulking past the bathroom without announcing that he was back had seemed furtive and sad. But he didn't feel it was appropriate to hammer on the door, trilling, 'I'm home, boys! Go easy with that loofah!' He hadn't lived in a house with other sexually active grown-ups since his college days, and in those distant times protocol hadn't been a matter that bothered people much. He couldn't help feeling that people over thirty-five ought to enjoy each other quietly if there was the least chance of being overheard. Even if they were gay.

So. Clarity and focus. It was now August; he'd been kicked out in April. Pursuing his current policy of drift couldn't be a long-term solution. At some point, he would have to take action, resume command of his life. However, even though living with Vinnie and Marc was embarrassing, moving out would mean paying rent. At the moment, all he had to contribute was a couple of bottles of vodka a week. Vinnie wouldn't allow him to give him any money, saying it would all come out of the restaurant anyway, which was true enough. And, as he had an overdraft of £7,000, it seemed foolish to move into a rented room just to prove a point. As for the sex ... Well. He could still feel the touch of Sorrel's cool arms. Still remember the last time with Rachel, a hurried, botched, early-morning encounter with the children liable to erupt into their room at any moment. Then, with a jolt, he thought of the lap-dancer. Last night he had had the strangest dream. She had been dancing towards him, a long slow dance along a corridor of pink blancmange. Her white, sweating breasts coming nearer, nearer, as she leaned closer, closer ... Disgusting, of course. Practically a nightmare. No wonder his pillow had been soaked with perspiration when he woke up. With an effort, he thought of Fay instead. But, considering she was his first true love, he felt surprisingly little lust towards her. Perhaps he didn't dare. Just as he was thinking this thought, his mobile rang again. With a sinking heart, he saw that it was his mother's number.

'Hello.'

'Stephen, it's your mother,' said Rose, unnecessarily. 'Where are you?'

'I'm lying in bed,' said Stephen, his mind not working quickly enough.

'Who with?'

'What d'you mean, who with? I'm on my own.'

'Not with Rachel, then,' said Rose, her voice narrow with anger. 'I can't believe you wouldn't tell me what was going on when you were here. Even after you knew I'd guessed there was trouble . . .'

'Yeah, well, why did you have to blurt it out in front of Fay and her mother? I thought you were the expert on relationships – I just don't get it.'

'It just came out,' said Rose. 'We've been over this already, Stephen. You know I can't hold a drink. But you're still being plain cruel, trying to keep me at arm's length. I'm your mother.'

'I know you're my mother. I've just been . . . trying to sort it out. I thought if I could get her back, it would all blow over; there was no need for you to be involved . . .'

'Never thinking I might be of some help, of course!' Rose was shouting now. He thought of those teenage years in Stoke, her hair bouffed-up in some insane style of the hour, her puffy face staring forlornly down at him as he sprawled in front of the gas fire, hating the world. Always, always, she wanted to help. 'I've had ladies close to suicide in my salon, talked them round, gave them a shampoo and set and they never looked back,' she said. 'Never. Looked. Back. It's a miracle, what human beings can do for each other if they only stop and listen. Even

Sylvia's started salsa lessons. It's given her a new lease of life.'

'Mum, I'm forty years old. Can't you let me mess things up my own way?'

'No I can't! What would you do if it happened to Elsie or Stan, years down the line? I know you, Stephen. Mr Softee, that's who you are. No. I'm coming down, and I'm going to get to the bottom of this.'

'Mum – you'll make it all worse. Please. I'm begging you. Don't come.'

There was a silence. 'How will your own mother make anything worse? Tell me the answer to that.'

'It's just not something you can put right. It's bad enough Carmel popping up all over the place doing her bloody compatibility charts and giving us zero.'

'I don't know if you're breaking Rachel's heart, Stephen, but I'll tell you this: you're breaking mine.'

And with that, she went.

Stephen lay back on his pillows again. He felt like making the sort of noise Lucky Jim specialized in, back in the days when men drank warm beer, Kingsley Amis was a bit of a sex god and women were good for nothing but standing around behind their breasts. His version would be a low-pitched yodel, hinting at thwarted Midlands savagery, emitted while doing a soupily stentorian fart. But such masculine prowess was out of fashion now. Instead, his mouth pursed with self-dislike, he squeaked out a lonely, uptight little parcel of wind. Then he realized he really did have to go to the toilet. A vague, circulating ache which had been pulsing around his gut for some time suddenly twisted itself into an urgent pain. Given that

Vinnie's only loo was in the bathroom, Stephen had no choice but to interrupt the gay sex-fun that had been going on for far too long.

15

He realized that something was wrong almost as soon as he knocked on the bathroom door and called, 'Sorry – really sorry. But I need to use the loo.' Asking your landlords to take a break from the joys of bathtime sex so that you can offload your poisonous shit into their lavatory is one of life's more embarrassing requests. However, as silent seconds passed, the atmosphere on the other side of the locked door suggested, he realized, the wrong kind of embarrassment. Motionless, he stood looking down at his pale knuckles, the sixth sense that women don't believe men possess prickling all over his skin. First there was no sound at all, then the splashing sound of a person climbing out a very deep bath. Then the noise of padded footsteps approaching, unwillingness in every tread. Finally, Marc's head appeared. 'Can't you wait?' he asked, nastily. Stephen tried not to look at his lardy white shoulders, his maternal breasts.

'No –' Stephen realized how urgent his situation was. 'I've got the runs, or something. Stress, eaten something crap, I don't know. I'm actually . . . desperate.' Another shaft of agony as these words reminded him of his urgent children. Every morning, there was a high-pitched tussle over toilet use, with one or other of them threatening to wee on the floor. He used to listen to this little ritual from his bedroom next door, smiling slightly into his pillow.

Now, he only heard them wake up on Sundays. He was disappearing to the margins of their life. During the time it took to suffer from this memory shard, Marc's head disappeared. This time, the quality of the silence suggested that he was in sound-free consultation with the person in the bath. Stephen was puzzled – why wouldn't Vinnie say anything? Was there some kind of homosexual sex act so outrageous that it rendered at least one of the participants mute after the event? But his stomach's hot twists were taking on a new and disturbing lease of life. 'I'm sorry to put you out . . . I'll only be five minutes.' Stephen called, beginning to wonder if he was about to soil his pants for the first time in his adult life.

Marc's head reappeared. This time, the rest of him followed, and he squirmed round the door with only a hand towel tied around his waist, if waist was the right word for his vast middle. In revealing his entire torso, he had also changed his approach. 'Stevie . . .' he said, smiling in a fake-animated way, showing his annoying little white teeth. 'It's a teeny, weeny bit difficult at the moment . . . Can't you just nip round the corner to the pub and use theirs?'

'No,' said Stephen. 'I really, really have to go now –'

With these words, he somehow surged past Marc's bloated body, squeezed through the barely open bathroom door and ran towards the toilet bowl.

Miraculously, he had taken his trousers and boxer shorts down in some unconscious, simultaneous movement. Like a skilled football diva, he managed to twist in midair, thus landing bottom-down on the seat. Something unholy swished out of him, completely liquid, taking with it small

213

parts of his entrails. For a moment, the relief of getting rid of this inner horror without being coated in his own excrement was overwhelming. He sat on the toilet seat, farting horribly, his face cupped in his hands. But he could experience relief in its pure form only for so long. After a while, other emotions came into play. Such as shame. And curiosity. He took his hands down, and looked towards Vinnie and the bath. While the bath was in its usual place, and in its usual unattractive shade of avocado, Vinnie was nowhere to be seen. In his place sat a young man, with close-cropped blond hair and steely blue eyes, who looked no older than seventeen. This was the owner of the falsetto voice singing the Kylie hit. He should have known that Vinnie would never have managed those high notes.

'Oh my God,' said Stephen. 'Who the hell are you?'

The boy looked at him, silent.

'Who he is is no business of yours,' said Marc, sliding back round the door. His skin, always bloodless, looked whiter than ever, as if his entire body was blanched with fury. 'Nor is what's going on in my life, or Vinnie's life, or any fucking thing connected to this house. You don't know the first thing about me, or him, or the way anything works in our relationship. So you say one thing to him, and I'll make sure you, my friend, are toast.'

'What on earth could you do that would make my life worse than it is now?' asked Stephen. He had never realized how much Marc hated him. He could see it now, of course. But he'd put the catty remarks, and the fact that Marc rarely addressed a remark at him directly, down to heterophobia or something. Marc was the sort of gay man who lived exclusively in a gay world. He had no contact with his family. He had no friends who weren't part of the Brighton scene. His only dealings with mainstream breeders were in his flower shop. Even there, his best customers were interiors-conscious queens with two incomes and no chance of having their lilies trashed by hyperactive under-tens. Stephen stared at him, wondering how to pull his trousers up in a dignified and manly way. He really didn't want Marc to see the size of his penis – it was average, he had always been led to believe, but still . . .

'I could tell him you've been borrowing money from your posh friends without telling him,' said Marc. 'I could tell him that you've never been honest with him about the way that place is losing money. There are two people in the world who Vinnie trusts. One of them is you. And the other – in case you hadn't guessed – is me. If you tell him about this, he'll find out that both of us are liars.'

'Nice,' said Stephen, leaping from the toilet seat, managing another midair twirl, pulling up his trousers and flushing the chain in one deft moment. God, the smell was bad. He turned back, zipping up his flies. 'Funny, I never really could work out what it was that Vinnie saw in you. Somehow, you always came across to me as a pointless, posturing little fat boy. Now I know. It's your inner radiance, your lovely, giving personality.' He began to wash his hands in the sink, keeping his eyes averted from the boy in the bath, who had still not said a word.

'Why don't you piss right off, you disgusting arse?' said Marc, coming up close behind him.

'Piss off yourself,' said Stephen, managing to wriggle past him again, and out of the bathroom door. For a second, he wondered when he had had this conversation before. Was it in the school playground? Or on one of his recent meetings with his lady wife? Maturity certainly did not seem to be his big number at the moment – perhaps this was the whole point of having a midlife crisis. The bathroom door slammed behind him, and he ran down the stairs and into the hall, pushed his feet into his shoes and his arms into his leather jacket and rushed into the street. It used to be only his mother who made him feel like a surly teenager. Now it was the entire world. The only way that Marc could have found out about Clive and the money was by going through the papers in his room. Once, Rose had read his diary. (Ironically, this was when he was sixteen, during the period when she thought he might be gay. Rose had realized Carmel was a lesbian only when she officially came out at Christmas at the age of thirty, by which time she had shagged most of Southeast London's Sapphic tendency.) These were the same emotions he had experienced then: rage, fear, disbelief. How could someone do that? Poking about in his room, among his private things. How could they have such moveable morals, such bad taste?

He paced along the road, then stopped abruptly. His mind – a whirl of abandoned children, newly austere gardens, errant wives who turned out to be lover-free, disturbed piles of admin and gay bottoms – suddenly alighted on something that wasn't completely depressing. Fay had phoned. What was that all about? Perhaps she fancied him, after all. Perhaps seeing him in Stoke had rekindled some unacknowledged spark from her schooldays. It seemed appropriate that, if everyone was conspiring to make him feel like a bonkers adolescent, he should get back in touch with the person who had driven him bonkers when he really was a teenager. Also, he felt obscurely that if, after all these years, he could impress Fay, then all the other people who were determined to humiliate him would cease to matter. Perhaps – and he hardly dared think this 'perhaps' – they might end up together. An image of the two of them came unbidden into his mind. Laughing in a carefree, tousled sort of way, they casually tended to some slices of aubergine grilled on a bed of fennel stalks.

The road was busy with evening traffic rumbling into central Brighton; he turned into a side road full of decaying houses with steep steps and rusty iron railings and called her number. He knew she worked late hours, and there was every chance she would still be at work.

'Fay Cattermole, hello?' Again, the citrus-cool voice. Just three words, but he could see her sitting there, at her desk, at the epicentre of the National Press.

'Fay, it's me again – Stephen.'

'I'm sorry? Stephen who?'

'Stephen Beckett. You phoned me.'

'Stephen Beckett . . . ? Oh my God. Yes. Stephen. *Hi.*'

His skin prickled for the second time that day. Was this lust? Or fear? Maybe there wasn't any difference. And his stomach had returned to form and was slithering around inside him. Perhaps his intestines were completely re-arranging themselves, just as Stan had flipped over from normal-way-up-baby to breech-baby just before he was born. 'Hello,' he said, in his John Major voice. Then, trying to go for a darker, ruder, Sean Bean type of tone, he said: 'I think you said there was something I could help you with?'

'Oh yes, yes, there was. Sorry to be so vague! I've been working on an Al Quaida colour piece, something to do with Scandinavian culture producing extremists, and my mind was . . . you know. Totally elsewhere. Just off to Stockholm to soak up a bit of that Stepford culture!' She laughed merrily. Stephen had no idea what she was on about, but assumed that this was just the way that journalists talked.

'I didn't know Al Quaida were based in Sweden,' he said. More laughter. The laughing thing was new, and quite disconcerting. Fay had never laughed at all when she was at school, as far he could remember.

'Oh, Stephen, you are funny! Osama Bin Laden lived in Sweden for a few years, with his family. As if you didn't know! We did a whole supplement on his teenage influences last week!'

'Of course,' Stephen chortled back, trying to mirror her tone, but was so unconvincing that a passing dosser gave him a very suspicious look.

'Anyway,' said Fay. 'The thing I was calling about was another piece entirely. We're doing a special feature on Sleazy Britain – a sort of round-up of the naughtiest places in the country – lots of pictures, wacky eccentrics, bit of lewd stuff. You know, born-again *Ice Storm* key parties, WI ladies who love going nude, saucy gay vicars who go cruising at weekends – that kind of thing.'

'Gosh,' said Stephen. Then, for some reason: 'Yah, right.'

'Which is where you come in,' said Fay. 'Or at least, I hope you do.'

'I'm afraid I don't know any gay vicars,' said Stephen.

'No! Absolutely not! No, I was wondering if you knew anything particularly outrageous about Brighton. You know, dirty-weekend capital of the universe. Graham Greene-land – forgotten corners. The Prince Regent – historic decadence. The story behind the story. Real south-coast sleaze, as opposed to the kind of south-coast sleaze that our readers think they know about already. Anything along those lines.'

Stephen's mind was reeling. Did she ever stop? Once, he had thought of being a journalist. But that was after watching John Pilger talking about nuclear war in 1983. He had assumed, in those days, that being a journalist meant dealing with hard information, proper subjects. What had put him off was the dreadfulness of the student wankers who ran the college newspaper. Puffed up with their own importance over nothing whatsoever, they had a special style of smoking, and never sat down in the refectory, but skipped about neurotically from table to table, as if they were looking for hot stories in a war zone. Now he knew that these people were on to something, because nothing whatsoever was the stock-in-trade of modern newspapers. And yet . . . The glamour of the occupation he had never dared to try still had its power. In another life, he would have liked to see his byline on articles about where to buy the best tepee or what kind of French dressing you should be making in a post-balsamic-vinegar society. It was in the natural order of things that Fay, aloof and poised as a teenager, should have her own restaurant column now. Whereas he was the eternal spectator, staring in a glazed way at the blur of famous anorexics and bleached interiors. He had read her food column faithfully for the last two years, even though food writing made him queasy and insecure. It was too late to get involved now – and life was complicated enough. Stephen wanted to say – indeed, he planned to say – 'Fay, I would really like to help, but I can't.' Instead, what came out was: 'Are you doing anything about lap-dancers?'

'Lap-dancers are very last year,' said Fay. 'But . . . I guess if we're doing a comprehensive trawl, we could have something in a box. Why, do you know about a club in Brighton?'

'Yes. Well, it's in Hove. I was there a few weeks ago.' Then he added hastily. 'You know, just to see how the other half lives. Depressed friend who needed a night out. That sort of thing.' He winced at his automatic impersonation of her conversational tic, but she appeared not to notice.

'Hove. Hmmm. I like that. More to Hove actually than the blue-rinse brigade . . . Brighton's sleaze seeps west . . . Hang on a minute.' He could hear her voice more faintly, saying: 'Sanjit. Lap-dancing. What do you reckon? Done to death?' Then she faded away completely for a bit. The dosser walked passed him again, carrying a tattered magazine. Stephen wondered if it was the *Carbuncle*. Then Fay came back.

'We like it,' she said. 'As long as I can go along myself, see the girls in action. Interview a couple of them about girl power, bulimia, celebrity tarts. That sort of thing.'

'I don't think women are allowed in there,' said Stephen, in John Major mode once more. 'I certainly don't recall seeing any.'

'Oh, we'll bluff our way in somehow,' she said. 'I'm a journalist, for God's sake. Think of Martha Gelhorn.'

'Yes, quite,' said Stephen, wondering what the connection was, exactly. 'Well . . . good luck with it. Shall I give you the address?'

'If you want to,' said Fay, with remarkable casualness for a news hound.

'Won't you need it?'

'Not if you take me there,' said Fay.

'But I . . .' Stephen's stomach was on the warpath again. 'I . . . I don't think I could go again.' The thought of Fay face to face with Gabrielle was just . . . Well, unthinkable.

'Whyever not? Red-blooded divorcee like you. I thought you'd jump at the chance. Lap-dancing is terribly mainstream, now. George Clooney puts money into his favourite club. When he thought it was about to close, he was desperate. That's the only reason I wasn't sure – so obvious, really. But Sanjit thinks it will work with the posh-totty-investigates angle.'

She was off again. His mind reeled – with journo-speak, with eager anticipation at the thought of an evening with Fay, with dread at the thought of the club, Gabrielle, the evil bouncers, the one-to-one room . . .

'So you'll take me, then?'

'I'll . . . well. I don't know . . .'

'Come on, Stephen, are you a man or a mouse? What's bugging you?'

'Nothing. Well – lot's of things. Divorce crap, work crap . . . I'm afraid it's all terribly boring.' God. How un-Sean Bean could you get?

'Divorce crap: no barrier at all. As a recently separated

male of a certain age, it's more or less mandatory for you to spend every waking moment in lap-dancing clubs, re-establishing your wicked sexist ways. Work crap: I know you've been having problems. How would a restaurant review go down? We're doing a slot on "Art and Food" – edible art, lunchbox chic. Get an exhibition in there, something Brighton-y, and I could come along with our art critic Erika Perspecua and cover it for you.'

'Could you? That would be . . . that would just be so wonderful . . .'

'You need some kind of selling point, remember. Something different. Erika has seen everything, and I have tasted everything.'

'I'll fix it,' said Stephen.

'You're a star,' said Fay. 'I'll call you next week and we'll sort it out.' And she was gone.

Whatever next? Stephen wiped the sweat from his forehead and looked up and down the street, unable to decide which way he should walk. He peered at his watch; almost nine o'clock. For a moment, he struggled to remember what day of the week it was. Friday. It would be mayhem in the kitchen at Earthsea. Of course he should rush down there right away. But he wasn't sure how he was going to face Vinnie again. So he loitered slowly down the hill, wondering what to do. He couldn't go to either of his non-homes, for obvious reasons. And he didn't want to go to work. One thing he had noticed about leaving his family was that suddenly he had a lot more choice in life. Pre-split, there was work and there was Rachel and the children. He divided his time unequally between the two, and wore himself out with the effort of keeping everyone unhappy. Post-split, he was quite often in situations like this one – unable to make a decision, marooned in suddenly plentiful time. However, the options on offer weren't usually all that attractive. For instance: he now had a choice, but it seemed only to involve deciding whether to walk up or down this hill. He tried to open up his existential horizons. Friday night. Single man about town. What would a normal bloke do in such circumstances? A picture of Nick rose up before him, and he had a sudden desire to see his one-time friend. It was true that Nick had avoided him since the lap-dancing trip – well, so what? They could go out, have a few beers, talk about it man to man. There was a chance Nick would be out, but walking to his house in Hanover at least gave Stephen a project. He turned on his heel and walked away from the glittering seafront.

Nick lived in a narrow little terraced house on Southover Street. It opened directly on to the steep pavement – the street climbed sharply from one flat park, the Level, to Queen's Park. At first Stephen thought all the lights in the house were out, but then he noticed a dim glimmering through the closed curtains of the front room, as if candles were burning in there. Stephen knocked on the door in a loud, butch way and waited. After a few seconds, Nick opened it, wearing a black silk dressing-gown, and holding a glass of red wine.

'Darling, you're . . .' he began. He looked at Stephen with horror. 'Fuck,' he said. Then. 'Steve . . . Pure accident – nothing to do with me . . . Who told you?'

'I'm sorry?' said Stephen. 'No one's told me anything.

Were you expecting someone – I mean – entertaining or . . . ?'

'Who, me? No!' Nick guffawed unconvincingly and slugged back the wine. 'No, just on my way out, mate. Want to come?'

'Well, I . . . Yes. I thought I'd drop round to see if you fancied a beer. Shall I come inside while you get ready . . . ?'

'Er, sure . . .' Nick glanced behind him. In the back kitchen, Stephen could just about make out a table laid for two, glasses winking in candlelight, white napkins on a dark tablecloth.

'Are you sure I'm not interrupting something? I can push off now if –'

'No-o-o-h! Nothing to interrupt!' Nick took a step backwards, drained the rest of the wine and said, in a desperately chirpy tone: 'Tell you what, I'll meet you in the Pub With No Name at the top of the hill. Just give me time to get my, er . . . things on. And I'll see you there. House is . . . you know. Terrible mess.'

'It looks incredibly tidy to me,' said Stephen, still peering past him. 'You must be having some kind of date . . .'

'No way!' insisted Nick, who was now actually pushing Stephen out into the street. Why were people always barring his way, pushing him out of doors? Perhaps he'd eventually develop door-rage. He wished he could find a nasty, mean, don't-mess-with-me-big-boy side to his personality. But it seemed he was the easiest person to mess with on the planet. After all, he was the man who had been ejected from his own dinner party by a pregnant woman.

'Okay, okay. I'll see you in there,' he said crossly, pulling himself away from Nick's grasp.

'Thanks, mate. Give me five minutes. Pint of Guinness'll go down a treat.'

16

By the time Nick appeared at the bar of the Pub With No Name, Stephen had already downed two double brandies. This made his stomach feel slightly better, and he had begun to look around the small, crowded, wood-panelled bar with the air of a man with a future. Speaking to Fay had given him some hope that things besides splitting up and going bankrupt might one day happen to him. As soon as he saw Nick, however, he took the instant-policy decision not to tell him about her or his planned return to the club. Although Stephen wasn't always good at reading his fellow human beings, he felt that Nick was not entirely to be trusted.

'God,' said Nick, after drinking most of his pint in a series of powerful gulps. 'That helps. What a night!'

'How d'you mean?'

'Oh, you know. Sorry if I seemed really weird just now. But Christ. Trying to relax before going out on the town, have nice glass of wine in the bath, then Clancy phones up and tells me she's pissing off to the States again, wants to take Poppy with her. Bloody bitch. That's why I was so, you know, when I opened the door . . .'

'Don't worry about it. You're no worse than me. But why did you call me "darling"?' asked Stephen.

'Erm. Good point.' Nick paused to drain his glass. 'Glad you asked me that. I called you "darling" because my brain is completely overloaded. It takes it out of you, being the ex-husband of a mad woman *and* an ethical estate agent. Especially in this town.'

'Why's that?'

'Why? Because Brighton is a shit-hole. Most of our clients are a bunch of chancers, you know. They think because we're ethical we'll be naive pushovers. Of course, where my dear old mate Keith is concerned, they're not wrong. He's a complete wipe-out as an estate agent. Born-again Christians should never mess with property. They should stick to the happy-clappy stuff and stay well away from bricks, mortar and cash. Keith wants to give money away. He thinks he's the fucking Messiah. Luckily, he works with me. I'm more your anti-Christ type of estate agent, which makes me a very tough customer indeed.'

Stephen wondered if he was ever going to spend any time with a human being who didn't speak in riddles. First unreadable Rachel, then incomprehensible Fay, now Nick's barrage of nonsense. He had the impression that Nick was trying to talk his way out of a tight corner.

'I'm sure you're very tough indeed,' he said, vaguely. 'Would you like another drink?'

'I'll get these,' said Nick. 'What's that – brandy?'

'For my stomach,' said Stephen.

'No need to make excuses; it's good to see you on the hard stuff.' Nick waved his empty glass at the barman and their glasses were refilled.

After sipping his brandy, Stephen said thoughtfully: 'What would you do if you knew something that would upset someone, but you don't know if they want to know the truth?'

Nick's drink appeared to have gone down the wrong way. He coughed and spluttered uncontrollably for a while. 'If I what . . . ?' he managed to say, finally.

'If, well. Say you had a friend, and you knew that their partner was being unfaithful, but if you told them, they would be devastated, but you're worried that if you don't tell them they'll be even more angry and more devastated in the long run.'

'Stephen, just what the fuck is on your mind? Has someone been spreading evil rumours?'

'No. Why would this have anything to do with evil rumours?'

Nick produced a packet of cigarettes, took one, and pushed the pack along the bar to Stephen. They both lit up. 'Let's get this straight,' said Nick. 'You really do have a friend whose "partner" really is being unfaithful to him or her, and you really do want to know what to do about it. Is that right?'

'Yes. Isn't that what I just said?'

'Yeah, okay.'

'So what would you do?'

'I dunno. Am I allowed to know who this mysterious person is?'

Stephen hesitated. But the brandy had done its work. His discretion was at a low ebb. 'It's Vinnie – the person I'm staying with. Plus I work with him,' he said. 'His boyfriend's got some other bloke, some young studenty kid. They were in the bath together just now. That's why I had to go out. In fact, I'm not sure how I'll ever go back.'

Nick looked relieved. 'Of course, the fucking fruity

queen on your answer machine! Rampant sex on the hearth rug!' he said. 'Christ, with your woofters, being unfaithful is the name of the game.'

'I really don't . . .' Stephen tried to say. But Nick was in full flow.

'If you will insist on shacking up with a couple of arse-bandits, then who knows what you're going to stumble on of an evening? Could have been a whole bunch of them, dressed as Carmen Miranda, rogering each other over the quiche.'

'Don't be so ridiculous. Vinnie loves Marc,' said Stephen, primly. 'Not all gay men rush around cruising and picking up strangers, you know.'

'Yeah, yeah, yeah. Maybe your mate and Fruity Boy have been the exception to the rule till now. Maybe they really do think they are Mr & Mrs. All I'm saying is, don't worry about all that moral shit. It's different for queers. They think with their pricks.'

'God, you can be disgusting at times.'

There was a pause. Two men with number-one haircuts and jean jackets were staring over in a hostile way.

'Oooh. Get you,' said Nick. 'A fucking fag-hag.' He looked pale and angry, and his glass was empty again – he was knocking them back even by his standards. He didn't notice the two men, who pushed past him when they walked out, pointedly leaving their full drinks on the bar. 'Maybe your mother was right all along. Maybe you'd like to join in with the fun yourself. Rachel used to say –'

'What? What did Rachel say?'

'I mean, she said to me, once, that . . .' Nick seemed unwilling to go on.

'What? That I was useless in bed? That I didn't really fancy girls?' Stephen felt his nausea return.

'No, mate, no. Calm down. I'm sorry. I mean it. Don't take me too seriously. I just say that stuff for a laugh. I'm sure your mate Vinnie is a really good bloke, for a poof. Sorry. Look, cheer up. Please. Let's have another.'

Glasses recharged, they drank again. Stephen realized he had already lost count. Nick looked as if he didn't care. With the sudden sharpness of vision that sometimes comes during the early stages of drunkenness, Stephen realized how bad Nick looked. The frown lines between his swooping black brows, always plain to see, were deep furrows as he dragged on his cigarette. His dark hair needed cutting, and straggled into his eyes. And his nails were bitten ragged. He wondered if he was still as widely fancied now as he had been at college. It seemed unlikely.

'Look at us both,' said Stephen. He patted Nick on the shoulder. 'I'm sorry. It's just that . . . I hate to think of Vinnie being hurt. On top of all the other traumas we're having, at Earthsea. This whole splitting-up thing is driving me over the edge. Till today, I thought Rachel was seeing Kris. Now it turns out she isn't, but she still seems to –'

'Seems to what?'

'I don't know. Not to want me. We nearly . . . nearly touched last time I saw her . . . But then this old schoolfriend of mine phoned on the mobile, and . . . then it was too late.'

'You're well shot of her,' said Nick firmly.

'She's certainly gone a bit hyper,' agreed Stephen.

Nick put his arm around his shoulders. 'What we need,

mate, is something to cheer us up,' he said. 'A project. Ideally, one which gives us access to nubile nymphets.'

Stephen froze, wondering if he was about to propose another trip to the lap-dancing club. But Nick was staring contemplatively at the row of pumps behind the bar. 'Something like a good party,' he said, at last. 'Not a "select gathering" that sucks arse. A proper bash. Rock and roll – the works.'

'Sounds fair enough,' said Stephen.

'Tell you what,' said Nick. 'It's my fortieth next month – September eleventh, would you believe. I was thinking of just curling up with a bottle of vodka and watching women's wrestling on Sky. But I could have a party instead.'

'Great idea,' said Stephen, imagining himself talking to a lot of backs.

'Invite some foxy ladies. Don't exactly have tons of close friends in Brighton – been here less than a year, of course. But you know me. Always could rustle up enough people for a good party.'

Stephen nodded, remembering that this was indeed true. In spite of Nick's rather solitary status at college, his parties had always been legendary.

'Could ask all kinds of people. Go for the universal approach, see who pitches up.'

'Right.'

'You're about ready for a new flame, wouldn't you say? After all you've been through with Rachel?'

'Give me a break. She only kicked me out in April.'

'But you'd come? Get off your face, in time-honoured fashion? Dance with some top totty, carefully selected by me and Ian?'

'Sure. Yes. That would be . . . just the thing.'

'Good one. Just what you need, you see, Steve. You're spending too much time either tearing yourself up over Rachel or playing gooseberry with our homosexual friends. When did you last have a shag?'

'Don't be so crass. As if I'm in the mood to sleep around.'

'There you are. I rest my case. No wonder you're behaving like a prat.'

Next day, Stephen dashed to the bathroom just as Vinnie was emerging, hair rumpled, wearing only black boxer shorts.

'Good night, was it?' he said.

'Erm. Yup,' said Stephen, striving for a normal, cheery tone. It was sod's law that he and Vinnie should meet outside the Bathroom of Sin.

'Glad to hear it. Let me know when you've got a window of opportunity to drop in at work again. Hate to impose on such a sought-after man-about-town as yourself – I know you've got a busy social life and all that.'

'Yes. Okay. I'm really sorry. I'll be in this morning.'

'Good. Because there's that bit of unfinished business to talk about. You know. Small matter of us both going to the wall.' Stephen thought of saying something about Fay and the review, but couldn't get the right words sorted out in his head. It was possible that Vinnie wouldn't see this as such a godsend, anyway. Somehow, Stephen needed to give the information the right kind of spin, and he wasn't up to that now.

It took him longer than he had hoped to get himself

together. Hangovers were part of his new life, but each one seemed to be slightly different and it was hard to get the better of them. This one seemed to have scraped out the inside of his head. Everything confused him. Breakfast didn't really help. It took him ten minutes to decide that he wasn't well enough to eat Coco Krispies and make himself a slice of toast instead. Another fifteen minutes went by while he waited for the kettle to boil, then realized he hadn't switched it on. Afterwards, he showered and lathered himself with as much of Marc's expensive soap as possible. Even that didn't help. His nostrils were too fouled-up with Nick's fags for the aroma of Eau Sauvage to make much difference. Downstairs again, he scanned the *Independent* for news about the war against terrorism, trying to feel like a sensible world citizen with global concerns. But he still felt as if his head had been turned inside out then heated in a microwave. Just as he was about to set out for Earthsea, and taking a few preparatory sips of painful Evian water, the phone rang.

'Stephen, it's me,' said a thick voice.

'Erm, who's me?' asked Stephen, wishing his brain would start connecting again.

'Carmel.'

'Right.' He waited for a second, wondering if she was going to add anything to this information. Was she testing him, leaving dead air on the phone to see whether he was capable of filling it up with touchy-feely words? 'Is there anything . . . wrong?' he asked, tentatively. A silent Carmel was a scary thing.

'Could say that,' said Carmel, even more thickly. 'Need to see you.'

'God,' said Stephen. 'Things must be bad. What about tomorrow night?'

'Need to see you this morning. Meet you in the Grand, eleven o'clock.'

'Okay,' said Stephen. 'Only, I need to go into work after that. And I hope you aren't trying to sort my bloody life out . . .' But when he put the receiver down, he realized that this was unlikely: Carmel sounded as if her own life was in worse shape than his own.

He felt a bit guilty as he hurried along the seafront to the Grand. It was a beautiful day: the sea was a shifting, glossy, cobalt blue, and delicate clouds were strewn across the sky like expensive shreds of underwear tossed around a room. Carmel must be having some kind of crisis, and yet he hadn't been able to put his grotty-younger-brother persona to one side, he realized. It was hard to ignore their shared history. Not only had Carmel always excelled academically, while he bumped along doing reasonably well, relying on late-night revision and the ability to turn a nice phrase, she had also done better at Sex. Someone always fancied Carmel, whether she was straight or gay. Her relationships tended to last, and sounded unreasonably torrid, though she did not go in for bedroom revelations. And, once she had come out, he had been amazed how many of her girlfriends had been good-looking, though he was ashamed to admit this, even to himself. He had never *really* thought that lesbians were a bunch of moustachioed hermaphrodites in baggy dungarees. Not really. Most of her lovers had cropped Hackney hairdos (shaved up the back but sprouty on top), chain-smoked rollies, wore biker jackets and had a host of well-advertised insecurities. Stephen found them rather raffish and charming.

He crossed the road just by the Palace Pier and had a sudden memory of himself and Carmel in their teens. Just before they all left for university, Fay Cattermole – heading for Cambridge, of course – had organized another Event. As with the fondue evening, this was an event which involved food. This time she had invited her fellow sixth-formers to a Chinese breakfast, somewhere in Hanley, though he never could find the exact same place again. He remembered the torture of trying to get the fragments of Peking duck into his mouth – using chopsticks – while simultaneously smiling winningly at Fay, who had seemed rather put out to find herself sitting opposite him when she had invited twenty other people. He remembered her eyes, cruelly navy around the edges, her small, neat mouth glooping up the shiny noodles. Presumably Carmel had also been getting on her nerves: she was sitting at her right hand and was struggling even more pathetically with her chopsticks than he was. In fact, he recalled now, Fay had had to hold Carmel's hands to help her manoeuvre them.

When he got to the Grand, he crossed the marble-floored vestibule and looked around the bar with its grand piano and high, vaulted ceilings, looking for his sister. At first, he didn't realize she was the scruffy figure sitting alone at a table near the window. It was hard to believe that her image was usually that of an international IT entrepreneur with a lesbian twist, whose suits were made to measure and whose haircuts were nearly as expensive as Bill Clinton's. She was sitting hunched up in a high-backed leather chair, looking like a bag lady who had wandered in from the cold, and wearing what looked like a dirty old anorak. By her side was a battered canvas hold-all. Stephen tried to imagine what event could have been so terrible that it had made her unable to locate a single one of her calfskin suitcases, which accompanied her on her frequent foreign trips like a set of Russian dolls. Then he saw that she had a tall clear drink in front of her – clearly not lemonade. Obviously, if she was boozing, he would be obliged to join in. He faltered, as if literally standing at the top of a slippery slope, then bent down and kissed her. Her face was cold and wet, and she smelled strongly of gin.

'Stephen,' she said. 'Thank you for coming. I won't keep you long.' The formality of her tone made him feel more guilty than ever.

'God, don't worry about that. I was being a prat on the phone . . .' He sat down in the seat next to her. 'Just tell me what's the matter.'

'Hard to find the . . .' Carmel gazed at him unhappily. 'I suppose this is what it feels like to be lonely.'

'Lonely? You know more people than anyone! You know bloody *everybody*! How can you be lonely?'

Carmel shrugged. 'It's a state of mind, I suppose,' she said. 'When you aren't . . . connected to the people you need.'

'But you've got the people you need! All your friends, all the people you work with . . . Lise, of course . . .'

'Yeah, right,' said Carmel. 'Lise.'

Stephen was at the outer limits of his ability here. He could tell there were loads of things he should say, questions he should ask. But he didn't know where to start. 'Shall we get a drink?' he asked. 'Only, I can see you are ahead of me, and if I'm going to have something alcoholic I need to psyche myself up.'

'I'm on double gin and tonics,' said Carmel. 'I've put my credit card behind the bar – put everything on there.'

'Wow. Serious stuff.' Stephen nodded, and waved at a waiter who was polishing glasses and watching himself in a vast ornate mirror. The waiter pirouetted towards them, camp in an uncompromising way that Nick would have enjoyed ridiculing.

When they had ordered drinks, Carmel gave a sort of shake, as if resigning herself to saying what had to be said. 'Okay. This is what it is. I expect you'll think it's quite funny. After all, I've been so much the expert on your relationship, and why it's gone wrong. You'll probably think it's just what I deserve.'

'Don't be silly,' said Stephen. 'Why would I think it's funny? I'm not your bloody enemy!'

'Maybe not. But I'm a lesbian – and I came out when you'd been with Rachel for years. I can't help thinking that you and Mum are still waiting for me to come out of this funny phase. Deep down, you think it's weird that I have sex with women.'

'That's complete bollocks! And it's actually really insulting. Why lump me in with Mum? She's a fucking recovering homophobe.'

For years, Rose had indulged in tears and tantrums relating to Carmel's immortal soul, and had come out with phrases like 'All I'm saying is that you're storing up trouble for yourself' and, more enigmatically, 'It can't end well – look at Dirk Bogarde.' But now she had adopted a strained truce in relation to Carmel's sexual orientation, putting

237

on what Carmel called her 'lesbian-lifestyle face' when confronted with uncomfortable realities like Lise and Carmel's double bed.

Carmel raised her shoulders again, and dropped them dolefully. 'I just don't think you'll understand.'

'Bit of a waste of time asking to see me then, isn't it?' said Stephen. 'I should be at work, finding out how deep in the red we are.'

Carmel agitated the ice in her glass to a fairyland tinkle. 'You know about me and babies,' she said.

'You mean the way you always ask to be moved in restaurants if there are any hideous children near your table? And your super little catchphrase "Thank *God* I haven't got kids!" I think I've got a pretty good idea where you stand on that one.'

'Yes, well. I couldn't put it better myself. Nappy-changing is for losers. The trouble is, Lise has decided she's feeling broody.'

'Broody? I thought the two of you were singing from the same adults-only hymn sheet.'

'So did I. So did I! But now – for about the last six months – she's decided that she isn't a "complete woman". Becoming a fucking mum is her new obsession. It's as if she's had a personality transplant – all she talks about is Baby, Baby, Baby!'

'But she knows you will never have children. Doesn't she?'

'Of course she does.'

'So why don't you . . . just chuck her out?'

'Oh, thanks, Stephen! Thank you for your concern! "Just chuck her out" – is this the same person who was crying on my shoulder about Rachel recently? Your relationship is serious; mine is just some vague shacking-up between dykes. Is that it?'

'Now, hang on a minute. I'm married. I'm already burdened with fucking progeny. I've made my bed, and I have to lie on it – without having any sex. Or so I thought. You are the lesbian champion of easy love. You are the person who set up a bloody dating agency so that gay people can move on to a new lover if they feel bored . . . Monogamy is fine for swans. Another of your catchphrases. Isn't it? Isn't it?'

Carmel said nothing, but took another swig from her glass. Stephen pressed on. 'Once the passion is over, the relationship is over? That's what you always say. But now you think you and Lise can survive Pampers, playgroups, fucking parents' night? *Do you?*'

'No.'

'Then why aren't you going to chuck her out?'

'Because I love her.'

'What?'

'It's more than passion. It's something for life.'

Stephen was speechless. He thought of Carmel the emotional buccaneer, Carmel who was touched by no one, Carmel who always had someone new. 'Too late now, though,' said Carmel. '*She*'s left *me*.'

'Oh. I'm sorry. You mean . . . For another woman?'

'She's left me for a bloody man! No need for IVF now! They've been together for two weeks and her period is late already. She's probably pregnant even as we speak.' A tear rolled slowly down Carmel's cheek, and plopped on to her neck.

Stephen stroked Carmel's shoulder, thinking of the kind little pats Elsie had given him when he and Rachel had argued in the hall. Then, suddenly, he felt that he was lucky. His own words came floating back to him: 'I'll always be their dad.' And he realized with a soaring joy that this really was true. When Carmel leaned over and hugged him, he found himself saying 'Don't worry, baby; don't worry, baby' over and over again. What with the morning gin and the hangover lying beneath it, he probably wasn't thinking clearly. But, somehow, he had the feeling that he was in the thick of life. And, although he didn't know why, the idea of Rachel had begun to loosen its hold. He had started to accept that the only life he could lead was a different one, a life-after-Rachel. 'We'll sort it all out somehow,' he said, stroking her hair, as she sobbed, helpless and heavy, in his arms.

'We haven't even talked about you,' sobbed Carmel, into his shoulder.

'There's nothing to be done about me,' he said. 'It's different for you and Lise. I can't believe she really wants a man. Not with that hairstyle.' He tried to imagine what Nick would make of a woman who shaved her head for aesthetic reasons.

'I wouldn't be too sure,' said the waiter, topping up their glasses with tonic water. 'Swapping sides is very now. I've got a wife and two kids in Market Harborough.'

17

When Stephen returned to the restaurant, after leaving Carmel on her third drink, he found that Nick had been true to his word. He was obviously determined to have plenty of guests. Not only had he been to the kitchen and personally invited the entire staff of Earthsea, none of whom he had ever met before, but he had also given everyone migraine-inducing, seventies-style invitations with 'NICK IS FORTY! IN THE BEST POSSIBLE TASTE (NOT)' inscribed on them in luminous orange and pus-green lettering. At the top of the invitation were lurid pictures of Mary Whitehouse and Kenny Everett – the latter sporting a feather boa, suspenders and little else. Presumably the fact that both were dead added to their cachet as superstars of naff. Underneath, Nick had written: 'It's time to cast off your mental chains, stick your caution where the sun don't shine and get ready to groove. Rocker, shocker, ex-punk or housewife superstar, the place to be on Saturday September 14th from 10 till dawn is the Rotunda Café, Preston Park. Theme: bad taste. Dress: nauseatingly. Booze: bring a crate (pina coladas provided). Sex: yeah, baby.' Below this Nick had listed his array of contact numbers, pagers, emails and faxes – the only clue that he was an estate agent. Stephen wondered if he had invited the hapless Keith. Probably. There was an atmosphere of unstoppable recklessness around Nick at the moment. It

241

was hard to imagine him feeling too embarrassed to do anything. He clearly wasn't getting much work done, either. He must have spent hours designing and delivering this missive. His party idea had certainly taken him over. Stephen himself hadn't managed to work up such a head of steam over a social event since his twenties.

'Are you going?' he asked Vinnie.

'Yeah, baby,' said Vinnie, but not in a very convincing way. 'Looks like a fucking shifty bloke, but I've got to have something to look forward to, haven't I?'

Stephen didn't dare speak in case he was forced to blurt out revelations concerning bathrooms, tiny hand towels or bloated torsos, like someone with Tourette's syndrome. He satisfied himself with: 'Mmm.'

Vinnie looked at him irritably. 'You certainly took your time. It's almost lunchtime.'

'I've been seeing Carmel.'

'Oh yeah? How's she?'

'She's . . .' Shit. She's been betrayed. She's been left in the lurch for someone totally unsuitable. She's been shat on from a great height, like certain other people I know. 'She's okay. Few work problems,' said Stephen.

'Is that all? Sounded pretty bad to me. She phoned here wanting to speak to you. Sounded like her whole life was falling apart.'

'Work *is* Carmel's life,' Stephen blustered on. 'You know all the trouble Internet companies are having now. Hers will survive – she thinks – but she's certainly lost a lot of business.' He was reminded of Nick's bizarre performance in the pub. Why had he started spinning a yarn to Vinnie? How was that going to help?

Vinnie looked at him, unimpressed. 'So, did you tell her all about you and Rachel? The continuing saga?'

'No. I . . . we mainly talked about Carmel.'

'About her completely boring work problems, rather than the fact your wife can't stand the sight of you any more.'

'Erm, yes.'

'You're a crap liar, Stephen. It's probably your most loveable feature. So Lise's dumped Carmel.'

'Yes.'

'Why?'

'Something to do with having kids. Lise wants them, Carmel doesn't.'

This seemed to cheer Vinnie up for some reason. He laughed mirthlessly. 'Fucking women!' he said. 'I've met that Lise woman – what? Three times? – and all she did was bang on about what a pain in the arse it would be to have children. Inconsistent or what.' He rubbed his thin hands in his eyes. When he took them away, Stephen saw that he had managed to make the purple sockets even darker and deeper. 'As we're nearly on the subject of boring work crap, let's have this conversation about the business that you keep trying to avoid,' he said, finally.

They trudged downstairs to the basement. If Vinnie really had got to grips with the minutiae of Earthsea's financial predicament, Stephen couldn't quite work out why he had failed to notice that they had acquired £30,000 from some unknown source. The fact that Vinnie clearly had no idea about this floating sum made him doubt whether any of his other calculations were worth worrying

243

about. As usual, Stephen's impulse was to not simply ignore the tedious issue of finance but to actively Not Think About It, as an act of will.

But it turned out that Vinnie's calculations didn't need to be that thorough to be credible. Without even turning on the computer, Vinnie indicated a pile of bills that lay on his desk. 'It's not rocket science, Steve,' he said. He paged through the pile, tossing each bill on to the floor as he talked. 'Look. Tomato man. Wine man. Cosima Fine Pastries. Fucking olive-oil man. Gas bastards. Water wankers. Laundry. Business rates. Need I go on? Not a single one of this lot has been paid for two months. And here –' he leaned down and fished a piece of paper from the seat of his office chair – 'is what we in the trade call a bank statement, Stephen. I don't know if you've ever come across one before?'

Stephen made one of his teenage mooing noises, calculated to reveal nothing. When he was at college, he had failed to open a bank statement for three years. Acquiring taste had proved an expensive business, and involved hanging out with people posher than him, who spent money on eating out and drinking wine that was a little more expensive than Black Tower or Blue Nun. Worse still, he had discovered a delicatessen in Blackheath in his second year. He must have been one of the few students at Goldsmith's who had run up an overdraft because of a taste for truffles and stuffed olives rather than Stella Artois. When he finally decided he had to face facts, he had to drink most of a bottle of grappa before looking inside one of those terrifying white envelopes. He still remembered the giddying sight of the black figures giving the total sum of his overdraft – £949.67. This was an unimaginable amount, comparable to the national debt. Perhaps this trauma had done him lasting damage. Perhaps this was why, to this day, he never opened any similar envelopes without hyperventilating.

Seeing that Stephen wasn't going to reply, Vinnie said, 'We are more than £32,000 overdrawn, and our takings have dropped, month on month, since the beginning of the year. Now, we can sit down at the computer and go over this in depth, but I don't really see the point. Unless you can come up with a brilliant rescue plan right now – like, this minute – then we may as well go upstairs and tell the staff to go home. Because we've got nothing to pay them with.'

'I see,' said Stephen. 'I must admit, things are a bit worse than I thought.' The reality still hadn't sunk in – did this mean his house would be repossessed? His family homeless? Vaguely, it occurred to him that he should sign the house over to Rachel so she and the children would have somewhere to live, even if they didn't have anything to eat. It was ironic that this was what she had asked for at the outset, and what he had objected to so strongly. But it also crossed his mind that it was about time that Rachel found herself a proper job, rather than counselling warring couples for 5 pence an hour – what a joke that was! – or cooing over swatches of designer fabric with expensive housewives who – after wasting weeks of her time – usually decided to use another interior designer with more experience or a double-barrelled name. She had two jobs, but a negligible income.

'You still don't look depressed enough,' said Vinnie.

'We're fucked, man. Does that mean anything to you? It's finished, *finito*. Up in smoke.'

'Of course it means something to me. This place is all I've got. But . . . I just don't believe it's that bad. We're always busy, aren't we?'

'Not busy enough. We need ten times the amount of trade, just to break even. We are in the shit. How many times do I have to say that to convince you?'

'There's got to be a way out.'

'Yeah, well, perhaps you'd like to tell me what it is. Because, I'll tell you this, if I didn't have Marc to keep me going, I'd fucking top myself tomorrow. It's closing in on me here, but at least I've got another life.'

'Don't be stupid, Vinnie,' said Stephen quickly. He shuffled the remark to one side. Vinnie was tougher than he was. Vinnie had always been tougher than he was. And if Marc and he did split up, he would find someone better. 'Of course I'm not amused. But I do have one more idea. It could help. It could even turn this place around.'

'Oh really? Amaze me.'

'Well, you know I met that old schoolfriend when I was in Stoke?'

'The one you've got the hots for?'

'Well, I used to. You know she works for the *Carbuncle*, that trendy arts magazine? It's all about modernism, being cutting edge, anti-Prince Charles traditionalism, that sort of thing.'

'I've got no idea what you're on about, but – yeah? – keep going.'

'Well, they're doing these restaurant reviews where food

246

and art are connected. And she's offered to do one here, as long as we can get an artist who's really radical and different. Then she'll review the food, and some arts person with a very strange name will review the art. It could cause a sensation. Some producer from Channel Four is interested in a series picking up on the idea. We could be celebrities. Everyone in the whole country would have heard of Earthsea.' Stephen was now exaggerating wildly.

Vinnie's expression was sceptical, but not hostile. 'What's the circulation of this exciting magazine – which I've never heard of, incidentally?'

'Huge – half a million or something,' said Stephen, who had no idea.

'Right.' Vinnie picked up one of the bills and stared at it for a moment. 'May as well give it a try,' he said. 'As long as we get plenty of warning. I don't fancy your friend turning up like some mystery shopper, picking all the stuff we've fucking run out of then slagging us off. Or coming in on one of our special nights when two of the staff decide to terminate their relationship just before the nine o'clock rush. That would be all we needed.'

'I'm not sure how we avoid that,' said Stephen. 'As we have no way of knowing in advance who is going to split up.'

'We'd just use our A-team on the night. Bit of warning and we could make sure that only the sensible, fire-proof people are doing the shift. On the minus side, even if she says we're running the best restaurant going I doubt if it'll be the answer to all our problems.'

Before Stephen could answer, a creamy, catty voice

came from the doorway. 'I know an artist who would be just right.' It was Marc, who had obviously been eavesdropping on the conversation in case Stephen revealed anything incriminating.

'Marc! What are you doing, creeping about the place? I thought you were at work,' said Vinnie. He rushed over and kissed him, full on the lips. Marc had the grace to look a bit bashful, and avoided Stephen's eye.

'Who did you have in mind?' said Stephen in a neutral voice.

'*Tiny* dyke who works in our shop sometimes,' said Marc. He twirled into the room, perched his large bottom on Vinnie's desk, and stuck his chunky legs out in front of him, feet crossed. This gave him the opportunity to scrutinize his feet. 'What do you think of these boots? I just got them. Too butch-without-a-twist?' he inquired of Vinnie, who peered closely at them, then shrugged.

'They look great on you. Sexy,' he said. To Stephen, they looked like hiking boots from Millets – but who was he to judge? Male fashion was something that happened at some distance from his Marks & Spencer's shirts and trousers, and this still worried him. He thought of the white shirts he'd sported at Goldsmith's, and the Kandinsky one he'd been looking at in the Lanes. Maybe he should buy it, just assume that it was tasteful, and branch out. He'd trained his palate, but not his eye, and was led blindly by Rachel when it came to choosing colours or knowing how things should look. Now he was on his own with his lack of visual awareness.

'What made you think of this woman?' he asked. It was hard not to be suspicious.

'Doesn't make a lot of money, but she's good,' said Marc, keeping his eyes on his new boots. 'She had an exhibition at Bag, that new place at Seven Dials. Does installations and stuff – very abstract. Sort of Jackson Pollock meets Frances Bacon, dear, if those names mean anything to you. And the reason I thought of her is that she's just finishing a whole load of stuff about food.' He smirked at Vinnie. Was all this just a ploy to impress his boyfriend with his fashionable arty contacts? Surely not: Vinnie was immune to all things artsy. Stephen scrutinized Marc's face, frustrated that not trusting someone didn't automatically provide any insight into their motives. But he didn't know any artists in Brighton, and the work he'd seen confused him. Everyone else in the town raved about the amazing quality of the stuff shown by open houses during the arts festival each May. However, when he had wandered round a few, the work he saw was mainly watercolours of fruit and flowers in pretty jars, which reminded him of something the Women's Institute might display in a village hall. That didn't seem at all the sort of thing that would impress Erika Perspecua. Whereas a Jackson Pollock approach to food might go down very well indeed. And he had no time to do any research. He would have to take a chance.

'Okay,' he said. 'Shall we go for it, Vin?'

'Yeah. Yeah, let's give it a try. And in the meantime, I'm going to do another special offer on the organic wine. Should get a few extra tight-bastard vegans through the door.' Looking almost happy, Vinnie went over to Marc and leaned his elbow on his shoulder.

'Let's go for it, then. What's her name?' asked Stephen.

'Gillian Smale,' said Marc, moueing a little silent kiss at his lover. 'I'll get on the blower right away.'

It turned out that Fay needed to do her lap-dancing piece for the following week's issue of the *Carbuncle*, and so a few days later Stephen found himself on the way to the club once more. He had arranged to meet Fay in a pub in Western Road; waiting there for her, he sat watching his reflection in the black window and wondering what the evening might have in store. When Fay finally walked in she looked frighteningly beautiful, her features brighter and more contrasting than he remembered. It occurred to him that perhaps she was nervous, and this made him more nervous still. Her hair was pulled up and pinned on top, and dark-red curls sprung from the top of her head. She wore a long brown leather coat, with big seventies lapels. Very *Carbuncle*, he assumed, and obviously expensive.

'Stephen,' she said. She bent down and kissed him. He was careful to have no physical reaction to this. It was just a middle-class girl thing, this kissing – he'd been around people who didn't have fitted carpets long enough to know that. She waved away his offer of a drink. 'Let's go to work,' she said, pulling a face that indicated that both of them were *au fait* with references to *Reservoir Dogs*.

'I still don't know if they'll let you in,' said Stephen as they strode along the street. He noticed with another deliberate lack of male response that she was exactly the same height as he was, in her flat shoes.

'Don't worry about that,' said Fay. 'Just watch me.'

It was an impressive performance. Stephen had no idea

what she said to the girl on the door – it was the same girl who had been there on his first visit – nor whether any extra money had changed hands. But it seemed that a bit of muttering and smiling were all that was required. Yet more proof that he had been right not to go into journalism in his youth – he had never smiled and chatted his way into anything. In the eighties, people he didn't know very well used to do something called 'ligging', which appeared to involve getting into clubs without paying (though he could never be sure and didn't like to ask). He had never ligged. He was born not to lig.

And yet, he thought, sitting at a table and ordering drinks from the semi-nude, semi-attractive waitress, here he was. Visiting Sin City with the most impressive woman he had ever known. In a way, he was for one evening part of the metropolitan media. It was a heady thought. But his satisfaction was short lived. Fay had whipped something out of her handbag which he soon realized was a mini tape-recorder. 'I'll leave this here for a bit,' she said, propping it up on the table between their bottles of lager. 'The music's quite low at the moment – it should pick our voices up without any problem.'

'Why do you want it to pick up our voices?' said Stephen, trying not to sound hysterical. 'You're not going to interview *me*, are you?'

'Don't be silly!' laughed Fay. 'Of course I'm going to interview you. You're the punter – part of a trend. New men who've suddenly realized that there is nothing shameful or sleazy about lap-dancing.'

Stephen nearly choked on his lager. 'Now hang on a minute!' he spluttered. 'First, I'm not a new man. My wife would be very amused to hear you say that. And second, of course lap-dancing is sleazy. It's a bloody disgrace. Just look at this place – it's hell on earth.' They looked around at the small circular tables, the *faux* antique, wood-effect chairs and the marauding waitresses in their tacky outfits, white breasts nearly exposed by their red net basques. In reality, it looked far too mundane to be hell on anywhere. 'I thought that was what you wanted,' said Stephen, trying hard to normalize his tone. 'If it wasn't sleazy, it wouldn't fit into your feature, would it? You don't need me to be in the feature; you just needed me to bring you here.'

Fay frowned, and then looked down. He had the sudden, chilling impression that she was trying not to laugh, and when she spoke her voice was full of suppressed something. Whether it was amusement or annoyance, he couldn't tell. 'Stephen. Please. I don't want to come on like Kate Adie here, but I have worked in Bosnia, you know,' she said. 'And Belfast – *before* the ceasefire. Colour pieces. Real lives, comfort food for the newly bereaved, the role of lipstick in a war zone. You know the sort of thing. I'm a real journalist. Do you seriously think that I couldn't get into a suburban lap-dancing club without a big strong man to hold my hand?'

Stephen shrugged. 'I just don't want to be interviewed. I'm sorry. I really don't have anything to say. I'm not a proper punter. I've only been here once . . . You should talk to some of these other –' He was about to gesture towards the yobby lager-swillers who filled the other tables, when another waitress appeared. She was carrying a bottle of champagne. 'What's this?' asked Stephen, incredulous. 'We didn't order . . .'

'On the house,' said the girl, placing two flutes beside their beer glasses. 'Compliments from Robbie. Says he's glad to see you in here again – and one of the girls would love to see you for a one-to-one. And he said to say that Gabrielle is in tonight.'

'What's a one-to-one?' asked Fay.

'Oh, you want to ask your boyfriend that,' said the girl, giggling to reveal slightly uneven teeth. 'It's what they all really come here for.'

Stephen was wordless as the waitress moved away, and Fay filled his glass. It was like one of the frequent dreams he had, in which disaster loomed and he wanted to run, even thought he *was* running, but found that his legs were immobile. 'Now, Stephen,' said Fay, in a firm, real journalist's voice. 'I'm so grateful for all your help so far, but we've got to stop playing around. We've agreed that you'll do me a favour, and I'll do something for you in return. We're old friends. No one is standing in judgement. No one's being politically correct. You like it here, and that's nothing to be ashamed of. Really.' She leaned forward and gave him the most perfect slice of a smile. 'Before you tell me about Gabrielle, let's talk about what *first* attracted you to the world of lap-dancing.'

18

Stephen's head was spinning. He was baffled – and felt the familiar fizzing sensation that heralded the onset of a panic attack. How could he avoid being interviewed by Fay without running away? He looked blankly at her professionally smiling face, all efficient edges and veiled impatience, wondering how he had managed to get into this without realizing he was getting into this. He looked wildly at the silently turning tape in the machine. He looked wildly across the bar.

'Nothing attracts me to lap-dancing,' he said at last, desperately. 'It's sexist, it's boring, it exploits women, it makes idiots of men, turns us into animals. It's just . . .' Then he saw her. Gabrielle, dancing her sexist, boring, exploitative dance. A wriggling simulation of sexual desire, first nearer to one table, then to another. 'It's just . . .' Hair swirling across her face. Tossed back to show her pert features, her dark eyes. She wasn't laughing tonight. His body seemed to swerve downwards, he gripped the edge of the table, then clawed his way to his cigarettes. Just like his dreams. Her breasts seemed to have a life of their own, seemed to be racing towards him across the tables, two perfect white orbs, dark nipples chasing after him like heat-seeking missiles. They knew. She knew. Everyone knew. His middle-class erection rose under the table, just like all the working-class ones all around him. He felt blank-faced passivity descend on his features, a mask of wanting, in spite of all his not wanting to want. He saw, without realizing he was seeing, Fay take a notebook out of her bag and start scribbling in it, watching him, like an artist taking sketches for a painting. He knew that Gabrielle hadn't seen him yet. And, somehow, he knew that she wasn't expecting him to be there. Why this should be an issue at all, given that she had only seen him twice, did not concern him. Neither did the fact that on the basis of these two meetings she had appeared to take a strong dislike to him. Stephen knew that she would be affected by his presence, just as clearly as he knew he would never seduce Fay Cattermole and that he and Rachel would never have sex again. As he stared across the bar at Gabrielle and Fay scribbled, hard-faced, at his side, it really did seem as though his sense of their connectedness was based in fact. Because she suddenly swung around, in the midst of a complex gyration next to a tableful of sales boys in identical blue shirts, and looked straight at him, as if she had felt his gaze physically. And, instead of carrying on with her dance, which was going down extremely well with the baying youths, she abruptly left the room, almost running out of a side door and disappearing into the darkness.

Fay was looking at him, shaking her head. Her eyes were glinting with malicious amusement. Notebook in hand, she had seen it all – both his reaction to Gabrielle and Gabrielle's startled response to him. 'Well, fucking Nora,' she said in her distinctly posh voice. 'I think your cover as a lap-dancing *ingénue* has been blown, Mr Beckett. I presume that is the girl the waitress was talking about. You are clearly having an affair with that poor, exploited young woman. This feature should be very interesting indeed.'

'Oh, for Christ's sake!' Stephen got to his feet. 'This was all a terrible mistake. I'm sorry I suggested it, sorry I brought you here. I'm going. You can stay if you like – draw on all your experience in Beirut or wherever it was. You don't need me. Or, if you have enough material for your exposé, we can share a cab.'

'I'll stay,' said Fay, taking a sip of her beer. (She hadn't touched the champagne.)

'Fine.' He turned on his heel and was about to leave, desperate to get away from Gabrielle, from the prospect of seeing her again, sick at heart at his stupid aspirations to be fancied by Fay. But, before he reached the brightly lit doorway leading to the outside world, a hand fell on his shoulder.

'Gotcha!'

He looked down at the hand, and then at the face. It was Nick. 'You old rogue,' he said, speaking to Stephen but looking with approval at Fay, who was regarding them both coolly from her seat. 'Not only here again, but here again with a delightful young lady. And not only here with a delightful young lady, but drinking champagne as well. Looks like life as a recently chucked-out man-about-town suits you, mate.'

Stephen took Nick's hand away. 'I was just leaving, as a matter of fact,' he said. 'You haven't caught me at a very good time, to be honest. But I can introduce you to Fay, if you like. She's staying. And she's not my girlfriend. She's someone I knew at school. Who's a journalist, so watch what you say.'

'Oh come on, mate! Ian's with me – and someone else you know . . . Don't be a pain in the arse; come and join us!'

Stephen paused, torn between the alluring sight of the exit and the worrying concept of Nick and Fay getting together and cooking up he knew not what. It occurred to him that Nick might make a far better subject for her feature than he would, but in his absence he had no idea what Nick might say. Incriminating, inaccurate stuff that would confirm Stephen as a pathetic sex-trade addict, perhaps. Safer, then, to hang around for a bit longer. Probably Gabrielle would lie low till he had gone, which was good. There was no need for him to ever know why the sight of him had caused her to run out like that. No need to ever ask, or to think about it again. But, looking across at the table that Nick was indicating, he finally decided he should stay. Sitting next to Ian, looking extremely lugubrious and very drunk, was none other than Clive, the most happily married man he knew.

'Steve. Oh. Shit,' were Clive's first words as Fay was introduced, hands shaken and tables merged. (She was looking very animated and pretty and had, Stephen noticed, put her tape machine away. He knew her well enough now to realize that this was for tactical not moral reasons.)

'What the bloody hell are you doing here?' muttered Stephen as he pulled up a chair next to Clive's.

'Could say same you,' said Clive blurrily.

'No, you damn well couldn't. I'm separated, on the scrap heap and a known associate of Nick's. You, on the other hand, are an upstanding father of four with a pregnant wife. Who you are madly in love with, as far as I can tell. Does Tamzin know about this?'

'Course not. Not speakin' her, currently, any case. Ships in the night, different agendas, not singing from same hymn sheet. Prob divorce when baby comes. Waitress — over here! More 'poo!' yelled Clive. His marital difficulties seemed to have pushed him back a couple of decades, to his wilderness years when he had worked as the ad manager for a double-glazing magazine based in Forest Hill.

Stephen shook his head emphatically at the waitress who was coming their way. But more champagne arrived in any case. Clive put a glass into his hand and filled it. 'This is mad, Clive,' said Stephen, keeping half an eye on Fay and Nick, who were already locked in deep conversation. 'Totally mad. How did you bloody meet him, anyway?'

'Buying buy-to-let flat. Felt so guilty about it that I thought I'd go to Ethical Estate Agency. Sop to conscience. And there he was. My rescuer. Found out we both knew you and — bingo.' He dropped his voice slightly. 'Other bloke a bit weird, though. What's he on about? All this stuff about ladders and seal cubs — can't make head nor tail . . .'

'Steve, mate, hi,' said Ian, who had just reappeared from somewhere. 'You look like a man who's got lost on the way to his execution.'

'You could be on to something there,' said Stephen.

'Just seen a friend of yours,' said Ian. 'No prizes for guessing who.'

'Well, I won't, then.'

'Gabrielle?' asked Fay, leaning across the table.

'The very same,' said Ian. 'And who might you be, beautiful lady? You look like the cheesecake on the hors-d'oeuvres tray to me.'

'I'm a schoolfriend of Stephen's. Who is this mysterious Gabrielle, anyway?' said Fay. Stephen could tell that, though neither her notebook nor her tape machine were on view, everything that was being said was being recorded.

'Some lap-dancer who Nick fancies,' said Ian.

'Not true,' said Nick. 'It's Stephen who's after her. She gave him hell last time he was here. Isn't that right Steve?'

'It was you who jumped on top of her,' said Stephen. 'And it was me who pulled you off. If we're at all interested in the facts.'

'Ah, but the sexual . . .' began Nick, but Fay interrupted him.

'Why are all of you so keen on lap-dancers?' she asked in an innocent voice. 'Are "respectable" –' (here she painted little inverted commas in the air, in the manner of the late Russell Harty) – 'women too boring? Too inhibited? Just not sexy enough?'

'Every man needs . . . an outlet,' said Clive, heavily. 'All that responsibility that's laid on us whole time. Plus, everyone's always on 'bout Men Are Crap. So let's *be* crap. Let's *be* fucking crap, and find an outlet that we can put our crap into . . . It's work/life balance thing.' Fay looked very impressed with this, and cosied up to Clive for an in-depth chat. Stephen regretted that he couldn't hear what they were saying.

'Bloody hell,' muttered Nick into his ear. 'Bit out of your class, Steve, isn't she?'

'Totally,' said Stephen, realizing that he was rather grateful for this.

'What a looker,' said Nick. Then he looked at Stephen as if struck by a bright idea. 'But I wouldn't rule her out. No way. I think she does fancy you. Bit of chemistry there, I reckon. Why don't you invite her along to my party?'

'She'd never come. She lives in Islington. All her friends are called Portia or Milo. Her whole life is like *The Late Review* without the baldies,' said Stephen, although he actually had no idea what Fay's friends were like.

'Still think you-Rachel best people f'reach other,' said Clive, leaning across and looking as if he was on the brink of tears. 'My ol' friends. Fiery but always together. Can't believe there's no way back . . .'

'Well, you'd better believe it,' said Nick.

'Sorry?' said Stephen. 'What's it got to do with you?'

'Hate to see a friend on the ropes the way you've been lately,' said Nick. 'God, this champagne is good. Let's order some more.'

'On me,' said Clive, firmly. 'All I've got is fucking money. May as well spen' it on my dear friends. Bonding session, team-building, put ourselves in new situation.'

'Champagne is lubrication for dry souls starved of the elixir of true friendship,' said Ian. 'Reminds me of something the Ice Maiden said to me around the time I was paying for her second abortion . . .'

'Her wha'?' asked Clive.

'Abortion. Second one. I wasn't the father either time. I was like a baby dodo in a battery farm full of . . .'

'Disgusting,' said Clive. 'Once bad, second totally . . . just ersponsible. Sick. Never consider it.'

'Clive,' began Stephen, 'I thought you were . . .'

'I'm totally against. Totally pro-life. Eugenics, Nazis. Woman's right to choose – choose what? Make selves Unpregnant? Get in fucking time machine, sperm swims backwards? Sorry, no way. Murder baby is all. Child-killing is all.'

'Calm down, mate,' said Ian. 'I'm apolitical. I'm like a general election with just one molecule of Tony Blair left inside it.'

Stephen pulled Clive to one side and hissed in his ear. 'Clive, you're not pro-life! You're in favour of abortion when it's necessary. For God's sake! You're angry with Tamzin because she wants the baby, not because she doesn't.'

'No I'm not!' shouted Clive. 'She wants . . . She had two . . . I said why two? She said, No business of yours. Didn't even know you in those days. Can't remember . . .'

'This time she wants to keep it,' whispered Stephen urgently. 'Her fifth child. Your fifth child. Remember?' But Clive was now knocking back another glass of 'poo and seemed to have forgotten what they were talking about. Nick was watching him, rocked as far back on his chair as he could be without falling over, blowing smoke rings, smiling quietly to himself. Then Stephen realized that Fay had disappeared.

'I think I'll just go and make sure that Fay is . . . okay,' he said.

When Stephen eventually found the ladies', which was hidden down several long and winding corridors, he knocked on the door. 'Fay! Are you all right in there?' he called.

There was no reply. 'Fay?' he called again. Then he tried a few more experimental bangs. Still nothing. After a moment, he gingerly put his head round the door and peered inside the room. There were two rather nasty-looking toilets inside, each of them clearly visible through the open internal doors and obviously empty. He withdrew his head and stood uncertainly for a moment. What should he do? He had a horrible feeling that Fay was up to something troublesome and underhand – digging around for some sex-trade dirt, presumably. Why he had ever thought she would be content to come along and soak up the atmosphere he had no idea. Perhaps it was because he had imagined that Fay had some interest in him. She was interested in him all right, but only as an example of the latest fad to hit confused New Men. Fancy imagining a new life, with a new woman who would replace his failed relationship, instead of trying to bring his family back from the brink! He hesitated for a moment, caught in a sudden hiatus of despair. But wallowing in self-hate wasn't going to help. He needed to find Fay and to persuade her to leave.

He walked along the corridor, knocking on each door. 'Fay? Are you in there? Fay?' he called. But he jumped when her head popped out of a door further ahead of him.

'Stephen! In here! Keep your voice down! I'm doing an interview.'

Oh God. Just as he had thought. He found himself in a small, boxlike, windowless room lined with mirrors and with a low-level shelf running around the walls, covered with cosmetics and squirty bottles and faced by a row of plastic garden chairs. Fay was sitting on one of the chairs, holding her tape machine in her hand, talking quietly to a painfully thin girl wearing a grubby white towelling dressing-gown. The girl had a gaunt, pale face and huge staring eyes, and her cheeks were streaked with tears. 'Then I left me mum, and then me foster mum came after me, and after that I told her about the abuse, and then my mum said I was a lying bitch, and then I went homeless again . . .' she was saying into the machine, unravelling a litany of misery which Stephen could barely hear. Fay gave him a look that told him to sit down and be quiet. 'This is Stephen,' she said to the girl who looked up nervously. 'He works with me. He's very discreet. Stephen, this is Kelly-Marie . . .' Stephen remembered her name from the fraught evening in Earthsea, but not her face.

'I don't mind,' said the girl. 'You get used to doing everything in public in this line of work.'

'So tell me more about Robbie,' said Fay. 'How did he persuade you to come and work at the club?' She shot another warning glance at Stephen, as if expecting him to interrupt.

'Didn't need persuading,' said Kelly-Marie. 'I was so fucking desperate. I'd been staying with these girls in Kings Cross who were both junkies, both on the game, and I met him through one of the punters one night . . . He seemed like a real pussycat to me. Didn't want sex or nothing like that. Gave me the money and then said he wanted to put a business proposition to me . . .'

'Which was?'

'That I could get a proper job, in showbusiness, and leave all that other stuff behind . . .'

'And did you leave all that other stuff behind?'

Kelly-Marie paused, staring miserably at her false nails.

'Sweetie, I don't want to push you, but this is an interview. That does involve you telling me things. Silence only works on TV.'

Still, Kelly-Marie was silent.

Fay sighed, and rolled her eyes at Stephen. He looked away, embarrassed. 'Look,' she said at last, taking the girl's limp hand. 'Tell me about a typical day. What's the first thing you think about when you wake up in the morning?'

'I don't know. I . . .'

'Come on. The sun's pouring through your window. It's another day in the life of a respectable lap-dancer. What do you think about?'

The girl seemed to gulp in too much air, or to be unable to take in enough. Something was wrong, in any case. Her face contorted, and then collapsed into itself. 'I can't . . . I can't . . .' She stood up, half turned and collapsed on to the floor, sobbing. 'I can't do it any more!' she said, at first barely audibly. Then her voice built and built in volume. 'I can't. I *can't*!' And she began to cry so loudly that her sobs sounded like screams, her breath came in great wrenches and she contorted herself into a foetal position, her hands pressed over the back of her head, as if she was being attacked. 'I can't do it any more! I can't do it any more! I want my mum! *Somebody fetch my mum*!'

'God! She's a fucking nutcase!' said Fay. Instead of going to comfort the weeping Kelly-Marie, she got up and stood behind her chair.

'Jesus Christ!' Stephen felt physically sick at the street-accident suddenness of the change. He leaped to his feet, wanting to run towards the girl but finding he couldn't. He reached out his arms towards her, took a solitary step, and the door flew open and another dancer ran into the room.

'Kelly-Marie! What's wrong? What's going on? Who are these —?' She looked from Fay to Stephen. 'You!' she said, giving him a piercing look. 'Now you see what happens when you bring your bloody nosy-parker girl-friend along.' She knelt down next to Kelly-Marie, half lifted her and took her in her arms. 'It's okay, darling,' she said, rocking her to and fro. 'It's okay. You don't have to think about it. You don't have to talk about it. It's me, Gabrielle. You're all right now.'

The girl wrapped herself around Gabrielle and her sobs, though still shaking her body, seemed to lessen in ferocity. 'I hate it here,' she said, raising her face to Gabrielle's for a moment. 'I fucking hate it.'

'That's okay,' said Gabrielle. 'Hating it is all right. Everyone hates their job sometimes.' She stroked the girl's hair. They were all silent for a moment. Stephen was trying not to look at Gabrielle. She had her back to him, but her hair was falling forward over her shoulders and he could see the freckles that dotted her white neck. After a while, she turned to look at them. 'You two had better go. Before you do any more damage. Or Robbie damages you.'

Fay was fiddling with something inside her leather bag. She handed Gabrielle a £50 note. 'It's for her,' she said. 'I promised to pay her for the interview.' She inclined towards the two women and said in a slightly higher voice: 'Er, thanks for your time . . . Kelly-Marie.'

'Fifty quid? Is that all?' said Gabrielle. 'No bonus for getting her into this state? I mean, she's only bloody suicidal.'

'I simply asked her a few questions,' said Fay. 'She was talking to me of her own free will.' But she was handing over another note. She looked chastened and pale. Gabrielle took the money without saying anything more.

'Let's go,' said Fay.

'Okay,' said Stephen, knowing that he had no intention of leaving yet.

They walked wordlessly down the corridor. Fay looked pinched and angry. Stephen wondered if she felt humiliated by the way her interview had ended. But perhaps this was unfair. Perhaps she was worried about Kelly-Marie.

'Poor girl,' he said, experimentally.

'Yeah, sure,' she said. 'Total basket-case. I suppose that's the sort of person you get in a place like this. Terrible. Still, I've got some good stuff on tape.'

'Good, good,' said Stephen. He could still see the white neck, hear the soft voice. Fay had faded from his mind into an old school photograph, even though she was walking next to him, perfect and Pre-Raphaelite as ever.

Outside, they walked towards the town centre, and Stephen hailed a cab. It veered out of the light-swim of the busy road, and Fay stepped inside. But instead of getting in beside her Stephen slammed the door and peered through the window at her. 'See you later,' he said. He realized his tone was distant, vague.

'Aren't you coming?'

'No. I . . . I think I'll go back to the others.'

'I thought you might like a drink somewhere. I'm staying at the Albion – come and have a nightcap there. We probably both need a drink after that bloody awful scene.' Was this the offer he had dreamed of for twenty years? Still, he hesitated only for a moment.

'That would have been nice . . . but no. No. Thanks.' The taxi pulled away before he had time to read her expression. Or maybe he just didn't care enough to look. Perhaps she liked him, perhaps she didn't. Perhaps she would review Earthsea, perhaps she wouldn't. His anguish and his energies were going in another direction now. He turned and headed back to the club, holding his fear carefully inside him like something precious.

19

Back in the club, Stephen checked that his friends were still watching the lap-dancers with the same gormless fascination as the other men. Clive was looking heavier and more confused than ever, staring at the girl currently dancing closest to him as if he wasn't sure what she was doing there. She was a redhead, Stephen noticed, like Tamzin, with gargantuan bosoms of the boob-job variety which poked unconvincingly forwards. It was obvious that Clive was going to need rescuing sooner rather than later. With a growing sense of urgency Stephen searched the corridor, opening each door as he went. But he couldn't find the dressing room. He felt he was losing control again. His head was swirling. He was going mad. Remembering the bottle of beta-blockers he carried with him, he stuffed a couple into his mouth. Where was she? Not knowing what else to do, he made his way to the manager's office.

Robbie was sitting at his desk, half visible behind a screen of cigarette smoke. His feet were on the desk, and he was peering at a bank of security cameras. 'Well, helloo,' he said. 'You should have told us about your friends in the film business last time you were here. We might have been a bit nicer to you.'

'Film business?' Stephen was in no mood for further complications.

'Your film-producer friend? Who you brought along tonight? She phoned yesterday, said you were looking for a location for a new British movie about lap-dancing.'

'Oh she did, did she?' said Stephen, trying to work out whether lying or not lying was his best bet. Fay, apparently, lied as a matter of course. 'I'm ... Yes, she's very impressed,' he said. 'Erm, look. You don't have any idea where Gabrielle is, do you? Only I really need to speak to her.'

'Is there a part for her?' asked Robbie. 'She's not the best-looking girl we've got, if it's a looker you're after. Have you seen the tits on Theresa? The redhead who's working tonight – she's a knockout.'

'It's nothing to do with getting a part,' said Stephen. 'It's a private thing. I just want to talk to her for a minute. As a friend.'

'Now I have seriously heard everything. *As a friend!* What are you like?' The cracked Estuary voice behind him was unmistakeable. He turned to see Gabrielle, staring at him with disgust. 'She's gone, by the way. Your little case study. Don't know where. In such a state that she could do anything. Thanks to you and your stupid-bitch girlfriend . . .'

'She's not my girlfriend, she's a . . .'

'Sorry, mate, you're confusing me with somebody who gives a shit.'

'Go easy, these people are doing a film here,' said Robbie. 'You could be the next Demi Moore, or . . .'

'They're liars,' said Gabrielle, her eyes glittering with anger. 'Don't believe anything he says.'

Robbie seemed to be unimpressed by this. 'You're too

emotional, girl,' he said. 'Always taking these total saddos under your wing. Kelly-Marie is a fucking nutter; there's nothing you can do about it. She's on self-destruct, and that's the way it is.'

'Yeah, right, which means you can carry on sitting on your fat arse, doing nothing as usual,' said Gabrielle. 'You may not care what happens to her, but I do. And I reckon I'm a better judge than you are of whether anyone can help her.'

'You're supposed to be working a fucking shift, in case you'd forgotten,' said Robbie, finally losing his cool. 'I can't have girls just buggering off in the middle of the evening! For Christ's sake, this is a business I'm trying to run here.'

'You can't stop me.'

'No, but I *can* sack you.'

'Sack me, then. I can do better than this.'

She turned on her heel and walked out. Stephen rushed after her. He caught hold of her arm, babbling, 'Please – this is all my fault. Don't go – I mean, let me come with you. It's late –' it's better to have someone with you.' Gabrielle was open-mouthed. He noticed for the first time what she was wearing. A short, belted mac, cream and shiny, and black stiletto boots. If Fay's long leather coat was at one end of the taste spectrum, this ensemble was at the other. Nonetheless, being close to her seemed to tighten his chest. 'I'm sorry you were sacked,' he said, lamely.

'He's full of shit,' she said. Her voice was sullen, and her body was half turned away from him, as if she was reluctant to acknowledge that they were actually speaking to each other. 'I probably know him better than he knows himself. He's got girls who are junkies here, screwing the punters and God knows what else. None of them are ever sacked.'

'So you've still got a job?'

'I'll be back tomorrow, and none of this will even be mentioned. So you can naff off back to your mates with a clear conscience.'

'Good. I mean, I suppose that's good.'

'Yeah, well, it's my job, isn't it? We can't all be Prime Minister.' She was still looking away from him.

'No.' Stephen hesitated, then decided he had nothing to lose. 'Let me come with you,' he said. 'To look for her.'

She stopped at last and turned to face him. 'Why don't you just piss off? Why would I need you?'

'I want to help – and I need to talk to you.'

'You're wasting your time, mate.'

'Why are you always trying to get away from me? Why did you run away when I came in?'

'Because I don't want to know you.'

'Why not? I could be better than I look. I hope I'm better than I look, anyway.'

She turned to face him properly. 'You're a bit of a sad fucker, aren't you, Stephen Beckett? Hanging around with that lying, stuck-up cow. But still playing the nice guy.'

'How do you know my name?'

Without a word, she began to rummage in the large shoulder bag she was carrying. After a moment, she produced a small brown book and handed it to him. It was his missing diary. He automatically opened it, and saw his name written on the inside cover in his self-consciously italicized handwriting. (As a teenager, he had worked hard at his beautiful script.) 'It fell out of your pocket when we were having our little barney last time you came,' she said. 'I would have sent it to you, only there was no address. So I just ended up carrying it round with me, along with all the other old crap.'

Stephen looked down at the diary, trying to work out what this meant. 'But why has seeing this made you decide you don't want to know me?' he said. 'Why would this make you run off when you saw me?'

She shrugged.

'Why? Why? I've got nothing to hide. The only dates in there are the days I'm meant to spend with my kids. I've got no life. I'm separated from my wife. She can't stand the sight of me,' he said earnestly.

'Yeah, well, fair play to her,' she said, smiling for the first time. 'That's about the worst selling job I've ever heard. What woman in her right mind could resist a man whose wife's sick of him, and who's already got kids? I already *know* you're a liar. Every girl's dream date, aren't you?'

'Yes. Well. I take your point. But I do have some redeeming features. I'm very tidy, for a start. And I'm a good cook.'

She stiffened again when he said this, and took a step away from him. 'All right. If it makes you feel better, then you probably are better than you look. And, as it goes, you don't look *that* bad to me. But, the problem is . . . You know someone I know – or used to know, in any case.'

'So what? Most people are pleased when they find they have friends in common,' said Stephen. Too late, he

272

realized that he sounded like Celia Johnson in *Brief Encounter*.

'Yeah, well this is a different situation. In my line of work, I keep things separate. Sorted. Which means I don't want to know you. Anyway, I *can't* know you.'

'Why? Do you think I'm a snob? There's nothing wrong with being a lap-dancer.'

'Yeah, I bet you'd like to see your daughter doing this in a few years' time. But it's not about that . . . as such. It's a bit more complicated.' She hesitated. 'Would you mind taking your hand off my arm?'

Stephen looked down at his hand, nonplussed. He hadn't realized it was still there. He removed it, and looked at her face again. 'Let me come with you anyway. It was my fault, and I feel bad about it. I'm not a liar, I'm not a film person, I'm just an ordinary bloke, and I should never have brought that woman along. I don't even go to lap-dancing clubs. Please let me help you.'

Gabrielle looked at him curiously. 'If you really want to, I can't stop you. It's a free country. But . . . I can't work you out,' she said. 'You ought to be a total creep. In theory, that's what you are. In every way.'

'Thanks.'

But she was still looking at him. 'Why did your wife leave you?'

'Because . . .' He paused, suddenly realizing that he had never asked himself this simple question. All his good intentions, all his determination to make it right, because it had to be right, because once upon a time, a very long time ago, he had decided it must be right . . . The truth loomed at him without warning. 'Because she didn't love

273

me enough,' he said. Then, to cover up the catch in his voice he said, as flippantly as he could: 'Plus, I think she wanted to go off with someone else and have lots of hot sex.'

'Sounds good to me,' said Gabrielle. 'So is she?'

'Is she what?'

'Having the hot sex?'

'I don't know,' said Stephen. 'I don't know what she's doing. I don't know anything.' He suddenly felt very foolish and pathetic.

Gabrielle smiled, slowly, as if she was finally starting to see the point of him. 'Oh, go on then you miserable sod,' she said. 'Come and help me find Kelly-Marie – before she does something even more stupid than usual. We are dealing with the original kamikaze kid here. She's probably in Whitehawk, setting fire to her boyfriend's car.'

He folded his arms across his chest, to stop himself from hugging her. 'Fine, good,' he said. 'I mean, how awful. Has she really done that?'

'Loads of times. Give her a box of matches and she's away. God knows what's eating her – it's beyond me, and I . . .' She broke off.

'You what?'

'I just know a lot of weirdos, that's all. Anyway. There's only one place she might have gone: her boyfriend's flat. She moved in last week, *against* my advice. We'll have to get a cab.'

'I'll pay for a taxi.'

'Okay.'

By now, they had reached the street outside. Only then, in a horrible flash, did Stephen think of Clive. He stopped in his tracks. Desire to be alone with Gabrielle for the first – and, probably, the only – time in his life fought with the knowledge that Clive should not be at the club. Disaster could be the only result. Clive, for all his failings, had proved himself a true friend in recent weeks, and Stephen didn't want to see his marriage follow his own into the abyss.

'What's up?' asked Gabrielle. 'Forgotten something else?'

'It's some*one* else,' said Stephen, reluctantly. He looked back at the garish sign – THE SUGAR CLUB – that twinkled on and off over the club's mauve double-doors. 'No, don't worry, I'm sure he'll be fine.'

'Sure who'll be fine?'

'My friend Clive. He's inside, having a midlife crisis.'

'So tell me something new. You're all having a bloody midlife crisis.'

'No, but he shouldn't be. His life is fine. He's having a row with his wife because . . . Oh, it's all very complicated. But he's madly in love with her. And he's very, very drunk. And she's not the forgiving kind . . .' said Stephen, with some feeling.

'So, looks like we've both got lame ducks to look after,' she said with a faint smile. 'You'd better go and get him.'

'Will you wait for me?'

'I'll think about it. Just get a move on.'

Stephen looked at her, her freckled face, her expression of guarded kindness. Her hair was a dark aureole around her. Then he did something very stupid. He stepped forward, took her in his arms and kissed her. Not gently, or nicely, or politely, or in an exploratory, tender-first-kiss sort of way. All his longing, his loneliness, his anger and his fear went into that kiss. His tongue twisted between her lips, his arms squeezed her to him. (She was lighter, skinnier, more fragile than he would have expected.) His arms were inside her coat; he could feel the shape of her breasts under her sweater. And her perfume – the cheap scent that he had had such superior thoughts about the first time he saw her – seemed to fill his mind. He thought of Fay, who wore real scent – Eau de Rochas – at the age of seventeen, when other, ordinary girls wore Charlie or patchoulli oil. He didn't care. The smell of Gabrielle, her skin, her body . . . he was possessed with pure, abstract lust. For a second, she didn't react. Eyes closed, he fooled himself that this amounted to a response. Then, with an angry wriggle, she pushed him away, fiercely, wiping her mouth with the back of her hand like a child.

'What the *fuck* do you think you are doing?'

His hands still clinging to her arms, he panted, 'I . . . I'm really sorry. It just . . . I couldn't help it.'

'Couldn't help it, eh?' came a voice from behind him. 'Can this be the same upstanding citizen who gave me such a hard time when I found myself in a similar situation?'

He turned. Nick was standing behind him, propping up Clive, who appeared to be focusing on Stephen with difficulty.

'Nick, why don't you just piss off and –'

'Bloody disgrace,' said Clive, disentangling himself from Nick, and staggering to the wall, which he clung on to with a pompous expression. 'Good mind to call Rachel on m'mobile right now. Tell her whole story. Molesting strippers in the vestibule.'

'Rachel doesn't give a shit what I do. She threw me out. Remember? You and Tamzin had ringside seats.'

But Gabrielle was clearly in no mood to listen to Stephen's friends. She pushed his hands away. 'I'm off,' she said. 'I don't know what I was bloody thinking of, hanging around with you. You think because I work here I'm some kind of pushover? You think I want you to snog me because I make a living out of waving my tits at a bunch of saddos?'

'No. No! Nothing like that. I completely don't think that.'

'Well, you have just proved everything I ever thought about men like you. The ones who think they're sensitive are the biggest wankers of the lot.'

'I don't think I'm sensitive. I just think I'm going mad.'

'You're not going mad, mate. Believe me. You're just one of those people who think too much.'

'Yeah, too right,' said Nick. 'You've always been one of those weirdo intellectual types. Trying to be something you're not.'

Stephen ignored Nick, and didn't dare look at Clive. The physical shock of kissing her had left him feeling weak, addicted. The thought of her walking away made him ache. 'Gabrielle, I was a prat. I'm sorry. Please don't think badly of me.'

'Yeah, well.' She belted her coat more tightly around her. 'What I think is that Kelly-Marie is the important person. Not you.'

'Right,' he said. 'Right, then.'

She turned to go. But he couldn't bear to think of her disappearing. The emptiness that would be left. Without stopping to think, he plunged on, speaking to her retreating back. 'The thing is, I don't know anything about you. I don't know why it's happened, but the thought of you haunts me.' He hesitated. She was still walking. He chased after her, whispering hoarsely to her retreating back. 'All my life, all my life . . . I've looked for a woman who's a perfect match, someone with taste, and discrimination. You know. Class. And then I saw you and . . . everything changed. For the first time, I realized that none of that mattered . . .' He broke off.

At the door, she finally turned to face him. 'Thanks a lot,' she said. 'Once you wanted someone upmarket. Someone better than you. Now you've seen me, common as muck will do instead. The female version of a bit of rough. Well, fuck you.' And with that, she was gone.

Behind him, Nick gave a low whistle. He had, Stephen realized, followed him to the door. He had heard everything. 'Well, well, Steve,' he said. 'First the lovely Fay, then one of the dancers – good on you, my son. Maybe there's hope for you after all. Let's go back inside and see if you can have your evil way with one of the other girls.'

Stephen stared belligerently at Nick, and beyond him at Clive, who was feeling his way along the wall, still with an expression of outraged moral grandeur on his face. 'I don't want another girl,' he said, furiously. 'I want Gabrielle.'

'It's totally disgusting,' said Clive, finally drawing near. 'Rachel, wonderful woman. Sorrel – girl's a picture. Totally not your league – used to go out with that French foot-baller, long hair, loves himself . . . But this is outrage. Have to tell Tamzin . . .'

'There's only one problem with that,' said Nick. 'You'll have to tell her you were here.'

'Oh yes,' said Clive, beginning to slide down the wall. 'Gorgeous redhead. Wibble wobble. Weeny thong.'

'You said it,' said Nick. 'She'll probably be able to retire after tonight.'

'Well, don't be discreet on my account,' said Stephen. 'I don't give a damn. Tell anyone you bloody like.' He went over to Clive and heaved him back on to his feet. 'Time to go home,' he said. 'This is no place for a happily married man.'

'Happily married, no, no, no . . .' said Clive, as Stephen dragged him along, step by heavy step.

20

The next two weeks passed painfully. As August drew to a close, the weather felt close and muggy. Stephen wondered when time would start to be on his side, when he would return to something he could call 'normal life'. Each day, he woke dehydrated, aching physically and mentally. He felt soiled by his trips to the lap-dancing club, not specifically because of what the girls did there but because of the way his emotions had been disturbed. He was no longer, purely, the dumpee, the rejected husband, the loser. He was now a man who would like something else to happen instead.

Or was he? The mental clarity he had experienced briefly in the club gave way to a feeling of permanent nausea. Thinking about the club made this nausea worse. He could hardly eat anything now – his problem with the physical act of swallowing had worsened, and he sometimes felt as though there was an airlock in his gullet. If he had been female, he would have been thrilled to see how loose his clothes had become, but, being male, he just tightened his belt and pretended that his puny white body wasn't there. Unfortunately, he was also pretending that his fellow humans weren't there either. Sometimes, idly, he wondered why Briony hadn't left yet, inspite of the fact that in the months since he had promised to train her as a chef precisely nothing had happened. Perhaps she was now hoping that Andy would come back to her. Also, Stephen couldn't bear to engage with Vinnie – was still terrified that he would let out the horrible secret about Marc, or that Vinnie would start nagging him about how badly they were doing. They had had to switch to new – lower-quality – suppliers for most of their raw ingredients, and some of the envelopes that dropped on the mat had a nasty, legal look about them. But it seemed as though Vinnie had lost interest in sorting out their financial problems himself. He didn't mention the bills or debts again, just tossed the unopened mail on to his desk. His mood seemed very black – there was no bantering with the staff, no casual leaning of the elbow on people's shoulders, and Marc's habit of dropping into the restaurant when his shop closed seemed to have been suspended. At home, the three housemates came and went almost silently. If the Coco Krispies hadn't vanished at their usual rate, Stephen might have thought that Marc had moved out. Vinnie he saw fleetingly on his way to the bathroom. Early-morning chat – never a big number *chez* Vinnie – was non-existent. The depressive torpor was contagious. When Gillian Smale's canvases were delivered, he watched them being unloaded and arranged around the bare orange and ochre walls without curiosity. In normal circumstances, he would have wanted to know what lay beneath the dust-sheets that were firmly taped over them. Indeed, he might have wondered why there was so much need for secrecy. But he never questioned the fact that no one was allowed to look beneath the heavy shrouds. He had too much on his mind.

One Wednesday morning in September, Stephen had

just put the phone down on Crispin, the organic man from Petworth, after hearing that there would be no more deliveries of curly kale, fennel or fruit until some money changed hands. He was standing, in habitual catatonic mode, listening to the staff winding each other up in the kitchen. Stephen had lost track of who was shagging who, who had been dumped by whom and the exact nature of the sexual quagmire that remained. But he had always assumed that two members of staff at least were above all this relationship rubbish. Briony because of her unrequited love, and Flint because – well, because he didn't really have a gender. Flint was a person who appeared to manage with very little but bone. His only possession was his mountain bike, and he appeared to have no other passion in life. And, although he slept on the floor of a flat rented by the evil love-god Andy, Flint seemed untouched by the operatic sex tiffs that preoccupied the rest of the staff. While Andy was at the epicentre of every sexual flare-up in the place, Flint seemed childishly removed from this semi-grown-up world of sudden obsessions and instantaneous endings. But now, Stephen realized, tuning more keenly into the cacophony of voices, both Flint and Briony seemed to be in the forefront of a row he couldn't quite understand.

'He did!' came Andy's voice, harsh and deep. 'He's a fucking gay boy!'

'Don't be so stupid! Stop trying to screw everyone up!' Briony cut in.

'I totally, like, have no idea what you're talking about.' Flint's voice was bemused, with an edge of panic.

Stephen hurried in, just in time to see Andy dry-humping the spindly Flint, leaning over him from behind and thrusting away with his burly buttocks in a fairly convincing impersonation of buggery.

'Get off me! What the fuck are you doin', man?' Flint's voice was a hysterical screech. He attempted to wriggle out from under his assailant, but he was too frail to throw off solid, fleshy Andy.

'Andy stop it! Stop it!' yelled Briony, tugging at his T-shirt.

But Andy was cooing into Flint's ear: 'Come on, now, gorgeous, you know you want it! We all know why you never score with girls, don't we? Mind not on the job, mate. But never mind, you can have me now . . .'

'For Christ's sake! Andy, what the hell are you playing at?' Stephen rushed over and — with some difficulty — pulled him away. All four of them stood silent for a moment, Flint and Andy panting heavily.

'Yeah, always there to defend good old Flint, aren't you, Steve?' said Andy. 'But you don't know what he's been up to. Fucking pervert.'

'Up to?' Flint's face was incredulous. 'Like, what have I been up to?'

'Playing silly buggers with certain people,' said Andy, glancing significantly into the restaurant, where Vinnie had reappeared, carrying a pile of clean towels.

'People who shall remain nameless.'

'I don't know what you mean,' said Flint. 'What people?'

'Yes, just what are you on about?' asked Stephen furiously. 'If you're trying to make out that something has happened between Vinnie and Flint, then you really are out of your mind. And you have picked a very bad time to come out with that sort of crap, Andy. So don't push it.'

'It wasn't Vinnie I was talking about,' said Andy, just as Vinnie walked back into the kitchen. 'And all I'm saying is I don't want stuff like that going on in my flat.'

'What do you mean, you weren't talking about me? Who *were* you talking about?' said Vinnie.

'No one, mate.' Andy affected a nonchalant expression. 'Just some bullshit Stephen's got the wrong idea about.'

Vinnie put down the towels and closed in on Andy, his eyes narrowed. 'Tell me what you mean,' he said, in a low, threatening tone. 'Something is fucking well going on round here, and I am going to get to the bottom of it. Tell me what you mean, big boy, or I will personally rip your head off.'

'There's no need to come at me like that,' said Andy. 'You know as well as I do what's going on. It's your boyfriend who can't keep his flies done . . .'

Stephen didn't see exactly what happened next. Vinnie moved so quickly that, although he wasn't aware of looking away, he missed the split second when Vinnie flew through the air and sent Andy toppling to the ground. And, before Stephen could stop him, Vinnie was on top of Andy, slapping him round the face.

'Leave my fucking lover out of this! You're a liar, you're a liar, you're a sick-bastard liar,' he shouted.

'I'm just saying what happened, mate. It's the God's honest truth. Ask Flint.'

Vinnie leaped up, dodged past Stephen and grabbed Flint by his shoulders. 'What's he talking about? What's going on?'

'Nothing, Vin, nothing, I don't know any more than you do,' said Flint, white as his apron. 'Andy's flipped – I'm not into that . . .'

'Into what?'

'Into, well . . . Like, we all know Marc will try it on with anyone. Even when he knows a guy is straight he still . . . You know. He puts it about a bit.'

Suddenly, the whole kitchen was silent. At last Stephen knew where all this had been leading. He saw the boy in the bath, saw Marc's smirking face, his fat white belly.

'You're out,' said Vinnie, very quietly to Flint. 'Scram. Now. And you,' he nodded at Andy. 'Get out before I kill you both.'

'I didn't do anything!' protested Andy. 'I only said Flint was a fucking queer.' Without a word, Vinnie grabbed him around his bulky waist and lifted him bodily from the floor, his sinewy white arms straining with the effort. He carried him to the back door, opened it and threw him out.

'Just one thing, surf boy,' he said to the pile of Andy lying on the ground. 'I'm a fucking queer myself. As you know. But I could beat the shit out of a nice breeder like you with one hand tied behind my back.' Turning back to face the others, Vinnie said: 'Flint, fuck off before I do the same for you.'

'You've got it all wrong, I . . .'

'Get out,' said Vinnie.

With a sob, Flint ran out the door, and Vinnie slammed it hard behind him. Briony looked from Stephen to Vinnie, eyes brimming.

'Well done,' said Stephen, who was looking over the

half-door into the restaurant. 'About six tables have just walked in, and we now have precisely two waiting staff on duty. And that includes me.'

'Yeah, and just how bothered do you think I am about that?' asked Vinnie. Stephen realized that Vinnie was untying his apron.

'What's this? For Christ's sake – you can't go as well!'

'Er, yes I *can*, Steve. I know you have trouble tuning into anyone's problems except your own, but did you have any idea at all what that was about?' Without waiting for Stephen to answer he went on: 'It was only about Marc, getting off with everyone he can. As long as they're male and under thirty. As long as they aren't me. Okay? Just in case any of that passed you by. I'm out of here. In fact, I'm out of everything.' His face seemed to have been swallowed by shadow.

'Oh come on! Andy was talking bullshit – Flint wouldn't do anything like that. You know that. He's not into other men, he's into mountain bikes and growing his own dope. Andy's just shit-stirring.'

'Stephen's right,' said Briony. 'I'm sure Marc would never . . .'

'Yeah, well. When I want your opinion, I'll ask for it,' said Vinnie, shrugging on his battered leather jacket. 'See you.' And, without another word, he was gone.

'Vinnie! Wait!' shouted Stephen, rushing to the door and looking out. But Vinnie had already disappeared. 'Shit,' he said. 'Shit. Shit. Shit.'

Fighting back a stronger feeling of giddy nausea even than usual, he went back to the half-door, trying to work out how many people had arrived. There were indeed six

286

tables with people sitting at them – mercifully, all were groups of two or three. Then – with a shock – he saw her. Sitting at table two by one of the floor-to-ceiling plate-glass windows that flanked the brightly painted door. Fay Cattermole. And opposite her, tall, narrow, spikily bespectacled and dressed, as she must be, entirely in black, was a creature who could only be Erika Perspecua. Fay had come, as she had said she would. But without warning him in advance, as she had promised.

'Stephen, are you okay?' Briony was standing next to him. 'You've gone a very funny colour. I mean, we can sort this lot out between us. It's only lunches, remember? I'll go out now and give them their menus. We can try to help Vinnie later.' She patted his arm kindly.

'I'm afraid things are a bit worse than that,' said Stephen. 'The two women on table two are the journalists we've been expecting. One of them is here to review all that art stuff that's still covered up. The other one is here to review the food we haven't got.'

'Right.' Briony peered into the restaurant. 'They do look a bit hard-faced,' she said. 'I'll go and be nice to them.'

While she was gone, Stephen checked out the fridges, freezers and storage cupboards. There really was remarkably little in there. In fact, the only dish that they had in any quantity at all was a simmering vat of borscht, which Vinnie had been preparing that morning. Apart from that, there was a quantity of stale bread, several fraying cabbages, some overripe tomatoes and the usually battery of beans and pulses, all of which would take far too long to prepare. In desperation, he looked in the back larder for their emergency supplies of tins. All they had were three cans of Tesco's own-brand ratatouille. At Tamzin and Clive's, presented with a similar challenge, he had had enough to go on – and an undemanding audience to cater for. Here, he had nothing. And this was to feed Fay Cattermole, the most exacting of all food writers. He went into the restaurant and wrote on the board, in shaky white capitals, 'WARMING HUNGARIAN BORSCHT'. He glanced over at Fay, but she was in deep conversation with her gaunt colleague. They were looking at the hidden artworks, and Erika was scribbling something in a little black notebook. He supposed that he should go over and shake them both warmly by the hand, but found that he was physically incapable of doing this.

Back in the kitchen Stephen took long, deep breaths and wiped his sweating forehead. 'There's the first order,' said Briony, spiking it on to the board. 'One bean and pasta soup, one spiced lentil cakes. Is that okay?'

'Er, no,' said Stephen. 'See if they'd like borscht instead.'

'Why? Are we out of those already?'

'We're out of everything already. Sorry, Briony. This is going to be the lunchtime from hell. I wouldn't blame you if you walked out as well.'

'Why should I walk out? It's just my job. If they can't have what they want, it's not the end of the world, is it?'

From the packet Vinnie had left behind, Stephen took a cigarette and lit it – despite it being forbidden to smoke in the kitchen. 'You are a life-saver,' he said. 'Let's think how we can do this.' He dragged the nicotine down into his system and thought hard. 'Look, go and get all the orders. Plug the borscht, but try not to sound desperate. Give everyone a complimentary glass of wine and some stuffed olives. Smile a lot and say it's Earthsea's anniversary.'

'Is it?'

'No. It's probably the last day we'll open. But let's go out fighting.'

'Like Butch Cassidy and the Sundance Kid?'

'Exactly like Butch Cassidy and the Sundance Kid.'

She smiled at him, and he realized that he had never seen blushing Briony so confident. Adversity was bringing out the best in her. Perhaps it would bring out the best in him too. When the orders were all in, he hastily picked up the one for table two. As he had expected, Fay and Erika had picked out the most complicated items on the menu: for starters they had ordered black pasta stuffed with spaghetti squash and corn-cakes rolled in chermoula cornmeal, and for the main course Jerusalem-artichoke soufflé and sumac-scented almond aubergine.

'Not interested in the borscht, then?'

'No – sorry. But I did persuade a few of the other tables to have that. And the lady with glasses wonders when you are going to unveil the artwork. She seemed a bit sort of huffy about it.'

'Oh God.' Hastily, Stephen scribbled a shopping list. He said: 'Briony, can you hold the fort here while I go and try and buy all the stuff we need?'

'Sure, but . . . you mean you're off to buy it all now? While people are waiting?'

'What else can I do? We've got nothing here. And no one will deliver anything, because we haven't paid them for months.' With that, he rushed into the restaurant,

Stanley knife in hand, and tore down the coverings from the paintings. He hared out into the street with only the vaguest impression in his mind of the pictures he had seen – a very thin woman and a very fat one; something that looked like a dead pig. There was no time to process this information, but just as he reached Infinity Foods a row of tiny words flashed into his mental vision: 'ALL FOOD IS FATTENING'. He registered that these words appeared alone on one of the giant blocks. It occurred to him fleetingly that Gillian Smale was not approaching the issue of food in a particularly celebratory way. Still, at least it was more artsy than the insipid watercolours he might have ended up with. Never mind. His entire mission would have to take less than half an hour.

Infinity Foods was a wholefood emporium that could hold its own with any other shop of its kind in the country. It was a Brighton landmark – a haven for intense vegan students with woolly condom hats and ethnic backpacks, paranoid organic parents in search of guilt-free chocolate cereals and low-salt crisps and gratuitously serene yoga buffs with shining eyes and low toxin levels. Its only drawback was that there were just too many people like this in the area, so most of the time it was packed with health-seeking counterculture vultures, and the aisles were strewn with their rucksacks and environmentally sound shopping bags. To make matters worse, everywhere you looked there were always buggy-loads of carob-smeared toddlers yelling for sesame snacks while their parents scrutinized the wheat-free pasta. Stephen pelted into this mêlée and began hurling packets and tins into his shopping basket, reading aloud from his list as he went. After a while, it became obvious that he would need not one but *two* shopping baskets, which slowed down his progress continually as he bashed his way past the other shoppers' shins, shedding packets of sunflower seeds and GM-free passata as he went. Finally, in a frenzy of tension, he dashed to the queue, only to find that waiting at the row of tills there were about thirty-two people carrying industrial quantities of sesame oil and silken tofu. Each of them, it transpired, was paying by credit card. Now, as Stephen was planning to pay in the same way himself, he had no justification for getting angry about this. But he felt his madness levels creeping inexorably upwards as dozy veggie after dozy veggie laboured over their signatures. When a particularly inane female, with long droopy hair and a Peruvian hat with earpieces, started feeling in her various pockets and pouches in a painstaking quest for the money to pay for her soya sausages, he let out an audible groan. A couple of people glanced at him over their vegetarian fun-fur shoulders; in others he detected the stiffening of the back that takes place when a normal citizen goes into nutter-avoidance mode. He was spreading alarm among the meat-avoiding classes.

In spite of noticing this, Stephen found he couldn't stop himself from making another, much louder noise, which sounded like an angry rhino preparing for battle. 'Errrrnnnngggghhhhhhhhhh!' he said, if such sounds are said at all. There was more shifting in the queue ahead of him. 'SOME OF US HAVE GOT BUSINESSES TO RUN!' he realized he was exclaiming, in full-caps, all-shouting Stan-mode. 'GET YOUR BLOODY MONEY READY, CAN'T YOU! VEGGIES OF

THE WORLD, GET YOUR DAIRY-FREE ARSES
IN GEAR!'

The next thing that Stephen noticed was that he was
being silently guided to the third till, which was empty.
'Thanks,' he said, in a more normal tone.

'That's okay,' said the small gingery man who had hold
of his elbow. 'It's Steve, isn't it, from Earthsea? Having a
bit of a stressful day?'

'You could say that,' said Stephen. 'There are people in
my restaurant waiting to eat this stuff.' He nodded at the
two overloaded baskets he was heaving on to the wooden
counter. The little gingery man (Stephen could not remember his name, though he felt he ought to) laughed at this
as if Stephen had made a very good joke.

'No, really,' said Stephen, hastily cramming his pur-
chases into used plastic shopping bags as the girl behind
the counter rang them through the till. 'I'm totally serious.'

The man laughed again, but with a worried look in his
eyes, then disappeared into the crowd. Stephen shrugged
and handed over his Switch card to the cashier. She was
the kind of hippie who had gone in for complicated
hair, and had a cornucopia of braids, dreadlocks and bits
of rag exploding out of her head, as well as sporting
what appeared to be a couple of knitting needles. After a
moment, she handed the card back to him.

'Sorry – it won't go through.'

Stephen thought he heard tutting of a distinctly non-
vegan nature coming from the queue. With a contemptuous glance behind him, he handed over his Visa card.
But that wasn't accepted either – nor were his Access,
his Amex and his Abbey National cards. As he peered

into his wallet for guidance, the desperation of his situation sank in. He couldn't pay. He had no money, not just no cash. No money. Nothing in the bank. Nothing anywhere.

He looked at the girl in horror. 'Look,' he said. 'Do you know who I am?'

The girl sighed. 'I'm sorry. If you can't pay, everything will just have to go back on the shelves.'

'But . . . the bloke who was here a moment ago – he knows me – can you fetch him?'

'What bloke?' said the girl. 'There are people waiting, you know.'

'I know there are people bloody waiting! There are people waiting in my fucking restaurant! I have to give them this food! Do you want me to go bankrupt? Go mad? DIE? Because I will, you know. All that's standing between me and the abyss are these baskets of food.'

Without speaking to him again, the girl waved her hand, apparently to someone at the back of the shop, and called, 'Miles! Over here! Bit of a problem!' Groaning again – and he could hear more restless noises in the queue behind him – Stephen tore off his gold watch and made to hand it to her.

'Take this as collateral. Take anything. Look, I'll marry you – after my divorce comes through – I'll do anything you like . . .'

Someone tapped him on the shoulder. Presumably the dread Miles come to eject him from the premises. But when he looked down he saw that it was a woman's hand, which was attached to a woman. Attached to Carmel, one of Infinity Food's most frequent customers.

'Carmel! Thank God! Quick – can you buy this food?'

She paid wordlessly, in cash. Taking two of the bags (he realized now he would never have been able to carry it all himself) she ushered him into the street. She was frowning. 'Thanks for bloody phoning me,' she said. 'I mean, I know you've never been one for workshopping emotional issues, but I thought even you might have liked to find out how I was after leaving me sobbing in the Grand.'

'I'm sorry, I . . .' There really wasn't anything to say. 'Just, everything is shit at the moment, Carmel. I just *am* a total waste of space. That's all there is to it.' He was fighting the temptation to look at his watch, which he still held in his left hand.

'What on *earth* is happening to you? Why were you offering to marry that woman?'

'Because I . . . Because . . . Oh, I can't go into that now. I'm just bankrupt, desperate, everything . . .'

'It would never have worked, you know,' said Carmel.

'Yes, I know that. It's really not important. We've just got to get this stuff to Earthsea, immediately, and I have to cook it slightly sooner than that. Fay Cattermole's there, to review it for the magazine she works for.'

'Fay Cattermole? However did she get involved in all this? Seems like there's a lot you haven't been telling me.'

'It's a long story. But, basically, there's nothing to eat at the moment except a load of borscht; Vinnie's left, along with nearly everyone else; and it's all chaos.' He was panting now as they hurried through the crowds towards Ship Street.

'God, Stephen. I thought my life was bad. This is just

ridiculous. When is it all going to end? You don't still fancy her, do you? Does she realize there's no food?'

'She may well suspect something by now,' he said, glancing at his watch at last. 'Since she arrived forty minutes ago, all she's had is a plate of stuffed olives and some organic champagne. On the house, of course. Quick – up here. It's a short cut.'

In the kitchen, Briony was ladling borscht into an army of small bowls. 'God, am I glad to see you,' she said. 'It's been kind of . . . a disaster zone out there. And this soup's nearly gone.'

'Jesus wept – how come we've sold so much? We don't usually get that busy on a Wednesday lunchtime.' Stephen was frantically emptying his shopping bags as he peered into the restaurant.

Carmel joined him, and scrutinized Fay. 'Hmmm. Gorgeous as ever, I see. She certainly looks pissed off, though,' she said in a stage whisper. 'Mind you, she always was the negative-energy princess. I thought you said she was with some art critic?'

'She's the spindly, spidery one. Over there, making notes. God, what *is* she looking at? Is that a pig's head?' Stephen nodded towards the far corner of the restaurant, where Erika Perspecua was studying an enormous close-up of the face of a dead pig, painted in with such hyperrealism that it looked like a colour photograph.

Carmel nodded calmly. 'You are in deepest shit, there is absolutely no doubt about it.' She gave his arm a re-assuring squeeze. 'You know, I *really* wish I could help you. But I've got to sort out this problem with Lise. She phoned me last night to say she really is pregnant. She sounded like crap. I don't think she really wants this man at all.'

'You're not still thinking of having her back?'

'I'm going to do my damnedest to get her back. This is the love of my life. Your friend Nick is trying to sell me a house in Hove. Perfect for a family – and I need to get over there now before it's snapped up by some hetero couple with two point four kids.'

'Christ.' Stephen looked from Carmel to the crowded restaurant and back again. 'Can't you still lend a hand? This is meltdown, Carmel. Even worse than the time when you didn't get a first for your dissertation on Female Circumcision and the Feminist Colonialist Mind-Set.'

'Don't be ridiculous,' said Carmel. 'Nothing could be as bad as that. It's only a restaurant. And as for the idea of me helping with cooking! Are you mad? Remember I was the only person in my domestic-science class who failed to make an egg sandwich.'

'Right. But what I need is someone to chop. There's no great skill in that, really.' He knew this was a lie.

'Don't you have to go at about 10,000 miles an hour? I'll probably cut my fingers off.'

'Just do it the way I do, and I promise you'll be fine. Carmel, I will seriously be in your debt for the rest of my life if you help me now.'

She was looking dubiously at the long knives hanging over the preparation table. 'Do you really need that kind of hardware just to slice a few courgettes?

'Will you, please?

'Oh, go on then. I'll have to think of something really horrible that I need doing in return, I suppose. Maybe I'll delegate the nappy stuff to you or something.' She picked up the knife that was lying on the chopping board in front of her. 'Just tell me what to do and I'll do it.'

The period that followed sometimes came back to haunt Stephen – the shouted instructions, the misunderstandings, the charred remains. Carmel, in spite of all her best efforts, was incapable of chopping anything to a consistent width, so that when Stephen fried the red onions or aubergines that she had prepared, the ugly and misshapen pieces cooked at different speeds. Also, her early wariness soon gave way to a devil-may-care insouciance under the constant pressure to go faster and faster. Stephen's aim, all the time, was to focus on what had to be done, and to do it in half the time it would normally take. His insane determination had some success. In fifteen minutes Erika and Fay's starters were sailing out of the kitchen. He hoped that this would keep them happy. Certainly, they were better off than the other diners. Few of them had ordered a first course, and Stephen knew that they wouldn't be getting any food for half an hour at least.

'How's it going?' he called to Carmel.

'Fine,' said Carmel, slashing at a pile of artichokes as if they were heterosexist *Daily Mail* editorials.

'Remember to keep your thumb out the way of that knife,' said Stephen. 'You've gone from being overcautious to not quite cautious enough.'

'Instead of patronizing me, why don't you go out there and have a word with Fay? I mean, you were out with her a few nights ago. It looks peculiar, you lurking in here. As if you're sulking, or something.'

'It might be worth having a look at those paintings, too,' said Briony, bustling in with a half-empty basket of focaccia. 'Some of them are pretty gross. Kind of a strange choice for a restaurant.'

'Okay, okay.' Wiping beads of sweat from his eyes, he sneaked a glance at Fay. She was picking at her black pasta with a superior expression. Unfortunately, a large group of NCT mothers had set up camp at the next table, and were now giving a breastfeeding display. He didn't want to talk to Fay. He didn't want to look at the paintings. He didn't want to even think about the mothers. But just then the telephone rang in the bar. He dashed into the restaurant and picked it up.

'Hello – Earthsea, how can I help?' he squawked, keeping his eye on the neat rectangle of numbers on the phone rather than make eye contact with any of his customers.

'Hello, Daddy.'

'*Hello!*' False brightness filled his tone. The children. Oh God, the children. He remembered one of Rachel's rants, back in the days when she still thought that ranting could make him be a better father. 'Children need your full attention,' she had shrieked. 'You can't avoid them all bloody week then, when you do finally see them, tell them you're too busy to talk. What kind of message is that?'

'Guess who this is, Daddy,' said the voice. The words sounded clear, sweet, distinct.

'It's Elsie,' he said, his voice catching. 'Isn't it, darling? Who else would it be?'

This was greeted with a wail of grief. 'YOU HORRIBLE! I HATE YOU! YOU ARE NOT A NICE DADDY! YOU ARE SHIT-FUCK DADDY!' The voice disappeared, and Rachel came on to the line instead.

'That was Stan,' she said, matter-of-factly. 'He wanted

to phone you up to show you how grown-up he was.' More screams in the background. 'Never mind. I'm sure it's nothing that twenty years of therapy can't fix. Your mother is here, by the way.'

'Fuck! Who the hell invited *her*?'

'I did. She only wants to help.'

'Well, I'm not bloody seeing her.'

'You're behaving like a child.'

'*Good*! Just bugger off!' He looked up. A steely-looking woman was standing at the bar, sleeping baby slung over one shoulder. She was staring at him meaningfully.

Then his mother's voice came onto the line. 'I knew you'd hate me coming down.'

'Well, why did you then?'

'I care about you, Stephen. You're my flesh and blood.'

'I know you care about me. I appreciate that. It's just –'

'Less of this go-it-alone attitude would be a step in the right direction. If you bend, you're less likely to break.'

'I am bending,' hissed Stephen. This was true: he was almost bent double, with the receiver clenched to his ear, avoiding the gaze of the hatchet-faced customer by pretending to look at the boxes of Fair Trade coffee that were stacked below bar level. 'I'm bending over frigging backwards, Mum. Well, forwards, literally, but meta-phorically backwards.'

'You've lost me now, Stephen. Is that one of your recipes?

'Bending won't stop me from going bankrupt. Bending won't make me into a better father.'

'Well, that's where you're wrong,' said Rose. 'These children love you. They don't expect perfection. They just want to see you sometimes.'

'For God's sake, Mum! Stop torturing me! What am I supposed to do? I'm trying to earn a living here! Rachel may think that money will just magic itself from somewhere, but I've got a business to run! Or to try to –'

'Just calm down. No one is torturing you. You could get through worse than this if you had to.' He straightened up and a tear splashed on to the phone's key pad. The woman at the bar, who had opened her mouth to speak, closed it again.

'Okay, okay. You've made your point. I mean, thank you. I'm sure you're right. But I've got to go –' He hesitated before putting the phone down, suddenly wracked with grief and love for Stan. 'Mum – hang on – I just want to know one thing . . .'

'What's that?'

'When did he stop speaking in capitals?'

'When did what? Oh! You mean, Stanley? Stop shouting all the time? I don't know. But he only does it now when he's upset.' In the background, he could hear Stan yelling, 'MY SKIPS! THEY'RE MY SKIPS! YOU HAVE THE RED BAG! POOH-POOH HEAD!' Obviously he had managed to arrest his son's development in a single telephone conversation. He put the phone down and wiped his eyes with the back of his hand.

'Are you all right?' asked the NCT woman. She had pink cheeks and small features, and looked like the sort of woman who kept her childcare manuals in alphabetical order and whose children would guzzle organic greens and go on to run the country.

'I'm fine, thank you,' he said, smoothing down his apron. 'Head cold, not a bad one. No food risk, or anything. No sneezing. Can I help you?'

'We've been looking at your artwork,' she said, in a clipped voice that hinted at generations of doctors in the family. 'Rather unsuitable for a family restaurant, don't you think? Not that any of ours are old enough to notice yet.' She glanced at her recumbent baby.

'I haven't studied them closely,' said Stephen, blowing his nose.

'Well, might I suggest that you rectify the situation?'

Stephen looked first to the kitchen, from where black smoke was beginning to emerge, then to the restaurant, where few customers were still at their tables. Some were looking at the pictures. Others had formed little knots of protest and were looking towards him.

Sighing, and avoiding eye contact with anyone, he went to look at the nearest picture, followed by his interrogator.

'It's quite disgusting,' she said. 'I mean, what is his point, exactly?'

'*Her* point,' said Stephen, who realized that he was looking at a cow, dangling upside down, presumably seconds after having its throat cut. 'The artist is a woman.'

'I find that hard to believe.'

Stephen looked around his small restaurant, realizing that he should have been suspicious of anyone recommended by Marc. Because the paintings were clearly designed to be a reflection on the dreadfulness of food, the damaging, cruel, unforgivable matter of putting stuff into your mouth, swallowing and submitting it to the processes of digestion. There were twelve in all. The first showed, in emetic Technicolor close-up, a typical motorway-caff all-day breakfast: a fried egg featuring an acid-yellow yolk, a sprawl of baked beans, a pair of fat-wallowing sausages, frazzled bacon, a lake of brown sauce. Next to it was a towering slice of chocolate gateau, flaunting its in-your-face cream filling, layer upon indulgent layer, calorie seams laid down like the fossil-loaded layers of chalk in a cliff face. And, next to that, a woman so thin that she was literally fleshless. Her giant distorted head had a corpse-like grin, her scanty black hair stuck out witchily around her. Most shocking of all were her eyes, meeting your gaze with triumph, as if to say, 'Look at me: I'm beautiful! Look at you: A mess of flesh!' The fourth showed a naked man, the fattest human being Stephen had ever seen. His body was a series of superimposed rolls, slavering down over itself. Gravity seemed to be sucking all this excess matter back into the earth. His head flowed into his torso, neckless, shoulderless, as if he had been melted with a giant blowtorch. His body billowed endlessly, so that his breasts sagged close to his navel, his legs clung together as if welded by body grease, and his stomach folds hung so low that his penis was obscured. Next to these were two enormous white canvases with the tiniest writing in the centre, only discernible when you came right up close. On the first were inscribed the words 'All food is fattening' and on the second 'Meat is murder'. But these were just the exquisite hors-d'ouevres compared to the rest of the collection. The remaining six paintings were like scenes from an execution: disembowelled sheep, decapitated chickens, lambs being fitted with electrodes and finally a calf screaming in close-up.

'Look,' he said. 'What can I say? It's bullshit. Have lunch on me. Have you had any wine? Champagne? Have more.'

'I don't drink. Alcohol is more of a societal problem than heroin, you know.'

'Well, if I had any heroin, I would offer it to you. I really would,' said Stephen. 'In the meantime, perhaps you would like to tell your friends about my generous offer while I cook some badly needed food.' Before she could say more, he dashed back into the kitchen and attempted emergency surgery on Carmel's burned offerings. The soufflé, which was meant to be crammed full of Jerusalem artichoke and Parmesan, was looking rather blacker than usual. The parchment pastry looked singed, and in places was peeling away from the contents. The dish was usually served with mashed baby potatoes with plenty of butter and roast artichoke. There was elephant garlic and artichoke veloute to go with it, which he splashed liberally with rocket oil. It didn't, in his eyes, look so terribly bad, from a distance. Although what it tasted like was anyone's guess.

The sumac-scented roasted aubergine was in an even worse state. The deep-fried garlic and chilli had been burned to a frazzle, and the spiced pakora and toasted cumin and tomato sauce had almost dried up. It looked like something nasty, dropped from a great height. But it would have to do.

'Okay, Briony, table two, the hags from hell, take it away!'

Giving him a reassuring smile, Briony ferried the food out to Fay and Erika. Stephen was tempted to collapse on to the floor, moaning with exhaustion and relief, but there were still five tables to deal with.

'How's it coming over there?' he said, turning towards Carmel. 'You know, you really need to get a move on if –' In a split second he saw her knife slicing its way through a cucumber – fast, but inconsistent still. She looked up at him, as if to speak, the knife fell and she gave a scream of agony. Blood poured over the preparation board, shockingly scarlet, dousing the cucumber she had been slicing with indelible ruby. Stephen dived across the room, clutching a towel, and grabbed hold of Carmel's arm. Her hand was still in place, and so, he saw, were all her fingers. But she had gashed the flesh between her first finger and her thumb. Stephen wasn't sure whether this meant she could have severed vital tendons or done something equally irreparable. He had a limited knowledge of bodies, as Rachel would have been the first to testify. Holding the towel tightly around her hand, he called to Briony: 'How many meals are there left to do?'

'Ten,' said Briony, her hands clamped to her face. 'Is she all right?'

'Not exactly,' said Stephen. Carmel's face was white with shock; she had sunk down on to a stool and seemed unable to speak. 'Tell whoever is still waiting for main courses that we can't do any more. They can have free pudding, but that's it. And they can take the fucking paintings home too, for all I care. I'm taking Carmel to hospital.' Briony whizzed back into the restaurant without waiting to question the wisdom of any of this.

'Who's going to hospital?' said a familiar, ice-cold voice. He turned to see Fay looking at them over the half-door. 'Carmel! I didn't know you were here! What's happened?' She looked shocked.

'She was helping me out, and slashed herself with a knife,' said Stephen.

'God. Carmel and cookery never did go together, did they?' Fay was apparently torn between hauteur and compassion. Hauteur won. 'I mean, frankly, Stephen, that partly explains it.'

'Partly explains what?'

'The fact that you have just served up the worst food I have ever tasted. That crap we ate in Stoke at that vile Harvester-type place was more acceptable.'

Stephen turned and looked at her full in the face. For some reason she was wearing a black beret, and her red hair came tendrilling out of it. Her eyes were smoky with immaculately applied liner. She was also wearing horn-rimmed spectacles. To Stephen, the whole thing looked like fancy dress.

'Just do me one huge favour and fuck off out of my life, will you?' he said. 'I don't care what you think. I don't care what you say. I don't care how impressive your friends are, or where you bought your coat. Just leave. And take that hideous, metropolitan stick insect with you.'

'I gather you are referring to me?' said Erika Perspecua in a cod-Central European accent, appearing suddenly behind Fay, pen in hand.

'Yes, I am.' He helped Carmel to her feet. 'Why don't the two of you go off and write the worst things you can think of in your circulation-free, up-its-own-arse little magazine? I'm sure you'll enjoy it.'

'I'm sure we shall,' said Fay, colder that ever. 'I'm sure we shall both have the time of our lives.'

22

''Scuse me, darling.' The tallest transvestite that Stephen had ever seen wobbled out of Oddbins, clutching a bottle of lager, a cigarette held between his scarlet lips. The door lintel grazed his head as he passed under it. He was wearing what appeared to be nine-inch towering platforms that would have toppled Naomi Campbell. But no one appeared to notice him. London Road, the busy shopping street leading to Preston Park, was packed with similarly dressed persons, male, female and everything in between. There were more wigs, fake tans, kinky boots and ironic tiaras embellishing the population that edged its way along the hot pavement than Stephen had ever seen. The crowd was drink-fuelled, E-crazy, borne along on a shameless wave of hysterical *joie de vivre*. Whistles and shouts filled the air – whistling being a newly traditional feature of these events, as Stephen knew from earlier jaunts in London. You knew, just looking at the snake-hipped boys in tight white jeans with par-blond hair, draped round each other's shoulders like so many feather boas, that there would be tears well before bedtime. But Stephen envied them for their fundamental, in-yer-face insecurity. Even tainted love was beige, not Technicolor, if you were a heterosexual, forty-year-old dad. And today, with his two children in tow, he was very much dad first, sexual being second.

'Now, stay close to me, and don't scurry off anywhere.'

'You're hurting my hand, Daddy; there's no need to panic.'

'I'm not panicking, Elsie, I'm just being a responsible adult.'

'About bloody time, some people might think.'

'Kindly refrain from swearing in front of my children, Carmel.'

'Yeah, or he'll rip your arm off at the fucking seams! Yeah! Like Indiana Jones in his cool bodywarmer!'

'Stan, stop that.'

It was a few days after the disaster at Earthsea, and the last weekend in August. To Stephen's surprise, Vinnie had not appeared since storming out of the kitchen. Neither at work, nor in the house. Marc, too, had gone to ground. It seemed to Stephen that he was coming and going into an empty house, though as he arrived drunk and left hungover, the impression this made on him was minimal. Where Vinnie had gone to he had no idea – presumably not to the same place as Marc. Stephen was stuck for ideas about what to do. Obviously, one did not call the police about an adult male who had fallen out with his boyfriend. But Vinnie's silence and continuing non-appearance was unnerving. As usual, he was hoping that Carmel might have some ideas about this – after all, she was the biggest expert he knew on gay relationships. But she seemed to be in a peculiarly ebullient and non-analytical frame of mind.

Pride had been her idea. Her injury had done nothing to dampen down the new vibrancy she was mysteriously exuding. The accident unit had been a mere blip on her trajectory to total mental health, and now, in her black leather trousers and denim shirt, she cut rather a dash with her heavily bandaged hand. She was also wearing a fetching leather hat, a Freddie Mercury memorial number, and quite a lot of make-up. Stephen realized that she had lost weight during her traumas with Lise. This was not her usual response to emotional pain – normally she would head straight for the biscuit barrel when love hit the rocks. Now she was stepping out alongside the other gays and lesbians who thronged the streets of Brighton in an annual celebration of their sexuality as if she really was full of pride and confidence. She had never looked better, and was unrecognizable as the bag lady who had cried in the Grand Hotel.

'So, just what *is* going on with you and Lise?' asked Stephen, still holding on tightly to the hands of his two children, and tuning out the resulting cacophony of complaint and protest. 'You've gone all mysterious about it.'

'Really? I don't think so. It's just that you are having the novel experience of being interested in someone else's life, for once. I'm being no more mysterious than usual,' said Carmel.

'Did Nick show you that house?'

'Yes. And I've put in an offer. All I have to do now is show Lise that I really do care.' She smiled at him, holding up her bandaged arm.

'You're not . . . you're not going to pretend you tried to kill yourself?' He glanced down nervously at the children, who were so busy gawping at the crowd that they failed, unusually, to pick up this gem.

'Erm, I wouldn't put it quite as crudely as that. Let's just say it's my fall-back strategy.'

'Blimey,' said Stephen. 'I always thought you were so scrupulously ethical, and that I was the morally shabby one.'

'Don't worry,' said Carmel. 'You still are. Some things never change. And I'm just bringing a little flexibility to the party. I want her back.'

'Foetus included?'

'Foetus included. Why else would I buy a four-bedroomed house?'

'Blimey,' said Stephen, again. They paused while they crossed the road to the park itself. It was hard to believe that this was the same place he had met Nick just a few months before. Now, with the hot sun beating down, its green swards of grass were invisible – a mass of bodies covered every available surface. Only the trees and shrubs stood out above the swarming heads of the revellers. From somewhere in the near distance came the throbbing sound of a band playing – some repetitive gay disco beat that Stephen couldn't place. The crowds were so dense that they spilled out into the road, stopping the traffic. It was hard to find a space on the pavement among all the grooving, swigging bodies, and Carmel had to walk slightly ahead of Stephen and the children, addressing remarks to them over her shoulder.

'Great, isn't it,' she said, surveying the jostling, hooting throng, 'to see all these people, just basically out for a good time. So many people who you don't know, but could . . . But, then again . . .'

'Then again what?' Stephen had to stop and pull the

children close to him while a posse of drunken boys rushed past, squealing and arm in arm.

'Jason's done it now!' shrieked one. 'Seventeen pina coladas in one afternoon!'

'Seventeen pina coladas and he's anyone's!' giggled another.

'Well, it gets boring in itself, doesn't it?' said Carmel. 'Looking for someone new. Different person, but the moves are the same.'

'I guess so,' said Stephen, wishing he could remember what these moves might be.

'Yes. It might sound like a climb-down to you, being my brother and having lived through all the crap I've spouted about there being no such thing as monogamy. About it being unnatural, I mean . . .'

'What's monogamy?' asked Elsie. 'Is it like Monopoly?'

'It's a bit harder than Monopoly, darling,' said Stephen.

'It's when grown-ups try to love each other for ever,' said Carmel.

'I know. Like at the end of fairy stories when they don't bother to tell you what happens next.' Elsie was interested in relationships, and resented not being allowed beyond the castle door once Prince Charming and Cinderella had tied the knot.

'Is it like Meccano, then? Or Bionicals?' Stan had gone all intellectual since dropping the capitals, but Stephen was anxious to get back to the conversation in hand.

'It's not like any game. It's when grown-ups live together. Very boring.'

'That's my point, though,' said Carmel, suddenly earnest. 'I thought that finding someone new was the interesting bit. I thought that, if Lise and me couldn't work it out, I would just find someone else who fitted the bill. Like I always did before. But this time . . .'

The children were pulling him towards an ice-cream van.

'This time what?'

'This time there isn't anyone else.' She looked at the crowd, frowning. 'No one else will do. There's only Lise.' A pretty blonde girl with bunches in her hair wearing denim shorts gave her a direct stare as she walked past.

'So *can* love last for ever?' asked Stephen, looking in his wallet for ice-cream money.

'Who knows? God knows. I'm just as much in the dark as you are. You've got to get over the idea that I've got all the answers to this love business.' Stephen did not say that, until recently, Carmel seemed to have been labouring under the same misapprehension.

'Right.' Absent-mindedly, he handed the ice-creams to the children. They walked towards the music, Carmel holding Elsie's ice-cream-free hand and Stephen keeping hold of Stan. The children were still overawed by the bizarre grown-ups on display. One shaven-headed man shimmied past them, wearing nothing but a pair of stripy boxer shorts, a white fur coat and an ornate diamante necklace. Behind him bloomed a giant peacock's tail. Another whistling group pirouetted by, wearing grass skirts and enormous, flower-covered hats, looking like Ascot débutantes in some parallel universe.

'Cool,' said Elsie, over-neatly licking her choc-ice. 'Why didn't you dress up too, Daddy?'

'Because I'm not gay, darling.'

'Are you gay, Carmel?' asked Elsie.

'I'm a lesbian,' said Carmel.

'Ladies *can* love each other,' said Stan, from somewhere inside his Cornetto.

'They certainly can,' said Carmel.

Perhaps it was the beer that caused the problem, but Stephen felt he needed one. He drained the can in a few, swift gulps, relieved to feel the fizzy lager sliding down his neck. Once he had emptied it, he scouted round for a bin, found one, balanced the can precariously on top of a lot of other empty cans, and then turned back to find Carmel and the children. Carmel and Elsie were standing by a rosebush, watching the dancers on the stage.

'Where's Stan?' he asked.

'I thought he was with you,' said Carmel.

Stephen wheeled around, so sure that he would instantly see his child's bright green T-shirt and tousled black hair that he thought for a second that he *had* seen him. But there was no child there. Holding his breath, he ran back to the waste bin, thinking that Stan must have followed him there without his noticing. But there were only discarded cans and chip papers scattered on the ground. No child. No Stanley. Stephen spun round again. It was as if he thought that Stan was trying to trick him, that if he moved fast enough he would outwit him. It was all a game, a trick.

'Stan?' he said. 'Stan?' Suddenly, the nausea hit him. Lost. The word started far away, then came rushing towards him with a horrible force. He felt his legs weaken, staggered for a moment and supported himself against a tree. All he could see, all around him, were adult bodies, dancing, gyrating, snogging, singing, whistling, laughing in exaggerated mirth. His child was somewhere among all those bodies, his lost, tiny child. He almost fell again, and crashed against a couple of women in matching black and orange leopardskin outfits. They gave him a hard, appraising stare. 'Have you seen a little boy? Little boy with black hair, green T-shirt? Boy aged about six?' he asked, his voice dry and unreal.

'No,' said one of the women, looking as if she thought this must be a trick question.

Carmel came rushing towards him, dragging Elsie by the hand. 'Have you found him?' she asked, idiotically.

'No,' said Stephen. He felt the panic coming more powerfully than ever before, he pressed his hands to his chest as if somehow that would relieve the sudden pain he felt in his body, as if Stan had been a physical part of him. Where was he? If he moved fast enough, he would find him. He must move quickly, and catch him, save him. Without thinking again about Carmel, he ran hither and thither through the crowd, banging into leather backs, naked torsos, kicking his way through half-eaten picnics. He wiped liquid from his face, not knowing if it was sweat or tears. Someone was bellowing, '*Stan! Stan!*' He thought that Carmel must have alerted the police, that his little boy was being tannoyed across the park, but realized the voice was his own, harsh and straining out his mouth. 'Stanley! *Stanley*! Daddy's here! It's Daddy!' He grabbed person after person, his face close to spider-eyelashes, the smell of garlic, orange foundation, perfect teeth, pock-marked skin, amphibian shades. 'Have you seen a little boy? Seen a little boy aged six? Little boy with black curly hair? Have you seen a little boy?' till he felt he must have asked everyone in the park, till his tongue was sticking to the roof of his mouth, till his head was spinning, he was throwing up on the grass, he was running, running, wiping the tears and the sweat away, great sobs coming out of his throat, till he crashed into another body, a girl in a short black dress, a girl with long, brown curling hair, small features, freckles . . . Gabrielle.

'Jesus!' she said. 'What the hell is wrong with you?'

'Lost my little boy,' he said. 'Little boy with black curly hair. Boy aged six.'

She took hold of him by the shoulders. 'Have you told the police?'

He shook his head. 'Don't know where they are. Just need to keep searching – can't stop now – gotta go. Got to find him . . .' He began to pull away, but she had him firmly by the arm.

'They're over here,' she said, dragging him towards two blue uniforms. 'Don't panic, he'll be all right. People will look out for him here.'

'Just want to find him,' said Stephen. But when they came closer to the police he had a sudden fear that they would keep him talking for too long, stop him from finding his son. What could the police do that he couldn't? Stan would be scared if an unknown grown-up tried to talk to him, an unknown grown-up in a uniform. He was shy at the best of times. So, just as they reached the two police officers, he managed to slip from Gabrielle's grasp and rushed away, back into the crowd. She followed him, chasing him along the concrete path. 'Stephen, what's up?

They can help you. What is it? Are you on the bloody run, or something . . . ?' Then her voice stopped. Stephen plunged on through the crowd, rushing towards something; he didn't know what – the elusive, shifting place where Stan was hiding, the fragment of space and time that held his son. The physical absence of Stan was like a wound, something so horrible that its existence could not be acknowledged. At last, he fell to his knees and lay gasping on the grass, eyes closed, breast heaving. When he got his breath back, he turned back. Asking the police to help was the only sensible thing to do. But where had they gone? He pushed his way through the crowd once more, through the bizarre, grotesque, beautiful faces, trying to keep his panic in one place, trying not to let it immobilize him. All he had in his mind now were images of Stan, his flat, flawless little face, his early-morning voice, pure and fluting, edged with the croakiness of sleep. 'Dad, guess what's my favrut dream. It's when I'm a Tyrannosaurs rex, right? And I bite a brontosaurus's head off, right? Because he's just a vegetarian.'

Stephen did not believe that he had a favourite child. The love he had for both of them was infinite, deeper and more painful than anything he had ever felt for a woman. But the two children made him feel very differently. With Elsie, it was admiration and wonder that overwhelmed him. From the very first moment he had felt her kicks through the taut skin of Rachel's distended belly, he had been astonished by her strength, her bravado and confidence. He marvelled that she was so like him in some ways – how many eight-year-olds kept all their shoes in the original shoeboxes? Or would only eat Gorgonzola cheese? – while in others she was so mysteriously self-reliant. With Stan, Stephen's overriding emotion was the urge to protect. At all costs, he wanted to keep his son safe.

The day he was born. The gay male midwife was sewing up the tear in Rachel's vagina, and Stephen was holding their brand-new child, damp black hair, little snarled-up face. The baby's nostrils were slightly flattened, his breath coming in quick little pants. The midwife stopped chatting to Rachel, lifted his head. 'There's something wrong . . .' They were out of the maternity room in seconds, leaving Rachel weeping on the bed, dashing through corridors to the special-care unit. He had known with bitter certainty, then, that his son would die. Elsie's birth had been perfect, problem-free. Stan's was blighted; he could not survive . . .

But he had survived. All that remained of the nightmare was a single photograph of him, lying under a plastic dome with tubes up his nose, hours after his birth. He *had* survived. He was alive now, crying, alone, somewhere in this park.

As he pushed his way through the crowds, Stephen made a promise to the God that he did not believe in, the Catholic Our Father who had distorted his childhood, warped his adolescence, made sex into guilt and guilt into a way of life. 'If I find Stan, nothing else will matter. Nothing else will matter. Just let me have him back, and I won't care what else happens. Close the restaurant. Make Rachel hate me for ever. Make me unemployable, mad, lonely, ill. I don't care. My children are the centre of my life. Just let me find my son. *Let me find my son!*'

Just as he saw a uniformed figure, and began to make

his way towards it, he noticed Gabrielle for the second time, walking towards the same policeman. The policeman was holding a child by the hand. A little boy in a green T-shirt. A little boy with curly black hair, aged about six. Stan.

With a cry of joy, Stephen rushed towards them. 'Stanley! Oh God! Stanley!' He snatched the child up into his arms and squeezed him tightly.

'You're hurting me, Daddy,' said Stanley. 'There's no need to squeeze like that. I wasn't even upset. I met a man who said he was a lady.'

'I love you,' said Stephen into his hair. 'I love you.'

Gabrielle stood back, took a step away as if she was about to leave.

'Friend of yours?' asked the policeman, who was looking rather bemused. Perhaps this was his first Pride.

'Oh no. I don't know him at all,' said Gabrielle.

Stephen looked up. 'Don't know me?'

'Well, I don't, do I?'

He stood up, lifted Stan on to his shoulders and held on firmly to his smooth brown legs. With his son on his shoulders, he felt that he had entered a charmed place. Nothing mattered now. He was strong. He had made his promise, and he would stick to it.

'Thanks for helping me.'

'I didn't do anything. This nice policeman found your boy.'

'You talked sense. Or tried to.'

'Anyone would've wanted to help.'

'But it was you.'

'Yeah. Coincidence.'

319

'Not the first place I would expect to see you.'

She stiffened slightly, and glanced over her shoulder as if worried about being watched. 'I'm looking for a mate of mine, as it goes. Thought he might be here.' She reached up and pulled one of Stan's legs affectionately. 'Bye-bye, Stanley,' she said. 'Don't leave your dad again, mate. All right?'

'Can I have another ice-cream?' asked Stanley, as they watched her hurry into the crowd again. For a moment, Stephen said nothing. He had noticed that the zip was coming undone on the back of her dress, exposing a few inches of secret white skin.

23

God was not slow to test Stephen's new-found resolve. The review came out in the *Carbuncle* the following Saturday. Fay had certainly tackled her subject with gusto. At the top of the piece was a monochrome photo of the author in tendril mode.

It is hard to identify the very best. Could I isolate that one, perfect meal – the most exquisite I have ever eaten? Hard, partly, because perfection is a two-way street, a partnership between the eater and the eaten. And because mood is all when dining. Sometimes, all that is required is pared-down simplicity – the omelette and the glass of wine so brilliantly conjured up by the sainted Elizabeth David. Sometimes, one craves sumptuousness, richness, gastronomic excess – conspicuous consumption, literally. And sometimes – oh! – one seeks comfort from food, comfort that it can so rarely truly provide. (Though my father's brandy-infused bread-and-butter pudding could soothe most broken hearts, as could his moistly rejuvenating Roman bread.) Thus, it is with some difficulty that one focuses on memorably exceptional meals. Was it the simple smoked mackerel and flatbread I ate last summer at an artist's impromptu barbecue in a tiny medieval village near Toulouse? Or the elegant perfection of the soft-boiled quail's eggs on a mushroom duxelles in the daintiest of pastry shells, followed by grilled Provençal vegetables with salsa verde, that I recently enjoyed at the Food Room, Deptford's modern fusion Mecca, which produces meals that equal in poetic creativity anything produced by Christopher Marlowe, famously stabbed to death in the time of Shakespeare just round the corner from this heavenly establishment? Delightful to recall, but impossible to choose.

Deciding on the worst meal, however, is a simpler matter. To succeed in this endeavour, all that was required was a lunchtime booking at Earthsea, one of Brighton's less prepossessing vegetarian eateries. My dining companion was award-winning art critic Erika Perspecua, and on the way through Brighton's bohemian North Laine quarter we agreed that we were seeking two things: a lunch that stimulated the interest and the palate, and the chance to sample the work of one of Brighton's up-and-coming young artists, Gillian Smale. The young iconoclast was showing twelve of her recent pieces on the walls of this small restaurant, and we approached its (slightly baffling) seventies exterior with a measure of anticipation.

Once ensconced, I ordered black pasta stuffed with spaghetti squash for a starter, followed by Jerusalem-artichoke soufflé, while Erika chose corn-cakes rolled in chermoula cornmeal and sumac-scented aubergine. Bizarrely, our overstretched waitress then tried to persuade us to restrict ourselves to borscht instead, and seemed quite put out when we insisted on our original choices. This was only the beginning of our troubles. Our arrival was followed by an influx of would-be diners, naïvely expecting a quick lunch, including a large number of new mothers touting screaming babies and recalcitrant toddlers, who stationed themselves at a table adjacent to ours. It rapidly transpired that the only food that could readily be supplied to any of these arrivals was the aforementioned borscht — whether the owner had been recently presented with a job lot of old beetroot one can only surmise. The toddlers among the group at the next table were soon stained purple by this all-purpose soup. Clearly, there was a staffing crisis under way — only one waitress was on duty and the background music (Courtney Pine, full marks for that at least) couldn't quite drown out the screams and shouts that emanated from the panicking staff in the kitchen. During the half an hour for which we sat before the starters began to dribble out of the kitchen, Erika was able to give her attention to the artworks. These — visceral, disturbing, challenging and fascinating though they were — were a surreal choice for this setting, presenting as they did a case for not only not eating meat, although this was arguably preaching to the converted in a vegetarian restaurant, but also for not eating anything at all. (See facing page for Erika's review.)

And so to the food. Our starters were passable – I found the textures uninteresting, and Erika's verdict on the corn-cakes was that they erred on the side of sawdust. But the real crime against humanity was the main course, which was of such a lamentable standard that my skills as a food writer are tested to the limit. How does one set out to describe the indescribable? To begin with, they had been incinerated, an eventuality we had begun to prepare for when the shouting in the kitchen reached a crescendo and smoke billowed into the restaurant. My burned soufflé had an intriguing taste somewhere between overzealously spread Marmite and boiled cereal packets. Erika wittily compared her almond aubergine to congealed vomit and told me it tasted worse than it looked. (She is peculiarly sensitive to texture.) Our lack of enjoyment of this almost comically execrable food was only impaired by the fact that further dramas were unfolding in the kitchen, with a fill-in cook managing to stab herself in the hand. The put-upon waitress then appeared once more in the restaurant to announce that no more main courses could be served, though we were welcome to a limited range of free puddings. The atmosphere among us was now that of plucky Londoners caught in the Blitz. Most of us accepted the offer of free dessert, and I must admit to some limited enjoyment of my ugli-fruit pavlova, while Erika was less impressed with her tofu and chocolate sundae, which she described as 'sickly and underpowered'. We finished our coffees as the proprietor was to be seen ushering his injured helper away, her arm covered in a blood-soaked towel. Perhaps Earthsea should forget about the food. The challenging artworks and the dramatic floor show were fascinating to behold; the meal, on the other hand, was the worst I have ever eaten. Nothing else has come close.

24

Once, Stephen would have been totally annihilated by this piece. As it was, he felt a curious sense of detachment when the biting, tiny words loomed up at him out of the page, as if he was observing the collapse of his own life through the wrong end of a telescope. Still, he couldn't shake his head clear of the venomous tone within, and he carried a copy of the article, neatly folded, long after it came out. At first, it seemed as if the review would have no effect. He comforted himself with the thought that hardly anyone would read it. The problem was that the sort of people who might buy the *Carbuncle* were exactly the sort of people who might – at one time – have eaten in Earthsea. In one newsagent's, he bought every copy of the magazine on the shelf, hoping to stop at least a few potential customers from seeing it. But business started to drop off almost as soon as it was published. Coincidence? Brighton was overloaded with trendy places to eat, so that was possible. Whatever the reason, the steady flow of customers he had relied on for two years started to dry up. Weeknights were emptier and emptier. Fridays and Saturdays – which at one time had been booked solid – rapidly went from quiet to moribund. He knew that there was little hope of the restaurant staying open till Christmas. He'd managed – God only knew how – to organize a stay of execution from his bank. He had until the end of

November to show that Earthsea was a going concern. But his office was still piled high with bills and demands. He knew that, in spite of everything, he wasn't really facing up to the fact that this was the end of Earthsea.

To make matters worse, there was still no sign of Vinnie. Stephen's mind slid around this fact unhappily. It was now more than two weeks since he had walked out. Stephen's detective skills were rather limited: he'd gone into Marc's shop once, but Marc was prissy and catty as ever, and obviously had no idea where Vinnie had got to. He persisted in flirting with his colleague and parcelling up a king-sized portion of sunflowers throughout their conversation. Stephen had even snooped round his land-lords' bedroom, looking for clues, but all he found was a collection of used condoms – in various colours – under the bed. But the late-night phonecalls stopped him from calling the police. There had been three now. When he picked up the receiver, there was silence. 'Vinnie?' he said the first time. 'Vinnie – is that you?' Something about the silence told him it was his friend. The second and third times, his frustration made him angry. 'Vinnie, I know it's you. Vinnie! Say something! Where the fuck *are* you?' But the line went dead every time. Stephen and Briony had to handle the cooking between them. Standards had slumped: there were now only half a dozen dishes on the menu. He had no energy left to feel sorry for Briony, or to feel guilty about not training her. She still refused to leave, saying she would hang on 'until Vinnie gets back'.

Now, heading for Nick's party, he tried to make his mind a blank. The only thing he was looking forward to was the booze. He planned to get stinking drunk and to speak as little as possible to anyone. Not wanting to leave anything to chance, he had invested in a quarter bottle of vodka, and stopped to take another swig from this when he finally turned into the rose garden which bordered the Rotunda Café, a circular, one-storey building. Wiping his mouth with the back of his hand, Stephen walked through the garden with lead-heavy legs.

As he came nearer, he heard the thud-thud of the sound system. He looked at his watch: ten o'clock. He'd stay for two hours, get hammered and then go. A few extra snifters would be needed just to cope with wearing his outfit – he had come as a rum baba. This was the same ensemble he had worn to the Cathcarts' seventies evening the year before. (The Cathcarts, having time on their hands, were keen on fancy dress.) Rachel had made it out of foam rubber and cheap fabric off-cuts from the Open Market, swearing and puckering the material as she worked. The final effect was anything but flattering – his body was encased in a squidgy gold satin cylinder, topped with an itchy layer of white fun fur intended to resemble cream. On his head was a red satin cap – the cherry on the top. The peculiarity of his appearance was increased rather than decreased by the overcoat that he had put on to hide this ensemble and keep out the cold wind. With it on, he looked like a very fat man with a tiny pin head and weedy, bandy legs.

Stepping inside, he had to admit that Nick had done a good job. He was certainly embracing bourgeois Bad Taste with a vengeance. It was ironic, really, this Bad Taste theme. His own quest for Good Taste, for bourgeois correctness in relation to style, had always seemed perfectly logical to him. Surely any discerning person would want to move away from hardboard room dividers? From a mother who had once had a purple perm? From Viennetta and tinned peaches? And yet real middle-class people seemed to like nothing better than dressing up as school girls! Vulgarity was positively hip. He was the only man he knew who saw Liz Hurley as Trailer Posh and disdained the trophy-tart image that celebrities liked to flaunt at the paparazzi. He was a man out of step with his own aspirations. What's more, he still couldn't get the memory of Gabrielle's partly undone zip out of his mind. There, in all its nakedness, the two inches of a back which any man in Brighton could look at every night. Thinking of her made his body swoon into itself with a thrill of pain. And Gabrielle must be the hardboard room divider of womankind. His naff past was claiming him still. He had learned to cook beautiful food, but was still the same, plain, bloke from Stoke.

He looked around the vast, circular room. It had been transformed – only the wooden floor was recognizable. Stephen tried to remember whether he had known Nick to approach any other project with such thoroughness. The only thing that came to mind was the seduction of one of the dance students at Goldsmiths, a girl with gold leonine hair who wore Lycra everything and smoked Consulate for breakfast. In the daytime, the Rotunda was full of small, noisy children busy dropping ice-creams on the floor and pushing their buggies over while their mums bonded over carrot cake, earnest and pink-faced and com-plaining about their sex lives. Now, all the tables had been lined up around the walls and were covered with an impressive array of alcohol: red wine, sparkling wine shoved into ice-filled buckets, and numerous brands of gin, vodka and tequila. The Bad Taste element was out in force: bottles of Bacardi Breezer, Hooch and ready-mixed buck's fizz stood in line like drag queens on parade. It was an astonishing collection, and a hymn to Nick's obsession with the demon drink. But he hadn't stopped there. The walls and ceilings were covered with a layer of helium balloons in a range of emetic colours – orange and lime-green, shocking pink and sludge-brown. (Brown helium balloons? Whoever came up with that idea really had an eye for detail.) And the walls were decked with lurid-colour posters of Bad Taste personalities – Neil and Christine Hamilton, Joan Collins, Anne Widdicombe, Paul Daniels and Debbie McGee, Geri Halliwell, George Bush; they were all there.

In the corner, the sound system pulsed away like a small nuclear reactor. Only the food was more minimal, consisting of some dips and salads on a single table. But even this was carefully presented, in a range of clashing bowls, and as he drew nearer Stephen saw that someone had bothered to give it a Bad Taste touch, with a massive prawn cocktail taking centre stage, next to which stood a hideous mixed salad (just like the ones Rose used to make) complete with chopped lettuce, bevelled tomatoes and thousand island dressing. Someone had clearly been helping Nick with all this. The whole thing was much more lavish and thoughtfully put together than Stephen had expected. How much had Nick spent? And why had he gone to so much trouble when a routine bottle party would have been enough? Stephen shrugged his shoulders, poured himself a large glass of wine and turned his attention to the humans in the room.

Nick – true to his form at university – had managed to assemble a huge number of people. Stephen wondered how many of his guests Nick actually knew. Carmel, for a start, was hardly a bosom pal, though Stephen knew she was invited. Their paths had crossed during their college days, and she had taken a dim view of him then. Now, their association had only been renewed because Nick was selling her a house. It was certainly an odd collection of people: large women in tiny leather mini-skirts and fishnet tights, and small men wearing large Hawaiian shirts and baggy shorts. Skinny men dressed as vamps and fattish women in voluminous shell-suits – surely this went beyond Bad Taste in the party sense and lapsed into actual bad taste? He had no idea whether Nick had any real friends. He suspected not. Perhaps this was really just a gathering of all the people he had sold a house to in the last twelve months. That would certainly be one explanation for the apparently eclectic group of people who were snaffling down the alcopops.

'Stephen, hi, glad you could make it,' said a peculiar-looking rabbinical character with a long beard and a white sheet over his head.

'Hello,' said Stephen, staring more closely at this strange individual, who had a sub-machine gun slung round his shoulders. 'Nick? Is that you?'

'Sure is,' said Nick, taking a pull from a bottle of San Miguel. He lifted his shoulders to show a T-shirt emblazoned with the image of the twin towers in New York. 'Got it now?' he asked.

Stephen scrutinized it. 'No idea,' he said.

'Oh, for fuck's sake,' said Nick. 'Osama Bin Laden, dumbo. The ultimate Bad Taste superhero.'

'Right,' said Stephen. 'Yes. Very good.'

Nick rolled his eyes. 'God,' he said. 'Useless wanker. And you are . . . Humpty Dumpty? In the snow?'

'I'm a rum baba,' said Stephen, glancing down at himself. 'Bad Taste food.'

'Of course,' said Nick. 'You would be.' He gave Stephen a quick, nervous glance, as if he had forgotten how weird and unpredictable he was.

'Great . . . setting,' said Stephen, indicating the room.

'Yeah, well, most of it was –'

'Was –?'

'A fluke. Fucking lucky to get this place. Expecting a hundred people, near enough. Lots of people known to you personally. Lots of *women*. Early days yet.' With that he wandered off, leaving Stephen feeling puzzled and uneasy.

Just as he was taking another slug of wine, he saw something that caused him to jolt and choke. A woman had just walked in – a woman with a definite look of Gabrielle. He knew it wasn't her; she was darker, and built on a slightly larger scale. But, in her basque and black fishnets, tippling on towering heels, she made his breath come in a gasp almost of protest. *What a slapper!* he thought to himself. Of course, the whole point of a party like this was that she was dressing up: she was a slapper only in quotation marks. He saw two people go over to speak to her: a tall, darkly beautiful woman who could have been dressed up as Cher and a black man who was almost certainly supposed to be Robert Mugabe (or was the wine already taking its toll?). With a shock, he realized that they were Sorrel and her fiancé Kris. With another, he saw that the slapper-with-irony was Rachel. Then he realized that he was standing right next to them.

'Hello, everyone,' he said, gesturing at them with his wine. 'Enjoying the party? Rachel, you look . . . fantastic. But I always thought you hated dressing like . . .'

Rachel looked at him dispassionately. 'Like a tart? Yeah, well, now it turns out that I'd have scored plenty of Brownie points with you if I'd done this years ago. We all know about your taste in women,' she said. 'When did you collect that costume? Have you been round to the house while I was out?'

'I took it with me in my first bag of clothes,' said Stephen. This was true. At the time, he hadn't known why it had been important to roll this up and stick it in along with the clean boxer shorts and balls of socks. The idea that this was because it was the only thing that Rachel had ever made for him was too hard to bear. 'But what do you mean, my "taste in women"? What is my taste in women?'

Rachel snorted and stalked off.

'Your outfit is very becoming,' said Sorrel in her precise, no-accent Euro voice. The DJ's flashing lights soaked her first in one colour, then another; now lime green, now bright pink. Her eyes were shining, she seemed to be laughing. At him? With him? Because she was young, beautiful and in love?

'Yeah, good to see you movin' forward,' said Kris. He moved towards Stephen and shook his hand. 'Sleaze is, like, you know, in the eye of the beholder. It's just a case of altering your mind-set.'

'I like my mind-set the way it is,' said Stephen coldly. His sense of bafflement and distance was increasing. Surely dressing as a rum baba didn't rate as a particularly sleazy activity? Unless there were aspects of food fetishism about which he knew nothing.

'Steve, I know you want to change,' said Kris. He took Stephen by the arm and spoke quietly into his ear. 'Sorrel told me about the way you saved that kid's party,' he said. 'Fantastic. That's not how negative people behave. That's the way rounded human beings spread love and under-standing.'

'Yeah, right,' said Stephen.

Kris squeezed his arm. 'Rachel's moved on. Now it's your turn. Learn to fly.'

'I'm a rum baba,' said Stephen. 'Strictly an earth-bound dessert. You're talking to the wrong pudding.' Then, registering something in Kris's tone, he said, 'What d'you mean, Rachel's moved on?' But Kris, too, had left him behind and swanned off into the increasing throng of people in the centre of the room, both hands furled around the back of Sorrel's neck as if taking part in some ancient ritual.

Stephen realized now that the throng did indeed include plenty of people he knew. In the far corner, Clive, gesticulating with a bottle of champagne, was talking to a bandaged mummy. He was clearly very much the worse for wear, and Tamzin was nowhere to be seen. Marc, dressed as a Hawaiian dancing girl, stood nearby, with Briony in head-to-toe silver with her midriff on display (Britney

Spears?). Next to them, Flint, in grey with a road sign on his head, was tucking into a plate of salad. Nearer to the sound system he could just make out Ian, who appeared to have come as himself, as he was sporting his usual check shirt and jeans. He was jigging about in pre-dancing mode and chatting to Dame Barbara Cartland. Suddenly, Stephen realized that this was Rose.

'Mum!' said Stephen, after squeezing through the crowd to reach her. 'What are you doing here?'

'Your friend Nick very kindly invited me,' said Rose. 'I thought it would give me a chance to catch up with you at last.'

'But how did you meet him?'

'He came to look at the house,' said Rose. 'Didn't you know?'

'Look at the house?'

'Rachel wants to put it on the market. You two need to talk to each other.'

'Don't start.'

'You can't hide from me for ever. Grow up, Stephen.'

Stephen said nothing, but scowled at his feet, exactly as he would have done at seventeen.

'Carmel says she's hardly seen you since the day she nearly killed herself trying to help you out.'

'I've thanked her about a million times. Anyway, I saw her at Pride.'

'She's had her own problems, you know, without trying to help you as well.'

'Yes, I know. It was heroic of her. It was just lucky that it wasn't even worse.'

'Maybe all this will teach you to appreciate your own

family, instead of being ashamed. Ashamed of me, in any case. Your own mother.'

'I'm not ashamed of you!'

'Yes you are,' said Carmel's voice. Stephen turned to see the bandaged mummy.

'Christ!' he said. 'Carmel? What the hell are you meant to be?'

'I'm the NHS,' said Carmel's voice through a narrow slit in the bandages. 'In honour of that wait in A&E. That's what *I* call bad taste. You've always been embarrassed about your background, Stephen. Always trying not to be naff.'

'You try too hard, that's your trouble,' said Rose. 'That time you brought all your things home from college on the train, just because you couldn't stand the thought of your own mother arriving in the Austin 1100 and your friends finding out I was a hairdresser. Then half of it going on to Crewe because you didn't have time to get it off the train.'

'You've always been a) a terminal control freak and b) a tragic snob,' said Carmel, going into bullet-point mode. 'Which is what makes the whole thing even more weird and unexpected.'

'What whole thing?'

'The lap-dancer thing,' said Carmel. 'Nick happened to mention it when he was looking round the house. And thank God he did. It certainly clarifies the situation for Rachel.'

'Fancy you falling for a girl like that,' said Rose. 'Rachel nearly fainted when she heard.'

'Great,' said Stephen. 'Not only am I kicked out of my

house, and not only is Rachel trying to sell it without telling me, but also everyone except me is hanging out in my kitchen, swigging tea and getting wildly exaggerated updates on my lifestyle from Nick, who is supposed to be one of my friends. Absolutely fucking brilliant.'

'Language,' said Rose. 'You're not with your low-life friends now.'

'Mum, I haven't got any low-life friends. Apart from Nick, that is. And I'm not . . . in love with a lap-dancer. I'm not in love with anyone.'

'Love!' said Rose, flipping her hand in front of her face as if waving away a fly. 'Love's not the issue. We're talking about good old-fashioned lust. You're chasing your youth, that's what it's all about. Throwing away your life, and all for nothing . . .'

'No need for being in love,' said Ian, his arm suddenly wrapped around Stephen's shoulders. 'Just think of it as the Vikings, arriving to rape and pillage and enjoy! You could even be the head Viking, the one with the biggest horns and his pick of all the chicks. Geronimo!'

'Had to tell Tamzin.' Clive had wavered over to his other side. 'Well, did my best to tell her,' he said. 'But she wasn't speakin' me, said I not allowed to speak her. Told me to go out tonight and never go back. I'm John Travolta, *Sat'day Night Fever*, by the way. She's got a right to know, if you're going to start bringing lap-dancers round for a fondue.'

Stephen found he couldn't speak. Had they all forgotten that it was Rachel's idea to split up in the first place? 'Just . . . just . . . Leave me alone,' he said, pushing his way back to the drinks table. He pulled out his cigarettes and lit one, feeling the walls pulsing around him. The music was getting louder. Emptying a bottle of lager down his throat, he turned back to the dancefloor and saw that the strangest people were now dancing together – he could even see Rachel and Nick stomping round each other, bumping and grinding like a couple of old rockers.

'You must be Stephen,' said a voice near to the table. 'I heard you were here as a rum baba.'

He looked down to see a very small woman, with short, straight hair cut close to her head and 1950s spectacles. She looked like a mini librarian. 'I'm not in fancy dress,' she said, apologetically. 'I'm on my way to another party at the Pavilion.'

'Right,' said Stephen. He was not in the mood for making conversation. 'Do I know you?'

'Nope,' said the small woman, unabashed. 'But you do know my work. I'm Gillian Smale.'

'Are you really?' said Stephen. 'Well, I don't know if you realize this, but you aren't exactly my top person at the moment. In fact, your paintings were – how should I put it? – the icing on the cake when it came to my restaurant getting the worst review in the entire *history* of restaurant reviewing.'

Gillian Smale did not look embarrassed. 'My work, on the other hand, got a rave review on the opposite page,' she said. 'I knew you'd be pissed off with me, but I wanted to say thanks anyway. Looks like this could be my really big break.'

'Well,' said Stephen. 'I hope you're not expecting me to congratulate you.'

'No, I'm not,' she said. 'I'm sorry it all worked out so

crap for you. That reviewer sounded like a right pain in the arse.' She picked up a bottle of beer from the table, opened it, and turned to go.

Then Stephen had a memory flash of the dead animals, the blood-caked torsos. 'Just one other thing,' he said. 'Are you a vegetarian?'

'No way,' said Gillian Smale. 'In fact, I'm one of the few people I know who still eats veal. And, as you can see –' she patted her flat stomach – 'I'm not one of those food-problem girlies, either.'

'So what were those pictures all about?'

She shrugged. 'They're not about me. They're just meant to make people think,' she said. 'Art's not just about painting pretty pictures, you know.'

'Yeah, right, thanks for that; I do watch the *South Bank Show*. But people don't want to think about stuff like that when they're eating. It's just . . . tasteless.'

'People don't want to think about stuff like that *at all*,' said Gillian Smale. 'At least when they're eating they're a captive audience.' Then she hesitated before saying, 'This is probably none of my business, but . . . You know it was Marc's idea for you to show my work. He's a good friend of mine, but he can be vindictive. Maybe he did think it would alienate people. I'm sorry, like I said. But what really worries me is your friend Vinnie. I think Marc has really dropped him in the shit this time.'

'I haven't seen Vinnie for weeks.'

'*Weeks?* I thought you two were friends. Don't you think you should try to find out how he is?'

'Excuse me. I know I'm a bloke and that makes me complete rubbish, but I've bloody well tried. I've asked

337

Marc. I've searched his room. He is a bloody grown-up, after all.'

'Yeah, *exactly*.' With an enigmatic, artist-type look, Gillian Smale left the building.

After she'd gone, Stephen drank purposefully for a while, following his beer with a vodka chaser and then pouring himself another large glass of wine. He realized she was right. He was being sucked down into his own vortex so quickly that he hadn't had time to worry about Vinnie, partly because he had always assumed that Vinnie was so much tougher than he was. And partly, he knew, because of his innate selfishness. It was tiring to think that, as well as being abandoned and trashed by everyone, he ought to start trying to be a better person. Just as he was about to try to track down Marc, he found that he had appeared beside him.

'Stephen!' said Marc, mock-effusive. 'How perfectly delightful to see you!'

'Fuck off yourself,' said Stephen, his voice coming through more thickly since his latest alcohol intake. 'Don't suppose you've heard from Vinnie?'

Marc didn't seem to hear this. 'Haven't got a fag on you, by any chance?'

Stephen gave him one, making sure their fingers didn't touch.

'Good news is,' said Marc, exhaling smoke, 'he should be coming along tonight. Phoned me from the airport this morning. Been to fucking gay Paree, would you believe.'

'*Paris?* Why Paris?'

'You paid, apparently. He was meant to go with me, but decided to fuck off there himself, on his own. And he ended up staying for two weeks. God knows what he got up to there.'

'I should think he spent a fortune.'

'Don't get the impression that would bother him all that much.'

Stephen dimly remembered promising to pay for a trip to Paris the night of the doomed dinner party. So that was where Vinnie had disappeared to. He had never thought of checking to see if he'd taken his passport.

'Anyway,' said Marc. 'It's all pretty irrelevant now.'

'Irrelevant?'

'Because I'm chucking him.'

'Well, that *is* thoughtful of you. Any particular reason?'

'New boyfriend,' said Marc, beaming. 'Twenty-two. Utter and total dreamboy, believe me. And he's not one of your waiters, in case you're wondering. Just moved down from Manchester. Came in and bought some gorgeous dwarf peppers from the shop three weeks ago and we've been hard at it ever since.'

'So he's not the man in the bath, either.'

'God! That strumpet! No. We are talking about the love of my life, Stephen.'

'Well. With any luck he'll dump you for someone younger and better-looking,' said Stephen. 'After all, he'll have plenty of choice –' But, catching sight of the latest arrival, he broke off. It was Vinnie, ashen-faced and ethereal as Christ, pushing his way through the crowd towards them.

25

When he reached them, Stephen saw that Vinnie looked even more cadaverous than usual. His olive skin was yellow under the party lights, his eyes hidden in shadow. And he was thinner – he looked wasted. Like a junkie, Stephen thought. Then he had a sudden, horrible vision of gay men in the last stages of AIDS. He saw, for the first time, that Vinnie could be vulnerable and frail. How could he not have noticed this before?

Vinnie spoke first. 'You're looking well, Marc. Somehow, I knew you would. Not the type to sit at home crying into your cocoa, wondering where the fuck I'd got to.' He took no notice of Stephen, apparently not even realizing that he was there.

'Yes, well, I was worried about you! A girl's got to have some distractions at a time like this. I'm up to thirty fags a day. Look!' Marc waved his cigarette in front of Vinnie's face.

'I've spent a lot of time thinking recently,' said Vinnie. 'Thinking about you till my head hurt. And now I've decided what to do.' Then he paused, as if he still hadn't quite mustered up the courage to take the next step.

Marc took a long drag on his cigarette, blew smoke into the air over their heads and said, 'Maybe I can help you out there.'

'How? By starting again? By going back to how it was?' There was a note of pathetic desperation in Vinnie's voice. Stephen, rendered invisible by the intensity of the scene, had never heard tough, cynical Vinnie sound like this. He hated it. He wished he could somehow stop the inevitable from happening.

'Not exactly.' Marc had the grace to look slightly self-conscious. He suddenly seemed aware that Stephen was listening. 'Let's go somewhere we can talk properly,' he said, taking Vinnie's arm. Vinnie, passive now, allowed himself to be led away. Stephen remained by the drinks table, feeling giddy and nauseous.

'What's going on with those two?' asked Carmel, pouring a drink next to him.

'Marc's chucking Vinnie,' said Stephen.

'About time they called it a day, isn't it?' She sipped her drink through a straw – presumably to keep the bandages clean. 'I mean, there's only so much talking through that you can do. Plus, they are a total mismatch.'

'I'm getting a bit sick of all this mismatch stuff, to be honest,' said Stephen. 'It's all bollocks, isn't it? You're mixing up compatibility and similarity – they're not the same thing at all.'

'So you don't agree that Vinnie is one of the world's top human beings and Marc is a complete shit-bag?'

'Erm, no. I mean, yes. I do agree.'

'Or that one person loving too much doesn't make up for the other not loving enough?'

'You've got me there as well. It's just that . . . I don't know. You always seem to want to tidy up relationships. The reason that Rachel and I split up wasn't that we were so different; it was that she decided she . . . She . . .' He thought of their earlier conversation and realized that he didn't know what to say. All he knew was that there was no going back.

'Yes. Like I said at Pride: sometimes it is right to hang on in there,' said Carmel. 'Making it work isn't about what personal qualities you may or may not have. It's about love. Wanting each other. Then you work out the rest. And that's what the problem is here – Vinnie wants a soulmate and Marc wants every boy he meets.'

'Well, you've certainly changed your tune,' said Stephen. On the dancefloor, his mother was now dancing energetically with Ian to the sound of Nirvana's 'Smells Like Teen Spirit' while Kris and Sorrel were smooching among the crazed dancers. Nearby, Clive was deep in conversation with a tall blonde he probably didn't realize was a transvestite.

'I've done a lot of brain-storming since that day we met in the Grand,' said Carmel. 'But I agree with you, for once. I have talked crap about relationships. I was wrong. And when you really love somebody, it doesn't matter whether your profiles match.'

'Well, thank you very much. This has to be a first. But I still can't believe you could bear to live in a house with children.'

Carmel lifted off the bandaged mask, and shook out her short, curly hair. She was smiling. 'You know who the first big love of my life was, don't you?' she said.

'Yeah, Farah Fawcett-Majors.'

'Close. Same period, anyway.'

'Who?'

'Fay Cattermole.'

'Fay? You mean – you had a crush on *Fay*?'

'More than that. We had a torrid affair, darling. We lost our virginity to each other. But she never liked the idea of "being a lesbian".' Stephen clutched the table, feeling that he would otherwise lose his balance. He couldn't speak. Carmel continued, in stream-of-consciousness mode. 'Always flirting with that awful Nigel Nunnelly, remember him? It broke my heart . . . All through my twenties, I only slept with men. Mainly because I didn't dare have sex with a woman again. It would have meant too much.'

Stephen frowned, trying to take this in. 'So, Fay is a *lesbian*?'

'Yes. She's been out for years now.'

'God.' Stephen couldn't think of anything else to say. He wondered if the offer of a nightcap when she left the club had been merely chummy, or whether she still had the odd bout of bisexuality. Why had he annoyed her by saying no? Perhaps she just hated the idea that he was no longer in thrall to her.

'What I'm trying to say is that I fell so hard for Fay that I haven't let myself fall in love again. It was more than ten years before I dared have sex with a woman. That's why I came out so late. But that's all changed.'

Carmel was still smiling. Stephen realized she was looking at someone on the other side of the room. 'I was wrong,' she said simply. 'True love *can* last. You just have to make sacrifices. If Lise wants babies, she can have as many as she likes.'

'So what about monogamy being a con? What about

343

sex-free relationships held together by fear? What about the joys of finding someone new when your old love goes stale? You built a whole business on that! Liberating lesbians from staying in a relationship because they feel guilty about moving on. Learning to live more like gay men. What happened to all that?'

'Oh, there's still a market for it,' said Carmel. 'It's just that I'll be doing something slightly different myself.'

'The complete opposite, more like! Think about it, Carmel. You'll be a mum, day in, day out,' said Stephen, in a vindictive tone that surprised him. 'Trapped for life. You'll go mad.'

'Actually, I'll be a *father*, which is slightly different. As you know, that's a role which is a bit more hands-off,' said Carmel. Stephen winced. 'Lise will be the mother. She'll be wonderful. Don't worry. I'm taking Lise to see the house tomorrow. Bit like yours, actually. Big surprise – so don't say anything.'

As she said this, Lise, bald head sprouting out of a froth of feather boa, came sweeping into her arms. 'Hello, gorgeous,' said Carmel, and they were lost to the world in an embarrassingly erotic kiss. Stephen moved away, scanning the crowd for Vinnie and Marc. But they had disappeared. He found himself standing next to Clive, who now had his arm around the tall blonde and was drunker than ever.

'Hello – Steve,' Clive said, as if taking a wild bet on this being the right name. 'Meet new friend Cecilia.'

'Hello, Cecilia,' said Stephen.

Cecilia gave him a cutesy wave with a vast policeman's hand, garnished with enormous rings. Her nails were carefully painted with fuscia polish. 'Nice to meet you,' she said. She sounded like Les Dawson.

'Cecilia top model,' said Clive. He took a swig from a bottle of champagne and offered it to Stephen, who shook his head. 'Knows Sophie Dahl, Kate Moss, Nigel Havers – everyone. Don't you?' he asked.

Cecilia nodded sheepishly.

Clive leaned towards Stephen and whispered in his ear. 'Fantastic, isn't she? Trying to get her take me home. Says she lives with her mother. No chance taking her back to Vinnie's, is there?'

'Sorry, Clive, no chance at all,' Stephen whispered back. 'Maybe you should arrange to meet her in . . . daylight.' He glanced across at Cecilia and she blew him a kiss. Deciding to abandon all attempt at subtlety, he hissed. 'Clive, go home, for God's sake. You should be with Tamzin. She's your wife. And you *love* her. You know that.' Clive just giggled and tipped his champagne bottle upside down. A few drops sparkled down on to his shoes, reflecting the disco lights as they fell. Despairingly, Stephen tried again: 'Look, why don't you come outside with me and look for Vinnie and Marc? There's some kind of bust-up going on, and I'm not sure how Vinnie's going to react.'

But before he could prise Clive away, he found that Nick had appeared and was topping up his glass almost to the rim. 'Hope you're enjoying yourself, mate,' he said. 'Weird fucking night at that club – bad scene for all of us.' He was swaying and had a cigarette between his lips which had burned down almost to the stub. 'Might have been a bit of a prat.'

'It doesn't matter,' said Stephen. He drank some wine to stop it spilling. 'I think I was temporarily slightly insane.' He wondered if that was true, or if he had in fact been temporarily slightly sane. That was certainly how it had felt. He remembered the sudden clarity, the focus, as if it had been one of those hyperreal dreams, suffused with inexplicable happiness, which you want to stay inside for ever.

'Yeah – we were all out of order. Look, Steve, there's something I've been meaning to say to you for a while now. Sort of a confession.'

'Confession? What could you possibly have to confess to that I don't know about already?'

This seemed to embarrass Nick. 'Well, believe it or not, Steve, there are things I could tell you that really would make you see me in a different –'

'Hello, boys,' said Rachel, suddenly zooming in between them. 'Having a manly heart-to-heart about the joys of lap-dancing?'

'Not exactly,' said Stephen. Then, suddenly he laughed. 'Oh – I know what you were trying to confess to, Nick.' Both of them stared at him, mouths open. 'I know it was you who told Rachel that I'd been to the club, *and* that I was allegedly in love with one of the dancers. *And* I know that she's trying to sell the house behind my back. I think you'll find that's illegal, Rachel. We have to agree about what to do with the house. When we're finally divorced. No need to rush into anything.' Their mouths snapped shut again, and Stephen found himself lost in the crowd. He realized that, instead of being blind drunk, as he had hoped, he was drinking himself sober. Something had just happened, or not happened. He tried to work out what it was. In her tarty outfit, with her shapely legs outlined by black fishnets, hair piled up on her head and spiralling down in tiny ringlets, Rachel had never looked more desirable; she glowed with a new confidence. Even so, seeing her did not tear at him. He felt curious about her, antagonistic towards her, even protective. But he did not feel love.

He made his way outside. Once out of range of the disco lights, it was very dark indeed. At first he couldn't see Vinnie and Marc. Then he caught sight of them, face to face, standing by the stagnant pool in the middle of the rose garden, talking intensely. Angrily. He looked from them to Clive, who was whispering coquettishly into Cecilia's ear. It seemed as though, because the pain of seeing Rachel had abated, he could see his two friends more clearly. Vinnie's face, white in the moonlight, desperate. Clive, chortling foolishly as he produced another bottle from somewhere. If he could, Stephen would help them. He took a deep breath, took out his mobile phone and pressed for Clive's number.

'Hello?' said Tamzin instantly. Her voice was tight.

'Tamzin, it's Stephen.'

'Oh.' He heard the dying note – knew that she was waiting for Clive to call. 'Where are you?' she asked. 'What's that awful noise in the background?'

'It's a party.'

'Is Clive with you?' she asked, suspiciously.

'Not with me *as such*, no,' said Stephen. 'But he is here. He said you told him to get out.' He could see Clive opening the bottle now, wiggling his tongue like Mick

Jagger. He'd pushed his glasses to the top of his head like a Sloane Ranger and his blond hair stuck out unbecomingly.

'I didn't mean out for good. I just meant out of my face. He's pissed all the time, and keeps going on and on about how we're bringing a monster into the world. One minute he was pro-abortion, next minute he was right-to-life, and now he's turned into one of the Three Witches in *Macbeth*. I suppose this is his version of a midlife crisis. This baby is the first thing that has ever gone wrong for him. Or for me, in fact.'

'But you still love him?'

'What kind of question is that? Of course I love him. All I'm saying is that he's an idiot. He's always been an idiot.' Stephen had never heard Tamzin talk like this before. There was nothing fey about her now.

'I think you'd better come and get him,' he said. 'Before he . . . does something seriously stupid.'

'A bit late for that, I should imagine. Has he hooked up with someone totally unsuitable? Before we got married he was always falling for mad women.'

'Something like that. Just get here as soon as you can. We're at the Rotunda Café.'

'I'll be there in ten minutes,' said Tamzin. 'Make sure he doesn't leave.'

As Stephen was returning the phone to his pocket, a terrible screaming tore into the air. He glanced into the club – the music was so loud that no one else had noticed. The dancing continued frenetically. Dashing into the rose garden, he saw that Vinnie had jumped on top of Marc and knocked him to the ground, and was lying on top of him, beating his chest with his hands. The screaming came from Vinnie, not from Marc, who was silent, staring in horror at his former lover's face. Stephen had never heard anything like it before – it was a primeval sound that made the hairs on the back of his neck stand up.

'Vinnie – for Christ's sake – get off!' he yelled. It took him a long time to pull Vinnie away. When he finally succeeded, Vinnie lay prostrate on the muddy grass, the horrible baying sobs still tearing out of his throat. Stephen found it hard to believe that he would speak intelligible words again – it sounded as if his brain had been destroyed by agony and grief. Marc scrambled to his feet, still not taking his eyes from Vinnie. For a while, no one said anything.

'I hope you're satisfied, Romeo,' said Stephen at last, taking hold of Marc's arm. 'You and your fucking pathetic little ego games.'

Marc wiped his mouth with the back of his hand. 'If it's any of your fucking business, I feel like shit,' he said. 'We just – I should have . . .' Stephen realized there were tears on Marc's face. 'I didn't know it would be like this,' he said, at last. 'Like someone dying.' He looked down at Vinnie. It seemed as if his sobbing would never stop. 'I need a drink,' said Marc, pushing past Stephen and disappearing back into the party.

'Vinnie?' Stephen bent down and touched his friend's shoulder, surprised that he felt so afraid. The cold leather shook uncontrollably. 'It had to happen . . . Please –' He bent lower so he was kneeling next to him and put his arm awkwardly around Vinnie's body. 'I'm so sorry. I'm really, really sorry . . .' Somehow, Vinnie slithered out from his grasp and turned his face towards him. His

349

eyes were ringed with scarlet, threaded with violent red veins. His face was twisted. Tears and snot covered his cheeks.

'You *knew*,' he hissed.

'What?'

'You fucking *knew* that he was screwing around behind my back. And you never told me. You fucking cold, selfish, miserable bastard. I'll never forgive you for that. Never.'

'I just didn't know how to put it – how you'd react –'

'Oh, *right*, yeah. Might have been a tiny bit embarrassing. Can't have that. Is that how much you cared? How can I trust you again? How can I trust anyone? I suppose you had a bloody good laugh about it, you and everyone else who knew what was going on and couldn't be *arsed* to tell me.'

'But, Vinnie – I –' Stephen began. However, just at that moment, he saw Clive tottering out into the street, propped up by Cecilia. Swaying and sniggering, they began to make their way out of the garden.

'Clive – wait a minute. I need to talk to you –' Clive, with great concentration, was licking Cecilia's ear. Stephen scrambled to his feet and chased after then. 'Look, erm – hello? Both of you. You can't leave now.' Clive and Cecilia turned to look at him.

'Checking into hotel,' said Clive. 'Best decision of my life.'

Cecilia smirked at Stephen. 'Love at first sight,' she said.

'Darling!' said Clive, and with that the two of them embarked on an enormous snog, hands snaking over each other's backs, tongues dripping with saliva.

'Clive, you do realize that you are grappling with a bloke. I mean, I assume even you know what gender people are.' Tamzin, looking about ten feet wide, was standing on the pavement in front of them. Her face was impassive.

'It's not a –' began Clive. Then he frowned at Tamzin, as information about who she was began to arrive in his brain. 'Blimey! Tamzin . . . Wife and stuff,' he said. Then, changing tack slightly, 'Hello, sweetness. Should you be out this late? How's the heartburn?'

'Clive, put that man down,' said Tamzin sternly. 'You pathetic little twerp.'

'Man?' Clive looked at Cecilia, brow still furrowed. 'Cecilia?'

'Afraid so, darling,' said Cecilia, disentangling herself and backing cautiously away on her wobbly stilettos. 'Bye for now.' Then she turned and fled, heels clacking on the paving stones.

Clive looked at Tamzin and Tamzin looked at Clive. 'Sorry,' said Clive, after a while. He wiped his hand across his eyes as if he had just woken up. 'God. I suppose "sorry" doesn't really cover it.'

'Sorry is a start,' said Tamzin. She sounded tired rather than angry. She took the champagne bottle he was still carrying and laid it sideways on the ground. Fizzy clear liquid seeped into the mud. 'Let's go home,' she said. Looping her arm through his, she led him away, his drunken, unstable weight supported by her magnificent, earth-bound bulk.

Stephen rushed back to the place he had left Vinnie lying on the grass. But Vinnie had disappeared. With a sudden, terrible foreboding, he rushed back into the café. 'Anyone seen Vinnie?' he said, grabbing Carmel.

'No. I don't think he's been back in at all,' she said. 'Why? What's wrong?' Stephen looked frantically around the room. Vinnie was nowhere to be seen. 'I don't know. Just – he's in such a state –' He dashed to the toilet – there was a Vinnie-free queue – then looked in the garden again, which was empty. Returning to the drinks table, he saw Marc swigging a Bacardi Breezer.

'Vinnie's disappeared,' he said. 'If he was going somewhere, where would he go?'

'How should I know? Anyway, he can't go far because I've got the car keys –' Marc patted his hip, then looked down in consternation. 'Fuck.' He pulled the contents of both pockets on to the table – screwed-up tissues, used train tickets, condoms, change, a picture of himself when considerably thinner. There were no car keys. 'He's nicked them,' he said. 'The bloody sneaky bitch.'

'So where would he go?'

'Maybe Abby's house – his friend, you know, the nurse who helped him. But she works nights, so she won't be there.'

'Nurse? Helped him? What do you mean?'

'He met her when he was in hospital. When he had his second breakdown. I can't believe you didn't know all this. Mind you, he always says he never tells you anything. Says it isn't worth it.'

'No, Marc, I did *not* know. I didn't know he'd had one breakdown, never mind two.'

'Christ! Weird friendship you two have. If you knew

more about his life, maybe he wouldn't be so pissed off with you.'

'One thing I do know is that he's beside himself. He could do anything.'

Marc looked sick. 'Don't lay this on me. He's tried before. It's not my fault.'

'Tried before? Tried to *kill* himself, you mean?'

'Yes. He took an overdose when his lover left him. Three years ago. I always thought you knew.'

Stephen tried to steady himself and order his thoughts. 'If he was going to do it again, what would he do? Where would he go? Has he ever *talked* about doing it again? Think about it. Think about him. *Think*.'

Marc was looking down, tears dripping on to his shirt. 'Well, we did have a conversation once. About what we would do if we wanted to top ourselves. But it wasn't serious –'

'And what did he say?'

'He said he'd never take an overdose again – too much chance of getting it wrong. He'd jump off something high. Said he dreams about those people on September the eleventh, just falling through the air.'

'Christ Almighty.'

'But – I mean, that's a joke. Not what you'd seriously do. It's so, well . . . So tacky. I thought, in a way, it was like him saying, "I love you for ever". He's a bit of a drama queen, you know.'

'What do you mean? What did he say, exactly?'

'He said if I ever left him he would jump off Beachy Head. It's just something you say for effect.' Marc's eyes were glittering with fear.

'Even if you've already tried to kill yourself? Even if you've already had two mental breakdowns? Jesus –'

Suddenly, Britney Spears appeared. 'You never deserved him,' she said in Briony's voice. 'He was always too good for you. If he does something stupid because of you, I hope you never get over it. I hope it haunts you for the rest of your life.' Stephen stared at Briony, realizing yet again what a lousy reader he was of his fellow human beings. She loved Vinnie, not Andy! Of course. How stupid he had been. He realized now why she had insisted on staying until Vinnie got back.

Marc's face was whiter than ever. 'I'm going outside,' he said. 'I've got to throw up.'

'Right – you do that. I need a car.' Stephen turned around, scanning the room, stuck for ideas. What should he do? Everyone was drunk. No one was in a fit state to drive, least of all himself. The walls were throbbing; the floor seemed to undulate beneath his feet. He didn't know if this was the effect of alcohol or shock. Should he call a cab? But this was hardly the time to involve a stranger. He scanned the crowd, desperately searching his brain. Rachel, catching his eye, came towards him. Her face was set. 'I hope you're satisfied with that smug little outburst,' she said.

'What do you mean?'

'About stopping me from selling the house. You can't control me now. If you are a free agent, then so am I.'

'Now look here, Rachel, it was you who wanted me to move out. We'd still be together if it wasn't for you.'

'Together! You mean living under the same roof, I suppose. Well, if that's your definition of "together", maybe we would. But some people demand a little bit more than that out of life, and I happen to be one of them.'

'Great. But you still can't sell the house behind my back.'

'Don't look at me with that snooty expression. I've done nothing to be ashamed of. Not like you. Scratch the surface and for all your jumped-up attitudes you fall for a lap-dancer. You of all people! After all those years when you were desperate to be more poncy than anyone else. You've spent so long ignoring your emotions that now you don't know what they are.'

Stephen was about to reply, but noticed his mother, edging past in her diaphanous pink, carrying an over-full glass.

'Dear me,' said Rose, taking a sip. 'Did you know that gorgeous blonde girl had a penis? I opened the loo door by mistake, and she was standing up to wee. Just shows it takes all sorts.'

'Right, yeah . . .' said Stephen, automatically filing her voice into the furthest reaches of his mind. He was half-turned towards Rachel. Then the glass of pineapple juice in Rose's hand zoomed suddenly into focus. 'Is that what you've been drinking all night?'

'You know I can't hold a drink – remember how I blurted out all that stuff in front of Sylvia Cattermole?'

'Look, Rachel, we'll have to discuss this some other time,' he said. Rachel frowned, but headed back to the dancefloor. Stephen turned to Rose. 'Did you bring your car?'

'Yes. What's all this about? You haven't done something illegal, have you?'

'No – *no* – I need you to help me. Vinnie's disappeared, and he said some stupid thing to Marc about jumping off Beachy Head – and it's probably mad, but I want to go there. Just to make sure that, you know . . . Nothing happens.'

'Beachy Head? The cliffs, you mean? Is that near here?'

'About twenty miles away. I need someone to drive me there. Now. Fast.'

His mother looked at him with an odd expression, put her drink down and took his arm. 'That poor boy,' she said. 'Of course I'll take you.'

'Thanks,' said Stephen, suddenly remembering what a liability she was behind the wheel of a car. 'You will keep your eyes on the road, won't you? There's plenty of time for me to explain everything later, when you don't need to concentrate.'

'Of course I'll look at the road! Let's go – I've parked just next to the wheelie bin outside. To tell you the truth, I could only get in at a bit of an angle, so I'll be quite relieved to move it sooner rather than later.'

26

It was a long time since Stephen had been driven anywhere by his mother. Partly, of course, because he usually drove himself. But also, he registered as the car juddered unsteadily into the traffic, because she was the worst driver in the world. Now, full of concern for Vinnie and overwhelmed by the drama of the situation, she was doing a worse job than usual.

'Come on, come on, missus – get moving – oh! Aaahhh!' she cried, as they sailed into the flow of car headlights. 'It just shows you: gay people – they're setting themselves up for disaster. Look at . . .'

'If you say "Dirk Bogarde" you can bloody well drop me off at the next taxi rank . . .'

'Well, maybe I'm old fashioned.'

'Maybe you are.'

'I'm not saying I don't care.'

'You always care.'

'And that's a sin, is it? Always caring?'

Stephen felt too sick to engage in a sensible discussion with his mother. Most of her speculations were based on her experience as freelance counsellor to every woman she managed to capture under one of her dryers, and on the women's magazines which were stacked around the walls of the salon. Was it wisdom that she had to share with people? Or second-hand, second-rate psychobabble?

His mother had had no education. She didn't know why Hamlet delayed. She had never read *Ulysses*, or '*To the Lighthouse*'. How could you know anything about human relationships if you fed your mind on Catherine Cookson? Yet Stephen had to admit that she also embarrassed him with her vulgar intuitions: knowing there was 'something not right' with the children that weekend in Stoke, for instance. Did he want to keep communication with her to a minimum because she knew so little, or because she knew too much? He saw, looking out at the night, that his passion to distance himself from all things naff was in a way an attempt to distance himself from his mother. She was almost professionally silly, pathologically trivial-minded. But that wasn't all she was. And perhaps, by ignoring her sanity, her kindness, her unstoppable flow of affection for other people, he had also ignored part of himself.

Now, he was afraid of what she might say. His composure was held together by gossamer threads. In his mind, he saw a tiny figure tumbling endlessly downwards in front of a white cliff. He sensed his mother staring at him, then her hand came across and patted his knee. Almost immediately, cars started hooting as she veered towards the oncoming traffic.

'Mum, for Christ's sake! Keep your eyes on the road! You want the third exit from the next roundabout.' Rose swore to herself as she steered the car into the right lane, but for the rest of the journey she lapsed into an unusual and discomforting silence.

Stephen knew only one way to Beachy Head, along the coast road through Saltdene and Newhaven. In the daytime, this was an easy if sometimes congested journey, the road ribboning along the tops of the cliffs, edged by retirement bungalows. At night, the experience was very different. Once they got beyond the suburban streetlights, all he could see was blackness and, to the right, the howling grey sea. Fear began to curl itself around him as the landscape opened up and they drove over flat scrubland which he knew topped the giddy white cliffs. The sky now came down all around them, dark and cloud-torn. Now and again, the car headlights glimmered on pale gateposts or dark humps of roadkill. Sea winds buffeted the car as they turned off the main road and down the narrow lane towards the edge of the land. A car horn screamed as they narrowly missed one of the few other night motorists on the road.

Rose's continuing silence fed Stephen's rising panic. He kept remembering Marc's words: 'He always says he never tells you anything. Says it isn't worth it.' Of course, he hadn't wanted to be told things. He was a man, after all. But he saw now how lonely Vinnie had been – how lonely he was at this moment. And the nearer they got, the more likely it seemed that Vinnie's words weren't an empty threat but were the simple expression of what he planned to do. Stephen knew that Vinnie wasn't the sort of person who said things for effect. He was action-prone – inclined to do things that were extremely ill-advised, like hooking up with Marc, or leaving the London-restaurant scene to throw in his lot with Stephen. He would do what he said he would do. The nearer Rose's car got to the cliffs, the more inevitable this seemed. By the time they arrived at the car park on the top of the cliff, Stephen was trembling from head to foot.

'Park there – outside that café thing,' he said, directing his mother to the brick-built visitor centre, constructed in the ersatz cottage style of a Tesco superstore. Over the main door were the words 'BREWERS FAYRE BEACHY HEAD' and below that ' NTRANCE'.

'Is that the car?' asked his mother.

He peered out and saw that Marc's VW convertible had indeed been left in the car park. One door was wide open, as if Vinnie had just left it and run headlong for the cliffs.

Rose stopped and turned off the engine. The banshee winds yelled around them. She turned on the inside light and looked at him again. Her face was collapsing with anxiety.

'I'd better get going,' said Stephen, but suddenly he felt too afraid to move. An intense wind came at them like a bomb blast, howling its way around the car. A half-moon jerked into sight when the clouds chased across it.

'You can't go out like that,' she said. He looked down, and realized that all he was wearing was the wretched rum baba outfit. His mother passed him a tartan travelling rug, which he draped over his shoulders.

'It might be too late already,' he said, staring out of the car's windscreen.

'Just pray to God it's not,' said his mother. She undid her seatbelt and began to open her door.

'Mum, you can't go out there! God! It's . . . dangerous.' He took his mobile phone out of his pocket and handed it to her. 'If I'm not back in fifteen minutes, call the police.'

'Why don't we call them now?'

'If I can stop him, we won't need them. It'll just be even more of a trauma if the police are involved.'

360

She nodded and handed him a torch. One of her Dame Barbara eyelashes was coming unstuck. 'Keep away from the edge,' she said. 'And stay low down. In this wind . . .' Her fears were whipped away by the gale, and by the slam of the car door.

The first thing that hit him when he got out of the car was the cold. Although it was only September, the temperature had plunged and the wind tore at him. For a second he couldn't move, and stood inert, his right hand still extended towards the car, and a voice, his voice, let out a sort of scream. With an effort of will, he turned on the torch, and pointed its beam to his left, towards the flat scrubby grass which he knew was the cliff edge. He remembered from his last visit there with the children that there was a footpath to the main drop itself – though you could in fact throw yourself off anywhere along its length, if you were prepared to negotiate a low, wire fence. But his hunch was that Vinnie would have gone towards the unfenced section of the cliff. He followed the beam across the empty road and on to the bouncy turf. The wind sliced into him even more keenly, as if other-worldly forces were trying to keep him away. Even in the daytime, the cliffs here had a bleak, eerie quality. Now, he remembered unwillingly that this was a spot which used to be popular with devil worshippers as well as suicides. It was an evil place, he thought, though he did not usually hold with such moral absolutes. He bent forwards, pitching each step against the force of the wind. He owed a debt to Vinnie. He owed a debt to friendship.

The torch beam showed up the muddy grass, sudden

pebbles, sparkling pale in the light, discarded lolly sticks. Slowly, he made his way to the edge. Finally, the grass came to an end, and he reached an area of rough, stony ground. Beyond it, he could see the sea, and the sky, but not where the two met. Below him, he could hear the waves beating the chalk with ritual force. But there was no sign of Vinnie. He took a step nearer the edge – he wasn't sure if where the land appeared to end was actually the drop, or if he needed to go further. A sudden rip of wind grabbed him and almost knocked him off his feet. He sat down heavily on the gravel. His mother was right: better to keep his centre of gravity low. Wriggling his way further towards the edge on his foam-covered bottom, he could see where the sheer drop began: it was still about six feet away from where he now squatted. To his right, he could now make out the cliffs themselves, sweeping down nearly 600 feet to the boiling sea below. Even in the darkness they glowed, a pale, creamy arc descending into the night. Further away, he could see the beam of the lighthouse, sending shards of brightness across the waves. And, outlined against the sky, standing on a little outcrop, just below the level of the cliff, he could see a motionless silhouette. Vinnie. Stephen felt a physical jolt of shock, even though this was what he had been expecting, even hoping to see. A sudden wave of referred vertigo threatened to overwhelm him, and for a second he hid his face inside his hands. When he took them away, he almost expected Vinnie to have disappeared. But the silent figure was still there. Taking a great gulp of air, Stephen began to shuffle closer. He stopped two feet from the first edge of land, from which the ground sloped down steeply to Vinnie's outcrop. 'Hello! Vinnie! It's Stephen! Hey! Can you hear me?' He did not look down.

There was no response. 'Shit,' he said. Studying the ground more carefully, he could see that there was a rugged little pathway from his position to where Vinnie was standing. So he slithered along it, until he was perched just a couple of feet from Vinnie's outcrop. Now he could see Vinnie in detail – his head was bent, as if looking downwards at the sea, his hands clutched what looked like a whisky bottle, and his hair was blowing flat against his skull.

'Vinnie! Vinnie! Can you hear me?'

At last, Vinnie turned. He gave a slow nod, but said nothing.

'It's a bit dangerous, standing there!' shouted Stephen. 'Why don't we climb back up on top, so we can have a proper talk?' Vinnie still said nothing, but took a swig from his bottle. It was a purposeful gesture.

'Fuck. Fuck.' Stephen tried to clutch the ground as another gust of wind blasted over him.

'I'm sorry you haven't been able to talk to me,' he shouted. 'I mean, not just recently. I mean, EVER.' He stared hard at Vinnie, but it was impossible to tell if he could hear him at all. 'I know what you think. And it's true: I did know about Marc – about one boy, that is. But I *never* meant to lie to you.' Vinnie still looked away, towards the bottom of the cliff.

Stephen thought hard. Thought of Rachel's parting shot at the party, her often-repeated litany of his failings. She was right up to a point. But he hadn't just ignored his emotions. Throughout his marriage, he had expected other people to tell him what they were. Working for some stupid goal had seemed easier. Now he was stuck on a cliff-top, trying to think of reasons to want to be alive. Even someone as emotionally super-literate as Carmel might be lost for words. But there was no way out. He had to think of something.

'I can't imagine what you are feeling . . .' he began. 'I mean, I've been depressed recently, but I know you're locked into something much . . . *much blacker*,' he yelled, suddenly worried that he just wasn't giving it enough volume. '*But . . . I've been dumped too. I mean, not two-timed, like you. I know you think it was some sort of conspiracy. But trust me – it wasn't!*'

Neither of them spoke for a while, then Stephen shouted: '*Rachel was the love of my life.*' He gazed out at the sea. '*And it's over. There's not going to be reconciliation. There's not going to be an "us".*'

'You're wasting your time,' said Vinnie, in a voice that was surprisingly normal in volume and tone. 'I can't trust anyone.'

'I'm trying to understand how you feel,' said Stephen. 'Trying to be . . . your friend.'

'Surprising how easy it is, really,' said Vinnie. His tone was almost chatty, yet there was a sense of him being far away, as if he was already halfway down the cliff.

'Easy?' Stephen felt another slice of wind go through him. Around him, some fragments of gravel started to slide down towards the precipice, and he tried to clutch the hard ground again.

'No fence. Always thought there would be some kind

of barrier. Warnings and stuff. But there's nothing. Land ends, drop starts. If you don't want your life, just chuck it over.'

'Not easy to jump, though. Not easy to end everything. Is it? The idea of it being forever. Freaked me out since I was seventeen.'

Vinnie swigged his whisky. 'Nothing freaks me out any more. It's like I've been going one way down a tunnel. Now I can see the way out. The only way. It's just about stopping the pain. Stopping being a pain to yourself, to everyone. Dragging them all down with you.'

'I know what you mean,' said Stephen. 'Feeling like there's nothing but filth inside you. Funny thing is, I thought I was the one who was depressed, and that you were the strong one.'

'Yeah, well. That's because you always go round with your head up your own arse.'

This sounded so much like the old Vinnie that Stephen was tempted to laugh. But something about the calmness of his friend's tone was frightening. Vinnie spoke with a detachment that made Stephen feel that the decision was made, that Vinnie was just killing a little time before leaping into the infinite darkness.

'Vinnie, I don't think I was so wide of the mark. So you've been ill before and I didn't know. You're still the strong one. You're still the person who runs the show. And you're still the best friend, the most important friend in my life. And I am truly sorry, Vinnie,' he said. 'I just got stuck with the idea that I had to concentrate really hard on one thing, be excellent at that one thing, and then my life would somehow fall into place. It would . . . work out. And I just saw you as the person who had to help me do it.'

'That's okay,' said Vinnie. 'I have to go.' He took a step closer to the edge.

Stephen, with a surge of nausea and horror, threw himself flat on to the ground and splayed his hands out so they were as close to Vinnie as he dared go. '*No! No!*' he shouted. '*Jesus! If you go over, Vinnie, you'll destroy me! I need you, Vinnie!*'

'Oh, Stephen,' said Vinnie, turning to look at him. 'If only that was true.' He put up his hand to wave, and in that split second Stephen managed to catch hold of his leg, holding it tightly in his two hands. He felt Vinnie losing his balance, begin to fall. Would they both go over? Which way was he going? Then he felt Vinnie sprawling on top of him. He wrapped his arms tight around his friend. But he knew who was the stronger. Eyes tight shut, he prayed, waiting for the inevitable, final battle.

'Can you hear me?' said a voice from above. 'We're here to help you, but you must stay calm. Can you hear me, Vincent?' Stephen kept his eyes closed. The police. Thank God. But he felt Vinnie begin to writhe in his arms. 'Can you hear me?' said the voice again.

'I can hear you,' shouted Stephen. 'But I . . . can't let go.'

'Vincent, we need to hear from you as well,' said the voice. It was a woman's voice. In a calm, spectating part of his mind, he wondered if women police officers were better at this sort of thing than men. She sounded strangely familiar. Vinnie said nothing, but started to wriggle in Stephen's grasp.

366

'He's pushing me away!' shouted Stephen. A rock scudded past them. 'Jesus! We're going to die here!' He felt as if there was already nothing between him and the sea. The sound of the waves was more real to him than the voice above.

'Vincent, you have to help us now,' said the voice. 'Stephen needs you. Can you do that for me? Can you help Stephen?'

Vinnie lay still, but silent.

'I know what you want to do, but it's not just your life that's at risk now. Do you understand me? Say yes if you understand me.'

Stephen, clutching Vinnie from behind, felt his captive's head move. 'Understand you. Yes,' said Vinnie, thickly.

'Good. That's really good, Vincent. Now, what you do in the future is up to you. No one's stopping you from doing what you think is right. But tonight you have to help us and we have to get you both off there. So will you do that for me?'

'Yes.'

'Thanks. Now, you'll feel something landing on you. It's a rope. Vincent, you need to grab it first. Please grab that rope.'

'I've got it.' Stephen could feel Vinnie's arms tense. 'You can let go of me now, Stephen.'

'Are you sure?'

'Trust me.' Stephen let go, and felt Vinnie's body being dragged away from him. He opened his eyes for the first time, and looked up at the sky. Vinnie had disappeared. Something dry and heavy fell on top of him. The rope. 'Now it's your turn, Stephen,' said the familiar voice.

Where had he heard it before? He grabbed it and let himself be pulled upwards, towards the top of the cliff. It was a surprisingly short distance away. He remembered now that he had only shuffled down a few feet. But the long drop into forever filled his mind. When he reached the top, he crawled to the turf and lay there, trembling in an ague of cold and shock. A blanket was wrapped around him. Some sort of liquid was poured into his mouth. He looked up and saw not uniformed police but his mother, bending over him, thermos flask in hand. Standing close to her was someone he recognized. It was Gabrielle. She had her arms around Vinnie, and was holding him close to her, sobbing bitterly. Impossible to believe that she had spoken those collected, professional words, and pulled them back into sanity. But he knew she had.

27

Gabrielle came out of the private room in the hospital and closed the door quietly behind her. 'He's asleep now,' she said. 'He didn't take an overdose or anything – just the whisky.'

'Was that likely?' asked Stephen.

'Sometimes people want to make sure they do the job properly.'

'So does that mean he didn't really want to die?'

'God knows. I'll stay here, though. He might need me when he wakes up. Thanks,' she said to Rose, who handed her a hot chocolate from the drinks machine. Rose gave her a warm smile. Gabrielle and his mother had forged the sort of womanly bond that would once have annoyed him. But now, still shaking from the cold and the closeness of death, he felt reassured by this version of normality. The hot chocolate, the smiles, the clinking gold bracelets they both wore. Gabrielle, he noticed, had a gold ring on each finger. He determinedly focused his mind on such details: being in the hospital unnerved him. A trolley carrying an old man, bleached by illness and age, went rattling by them. Stephen's eyes followed the hopeless, limp figure sprawled under thin blankets.

'Are you sure you are all right, Stephen?' asked Rose. 'I still think you should be in bed or something.' She took his hand and held it close to her body, her plump fingers gripping his. 'You were always useless with heights.'

'Honestly, Mum, there is nothing wrong with me! I'm fine. Completely fine.' He knew she could feel him trembling.

'I'll drive you home now. If you're ready.'

'Thanks, thanks.' He looked distractedly at Gabrielle, desperate to speak to her alone, but not knowing how to ask. His mother gave the two of them a sharp glance. 'I'm just popping to the ladies',' she said, releasing Stephen.

'Well,' said Gabrielle. 'I expect you're feeling a bit confused.' She sipped her drink, watching him over the plastic rim of her cup. Her eyes were still piggy and red from crying, but her voice was calm.

'You could say that,' said Stephen. 'Does this mean you aren't really a lap-dancer? A plain-clothes policeman or something?' He thought of Angie Dickinson, going under cover as a vice girl every week in the seventies. Gabrielle's present outfit – flouncy white skirt, red cowboy boots and gypsy-style top – was one which Angie might well have chosen. 'Policewoman, I mean.'

'I'm a psychiatric nurse,' said Gabrielle. Her tone was flat and resigned. 'And a lap-dancer as well. Only, Vinnie doesn't know about the lap-dancing bit.'

He thought about this, or tried to. Thought of her in white coat, wheeling nodding nutters about in a mansion. But he assumed her job was nothing like this. All the time, he could hear waves crashing on rocks, feel the searing wind. After a while, he asked: 'Is Abby your real name?'

'Yeah – kind of. Gabrielle's a bit of a bloody mouthful. All my friends outside the club call me Abby.' She was watching him carefully, as if he was a child emerging from a tantrum.

'And you helped Vinnie . . . before? When he was ill . . . the last time?'

'When he tried to top himself last time, yeah. That's how we met.' She drained her hot chocolate down to the last dregs. When she removed the plastic cup from her lips she had a little brown moustache. It suited her. 'He's a manic depressive. Manic depressives are sometimes suicidal. And Vinnie's taken a lot of knocks. Some really hard knocks.'

'Why did you go to Beachy Head? I just can't work out why you were there – or how you got there so quickly.'

'Marc phoned me. Can't stand me, so he doesn't usually get in touch – I knew it must be something bad. And he sounded terrible. I just jumped in the car and got over there as fast as I could.'

Stephen paused. He was still confused, still in a state of shock, he supposed. It might be weeks before he felt normal again, whatever 'normal' was these days.

'How do we know he won't try it again?' he asked at last.

'We don't,' said Gabrielle. She wiped her eyes with the backs of her hands, and he realized her tears were flowing again. 'So fucking unprofessional!' she muttered angrily to herself. Then, more clearly, she said: 'The doctor says he needs to rest, which anyone with half a brain could see anyway. We just have to take it day by day. He's come out of this before – we'll just have to help him come out of it this time as well.'

He looked at her, wanting to drink in all the visual

information he could. There was so much he wanted to know, but the right questions wouldn't come.

'Why doesn't Vinnie know about the lap-dancing? I thought you were proud of it.'

'It's not me I'm thinking about. He sees me one way; he couldn't cope with seeing . . . the other side. We'd lost touch for a while, then I came into your restaurant with the girls from the club and he walked up to our table. I dived under it without even thinking – just knew I had to hide from him! After that, I bumped into him, accidentally-on-purpose, when he'd finished work one night. I could see he wasn't right, straight away.'

'But you can't live like that!'

'Like what?'

'In different boxes.'

'I don't know what you're on about.'

'Look, I upset Vinnie because I lied – lied by omission, anyway. And I only did that because I was worried about how he'd react. I was trying to protect him. Bad decision. I totally agree. But aren't you doing the same thing? Isn't it patronizing to keep him in the dark? You're being just as dishonest as I was.'

'Yeah, right, you can make it sound like that if you want. But when it comes to keeping Vinnie in one piece, no one knows more about it than me. Okay? And if a little white lie is in order, a little white lie is what he gets. Now, piss off and leave me alone.' Her tears were flowing again.

Stephen bitterly regretted the change in her tone, but he knew that what he'd said was true. He looked down at the back of his hands, at the ropy veins and bitten nails. Girlie hands, nonetheless. 'Right – fine – I'm going. But I still don't see the difference. I care about him too, you know. The whole restaurant thing was a complete cock-up, true. I ignored all the people who mattered, trying to keep it going. But only because I didn't know what else to do.'

'So you're the sad little victim, are you? None of it was down to you?'

'I didn't say that. I've made some terrible mistakes in the last few months. But I know what matters now. My family. My friends. And Vinnie is the best friend I've got.'

Gabrielle looked down into her empty cup, as if determined not to catch his eye. 'Okay. Well. The last thing he said to me before he fell asleep was, "Make Stephen go away",' she said. 'He's just tried to bloody kill himself. If he doesn't want to see you, I'm not going to force him.'

'What about you? Don't you want to see me again, either?'

'Why would *I* want to see you?' She looked up at him at last, and he felt a shot of sheer joy when their gaze met. It was as though they were enclosed in an almost unbearable intimacy, but one so fragile that it barely lasted a second.

'You're right,' he said, shaking himself. 'Silly question. But, will you tell him that I – that he . . .'

'What?'

'That he's the only real friend I've got.' Were these the best words he could come up with? 'That he's my . . . He's like my brother.'

'Right.' She was looking away again, at a couple of

nurses hurrying along the corridor, laughing, arms folded. 'I'll tell him that,' she said.

It was almost four o'clock in the morning when Stephen finally turned the corner into Canning Street. Wearily, he climbed the steps to the front door and let himself in. The emptiness of the house seemed almost sinister. He knew without checking that Marc wasn't there – the stillness and silence hung within the walls as if Vinnie really had died that night. And he knew that something *had* died: the old way of life. All those years – ever since the fateful Fay Cattermole incident with the stewing steak and the Arctic roll – he had been trying to achieve something that was worthless. Taste. Taste to him was about creating a life that made him better than other people. It was a goal he had never reached. He was still insecure about his naffness and gauche mistakes. He could never be tasteful enough, just as an anorexic can never be thin enough. And when his taste faltered – or his concentration wavered – he would be sent into a state of panic. Soon after Earthsea opened, he had gone out for a picnic with the Cathcarts. He'd left some of the catering to Rachel, thinking that she would be able to produce child-friendly food. And he'd nipped into Sainsbury's on his way over and bought some grapes and bags of Kettle crisps. When the picnic cloths were laid out and the respective picnics displayed, he had felt physically ill. Rachel had produced cheese rolls and – blast from the past – mini-pizzas. While Clive and Tamzin had gathered together a positive cornucopia of goodies: homemade spinach flan, couscous salad, strawberries and cream, smoked-salmon bagels for the kids and even –

another death-knell – *sushi*. That night he and Rachel had argued bitterly. She had called him a narcissistic little twat, he remembered. He had called her a stupid, lazy bitch. Those were – yes – those were his exact words.

The desperation of his lifetime's ambition now stared him in the face. Tomorrow might not be good, but it would be different. He stood in the dark hall for a moment, unwilling to turn on the lights. But as he moved forward, groping his way towards the stairs in the soothing dark, there was a loud knock on the door. He turned – who could it be? Perhaps Marc had come back after all, and had forgotten the key. Switching on the hall light, he opened the front door, blinking. It wasn't Marc who was standing there, but Nick.

'Hello, mate,' said Nick. As his face came into focus, Stephen noticed the black rings under his eyes and shadows under his cheekbones. He looked as though something was eating him alive from the inside. 'Can I come in? Fucking miserable out here.'

'Yeah – sure – sorry –' Stephen waved him in and closed the door. 'Come and have a cup of tea or something.' He was too tired to be truly curious about what Nick was doing there.

In the kitchen, Stephen put the kettle on while Nick sat slumped at the table, playing restlessly with Marc's retro seventies place mats adorned with emetic swirls in browns and dull greens. 'I've been waiting out there for nearly two hours,' said Nick. 'Thought you might not be coming back at all. In fact, I kind of hoped you wouldn't.'

Stephen paused to look at him with two mugs in his hand. 'I was at the hospital. Vinnie tried to kill himself.'

'Jesus Christ.'

'He's all right.' He didn't want to say more – certainly didn't want to mention Gabrielle, the secret psychiatric nurse. 'So why were you waiting for me?'

Nick flipped a mat nervously. It landed on the floor. 'Oh, you know. Wanted a little chat.'

'About . . . ? What, exactly?'

Nick scraped his chair back from the table and wandered to the kitchen window. As they were in the basement, all there was to see outside was the tiny back yard, empty plant pots marching up the steps to street level. He stared out at this unengaging scene for several moments.

'Look – I don't want to be rude, but I've had the worst day of my bloody life and I really need to sleep,' said Stephen. 'If you want to do Pinter silences, you've picked a bad time.'

Nick spoke without turning to face him. 'I've been meaning to say this for a long time. A very, very long time, it feels like. Although, in fact, it didn't really start till a few months ago. The day after we went to the club for the first time. Remember that?'

'Of course I remember it. What are you talking about? I don't understand.'

'No. No. You're fucking right you don't.'

Stephen was beginning to lose his temper. 'What the hell have you come here to tell me, Nick? Whatever it is, why don't you just get on with it?'

'I'm in love with Rachel,' said Nick in a high, strange voice. 'And she's in love with me.' He was still looking out at the yard.

'*What?* You mean . . . Are you having an affair?'

Nick turned at last. 'It's a bit more serious than that,' he said. 'We want to get married. When your divorce comes through.'

Stephen sank down on to a chair, two mugs still in his hand. He realized, somewhere inside, that this information was more shocking to him than seeing Vinnie standing on the cliff edge. He felt as if Nick had just told him that Rachel was dead. Looking up at Nick, he tried to focus on his face. Tried to see the past, but found that it had disappeared. 'How did it . . . how did it start?'

Nick closed his eyes, obviously girding himself up for yet another revelation. 'It started at college,' he said. 'During Finals.' Stephen's world took another jolt. The room seemed hazy, as if the world was literally fragmenting around him. He saw Rachel's face, laughing, halfway through a kebab. He saw Rachel, naked in the shower, pouting her lips for his kiss. He saw her sitting in her revision headscarf, scrawling furiously in her copy of *Daniel Deronda*. In 1984. The year she started screwing Nick.

'At college? But we were already . . . You weren't . . . sleeping with her behind my back?'

'Yes.' Nick began walking up and down the kitchen. 'Please don't think I've been enjoying this! It's been like – I can't say – just purgatory for weeks, months. The guilt, the not knowing if she really cares. Stephen, I have never felt like this about anyone. Not anyone. And I would have given anything for it not to be her. I wanted to be a good friend to you – I could see you were fucked up – and then the next thing I knew, I was in too deep to turn back . . .'

'So why – how come she never told me?'

377

'She broke it off with me when we all left. Told me she preferred you. I never got over it. Shagged around, pretended to be a lad, met Clancy, thought she was a laugh . . . Biggest joke of all, that one . . . Next thing I knew, she was pregnant, and we were having one of those American weddings where you make up your own vows. Only it was in Crouch End.'

Stephen tried to think. If Rachel had lied, and lied, and lied, how could anything be true? Her face was more vivid to him now than it had ever been – but was that really all he knew about her, her face? All those years of thinking that women could tell him, if he could be bothered to listen, how he should be living his life. All those years of thinking that she was the best, the finest, the most exacting person in the world. And he knew nothing about her at all. The sudden loneliness, in the past as well as the present, was overwhelming. His history would have to be rewritten, made clean. He knew that he should ask more questions, but couldn't think what they might be. Dates, places, number of times? It wasn't relevant. All that mattered was that he had based his life on a woman who was a stranger. First he had put shallow, cold Fay on to a pedestal. Then he had substituted Rachel, with her loud, overbearing family and her indelible confidence and splendid rage. And for years he had worked at his restaurant to make himself a worthy, successful, solvent spouse. In spite of his efforts, the only real achievement in his life was being a father.

'Aren't you going to say anything?' asked Nick. He looked more nervous than ever. 'You're not ill, are you?'

'Not ill, no. She really loves you?'

'Yes.'

'Jesus God.' He wanted to be alone. He wanted to turn all the lights out, crawl under the kitchen table and bay like a mad dog. He wanted to be dead. He wanted to go back to Beachy Head. He knew the spot now. There would be no prevarication. He would need no whisky. One step into the darkness and he could plunge into the steaming foam. There would be no need for words then, or explanations. 'I don't expect we'll be seeing much of each other in future,' he said flatly.

'Is that it?'

'Is that what? Were you expecting me to beat you up?'

'I don't know – I suppose I did think you'd have a bit more of a reaction than this.'

'I've had a fuck of a lot to react *to*, lately,' said Stephen. 'I mean, if it's any comfort to you, I feel physically sick. But I've been feeling physically sick for weeks.'

'She's . . . she's a great woman –' said Nick.

'Yeah, well, spare me the eulogy.'

'And your kids are so brilliant! If Poppy was half as bright as Elsie, I'd be more than –'

With a sudden cold flash, Stephen realized what Nick was really telling him. That he, Nick, was to be the father of Elsie and Stan. That when they squabbled over the toilet, it would be Nick who heard them from the bedroom. That while Stephen would be Weekend Dad, Nick would run them to school, empty the uneaten contents of their lunchboxes into the bin in the evenings, take them to their swimming lessons at the end of the day. That, while Poppy lived with Mad Clancy, his children, his dear, precious, eccentric children, would live with Rachel and

Nick. Probably in his old house, under the ceilings he had painted. He would be reduced to a sideshow in their lives. The extent of Rachel's power to destroy him left him winded, marooned. 'Get out,' he said hoarsely.

'What – I – I thought we were having a civilized discussion. Cards on the table, man to man . . .'

'Just get out. Get out of this fucking house, and leave me alone.'

'I'm sorry. It was just . . . I can't explain it. The emotions between us – like nothing else I've ever known – you can't imagine how she makes me feel.'

'Oh, I think I can.'

'Please believe that I'm sorry, Steve. You've got to believe I'm sorry . . .' To his surprise, Stephen saw that Nick was crying.

'Get out of here. Go and cry on *her* shoulder. Your tears are wasted on me. Mate.'

After Nick had gone, Stephen sat in the kitchen for a long, long time. Only when the sky was paling outside to a drizzly autumnal dawn did he stir. The pieces of his life lay around him, fragments that it would be impossible to rebuild into any new whole. When he stood up, he realized for the first time that he was still wearing what was left of the rum baba costume, now reduced to a tube of wet foam rubber which encased his aching body in a damp, deadening grip. He took a pair of scissors and cut himself out of it, then stuffed it into a bin liner and put it outside in the yard, noting the efficiency of his cold, white hands, which seemed to live on without him.

28

It was Christmas Eve at the Cathcarts', and Stephen was there with his children. The evening meal was in progress – the children's meal, that is. The Cathcarts practised the sort of gastronomic apartheid forced on most families with young children, with an early sitting, before bathtime, of small people eating fish fingers and – under protest – some form of vegetation, and a later one when the children were safely in bed. Or at least out of sight, so that food with a proper taste could be prepared, and fresh herbs finely chopped to the sound of bottles being uncorked. But as yet, they were still experiencing what Rachel – now absent somewhere with Nick – called 'poison hour'. Six children sat around the Cathcarts' long oak table. Six mouths were yelling and disputing and challenging the status quo, and six little bottoms were rarely anywhere near a chair.

'Dad! Dad! Elsie's a pescatarian too! Dad! She can't have sausages!' In spite of dropping the capitals, Stan had only one note: earth-shattering urgency.

'Stephen, pass the broccoli down this end, can you?' Clive was already sipping a gin and tonic. His glass tinkled alluringly, but Stephen, who had started drinking at lunchtime, had declined one.

'Zuleika *hates* broccoli, don't you, Zuleika?' This was from four-year-old Tallulah, a pale fairy in a gossamer-pink gown now covered in baked beans.

'Actually, I only like vegetables that are orange or yellow, not green stuff. Like corn on the cob, raw carrot, whatever . . .'

It was tempting to tune out. At meal times in the old days, he had tried to get involved, be the professional foodie father. But there was only so much interest he could summon up in a child refusing to eat a plate of plain pasta with Edam cheese. Often, he would end up flicking irritably through a recipe book, trying to fade his recalcitrant children into the background. But now . . . He had them for only a couple more hours. Then they would be spirited away – and he would need a great deal more gin. He put his arm around his daughter's shoulders. 'Elsie, why aren't you eating your sausages?'

'Because I'm sorry for *mammals*, Daddy. Don't you ever listen? Because I'm a *pescetarian*, for God's sake!'

'What on earth is a pescetarian?'

'Dur, a fish-eater, dumbo. Haven't you even heard of that?'

'Zuleika started it,' said six-year-old Noah, waving his fork.

'Actually, it was Ruby who started it, in my class.' Zuleika tucked her long pale hair behind her ears with her narrow white fingers. 'She's very sensitive. She can't even be in the same street as an abattoir. When we went on the school trip to the Open Market, she, like, barfed when she saw a pig's head.'

'Gross,' said Elsie, smugly. 'Some people say it's okay to eat chicken. But I say why don't people feel sorry for chickens? Haven't they got feelings too? I don't see why they should miss out on the kindness of vegetarians.'

'Yorick, have you eaten *any* of that mashed potato?' Yorick, till recently the youngest of the Cathcart brood, looked up at his father with round, submissive eyes. He had eaten nothing from his plate at all, but was in the process of dropping it, spoonful by painstaking spoonful, on to the retro-chic marmoleum floor.

Stephen took Elsie's plate over to the Aga and replaced her sausages with fish fingers. He was on the margins of their Christmas, not part of the real event. This was to happen in Winchester, with Rachel's overbearing parents. Nick, Rachel had informed him crisply on the phone the day before, would be there as well. The bitter harshness of this seemed to be something he could do nothing about. He had no rights over the way the break-up was conducted. Evicted from his home, and now excluded from Christmas with his own children. 'Gravy, Elsie?' he asked.

'Is it vegetarian?'

He wrestled with his conscience, accepted that the days when he would tell little white lies to give himself an easy life were over. 'Er, no. Probably not. Have some butter on your potatoes instead.' He dropped a generous dollop on to the snowy mash. He wanted to be a good father. If he did nothing else in his life, he wanted to achieve that.

'How's everything going?' Tamzin came in as he returned the food to Elsie.

Clive laughed hollowly. 'I see you made yourself scarce, darling.'

'Very funny. I've just been feeding Dido.' She smiled at the baby now sleeping on her shoulder, whose head was turned away from her and towards Stephen. So far, she looked almost like any other baby, especially now, with her scrunched sleeping features, her eyes tight shut. Only when she was awake could you see her round, lidded eyes, the characteristic sign of a Down's child. Tamzin, once too groomed to be true, had her hair roughly tied back in a slightly fraying hairband. Still big after the birth – Dido had been born four weeks earlier – she was wearing a check maternity frock that made her look like a text-book frump. But Stephen thought she had never looked better. Strands of hair hung around her smiling face. Her eyes were full of a new calmness, a sort of peace. She loved her flawed baby with a kind of acceptance that Stephen had never seen in her before. It was as if no longer having a perfect life had come, finally, as a great relief.

Clive went over to her and held one of the sleeping child's hands in his own. He looked into Dido's face with an expression of almost unbearable tenderness. 'Such a . . . such a little *miracle*,' he said.

Upstairs, Stephen packed the presents he had brought for his children into a bin-liner for the hundredth time. It was hard to stop counting them, wondering if he had bought too few, or too many. He had never bought them presents independently before. In the past, he got them the odd book that he liked the look of and left the serious, guerrilla-style missions to Toys 'R Us to his wife. On Christmas Day, he had often been appalled by the sheer volume of toys they had been given. In those days, it seemed like vulgar excess. Why, for instance, did Stan have six Action Men, who between them shared two motorbikes, a jeep and some kind of missile intended to disrupt bathtime but which usually had no batteries? Why did each of his children have sixteen Beanie Babies? Why was the house – already stuffed with baskets of soft toys – expected to cope with another tidal wave of cute teddy bears and babies that really cried and crapped, just because it was the festive season? But this year had been different. This year, he had gone all the way to Hamley's in Regent Street and had stayed there for five hours. He had started with presents he approved of, or considered tasteful: a hardbacked edition of *Pippi Longstocking* (for Elsie) and a book about dinosaurs that unfolded into a giant model of a Tyrannosaurus rex (for Stan). Then Monopoly and Scrabble, bringing back memories of his childhood games with Carmel, who always beat him at everything. But after a while he weakened and other, less admirable presents had followed. His first lapse was Harry Potter wizard outfits, though the book was very overhyped and he was strongly opposed to the associated merchandizing. Then he loitered by the Beanie Baby counter and his resolve crumbled. Some of these toy animals had such mournful eyes. You couldn't look them in the face and stay un-moved. Of course, he ended up buying four – two for each of his children: a tiny black Labrador puppy, a baby reindeer, a mini chimpanzee and droopy little donkey. After that, he had got the spending habit and had splashed out on videos of *Spider-Man* and *Scooby Doo*.

It had crossed his mind that they could open these tonight – now – before Rachel and Nick came to collect them. Sort of Scandinavian style – maybe he could start up a new family tradition. But he knew that this would have been wrong. They must open their presents on

Christmas morning, in the time-honoured fashion. It was probably more important this year than any other that the rules of Christmas were sacrosanct. All of them except the one that suggested that their father should be with them, he thought.

He looked up, and saw Clive hanging around uncomfortably in the doorway. 'How are you?' he asked. 'Ready for another gin?'

'I'll wait till they've gone, thanks. Don't want any comments from Rachel about me being drunk in charge of the children.'

'No. Probably right.' Clive paused. 'I think you're handling all this incredibly well. Can't think of anything worse.'

'Neither can I.' He took his cigarettes out of his jeans pocket and lit one. 'Don't mind me smoking up here, do you?'

'God, no, go ahead. God. Have four at once if it makes you feel better.'

'One is fine.' He exhaled the smoke. One did make him feel better. It was a strange truth. Smoking was the best panacea he knew for this fizzy, damaged feeling. 'The thing is, he is such a wanker, Clive. How could she do it? How could she fall for somebody like that?'

Clive shook his head. 'Sex appeal? How can you tell with girls? Money?'

'He's not exactly loaded, as far as I know. And that's so much not Rachel's thing.' He shrugged heavily. 'To be left for him . . . it's beyond belief. It's almost comical.'

Clive sat down next to him on the bed. 'There's no sense in it. It's not that she wants him more than you, anyway. It's that she wanted someone new. And he came along at the right moment.'

'I suppose so. Rekindling their college crush. Can you believe that? Charles and Di were still in love with each other when I first achieved the status of class cuckold.'

'Rekindling! Nice word.' Clive gave an abrupt laugh and said, almost as if thinking aloud. 'Before Dido was born, Tamzin and I were talking about renewing our vows? Remember that? How we were going to hire a string quartet? We've quietly dropped *that* idea. You're not the only person who's learned a thing or two in the last year, Steve.'

They both fell silent for a moment. Stephen flicked ash into the bin that stood by his bed, wondering if this was actually driving Clive mad. 'Thank you for having us today,' he said. 'It would have been hard to make it into a fun event in Vinnie's house. No one there, all the marks on the walls where Marc's pictures used to be. Like a bloody morgue. Even the heating's broken.'

'It's been a pleasure. I wouldn't have had it any other way.'

'I mean, this isn't an easy Christmas for you. With all the worry about Dido and everything.'

'Best Christmas we've ever had. We've never been happier, mate. Never been happier. She's a little angel from heaven.' Clive wiped a tear from his eye. 'Good job Tamzin's driving down to Cornwall tonight. I'm a bit more plastered than I thought.'

Downstairs, the doorbell rang. Stephen scrunched out his cigarette and stood up, feeling as if he was walking to his execution.

*

Rachel stood on the step, muffled into a long fur coat he had never seen before. He assumed it was a fun fur, but of course anything was possible now. Maybe she had a passion for musquash and mink as well as for Nick. Maybe she'd started eating veal again. Not that she looked as if she'd been eating anything much recently. She was thin and pale, and her eyes were circled with red.

'Hello, Stephen,' she said.

'Hello.'

They looked at each other for a moment. For some reason, he remembered her crying over Elsie's hamster, which had died after falling into the bath. Its name was Helen. That had been Christmas Eve, too. He thought of the little wet body, curled up in the palm of her hand. He had reached out and touched the wet fur. Still warm – or perhaps that had been the hot water. Futile little trails of memory, but they were his life. And so was Rachel. She was waspish, she was tricky and she had never *really* liked seafood. But she was his wife. He wanted to say, 'Let's turn the clock back. Let's forget all this splitting-up stuff. I love you. I need you. This is mad.' Where was all the certainty about being over her he had felt at the party? Where was his resolve?

'Are the children . . . ready?' she asked. She didn't call them. Her eyes were locked on to his, full of tears.

'I think so.' He closed the door behind her. She kept her coat muffled around her, although the house was warm. It seemed suddenly empty, as if everyone else was shrinking back into the high, square rooms, anxious not to be part of this scene.

'Elsie! Stanley! Mummy's here!' he called. Silence followed. 'Can't imagine what they're up to,' he said heartily. He thudded up the stairs to the first landing. In the playroom – which was the size of a small church and boasted such wonders as a doll's house as tall as the bunk bed and a multicoloured rocking horse that would not have looked out of place on the seafront carousel – the six children were sitting, silently, in a little circle. It was a spookily uncharacteristic sight. Elsie and Stan were clutching their little backpacks, which he knew were stuffed with their favourite toys. They looked like little wartime refugees, about to be sent into the unknown.

'Come on, kids,' he said, in a big, insincere voice. 'Mummy's waiting.'

'We don't want to go,' said Elsie. A tear rolled down her face. 'We don't want a Christmas with half our parents. We want a Christmas with both our parents.'

Stephen squatted down beside her. Was this where the damage really started? Was this the coastal shelf of misery that Philip Larkin talked about? 'They fuck you up, your mum and dad / They may not mean to, but they do.' They were fucking up their kids big-time, now. No more piffling about with trivial mistakes, like getting angry if they wet the bed. No. This was emotional Exocet.

'Elsie, darling . . .' Elsie, darling – what? What the hell were you supposed to say at times like this? We, your parents, have failed you, but we'd like you to put a reasonably brave face on it for our mutual convenience? Don't worry, lots of kids have to deal with this kind of shit these days? Don't give me a hard time, I've been drinking all day? 'We didn't mean this to happen,' was what he did say. 'We both love you, but we need to sort ourselves out.' Behind him loomed the spectre of their combined uselessness.

'But what's the point of Christmas if you can't have all the people you need in the same place?' said Elsie. Her grim little face was adolescent already. He told himself not to read too much into this – that way, madness lay. He would deal with guilt drip by drip. One drip at a time. He could not allow himself to be swept away by the knowledge that she had lost her innocence.

'Yes, well, you'll have a lovely time with Mummy,' said Stephen. 'And I'm still your dad.'

'But you won't see Santa!' said Stan. 'Nick will see Santa!'

'I'll be . . . thinking about Santa,' said Stephen. God. Was this really the best he could come up with?

'Nick won't necessarily *see* Santa anyway,' said Elsie. 'Only if he happens to be awake, like that time you were and you gave him some extra sherry and he talked to you about what he eats in Lapland.'

Stephen had forgotten about this particular flight of fancy. 'So, what do they eat in Lapland?'

'Dad! Dur! How can you not know? Reindeer rissoles and apple snow. He only touches mince pies on Christmas Eve – he can't bear the sight of them the rest of the year. Fancy you not remembering that!'

'Sorry, yes. Yes, I remember it now. Look, you have to go now. I'm really, really sorry, but you have to go.'

The children stood up and clung to him, their heads nestling into his thighs. He felt stifled by grief, tried to take a deep breath but to his horror heard himself sob. Their two faces tipped up to look at him.

'Are you crying, Daddy?' asked Stan.

'No! Far too big and old for that sort of thing.'

'Everyone cries sometimes,' said Elsie. 'Even the Government.'

Rachel appeared round the door. 'Hello, you two,' she said. 'Time to get going.' They disentangled themselves from him and went to her mutely, each taking hold of one of her hands. But they didn't take their eyes off Stephen's face. 'I'll bring them back on New Year's Eve,' said Rachel. 'Like we said. And I'll get them to phone you tomorrow.'

'Right.' Should he say Happy Christmas? Surely that would just sound like embittered sarcasm? Instead he said, 'Drive carefully.' Only it was Nick who was in the driving seat, he supposed.

Rachel still seemed to find it difficult to look away from him. 'I didn't mean this to happen,' she said, her voice ending in a little wail.

'That's what Daddy just said,' said Elsie.

'Oh.' As they went, it seemed suddenly as if it was the children who were carrying her away, not the other way around. When they had gone, Stephen looked at himself in the bathroom and stared into his own eyes for a long time. Then, a niggling half-thought started to bother him. The presents. He had forgotten to give them the presents.

He went downstairs and showed the bag to Clive without saying anything. 'Shit!' said Clive. He already had his coat on, and was loading the Cathcart goodies into the new Renault Espace he had purchased the week before. 'What a nightmare! All those wonderful toys! All the thought you put in.' He looked at the bin-liner with an embarrassed expression, as if he couldn't really deal with that much pain.

Stephen stood, holding the bag, swaying gently to and fro. He wondered if this could be the final straw, the crisis that finally tipped him into what Carmel had informed him one no longer called a nervous breakdown. (The term was, apparently, at once pejorative and vague.) Many years ago, his father had had one of those, when you were allowed to have them, and had run away at Christmas with a month's profits from the salon. Or that was the story, anyway. Perhaps Stephen was now, in his fortieth year, turning into naff, cowardly Giles, who had left their mother and somehow vaporized, disappeared into a long anecdote about wasted promise and youthful good looks.

Tamzin, now wearing a long cream cardigan over her dress, came rushing into the hall. Dido was still on her shoulder. 'What's happened?'

'Elsie and Stan have left without their presents,' said Clive. 'Just really is the icing on the cake.'

'They'll come back,' said Tamzin, with complete certainty. 'They'll realize what's happened, and come back.'

'They didn't even know I was giving them all that stuff,' said Stephen. He sat down heavily on the oak settle which dominated one side of the tiled hall. 'It was meant to be a surprise.' He looked down at the ugly, bulging bag. Was that really the best way to express his love? Too late for that now. Too late to try and undo the past with a sack full of semi-durable toys. Just then, the phone rang.

'Yes?' Tamzin adjusted Dido's position on her shoulder.

'Nick, hi. Yes. It's Tamzin. Mm. We were just talking about that. Mm. Do you want to speak to him? No? Okay. Okay. I'll give him the message.' She replaced the receiver. 'They're coming back. Only got as far as Worthing. Elsie seems to have been doing a bit of pre-Christmas espionage – your present cache wasn't such a secret after all. She suddenly realized that you'd forgotten to hand over the loot.'

'And Nick's coming back? Just to collect the presents?'

'I don't know why you've got that expression on your face,' said Tamzin. 'He's still a shit.'

After that, Stephen poured himself a large gin, lit a cigarette and stretched out on the floor of the living room. The bag of presents was still by his head. He would not be letting it out of his sight until it was safely in the boot of Nick's car. He listened to the sound of the Cathcarts coming and going, running up and down the stairs, squabbling, sorting out crises and developing new ones. Dido cried at one point, then was quiet. He thought of Tamzin, breastfeeding her in the kitchen in the midst of all the chaos. It was odd that the Cathcarts, the vulgar, materialistic Cathcarts, were having an old-fashioned Christmas which would have impressed Charles Dickens himself with its warmth and togetherness, while he, Captain Taste, was pinning all his Yuletide happiness on handing over a bag of shop-bought tat to the children he no longer lived with. But so fucking what, frankly. He was bored with drawing up interesting little parallels in his mind, especially ones that showed him in a bad light. He was getting pissed. He was going to spend Christmas Eve on his own, and so what if he was an entirely crap person who was doing all the things he had always assured the world were anathema to him. So bloody what.

After a while, he realized that Nick was standing near his head. He struggled to his feet, dusting ash off his jumper. 'Here they are,' he said, holding out the bag.

'Are you okay?' asked Nick.

'I'm fine. Festive lie-down. Thanks for coming back.'

'It's nothing. Nothing. Got to do everything we can to make it better for the kids. For your kids, I mean.'

'Right.'

Nick held the bag up in his hand in an odd gesture of farewell. He turned as if to go, then seemed to think better of it and turned back again. 'She still loves you, you know,' he said. 'I think she always will.'

'Which explains why she's ended up with you, I suppose,' said Stephen. The scene seemed to be swimming into dream territory; it seemed not to matter what he said.

'I know you can't work out what she sees in me.'

'No, you are absolutely right. This is a mystery to me.'

'It's not what I am, it's what I'm not. As in, not a perfectionist. Not someone she has to work hard to impress.'

'Oh fuck off! As if Rachel was trying to impress me! I was the one who was out of my league. I was the one who never really felt . . . safe. What a load of shit!'

'Why don't you ask her yourself? Ask her.'

'I will. Don't worry. I will.' But, after Nick had gone, Stephen wondered if he ever would. Perhaps it was better not to know. He lay down on the floor again, and when the Cathcarts came to say goodbye he was too tired to get up again, but listened to them, still feeling as if he was in a dream.

'Seems awful to leave him here like this,' whispered Clive.

'He's positive that he doesn't want to come with us,' said Tamzin quietly. 'And, think about it. Would you want to spend Christmas with a big, happy family if you were going through what he's going through? The happier we are, the worse it is for him. This year, at least, he's better off on his own.' He heard them put something on the coffee-table, and tiptoe out into the cold.

29

Stephen woke up with a start, furry-tongued and stiff. He could hear knocking. Where was he? He sat up, stared round the room. On one side, the marble fireplace, topped with a gold-framed mirror. By the window, the enormous Christmas tree, its red lights glowing against the silver decorations, which glimmered like sweets in a jar. The Cathcarts. Of course. He struggled to his feet, staggered for a moment, and walked over to look out of the window. The heavy curtains were still drawn back, and outside the streets were dark and still.

Looking out, he saw a bulky figure wrapped up heavily against the cold. Who the hell could it be? He glanced at his watch. Just after midnight. Christmas Day. Still not fully awake, he went to the front door and opened it.

'Hello, Stephen,' said a voice.

'Carmel!' he said. 'Bloody hell! This is a surprise! Why aren't you at home, all snuggled up with Lise and the bump?'

'She's asleep. Pregnancy is like one long Mogadon, as far as I can see. And I've been to Midnight Mass. Merry Christmas, by the way.'

'I suppose it's still merry for some people.'

'Yes, I thought you might take the Ebenezer Scrooge line, once Your Children had been spirited away. So here I am. Offering you a little bit of seasonal company.'

'That's very nice of you. I do feel a bit – I dunno – sick, I suppose.'

'Aren't you going to invite me in?'

'Actually, I need to get out of this house.'

'And go where, exactly?'

'Earthsea. See how it's doing. How much dust has piled up since it closed.' The restaurant had closed one week before, as he had known it would, without really facing up to it till the last diners had finally left. It was a trauma which seemed insignificant now, compared to the loss of Elsie and Stan. But his life seemed to have drifted into nowhere, now that his poor old Earthsea was no more. The restaurant also seemed to represent his relationship with Vinnie, flawed though that had been. And Vinnie was still refusing to see him. His life was all endings.

'Sounds just a bit depressing to me,' said Carmel. 'I'll come with you. Maybe we can workshop some ideas for the New Year on the way down.'

'Workshop away,' said Stephen. From the living room he grabbed his leather jacket and the card the Cathcarts had given him, then set out into the night.

They walked towards the seafront. There were still knots of seasonal revellers wandering along the road, some tottering unsteadily, some with arms wrapped around their friends. Young people, of course, who didn't have stockings to fill or turkeys to stuff. Stephen remembered the odd hiatus that was Christmas when there were no children to wake the house at five a.m., just a few hungover grown-ups smiling sheepishly over gifts they had chosen themselves or record tokens. Now, he was back there again, child-free, with the festive hours to fill, the lure of terrible television and drink likely to suck him into a stupor.

'I suppose I'll learn the real meaning of Christmas, now I'm going to be a mother,' said Carmel, echoing his thoughts. Stephen noticed she had stopped referring to herself as a father – another step on the road to commitment.

'You know it's really Christmas when you can't be bothered to open the Baileys because you're too busy stopping your toddler from eating the tree,' he said.

'Baileys? Bit *de trop* for you, isn't it?'

'Nothing is too *de trop* for me now, thank you Carmel,' said Stephen. 'I am a changed man. I *want* to be naff. I love, crave and embrace naffness. I am Mr Naff, of Naffsville.'

'No need to go too far.' She put her arm around him as they walked. 'You're not all bad. You just got your priorities wrong.'

'Like you did?'

'Exactly like I did. Both of us were trying to tidy life up, somehow. Get the better of it.'

The thought of an anal past did not seem to depress Carmel. 'Remember that time Mum invited Albert Cattermole in for a drink on Christmas Eve? And gave him the cooking sherry left over from the trifle?' Her voice was bright.

'How could I forget? "Dear lady, I believe you have made an error with my drink."' Stephen was shocked to find himself laughing. 'Why was he bloody well there in the first place?'

'He brought me home. I'd been carol singing with Fay,'

said Carmel, smugly. 'We made £9 for Oxfam and had a big snog outside the Crystal Ballroom. Hiding in the doorway. Our first date.'

'Blimey. It really is the sodding secret history round here. Lesbian life as I never knew it.'

'Mum gave him a bottle of Ansell's bitter instead,' said Carmel. 'No wonder he never came near our house again.'

'Makes you sort of proud of her, in a funny way, doesn't it?' said Stephen.

'And protective, at the same time,' agreed Carmel.

'But still embarrassed.'

'We'll always be embarrassed. But we love her.'

'Yes,' said Stephen. 'I'm afraid we do.'

As they got nearer to the restaurant, Stephen suddenly felt that he would rather be alone. 'Carmel, I do appreciate you coming round. And you've cheered me up incredibly – in fact, I'm amazed how much better I feel. But I would like to do this by myself. This visit to Earthsea, I mean.'

They had stopped at the top end of Ship Street, with the glittering sea behind them. Carmel searched his face for lurking signs of depression.

'Are you all right, though? Will you be all right?'

'I'll be fine.'

She kissed him on the cheek. Then smiled, and marched off into the night. When he reached Earthsea, he found that a large orange van was parked directly outside – though parking was strictly prohibited. Approaching it, he saw that it was painted with splodgy purple and lime green flowers. It looked a bit like he had expected the Magic Bus to Greece to look, years before. A hippy bus, for dozy people. Along one side, painted in uneven, messy lettering, were the words 'AL'S MOBILE DISCO'. He peered in through the windscreen. Someone had propped a piece of paper inside, with a scrawled message for passers-by. It read 'YOU SMELL OF PISS'. Once, this would have infuriated Stephen beyond words. Now, he stood back, letting his breath frost the air, and wondered what this Al character was like. Presumably he was a drug abuser with a chip on his shoulder, who wore dodgy woolly hats. Where was he now? Had he got children? Chances were, if he had, they weren't living with him either. He and Al had the night to themselves. He turned, unlocked the restaurant door and stepped inside. He switched on the lights and looked around. It was a lonely sight: Christmas Eve was usually a busy evening, and at this time there would still have been the odd table finishing up but a growing feeling of excitement and hilarity among the staff. He remembered Vinnie sweeping up last year, with swathes of tinsel looped ironically around his neck, and Flint making them all a Margarita as soon as the last diners had departed. Now a neglected gloom hung around the restaurant – it was as if a layer of dust had already settled on everything, although it had only closed down a week before. He felt as if he was stepping into another age. At the same time, it looked as if someone had just rushed out, expecting it to open as usual the following morning. Chairs were standing on the tables, alongside the lunch-time menus in their wooden stands. At his feet were piles of unopened mail, surging across the floor. Bills, mostly, he suspected. He kicked them to one side, went to the bar and poured himself the large gin he had been looking forward to. He sat on a bar stool, smoking and letting the alcohol swirl in his head, keeping his mind blank. With no future to look forward to, and a past that ached, it seemed to him that this was an eminently sensible thing to do. He told himself this as he poured himself a second glass. He would drink until the sun rose. That was about as far into the future as he was prepared to go. But, after a while, he detected an unfamiliar sensation in his stomach. Hunger. He was so used to ignoring hunger pangs and replacing food with booze or fags that he had almost forgotten what it felt like. Food. Surely he wasn't interested in eating anything at a time like this? He wouldn't be able to swallow. He would vomit, instantly. But he found that the insidious feeling would not go away. He heaved himself off the stool and clattered down the stairs to the kitchen.

This presented an even more pathetic sight. The stations and worktops were all empty, except for a few cardboard boxes which had been dumped on top of them. A pile of freshly laundered aprons had been left on top of one of the hobs. The fridges and the cold room were locked and bolted. He took out a key from his clanking bunch and opened one of the fridges, looking for food that had survived for a week. He found a lump of vegan Cheddar, hacked a piece of it off and stood chewing, staring into the fridge like a teenager with the munchies. It was then that he heard the door of the restaurant open. Shit! Had he locked it? He wasn't sure. Could this be Al and his cronies, come to trash the place or drink it dry?

'Hello?' he called, experimentally. 'Who's there?'

There was no reply. He slammed the fridge door shut

and ran back up the stairs. When he reached the top, he saw one solitary figure, standing in the middle of the restaurant. It was Vinnie.

'Vinnie! Christ! What are you doing here?'

'Same as you, probably. Soaking up the atmosphere.'

Stephen shrugged and smiled. 'Yeah, right. There's nowhere else to go, really, is there?'

'Absolutely pissing nowhere,' agreed Vinnie. 'Funny to think: this time last year we both had homes to go to. But we weren't there. We were here.'

'Was that bad? Was that why it all went wrong?'

'Search me. Feels kind of lonely now, though,' said Vinnie. 'Marc's gone to the States. Flew off yesterday. I don't think he'll be back.'

'What'll he do?'

'Sell flowers to queers in San Francisco, I expect. He's the type who gets a green card without even trying. He's probably already found some dippy Californian fag hag who's agreed to marry him. It's over, anyway. *Finito*.' He sat down at the bar. 'Let's both have a drink,' he said.

Stephen refilled his glass and passed one to Vinnie. They sat smoking for a while, side by side on their bar stools.

'I didn't think you were speaking to me,' said Stephen at last. 'Thought . . . we were over as well.'

'We were,' said Vinnie. 'It was Abby who talked me out of it. She made me realize that – I dunno – we all fuck up, don't we? You should have told me about Marc. Everybody should have told me about Marc. But no one did.'

'I'm sorry. I was too scared. Too much of a coward. And I could only think about my own problems.'

Vinnie nodded, looking ahead of him and not at Stephen. 'What really got to me was the idea that you thought it was okay because we were gay. Like, I wouldn't mind because gay men are never faithful. I thought you were making me into some foul fucking nancy stereotype. After all the years we've known each other.'

'Did we know each other? Did I know you? It makes me feel so bad that I just ignored the missing years, when it turns out you were . . . ill. Never asked what you did. Just always thinking about myself.'

'You knew what you wanted to know. That's what it felt like. I thought you just gave me as much attention as you had to spare. Which wasn't much. And if my boyfriend was playing around, what was it to you?'

'It wasn't like that, Vin. Honestly. It was just funk – fear. I knew you'd be horrified. I knew you'd be hurt. And I didn't want to be the one to rock the boat.'

'Yeah, well. I can't blame you for that. I probably would have killed you if you *had* told me . . .'

'Yes,' agreed Stephen, looking round at his friend's hunched, still body. 'I think you would have done.'

'I really loved him,' said Vinnie, quietly. 'Never loved anyone before. Never felt that – what is it? Like part of you disappears. The edges between you disappear.' His voice cracked and he stubbed out his cigarette fiercely in the ashtray.

'I'm so sorry.'

'It's okay.' Vinnie turned towards him, gave a sheepish

403

half smile. 'I mean, *now* it's okay. Now I realize that . . . none of it was your fault.'

Stephen wondered if they should touch. Should he put his arm around Vinnie's shoulders? He wanted to. But he was afraid it would look like wanting to win Brownie points for not being homophobic. Instead, he said: 'Maybe we can still turn Earthsea around. Still, you know, pull ourselves out of the mire.'

Vinnie was lighting another cigarette. 'Maybe,' he said. 'What we need is someone who knows about money. We're just two daft fucking chefs.'

'So no hope then? Declare ourselves bankrupt and that's that?'

'I don't see why,' said a voice behind them. Stephen turned to see Gabrielle, surveying them with her arms folded. On her face was a quizzical, half-amused look that didn't go with her head-gear. She was wearing glittery reindeer horns. 'Although, if you want to get canny, you could start with locking the door at night,' she said. 'Anyone could walk in here – even trash like me.'

Vinnie squinted round at her, smiling. 'How did you know I was here?'

'You haven't talked about anything else for days! How could you not be here? Anyway, it wasn't just you I wanted to see.'

Stephen felt something lurch inside him. He suddenly felt self-conscious and fingered the Christmas card the Cathcarts had given him as if it was an object of fascination.

'Yeah, right. I've noticed the bond between you two. Really touching,' said Vinnie, with a sarcastic laugh. He sounded like himself. He was all right. Not just not dead, or not mad. Stephen tore at the envelope to stop himself from crying. Inside was one of the Cathcarts' super-expensive cards, gold-leaf angels looking pleased with themselves and flaunting trumpets. He opened it. In one corner it said: 'This card is based on a design by Zuleika Cathcart. All proceeds will go to the Down's Society.' He looked at the message in Clive's handwriting. It was longer than he had expected. It read:

To dear Stephen, wishing you a happy Christmas and the best New Year yet. It's been wonderful having you to stay, and I hope we will always be the closest of friends. And I also hope that you won't be offended if I include our Christmas present to you in this card. Tamzin has had one of her Ideas. Remember you talked about an NCJ woman who was driving you mad the day of the restaurant review? She is one of Tamzin's friends, and afterwards she kept going on about how her children loved that borscht. It occurred to us that, although there are probably too many restaurants in Brighton, and veggie ones seem to be opening up every day, there isn't one for children. Our suggestion — and it is JUST a suggestion — is that you reopen as a restaurant selling real food to kids — veggie, organic, cutting edge, whatever you like. And I'd like to come in with you and Vinnie as a third partner. I won't interfere, but I'll invest as much as it takes to get the thing going and I'll be the money man. The entrepreneurial genius, if you like. (Only joking.) You could open in the early evening, for older kids. You could do parties. Tell me if it sounds like hell on earth, but I think it could be a real winner. Not to mention a real earner. And

405

you could run it in a more laid-back way — see more of Elsie and Stan, who by the way are the world's most fantastic kids (well, in the top seven, anyway). Tell me what you think. In the meantime, we'll be thinking of you.

   Love from your friends Clive, Jamzin, Zuleika, Tallulah, Noah, Yorick and Dido.

'Who's it from?' asked Vinnie, craning to look. 'Why have you got that weird expression?'

'From Clive. He's offering to back the restaurant.'

'Fucking hell!' Vinnie scrutinized his face. 'But there's a catch.'

'Er, yes. He wants us to reopen as an upmarket children's restaurant.'

'Fucking hell,' said Vinnie again, in a different tone. 'Is he trying to kill us?'

'He thinks it's a financial winner,' said Stephen. He looked at the card again. 'I mean, could he be right? You were saying just now that we need a money man.'

'But kids! All day! I mean, I'm not a masochist.'

'Don't just write it off, Vin,' said Gabrielle, who had been watching them closely throughout this exchange. 'It could be brilliant. It's the one type of restaurant that Brighton hasn't got. And this town is full of people who are obsessed with their kids' health. Buying Organix baby food that costs an arm and a leg. Or that Green Parrot Café crap in Sainsbury's.' Stephen looked at her in surprise. 'I *do* know people with children, for your information,' she said. 'I don't only hang out with lap-dancers and mad people.'

'Thanks, sweetie,' said Vinnie.

Stephen shot a glance at Gabrielle.

406

'Yeah,' she said. 'I took your advice. Told Vinnie about my second career and made an honest woman of myself.'

'Didn't bother me in the least,' said Vinnie with a dry laugh. 'Don't know why you thought it would. Let's face it, anyone who works in mental health needs some kind of escape. Anyway, does this mean you'll come and work for us, then? Wipe snotty noses while kids chuck lentil bake around?'

'Yeah, I'll work for you,' she said. She crossed over to the bar and poured herself a drink. 'Just gave in my notice today, as it goes. Decided to stick to what I'm good at.'

Stephen stared at her. 'So no more lap-dancing? No more Robbie? You must be relieved!' He realized he meant that he was relieved.

'I am relieved, but I'll still be dancing round that pole. Whatever you might think, Stephen, I reckon I'm an okay lap-dancer. Not top notch, but I can do the business. The thing I'm useless at is being a psychiatric nurse. Can't do it. Just can't keep doing it any more.' She wiped the tears from her cheeks with the palms of her hand, her reindeer horns bobbing up and down incongruously as she did so.

Vinnie pushed his stool away and went over to her. 'Is this because of me?' he asked quietly. 'Because . . . you saved my life, Abby. Twice you've saved my life. How useless is that?'

Her voice rose to a wail. 'I know I did, Vinnie! I know I did! And if I don't do anything else in my life, I'll have something to be proud of. But I got involved. That's my bloody point. You can't do that job if your emotions keep getting mixed up with the patients. I'm not a professional. I'm a bleeding stupid amateur. I cared about you, and now you're my best friend. But it keeps on happening . . . I dream about the people in the unit, the things they tell me. I'm obsessed. It's dancing that keeps me together – so easy, so mindless. I've got to walk away from that job.' Vinnie put his arms around her and hugged her.

'It's a shame,' said Stephen, 'because, I was thinking the other day, you are the only person I know who does a job that is any use to anyone. All my friends are estate agents, management consultants, dot-com whiz kids. Even my mum is a hairdresser.'

'Nothing useless about hairdressers,' said Gabrielle, pushing Vinnie gently away. 'Anyway. It means I'll be free in the daytime. Bit of light waitressing should suit me down to the ground.'

Vinnie looked at Stephen. 'What do you reckon? Shall we go for it?'

'I think we should.'

'And take on this new staff member?'

'Why not?' Stephen began to laugh. 'I just came in here for a quiet drink. Never thought . . .' His words tailed away. He was thinking of his far-away children, sleeping with their stockings heavy on the end of their beds.

Vinnie came over and offered him a cigarette. Pulling a third stool over to the bar, he waved Gabrielle to a seat. 'Let's all celebrate,' he said. 'Tell you what, I'll open some of that organic champagne. Drink a toast to – what are we going to call this place, anyway?'

'Elsie & Stan's,' said Stephen, in a tone that did not encourage debate.

'Elsie & Stan's it is, then.' He disappeared to search for a bottle.

For a while, Stephen and Gabrielle sat at the bar. Their stools were close together, but not touching. Both looked ahead, at the glistening bottles, the stash of menus, the wine glasses. Stephen resisted the temptation to leap up and start polishing these.

'Elsie – that's your little girl's name, then?' said Gabrielle after a while. 'Of course, I've met Stan.'

'Yes.'

'Nice names.'

He wondered if she meant this. 'My mother thinks they're horrible. Asked me why I stole the names of two characters in *Coronation Street*.'

'Oh God! Yeah! Elsie Tanner and Stan Ogden.'

'I thought you'd be too young to remember them.'

'I'm older than I look, you know. Wrong side of thirty. I used to watch them on Granada Plus, anyway. I still think they're great names.'

'Thank you.'

She turned to look at him. 'I'm really sorry about you and your wife. About . . . not being with your children.'

He didn't look at her, but fiddled with his cigarettes, lit one, then offered the packet to her as an afterthought.

She shook her head. 'Terrible for the skin. Haven't touched one for years. Not since I stopped going out with a bloke who basically hated my guts.'

He found he was laughing. 'We've all had relationships like that,' he said. 'Poisonous ones.'

'Yup. I think I've had more than most. Maybe it's the job. They fancy you, but they're ashamed of fancying you.

409

Think they should do better. The worst thing is when they decide they can make you a better person. If I had a pound for every man who'd told me I was too clever to be a lap-dancer, I wouldn't need to do the Lottery again.'

Stephen was looking at her now, at her neat, freckled features, the tumbling hair, which she was wearing in comedy bunches, at the bobbing, flickering red antlers. But all he could really see was her brown, expressive eyes, each lash identified by a layer of black mascara. He didn't want to know how many men there had been. He thought of them, the embarrassed, the sexist, the would-be Pygmalions, and then consciously evicted them from his mind.

'I wouldn't try to change you,' he said.

The atmosphere between them tightened. Gabrielle leaned across and took a cigarette, lit it. He noticed that her fingers were trembling. He noticed that his legs were trembling too.

'Is that a proposition?' she asked.

He hesitated. 'Well.' He paused. 'It would be. I mean – if I was in any fit state to have a relationship with anyone. Except that . . . I'm just so fucked up. All I can really think about is my children.'

She nodded, but shifted slightly closer to him on the stool.

'And . . . I haven't recovered from all this terrible stuff with my wife. Leaving me for one of my friends. All of that.'

Gabrielle said nothing, but again he felt her weight almost imperceptibly shift in his direction.

He went on: 'And I'm broke, of course, and God knows whether this brainwave of Clive's will actually work. Plus,

410

on top of that, it would be entirely unprofessional for us to see each other if you're working here.'

'Bound to be a total disaster,' said Gabrielle, reassuringly. 'Then there's the fact that we've got nothing in common.'

'Exactly,' he said. They were leaning forward, with their arms resting side by side on the bar. The cigarettes smouldered in the ashtray. Their bodies were millimetres apart. On the bar, he watched his right forearm and her left move closer.

'I mean, if there is one type of person who seriously gets on my tits it's up-their-own-arse middle-class men who spend the whole time going on about their ex-wives.'

'Quite. Keep well clear.'

'And as for these anal frigging foodies! I'm all for detox and a bit of organic, fine. For health reasons. But in this town, you get people who don't think about anything else. It's their life! Drives me mad. Nothing wrong with a nice bit of junk food on a rainy day, and I don't even care if it's got GM or a load of dolphins got killed.'

'Absolutely. People like me are the scum of the earth, and completely unsuited to normal dating.' His hand lay on top of her hand now. His fingers were tangling into hers. 'As for you. Not just a lap-dancer, but someone who actually wears reindeer antlers. And bunches . . .'

'They're wearing bunches in *Vogue*, for your information, mate. It's the prairie look. Cowgirls.'

'You do realize that my ideal woman is Nigella Lawson.'

'And my ideal man is George Clooney. Of course.'

'Of course.' He took her in his arms. 'There's no hope for us whatsoever. We're totally and utterly incompatible.'

'Totally and utterly,' she said, impersonating his voice.

When they kissed, he felt the joy surging slowly throughout his body. He felt the grief and anxiety subside. He felt . . . What was that feeling?

'I know we're not having a relationship or anything,' said Gabrielle, drawing back momentarily. 'But I like you. I liked you the first time I saw you, with that stuck-up expression on your face.'

'I like you,' he said. 'Although I must admit, I didn't warm to you on that particular evening.'

'Nar. Well. Maybe now you'll *have* to put veg lasagne on the menu.'

Stephen laughed. 'Yes. We'll call it Pasta Gabrielle.' Then he hesitated. 'Would you mind if I did something?'

'Depends what it is. Why don't you do it, and I'll tell you if it pisses me off?'

Very gently, he removed the reindeer antlers from her head, and positioned them carefully on his own. They were surprisingly comfortable. 'That's better,' he said.

Once more, they kissed, and this time he felt himself swooning away into another world. What was it – that feeling again? The real world, the world he knew, seemed to be falling away. Like someone drowning, he saw a series of images flash before his eyes. His life in pictures. Rose, parking her car at that mad angle outside their pokey house. The Holy Mother, following his teenage moves with her uncanny, reflective eyes. Rachel, laughing in bed and making a mess with the toast. Stan, found again at Pride, solemnly scoffing an ice-cream. Elsie's face, the last time he saw her. And Carmel, slashing away at a courgette and slicing her own hand. Last of all, there was Fay, feeding Nigel Nunnelly with those bloody olives, long, long ago. His eyes fluttered half-open. All he could see was the panorama of Gabrielle's cheek. He suddenly remembered Vinnie's words. It was as if part of him had disappeared. As if the edges between them had disappeared.

So much so that it was a long time before either of them noticed Vinnie himself, standing in the doorway, smiling and cradling a bottle of champagne as if it was a newborn child.